A LILY PAD is a floating leaf of the white water lily family. The scientific name of lily pad is *nymphaea odorata*. A bullfrog sits on a lily pad in a pond. The lily pad does not sink under its weight. The giant water lily, *victoria amazonica*, has the world's biggest lily pad, up to four feet, which can support the weight of several people at once. The lily pad is quiet. It lies tranquilly on the surface of the pond water, offering refuge and camouflage for the frog, protecting it from predators. The lily pad fits in with its natural surroundings, as does the frog.

Human beings are the only creatures which do not fit in with the rest of nature. Nature is simple. But mankind rejects simple living. Now, suppose a pond has one lily pad in the beginning. Suppose that single lily pad becomes two in the course of a day. And then, suppose each of those lily pads spawns another one. Suppose this occurs day after day after day. Soon the pond will be full of lily pads.

The American military has adopted the lily pad concept. In military jargon, a lily pad means an outpost, an advance camp, a foreign base, or a staging area, only one in a series. It means a scaled down military facility with *theoretically* little permanent personnel, often used as a staging ground for Special Forces and Intelligence operations. Soldiers may then leapfrog from one lily pad to another. The outpost aspect of the military lily pads follows the model of the multiplying lily pads. Especially the giant water lily leaf. They not only multiply but also grow in size and in time tend to become permanent military bases now encircling the world. For example, Afghanistan is a gigantic lily pad; permanent, also a place to move out from, a place from which soldiers go out to 'conduct operations' against other people around that part of the world.

In American military thinking, the huge city-like bases for 100,000 troops in Germany are no longer necessary. So America is "reconfiguring its footprint"—that is, reviewing its global deployment of troops in order to be able to apply military force anywhere rather than be tied to a small number of bases. That is the lily pad concept, the analogy of frogs hopping around a growing number of foreign bases. Frogs equal battle-ready troops. Saudi Arabian restrictions on the use of U.S. bases there resulted in the construction of the Qatar lily pad. The air war against Serbia and the theft of its historic territory of Kosovo made possible the creation of the giant lily pad-state in the Balkans. Lily pads now dot Bulgaria, Romania and the Czech Republic, northwards to the Baltic States, across the Black Sea to Georgia, another lily pad-state, to lily pad-state Iraq, and on to Kyrgyzstan and Afghanistan and to Singapore. The only limit today is the surface of planet Earth, but the moon and Mars are not excluded from military "Strangelove" ambitions and dreams.

At the last count—no one can be precise since the U.S. maintains secret bases and Intelligence installations all over the world—the United States of America had 737 bases and more than 600,000 soldiers manning garrisons or involved in countless operations in some 200 nations, spanning the globe from Europe to Iraq and Afghanistan, to the Far East, the Pacific, Africa and Latin America. To this figure one must add hundreds of thousands of "private contractors", aka mercenaries—their exact number is also secret—serving the interests of the global American empire. Like the lily pads. It is safe to assume that their number is growing.

PRAISE FOR LILY PAD ROLL

An American's anti-American probe into the secret world of US military bases spreading eastwards from the Balkans, *Lily Pad Roll* is also an intriguing exploration of 21st century post-Soviet Eastern Europe. Gaither Stewart's characters, grappling with problems of time, memory and exile, are often fractured souls seeking a centre for themselves in a geopolitical world in turmoil.

—DESMOND O'GRADY

Rome

Correspondent for *The Sydney Morning Herald* and

Author of *A Word in Edgeways* (Connor Court)

* * *

A finely balanced political and psychological thriller, written with direct insight and intimate knowledge of the countries in which the action takes place. The intellectual sophistication of this novel equals or outshines works by Le Carré, whose spy books reveal the tawdry underbelly of the international undercover machinations to detect an adversary's internal decision-making. *Lily Pad Roll* reveals the glamorous fictional auras traditionally attached to spy stories for what they are: full of pitfalls and imbued with the spiritual damage they cause to the protagonists. It makes this book and its predecessor, *The Trojan Spy*, absorbing and fascinating, while the mise-en-scenes are exceptionally realistic and of a cinematic immediacy.

—GUI ROCHAT

Former Senior Editor, *Cyrano's Journal Online*

Art Critic, and specialist in Old Master French Paintings.

Rochat was brought up and educated in Holland,

France, Iran and Lebanon and has lived on and off

in North Africa as well as in the U.S.

Working on many levels, but always absorbing, *Lily Pad Roll* is complex but luminously accessible like a long awaited epiphany. The book's atmosphere and saturation recalls Graham Greene's *The Human Factor*, Celine's *Journey Into the Night* and the plays of Slawomir Mrozek. *Lily Pad Roll* is like an original scene out of *Doctor Strangelove*, when the Soviet Ambassador, in the War Room, photographs the scenes of the final minutes of life on our planet. Life is ending, but the photographs will be useful. The Cold War is over. Nonetheless in the American military mindset every new Lily Pad will be useful in the future. American "lily pads" play the Dr Strangelove role here.

—BRUNO MIRKOWSKI
Russian-American Warsaw resident
Former producer of *Voice of America*, and formerly affiliated
with the Russian service for French language Africa.

* * *

Gaither Stewart's new novel *Lily Pad Roll*, offers a fresh perspective on world events, unraveling layer after layer the deceit concealed in the imposition of "democracy" on a recalcitrant world. Georgia, Serbia and Iran may not seem to have much in common, but all three are influenced by the same forces. When a young journalist travels through Eastern Europe to investigate America's new military presence among post-communist countries torn between fragile democracy and a shifting geopolitical situation, he himself falls into the murderous sights of US secret services. The author's deep understanding of the region enables him to present the story behind the story, from the perspective of local people, without ever losing sight of breaking events and the reality that the US continues its century-old containment of Russia by any means necessary.

—SASHA ARSIC
Nish, Serbia
Political Activist

OTHER TITLES BY GAITHER STEWART

The Trojan Spy
(Book One of the *Europe Trilogy*)
a novel

Icy Current, Compulsive Course
short stories

To Be A Stranger
short stories

Once in Berlin
short stories

Asheville
a novel

On The Side of the Losers
essays

LILY PAD ROLL

by
Gaither Stewart

Trepper & Katz Impact Books
A DIVISION OF PUNTO PRESS

New York

Lily Pad Roll

Copyright © 2012 by Gaither Stewart

Published in the United States by Trepper & Katz Impact Books

Trepper & Katz Impact Books is an imprint of Punto Press, LLC.

Punto Press Publishing
P.O. Box 943, Brewster, NY 10509-9998, USA
www.puntopress.com

Address all inquiries to: admin@puntopress.com

Library of Congress Control Number: 2012945383

ISBN: 978-0-9840263-2-6

Cover art, book design, and interior pages illustrations by
Sarah Edgar

Printed and distributed worldwide by Lightning Source, Inc.

Political fiction | Historical fiction | Cold War | Espionage |
False Flag Terrorism | Strategy of Tension

* * *

Trepper & Katz Impact Books pays homage to Leopold Trepper and Hillel Katz, two heroic fighters against fascism in World War Two. May their example guide those who, in every latitude, struggle today against great odds for world peace and social justice.

"A book is the product of a different self
from the one we manifest in our habits,
in society, in our vices."

—*Marcel Proust*

Russia's whole power, her whole personality,
so to say, and her whole future mission lie in
her self-denying unselfishness.

Our People love truth for the sake of truth and not for
show … you will be astounded by the degree of freedom
of spirit which they will show before the burdens of
materialism, passion, the lust for money, and possessions,
and even before the fear of the cruelest martyr's death.

—*Fyodor Dostoevsky*

PREFACE
Paul Carline

ILY PAD ROLL is the second part of Gaither Stewart's *Europe Trilogy*. It was born, so to speak, out of the characters of the first novel, *The Trojan Spy*. According to its author, there was, to begin with, no intention of writing a trilogy. *The Trojan Spy* was completed and first published as a stand-alone 'spy' novel in 2010, but it seems that both the characters—and the evolving political background—presented cases of "unfinished business" for the author. Although the central character of *The Trojan Spy*—the Russian double-agent Anatoly Nikitin—was no longer around, having met a violent death on a mountain road in Italy, his ghost hovers over *Lily Pad Roll*, and his intimate connection with later events continues in the destinies of Elizaveta and Masha.

In his review of *The Trojan Spy*, Australian novelist Desmond O'Grady writes of Nikitin's self-appointed mission "to uncover the deadliest of spy rings, the organizers of terrorism". He observes that "the brutality and menace of terrorism has only increased since spies were supposed to have disappeared with the end of the Cold War, and that much of the world is hostage to a strategy of tension in which terrorism provides the pretext for creations like Homeland Security in the USA".

Although the application of the "strategy of tension" to which O'Grady refers has become global, especially since 9/11, with major elements of it in operation in the so-called "Arab Spring" events, it originated in a specific European historical and political context which has direct connections to the issues raised in the *Europe Trilogy*. Wikipedia defines the "strategy of tension" as a method for "dividing, manipulating, and controlling public opinion using fear, propaganda, disinformation, psychological warfare, agents provocateurs, and false flag terrorist actions" — thus by definition a conspiracy by those who plan and execute it. NATO was formed in 1949. Its clearly conspiratorial mission, formulated the same year by its first Secretary-General, Lord Ismay, was to "keep the Russians out, the Americans in, and the Germans down". In post-WWII "Cold War" Europe, the NATO powers used the largely manufactured "Red Menace" — the supposed threat of a Soviet takeover of the whole of Western Europe — to sway public opinion against Communism in general and radical left-wing/communist political parties and candidates in particular.

By the late 1960s, communist parties had gained some ground politically in Europe, i.e. they were popular with the voters; nowhere more so than in Italy, where the "strategy of tension" was played out in its deadliest form. The Piazza Fontana bombing of December 1969 in Milan (16 dead, 90 injured) was followed by the 1974 bombing of the Italicus Express train (12 dead, 105 injured), the Piazza della Loggia bombing in Brescia the same year (8 dead, more than 90 injured), and the 1980 Bologna railway station bombing (85 dead, more than 200 injured). At the time, these and other attacks were blamed on "communists" (Baader Meinhof, the Red Brigades), but were in fact carried out by members of right-wing/fascist paramilitary groups, trained and armed by the CIA and British MI6 and working through NATO i.e. classic 'false flag' events which were also clearly conspiracies.

In 1984, questioned by judges about the Bologna bombing, far-right activist and member of both the neo-Fascist Avanguardia Nazionale and the Ordine Nuovo and the infamous P2 Masonic Lodge, Vincenzo Vinciguerra said: "With the massacre of Peteano [the murder of three policemen in 1972, for which Vinciguerra received a life sentence], and with all those that have followed, the knowledge should by now be clear that there existed a real live structure, occult and hidden, with the capacity of giving a strategic direction to the outrages ... [it] lies within the state itself ... There exists in Italy a secret force parallel to the armed forces, composed of civilians and military men, in an anti-Soviet capacity ... A secret organisation, a super-organisation with a network of communications, arms and explosives, and men trained to use them ... A super-organisation which, in the absence of a Soviet military invasion which might not happen, took up the task, on NATO's behalf, of preventing a slip to the left in the political balance of the country. This they did, with the assistance of the official secret services and the political and military forces". Referring to the Piazza Fontana bombing, Vinciguerra said: "The December 1969 explosion was supposed to be the detonator which would have convinced the political and military authorities to declare a state of emergency" — similar to the effect of the 1933 false-flag burning of the Reichstag in Berlin which allowed Hitler to pass the "Enabling Law", whose modern parallel is the Patriot Act. Vinciguerra made it clear that the attacks were supported by the political and military establishments, not only in Italy: "The Carabinieri, the Minister of the Interior, the customs services and the military and civilian intelligence services accepted the ideological reasoning behind the attack[s]".

After then Prime Minister Giulio Andreotti had formally admitted — in 1990 in the Italian Parliament — the existence of the "Gladio" armies, investigations were carried out in a number of European countries. In 2000, the Italian government published a 300-page report on the Gladio operations in Italy, documenting connections with the United States. It attributed responsibility for the "strategy of tension" to the US. Having examined why those who committed the bombings in Italy were rarely caught, the report concluded that "those massacres, those bombings, those military actions were organised or promoted or supported by men within Italian state institutions and, as has been discovered, by men linked to the structures of US Intelligence".

The "stay behind armies" linked to the terrorist bombings and assassinations were subsequently found to have existed in no less than seventeen European countries, including even Switzerland. The most comprehensive examinations of the history of "Gladio" are contained, firstly, in the book *NATO's Secret Armies: Operation Gladio and Terrorism in Western Europe* by Swiss historian Daniele Ganser, and secondly in the three-part documentary by American director Allan Frankovich broadcast by the BBC in 1992 and entitled: "Operation Gladio—The Hidden History of US Sponsored False Flag Terrorism in Europe". The broadcasts stated: "This BBC series is about a far-right secret army, operated by the CIA and MI6 through NATO, which killed hundreds of innocent Europeans and attempted to blame the deaths on Baader Meinhof, Red Brigades and other left wing groups. Known as 'stay-behinds', these armies were given access to military equipment which was supposed to be used for sabotage after a Soviet invasion. Instead it was used in massacres across mainland Europe as part of a CIA Strategy of Tension. Gladio killing sprees in Belgium and Italy were carried out for the purpose of frightening the national political classes into adopting U.S. policies." On a return to the USA in 1997, Frankovich suffered a possibly suspicious 'heart attack' at Houston Airport and died one week later. His "Gladio" film was never shown again by the BBC, but is available on YouTube. Frankovich also made the film "The Maltese Double Cross" which questioned the official story of the Lockerbie plane bombing (Pan Am flight 103).

In an interview given in 2005, Ganser said: "People often say to me: It is very interesting what you write about what happened in the 1970s, but I am living now. What is going on now? My usual answer to that is that 'stay behind'/ Gladio as such is not operative any more, but what obviously is still going on is secret warfare". As an example, Ganser spoke of events in the Balkans which also figure strongly in

Lily Pad Roll: " ... we had the Kosovo operation when, on March 24, 1999, the NATO bombing of Serbia started. I looked at what exactly the OSCE [Organization for Security and Cooperation in Europe] did in the weeks before, because William Walker, the U.S. representative to the OSCE, had been linked to covert operations in Latin America. The data I found showed that Walker had the Racak massacre in Kosovo manipulated in order to spread a 'genocide' claim. [This] impressed German Foreign Minister Joschka Fischer, despite the fact that the data on the ground did not support this claim". Ganser added: "The rule with Gladio is that you cannot rule out anything, that's exactly the point. After all, secret armies have existed for 40 years in all countries of Western Europe outside of any control of parliamentary democracy. If that's possible, you can't rule out anything."

After the Andreotti revelations, the matter was debated in the European Parliament (on 22 November, 1990). The eight-part resolution with which the debate concluded called upon the governments of all the EU member states and the Council of Ministers to carry out in-depth investigations and provide "full information on the activities of these secret intelligence and operational services". The resolution was forwarded to the European Commission, the Council of Ministers, the Secretary-General of NATO, the governments of the member states, and the United States government.

Predictably, perhaps, nothing happened. As Ganser wrote later: "The dog barked loudly but it did not bite. Of the eight actions requested by the EU parliament, not one was carried out satisfactorily. Only Belgium, Italy and Switzerland investigated their secret armies with a parliamentary commission, producing a lengthy and detailed public report". Meanwhile, the campaigns for independent inquiries into the major 'terrorist' incidents in New York, Madrid, London, Bali and elsewhere continue. In none of those cases — or of the many 'minor' ones, like that of the "Christmas/Underwear Bomber" — has the truth been told.

In the course of researching for this preface I came across the work of another author and journalist, Hunter S. Thompson, who, despite his various addictions, had the great virtue of a passionate commitment to getting below the surface of things to reveal the truth, however dirty it might be. One quote of his leaped off the page: "Fiction is based on reality unless you're a fairy-tale artist. You have to get knowledge of life from somewhere. You have to know the material you're writing about before you alter it". Gaither Stewart has an unusually wide (and long) life experience on which to draw. He has been to most of the places he uses as settings for his stories (and the few exceptions have been minutely 'walked through' with the aid of maps). Indeed, his sense of place is legendary—one reviewer suggesting that the places could be seen as extra characters. He is also clearly very familiar with the inner landscape of the mind and soul, with its dark and light places, its abysses and its high peaks.

I referred above to the "evolving political background". Perhaps I should have said: "geo-political and military background". *Lily Pad Roll* takes us into the world of the inexorable spread of American and NATO bases around the world, and in particular in those countries which form a kind of crescent surrounding Russia on its south-western, southern and south-eastern borders. The exact number of such bases is unknown (except presumably to the Pentagon and the White House), estimates varying from around 740 to over 1000, with new bases continually being created or older ones extended—such as those on the Yemeni island of Socotra and the Omani island of Masirah, both situated strategically at the southern exit of the Strait of Hormuz, within easy striking distance of Iran. The base on Masirah is (with a sense of irony perhaps) called Camp Justice.

Then there's Camp Bondsteel, in Kosovo, one of the largest, of which the character Ilya in *Lily Pad Roll* says: "Our Kosovo, the cradle of my country, is one great NATO base. Camp Bondsteel. 'Beautiful CBS', they call it. And I do not mean the TV network. That is what is happening. It is like going abroad ... if you can even get in there. The Kosovar workers on the base are the new Negroes at one dollar an hour. On the base Americans even have separate toilets. And Burger Kings and movie theaters. The base even runs its own Marathon. The Kosovo Marathon! Camp Bondsteel has a downtown, a midtown and an uptown, dance halls and bars and baseball fields, University of Maryland and Central Texas College courses, while Thai girls give massages, allegedly controlled by military authorities. I wonder. And gigantic helicopters that can fly to Tehran ... with a few stopovers in the string of American outposts and bases along the way. But also nearly to Russia. The whole base is surrounded by a 2.5-meter high earthen wall, seven miles in perimeter. The largest base in the Balkans."

According to Iraklis Tsavdaridis, Secretary of the World Peace Council (WPC): "The establishment of U.S. military bases should not of course be seen simply in terms of direct military ends. They are always used to promote the economic and political objectives of U.S. capitalism." Imperialism, in whatever form, always needs force or the threat of force to sustain itself. If this can be done under the guise of bringing "freedom and democracy" to 'oppressed' peoples, then it becomes much easier to sell the scam to gullible people, especially when the mainstream media, through which they acquire most of their news and which is part of the same rapacious global corporatocracy, feeds them continuous disinformation and outright lies.

Writing in June 2011, another journalist, Chris Hedges, lamented the death of traditional (especially investigative) journalism: "The steady decline of the news business means we are plunging larger and larger parts of our society into dark holes and opening up greater opportunities for unchecked corruption, disinformation and the abuse of power. A democracy survives when its citizens have access to trustworthy and impartial sources of information, when it can discern lies from truth, when civic discourse is grounded in verifiable fact."

The novel has long been a medium to which concerned or angry writers could turn to bring their concerns and anger — about social injustice, political corruption or an assault on human values — to a wider audience in a form which allowed the potentially dry polemics of the argument to be given life through the characters and a hopefully engaging plot. Hunter S. Thompson did it; so did George Orwell, another journalist-author, whose *1984* became the classic representation of a totalitarian society, including the original "Big Brother". By 1989 it had been translated into 65 languages. Orwell was well aware of the 'false flag' device. The girl Julia, with whom his hero (or anti-hero?) Winston has an illicit sexual relationship, surprises him one day by speculating that "the rocket bombs which fell daily on London were probably fired by the government of Oceania itself, 'just to keep the people frightened'." Working as he did for the BBC, Orwell was probably aware of the revelation made by one of the Germans interrogated at Nuremberg. Bernard Naujocks that the incidents which Hitler used to declare war on Poland — especially the faked attack on the German radio station at Gleiwitz on the Polish border — were 'false flag' attacks. He may also have been familiar with Nazi Propaganda Minister Joseph Goebbels' statement: "If you tell a lie big enough and keep repeating it, people will eventually come to believe it"; or with the declaration made at Nuremberg by Hitler's deputy Hermann Goering: "Voice or no voice, the people can always be brought to the bidding of the leaders. That is easy. All you have to do is tell them they are being attacked and denounce the pacifists for lack of patriotism and exposing the country to danger. It works the same in any country."

As Orwell and others have shown, fiction can be an effective way of bringing suppressed truths to a wider public – bringing some light to the "dark holes" referred to by Hedges. Orwell himself acknowledged the polemical purpose of his later work, stating that all the "serious work" he had written since the Spanish Civil War in 1936 had been written "directly or indirectly against totalitarianism and for democratic socialism". Stewart's trilogy is in august company. Perhaps it may help to inspire a new generation of journalist-novelists committed to filling the gap created by the death of mainstream journalism. Perhaps honest novels—at any rate if they are as well-written as those in Stewart's trilogy—can add a clearer and more appealing message to the often confusing and shrill voice of the Internet. As Oscar Wilde playfully observed: "Anyone who tells the truth is bound to be found out sooner or later". It is certainly true that human society stands in great need of the truth, perhaps more than at any time in the past.

Other contemporary novelists, such as le Carré and Ludlum, have skirted around the issues. So far, only Stewart has had the courage to nail the lies directly. The encirclement of Russia (and, to an extent, also the other great nations of India and China, seen by America as threats to its global hegemony) and the surreptitious expansion of American military and economic power worldwide in defence of an obviously corrupt and failing global capitalism—including through its multitude of 'Lily Pad' bases—is the major, as yet insufficiently told, story of our time. The three stories of Gaither Stewart's *Europe Trilogy* should be read widely. They would also make wonderful films.

Newhall
04/04/2012

ACKNOWLEDGEMENTS

Not for the first time I am indebted to Remi Stewart, my daughter-in-law, for her patient and as usual thorough editing of this volume and her countless suggestions on style and content. My deep gratitude also goes to Paul Carline in Scotland first of all for his preface to this volume, secondly for his several readings of the text, a second edit of the final text, thorough background research concerning content and his constant and patient advice and suggestions. Thanks are also due to the publisher Patrice Greanville for his back cover center piece and his unerring guidance in the preparation of the final manuscript. For their encouraging and often stimulating endorsements for this second volume of the *Europe Trilogy* my appreciation to Bruno Mirkowski in Poland, Sasha Arsic in Serbia, Desmond O'Grady in Rome and Gui Rochat and Mike Hopping in the United States. The helpful friends and acquaintances, writers, journalists, political activists and people on the streets of East Europe are too numerous to mention by name, but I remembered and saw them in my brain's eye in the writing of this novel. Lastly, my special thanks to the artist Sarah Edgar for her exquisite cover art and the general layout of the book.

LILY PAD ROLL

by
Gaither Stewart

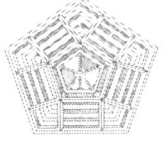

1

THE sun has reawakened. Rekindling the promise of the most spectacular new dawns of recent years. After a long sleep, the activity of our central star has resumed. Scientists have observed solar eruptions on the sun's surface, launching charged particles into interplanetary space. This cloud of particles is now heading towards Earth. Scientists claim its arrival will cause a new and beautiful dawn visible in North America and Northern Europe. However, within the beauty is also terror. Apparently such solar activity is cyclical, repeating about every eleven years. The last time this occurred was in the terrible year of 2001.

I don't know what to make of that scientific-social-political coincidence—I mean the turbulent solar activity coupled with the explosion of homemade terrorism. Nor do I understand the apparent self-satisfaction of the scientific world with this discovery. Allegedly the eruptions are one of the clearest signals of the sun's reawakening, as a result of which Earth could cease to orbit the sun.

But stop! Imagine! Our planet would then again transform. Gravity, scientists report, would become enormous at the poles, which would attract all the abundant water of our planet. Much of our planet would be submerged, including most of Europe. And in place of the many contours of the maps to which we're accustomed, one great continent would appear at the equator. The beautiful new dawn at the poles would be the result.

At the same time as such solar activities are going on, our moon is getting smaller and showing its wrinkles, pittings and swellings. In other words, aging. Besides aging, the moon is moving away from Earth at the rate of four centimeters a year. So what do these cosmic alterations mean to us today? Four centimeters do not sound like much change. Yet we all know that the universal environment is changing. That other interplanetary mutations are occurring in the same way that our own Earth changes from year to year.

The sun reawakening. The moon abandoning us. Also the gods. The signs are accumulating that mankind is indeed lost. Yet we human beings are unaware of our growing solitude.

2

CLIFF

THE gossamer threads of the pathways and the highways all seem to lead back to the St. Moritz of my youth. To the corner of Switzerland that haunts the web that is my life. The entanglements of slippery threads lead back to the lie, to the brutalities and the intrigues which shaped me. Away into the mist first fled my mother. While her hair was still fiery red she escaped, leaving my self-deceived father to wait for her. Hanging onto her portrait and predicting her eventual return. Within the gray Engadine shadows that the sun leaves behind as it abandons the Lei da San Murezzan and transforms the snowy peaks of Corvatsch to a pink glow, there under the bowers of the Hotel Palace and the Chadafö and along the spidery streets of my life's cities, reverberates the mystery of who I am.

I stand in the oval bathroom under the yellow and blue and green nuances of Elizaveta's skylight and stare into her mirror framed in yellow hanging symmetrically under the skylight, the mirror which asks me the same question every day: "Who is that?" I wait and listen, still hoping for an answer. I mean, what is my life about anyway? Who is that looking out at me, a question mark in his eyes, asking those uncomfortable questions about what he once thought he was doing in his life? I, who thought it was only a question of me against the authority of the rest.

Yes! Who is that looking in at himself?

In my former life, it was I instead who asked the mirrors the questions: "Where do I go from here? What is next?"

Today, my breath casting opaque clouds on Elizaveta's

mirror, my answer to the old question is: "Not back to that life of sham." At least I know my new goal: to distinguish my genuine life of today from the fictitious world of my life of yesterday.

Since my defection—senseless and infantile, *they* thought— my goal has been to destroy the myths inculcated in my psyche, to construct protective barriers in my mind and to separate today's me from the shadow of the me I left behind.

Though *the events,* as they came to be called, happened over a year ago, the memory of the bombings survives in the minds of all Westerners. No serious doubts about their nature or their reality have arisen. If they of Power say there is a worldwide conspiracy against us and our way of life, then there is. No inquiries necessary. Fact is fact, *they* assert.

Their alleged facts, I answer. Innocence, gullibility, sheer ignorance and optimistic Americanism know no limits.

No, even if I wanted to, I couldn't return to that point again. The nadir of my life. A bellyful was a bellyful. Revenge didn't erase the memory. Madness waited in ambush.

I know what happened that tragic day before Christmas. I know where the bombs came from. Not from Afghanistan or Al Qaida. I'm proud that I killed some of those responsible. But not all. I know how things work. I know the competition for power and prestige. If *they* who once comprised also me succeeded in first concocting worldwide terrorism and consequently the universal, eternal wars against it, wars accepted and abetted by our civilization, of what are *they* not capable in order to extend their empire?

Now I realize that the *events* were not a conspiracy of only a rogue part of the Agency. No longer do I believe the rogue agents I killed bore all the responsibility. Now I know there is no rogue Agency. There is only The Agency. That changes everything. How naïve I was. How little I took of my mother's prescience to get out before it was too late.

3

CONSPIRACY is in the very air we breathe. It runs through our veins. Conspiracy is the dark stain in man. Real life is not what the naïve believe it is. The stain runs deep. Real life is not straightforward. After the fact, things can appear so vacuous, so different and so remote that even the most terrible events come to seem to have occurred in a completely different manner. As if they happened in a life where neither people nor happenings were real but were only the fictional abstractions created by criminal leaders.

No wonder I'm not situated in real life. Still, I had the good fortune of experiencing—just barely in time—the crisis and the rupture in my life, my separation from that life and the conjoining with a new one. Long gone is that life when I felt all-powerful. Beyond laws, codes, rules and regulations. Now I know that my self of then—then, when I didn't know the meaning of loss or losing—was my worst self. Nor did I realize the existence of another "I" inside me. Yet I escaped.

I came away physically and spiritually damaged. Though I believe I've now recovered—yes, yes, I have. Hmm, yes, I believe so. Then, if not, who is that looking out at me from the bathroom mirror? I peer at the image. I examine it. The more I study the image, the more I realize how far I am still removed from my real "I." I realize that my past remains as part of my present.

"Who is that?" I ask in turn. Who is that in the image— the "I" in the mirror looking so cynically back at me—the

"I" who I once thought had discovered what I once thought of as his enchanted self? I know, I know. Ridiculous assessment. Mad conclusion. That is not to say that I believe that full truth about the self is possible. Nor even probable. The Dane noted that it is no pleasure to recall old thoughts. In fact such truth would most likely be unbearable. But if truth does live in me, I hope to reduce the distance between it and myself. My difficulties in grasping truth are not surprising. That I have doubts about its existence. For in my father's world, a world of intrigue in which I grew up, truth was never a factor. Nor did it exist in my life in the Agency. Maybe it will remain a chimera. Forever an unobtainable goal.

I've always thought that at a certain stage of life we all need to situate ourselves. To reclaim, let's say, our true selves. It's no small achievement to be able to embrace the positive aspects of your self and abandon the negative ones: to reacquire oneself, so to speak. I'm fortunate in that I'm now free to try to realize my own potential. That I recognize the right path even if I don't always follow it. As psychoanalysts love to discuss and theorize, I too try to cultivate the concealed powers of my creative unconscious without letting go the reins of self-control. The discovery of the existence of those latent powers was, I think, more confusing than anything that occurred in my former life.

I just told myself that I was finally free. But actually I'm not. I'm not satisfied with my situation. Nor with myself. And I know I will never be. But I have crossed the threshold.

So I proceed stealthily, a shadow, a shell of my former self, observing the realities of my new life as well as the results of my former actions. I don't live with nostalgia. I live for present. And the future. Though I resurrect my former life from time to time, it appears to me distorted as seen through a dark veil. I hope that is a sign of progress.

They might think I'm savoring my revenge — in silence. But that's not the case, I tell myself, nose to nose with my silent image. I don't seek revenge anymore. I seek my own authenticity, a recognition of and participation in reality. Reality is my goal. So, though only partially redeemed, I feel I have a hold on the keys to my own life. And today I feel responsible also for the life of Elizaveta. Maybe that is arrogance, but I confess it makes me feel noble.

That my spymaster father died crazed by urgency and time and loneliness, that Nikitin vanished in the explosion in which I too should have died, that I killed other men on the midnight streets of a hillside town in Italy—those things really happened. I remember.

Now I, a willing witness of my former "I", know that my former life was also theater. And I, an enthusiastic actor. A deadly actor, an operative of a secret American government agency operating on the borderline between legality and criminality, which lied, stole and killed.

Yet I learned, finally, very late, when all the disparate events of my lived life seemed to cohere, that criminality is always criminality, no matter whose interests it serves. It is the very reality of those bewildering events that casts the light necessary to concretize those interests, to stretch them out in time and reveal them for what they were.

"Did I—Did you?" I ask my voiceless and uncommunicative self looking out at me. Did I share *their* blind faith in our indifferent and loveless technology vis-à-vis the depths of the mystery and the potentiality of magic? I would like to hope that I secretly hated it.

I no longer know what I thought I knew back then. I just acted. Does a voiceless automaton think? Or just act? Does the soulless feel? Or just act? The dread I came to feel of the vertiginous heights of *their* technology and *their* faith in it now seems insignificant in comparison to the tremendous task it set—that of monitoring the world— while in reality *they* remained ignorant of the immensity of the magic at work around us.

I used to feel I stood in the middle, between the lines,

suspended between two worlds, the in-between-person, neither here, nor there, as if I could somehow unite opposites. In reality I knew what *they* were doing: those imbeciles were preparing tragedies.

Yet I stayed on, unthinkingly caught up in *their* fairy tale. But today, trying to recall and describe the brutality of the reality, I believe I discern the lines of the presence of another "I". I always knew—well, at least since I arrived at an early stage of self-realization—that I had within me an "I" different from the one existing in *their* world. From one day to the next, it seemed, the other "I" acquired the capacity to distinguish misconceptions from comprehension. Fiction from reality. Lie from truth. Another actor, another narrator, materialized from the nothingness. An actor still distant from the real me.

The porous interface separating things, the boundary line, the divide between peace and violence—but also the meeting and gathering place—is as equivocal as this mirror. Often I wonder about the distinctions. And I hope for the best for me, that I will make a better showing. Still, it's no wonder I'm still un-situated. And no wonder that the shadow of violence remains.

4

J AGGED edges of ice reaching out into tram-lined cobbled streets. Sidewalks frozen. Short careful steps of elderly shoppers pulling bulging carts. Beer-laden old men. Despite the enduring winter, the change in the air is palpable. By now the snow and ice in the city should have transformed into slush. Instead the white remains in all its splendor. Cold, packed, white snow over thick beds of ice. The ground-hog appeared and saw its shadow. Or it did not. I never remember which is the sign for change. What remains is the wintry glory I prefer. No unpleasant signs announcing the warming of the sun to come. We can do quite well without the slushy ugliness of the passage to the season of the sun due to follow the pristine beauty of today.

I slide my feet over a solid sheet of ice on the untrammeled and sunless street. I'd left the car blocks away from the apartment, this time in the Rauch Strasse. I keep a calendar-map in mind to remember where my car is each morning. Now I drive an old, nondescript Opel. No more Porsches mark my presence. Always park in a different spot on a different street. Old habits hang on.

Hopefully no nosey spy in the neighborhood will rec-ognize me. I touch my heavy beard for reassurance. It's frozen stiff. From time to time I look over my shoulder. On the qui vive for shadows standing immobile in darkened doorways. For darting silhouettes against dim lights in isolated upstairs windows. Tenacious old habits. Times and events are so confusing that I sometimes even forget who the enemy is. That's old thinking too.

My new life position is still ambiguous. New wife, new job, new direction, but my situation remains obscure, unclear to me, suspicious to Elizaveta.

No matter how cautious I am, unusual things continue to happen to me. It has been that way my whole life, since the village school in St. Moritz, in my former work and still today ... and especially since Elizaveta came into my life. Unclear if I attract the strange occurrences or the occurrences attract me.

Then because of my tendency to implicate others in the things happening to me, the singular occurrences become a kind of complicity. People and objects in my orbit have a way of going haywire and then having their way with me. No wonder I easily lose all normal sense of orientation, as if anything at all could happen at any time. That has to come to an end.

The same moment I turn into the Holbein Strasse, still lined by the familiar mix of contemporary and pre-war apartment houses, it comes back to me: I shouldn't have done what I did. But as usual I did it anyway. Without reflection, instinctively, like much of my life action, not only did I return to the same city with another woman but also back to the same street. Any analyst worth his diploma would grab that and run with it. The street where twenty years earlier my life swirled out of control and ended in tragedy. There must be some morbid but irrepressible destiny, a kind of fatalism in which I proclaim not to believe — an inescapable attraction to the same place where I once experienced a life-changing tragedy.

Still, despite the sense of guilt that hangs over my relationship with Elizaveta, I'm inexplicably optimistic. About my new happiness, I mean. It's a kind of utopia. The euphoria of our togetherness simply outweighs my former unhappiness and my sorrow, misery and failures experienced on this same street.

Even though the past is not static and seems to change

as I change, I believe that in the long run Elizaveta will overcome the violence of my nature. She promises me that. Not only am I already becoming more perceptive of my elusive self, but I also believe she will root out my blood-sucking guilt that has begun infiltrating, bit by bit, through imperceptible cracks and crannies here and there, into our relationship.

In these new times with Elizaveta, in our vertiginous moments of bliss, I instead act as if I had no past at all. Otherwise how could I permit myself the luxury of wallowing in this new happiness?

I do feel guilty. At least that! Guilty that I grieve less over the breakup of my former family. Some mornings I look at myself in the mirror and realize I'm not terribly afflicted. Not like before. I should suffer more. I should still be desperate over the loss of my daughter. I regret that my phobias and obsessions and manias have lessened their grip on me. I should have hung onto them. I need them. Still, I have to accept the fact that my daughter will never return and that nothing in my world will ever be the same again.

Sometimes I, Clifford Beecher, think it doesn't matter. Sometimes I still feel I'm invisible. I know the problem is that I don't know who I am. I would like to be indifferent to what I feel I am. But I know I am not. I can't accept that I am what I was destined to be and do the miserable things I do and that my life—as it is—is a necessary part of the order of things. I have never even considered fate. Fate, ambiguous or unequivocal, doesn't exist for me. Or hardly.

* * *

The senseless, unnecessary what-if questions continue to plague me. What if I hadn't thought of going to Dubrovnik that day? What if I hadn't seen Elizaveta in the travel agency window? What if I hadn't spoken to her? What if? What if? If not, would I be down in Turin tonight trying to put a failed marriage back together instead of forgetting Giuliana and trying to find myself? Or, if not for Elizaveta would I still be out there betraying people? Killing people? One day I should isolate myself on the top of a mountain, maybe retire to a Benedictine monastery, and try to record those things. In any case, if not for Elizaveta, my life today would be destinationless. Navigation without a rudder. Like a speedboat turning in circles, round and round until overcome by the clash of momentum with the crest of its own wake, I would spin off course, beset by moments of madness.

5

ON THE first evening in our first home together I went out to reconnoiter the familiar surroundings. This was a necessity. And habit. In the hotels and safe houses of the world of my former life, I explained to Elizaveta, I always did that. I have to know exactly where I am. Europe, Germany, Bavaria, Munich, Bogenhausen, Holbein Strasse, number 36, sixth floor penthouse, in the year 2011. I am constantly driven to situate myself in space and time. It's more than my sense of place; it's a compulsion to know the physical spatial reality of my places, even of the temporary ones, which through sight and touch I try to make mine. It's also my insecurity, as my old partner Franz used to explain. In any case, though my present time and space have a tendency to fragment and overlap past memories and become evasive, I still consider this part of the city my territory.

That evening Bogenhausen seemed strange. Like a no man's land. I was surprised at my reaction. Maybe it was because I hadn't revealed to Elizaveta that I'd lived on this street in another life. With another family. In a different situation. I don't know why I hadn't told her. Truly bizarre, for reticence has never been one of my characteristics.

It had been dark for hours. An icy wind blew up Holbein Strasse. The lights strung across the face of an apartment building illuminated scaffolds along the edges of the roofs. No matter the cold, the wind and the ice, men were working up there. I pulled my sheepskin coat high around my neck and stopped to observe the bundled figures of workers carrying materials moving back and forth along the boards. Turks or some other Middle Easterners.

Unthinking, again out of habit, I stepped into the Gaststube down the street in the direction of the Ismaninger Strasse. The pub was once my favorite hangout. The last thing I needed today was to become known again on my own street but 'What the fuck!' I thought. Once this was my place, but now the scene inside bewildered me. The officious-looking young woman in red who popped up at my side looked up at me seductively and asked if I had a reservation or perhaps I would like a table in the Winter Garden?

"Winter Garden? Here?"

The hostess peered at me curiously.

I hesitated, staring open-mouthed at the slick mahogany bar along the side wall, the soft indirect lighting and a swarm of chic little iron tables painted dark green filling the long room. The heat was oppressive. Dig that new bar, dig that lighting, I repeated to myself, just for the sensation of using the for me new English word that actually fitted my former self more than me today. When I think in English I practice words I've never uttered in the English I almost never speak anymore. Not since English-speaking Franzi and I closed our shop in St. Moritz. I make lists of such words and expressions I read in American novels: Dig this. Scope that. Clip him. Words describing my old life.

The heavy dark wooden tables and benches once bearing my carved initials had vanished along with the old proprietor and his deep bass voice: *"Grüss Gott, Clifford, wie geht's der Familie, hoch di hie."* The pub's former simple *Gemütlichkeit* was more my style.

Standardization, homogenization, uniformity. What can you do about them? *Menschenskinder!* You have to go to Paraguay or Argentina or even the Amazon to rediscover anything genuine. All of Europe is fake chic ... or fake American. Or was the past style I had in mind itself false? Are the cute little tables and slick bar now genuine?

"*Vielen Dank, gnädiges Fräulein, aber ....*" Forget this pub-bistro! No longer my place. Neither past nor present, certainly not my future.

A few streets over, the Prinzregenten Theater was resplendent. Christ Almighty! Cars everywhere. The row of old shops and my barbershop of back then had vanished, making way for a metro station. The illumination of the area around the entrance to the U-Bahn and the great theater made the square resemble the Champs Elysées. So different from the time back then when Giuliana had gotten tickets for the reopening of the new stage in this old opera house. For the sake of my ex-wife I'd suffered through the endless hours of *Tristan und Isolde*. And even though she then played the record for months afterwards, today I don't remember one single musical theme from the opera. Never understood why I'm good with languages but simply can't retain music. It's a mystery. Heavy stuff, *Tristan*. The kind of love I doubt artistic Elizaveta would want to comprehend. You have to be very German to appreciate it.

Looking over the billboard I realized I had to make a special sacrifice for Elizaveta also. Not the theater though. I had to take her to Russia! That will come out in the wash, as my mother once liked to say when I was a tot. Look at it any way you want but old Nietzsche was right: things do indeed repeat themselves. Thank God *Tristan* was not on the billboard.

6

E LIZAVETA says I'm just confused. Actually she knows so little about me. I have to fill in the gaps. Sometimes she accuses me of making things up. And sometimes I too wonder if my past even happened. Is the past as I remember it necessarily reality? Or has memory warped the reality into fantasy? Was that ugly world of the dark palaces I frequented real reality? Or is that just my personally biased illusion of what might have happened? Only a dream? If so, it's a lasting one.

Anyway, one thing is certain. I didn't dream the tragedy. It happened. She's gone. Never to return. Even her grave disappeared. Every day since she has still been gone. And her death left behind a trail of destruction and hurt and pain and sorrow and lasting trauma that swept away the little in common Giuliana and I had. Sharing that kind of tragedy, I learned then, impacts a relationship more than sharing successes.

I never seem to get things straight in my mind. I can never distinguish between what is real reality and what is fantasy, between what is reality and what is only my fertile imagination of what might have occurred. Are the things I love most in life today destined to morph into fantasy in an unpredictable future? A chimera? Is my love for Elizaveta real? Is romantic love itself reality? That, Clifford, is the question of questions.

My friend Franz was right about me: my mind is a bloody mess. A quagmire. A battleground where reality and fantasy fight for supremacy. Franz likes to compare me to a speeding tram on the edge of a cliff. A Cliff! But a fucking tram! He explains that a tram is unaware of where it's going or of where it's coming from. It just moves along its repetitive rails, always in the present. So the images of the different times and events in my life overwhelm me and become my present, in the same way as the illumination Elizaveta so loves overlaps the darkness creeping toward us from the direction of the Friedensengel hanging over the River Isar. So I continue to move ahead, despite my dark past.

Oh, I was once cocksure of myself and the future. Elizaveta says I still am. Once the world was never big enough. I had to live more than one life—two, three and more lives. Everything easy. Easy. At some point in life I began to feel I was immune to the ills that strike less fortunate people. I've often wondered: do other people at certain times in their lives feel the invulnerability I once felt?

Maybe I once believed that Fate—even if I claim not to believe in her—was on my side. Actually I don't claim that Fate doesn't exist, but the doubt exists. Fate exists … and doesn't. In any case, either I'm strong enough to master my fate—if it exists—or it is more powerful than my will. Destiny is something else. Franz often quoted the French proverb that people often meet their destiny on the road they take to avoid it. Like the soldier in the tale of his appointment with Death in Samarkand. It's along that precise road of seeming escape that fate can step in to give you a hand, Franz says. Because, he believes—like Heidegger, he says—that though you can't change your destiny, you can challenge it.

Still—and this is what is so curious about destiny and fate in my opinion—how am I to know what my destiny has in store for me? Was it just my destiny or did fate prompt me to squeeze the trigger on the hill of Perugia? Is there really a difference between the two? Fuck it! Maybe these are the futile questions of age and circumstances.

When that first night I returned home around midnight, Elizaveta was still re-arranging her studio. She still wasn't satisfied. Too much a perfectionist for me. But I seconded her. Worktables, palettes and paints, canvases, an easel here and a pedestal there, and paintings stacked against the walls. She only glanced at me with unseeing eyes, engrossed as she was in momentous decisions.

"In your own world now, eh, Lizzy?" I say with the immense affection I feel for her. Maybe it's because of her detachment in such moments that I feel uneasy around her works of art. One of the last things I learned about her was that her real life is her art.

"Only one of my worlds, Clifford. Only one of them."

"Am I in it too?"

The truth is I don't know how I feel about her artwork now that we live together. Or how she can separate art from her lived life ... and from me. While I was still at home in Switzerland and she here in Munich, her paintings made her seem even more exotic and fascinating. Her job in a travel agency was a front, the sacrifice that made her artist life possible. Now her art is a thing apart, and at times, it seems, divisive. She can disappear into it, into a seclusion from which I am excluded.

"Oh, don't worry, you're there, my love, fixed."

"I wonder."

Should have told her about my dream. I've had it before. We're on a bus; I, in a front seat, she, somewhere behind me. The bus stops and she is getting off. We both reach out toward each other and hold each other's hand. She begins pulling her hand away. Slowly it slips from mine, and she says *Lebewohl*, Clifford, and begins to descend the steps of the exit. I know she is leaving me forever. I plead, "Wait Elizaveta, wait." But she leaves the bus. I jump down after her and call her name as she walks away. "Liza, come back! Liza!" At some distance away, she turns and looks back at me, sadly, then again turns and walks away, away, away, and I call "Liza, Liza, Liza," until she disappears. The aftereffects of my dream hung on. Representative of my insecurity, Franz would repeat. It seems to presage a new reality. I fear that now that she no longer works in the travel agency, her isolation will expand and the walls around her thicken.

I wonder if there is some spite and vengeance of fate at play here?

"I now have two things I never had before," Elizaveta says in her melodious German, "you ... and a lot of natural light." For her it was love at first sight for the roof garden apartment we moved into just before Christmas. She loves the morning sunlight flooding the apartment these recent days just as she loves white and yellow colors. She loves the bright light reflecting from the glass doors facing the terraces, the piercing white from the skylights in the long mansard room now her studio, the white of her favorite decorations throughout the apartment and the daffodil yellow of her dresses. Even at night Elizaveta refuses to close the blinds, so that our Bogenhausen penthouse is illuminated like Marien Platz.

I understand her love for light since she, the artist of bright colors, had lived the last ten years in a dim basement apartment on a narrow Schwabing street. But her love of me? "Why me of all people?" I ask again. For, as my ex-wife testified many times, I'm no prize.

"Why you? You're my soul mate. And one of my alter egos. I mean, the spy you say you once were but are no more ... you claim. The man you are today. The prophet you are becoming."

"A spy, well, uh, that makes me laugh. Seems like a joke. I wasn't even a decent intelligence agent. Nor a diplomat. Though they tried to make me one. A habit does not a monk make, Rabelais said. But a prophet? That's another fictitious me, like one of your artistic creations."

If anything I'm more gangster than policeman. Giuliana thinks so too. And she knows me pretty well. She knows I once liked it that way. Half diplomat-spy, half criminal.

No wonder Giuliana's goody-goody Papa and Mama detested me. Now that's a matter of Fate, for sure. A thin line separates me from a completely different life. Maybe only because of Big Cliff I didn't step over that line definitively. Now I'm reformed, of course. Thanks to Elizaveta.

"*Nein, nein, durchaus nicht.* Not at all. My creation is one thing, Clifford. You are another. That is, if Clifford is your real name. I might start out a figure *modeled* on your huge figure but that image transforms and becomes something totally different. So none of my creations are the you I know. Not yet anyway. No more than are you yourself my creation."

"Do you mean creation like God's work?"

Standing taller than usual under the skylight, her blond hair reaching the ceiling at the place the mansard roof dips sharply, dressed in her habitual yellow, Elizaveta looks like a goddess reaching toward light.

"You look like I imagine Artemis, old Zeus' daughter, standing there with her bow and arrows, the protector of gentle animals, whose job was to bring light into the world. You are her, and she, you." That's one thing I especially love in Elizaveta: I can talk about anything; she has taken Franz's place; he's like that too. Yet there are limits, I warn myself. Old Cliff was right; you don't have to share every fucking thought.

"You mean my work. Yes, Clifford, it's godlike. My art, my bow and my arrows. But your image is not bad either … you with your Odysseus beard and all that hair."

"For Chrissakes, Liza! You'd better leave me out of your art."

"I do. I do. As I said, you, Clifford, are another matter."

* * *

The next afternoon I found her sitting at her studio work-table, spotlights from the corners zeroed in on three black and white photographs spread before her. Oh no! The pictures! That means Russia, again in my life. I'd left them lying around somewhere during the move. Just like me. Never do things in proper order. Never have. Hate order, in work and in play. Probably the reason I was a bad husband to Giuliana—talking too much, revealing everything. My young age wasn't the reason, though I tried to justify myself with the age issue. What a liar. Big Cliff's teaching. Never tell it straight unless it's part of a plan. There are ways and ways to do things. I wanted the different way. No repetitions for me. That things occurred in the same way each time drove me crazy. No bureaucrat, Cliff! Nosiree. Not Cliffy. Not Golden Boy.

I never hide documents. Especially not secret ones. Never put them in envelopes with innocuous labels. My stupid theory is that things left open and exposed can't contain great secrets. I brought the iron safe from St. Moritz but hadn't put the photos there either. A bad habit. A stupid mistake. My usual arrogance. She wasn't supposed to see them, not yet anyway.

"How do you happen to have these photos that I've never seen? What does it mean?" she said, looking up interrogatively, pointing a finger at each. "Mother, Mother and I, and the third is of my father, the stranger."

Why did I have them? They are echoes from the past— an explosion on Mount Subasio; gunshots on late night streets of Perugia. People appearing in my life and soon vanishing. Not only the persons in the photos but why I had them was the point. I felt like a piece of *merde* that I hadn't told her about her father. And about her mother too. I hadn't had the courage to tell her that in my former life I knew her father, that I had worked together with the man she hardly knew, that he was once on my spymaster father's payroll. It was pure chance that I got my hands on the photos revealing that the man I'd known practically all my life, like my uncle, was her father.

I myself don't know what to make of the chain of circumstances linking me to her parents. Her mother had long since disappeared, back to Russia they said, and her father was dead and gone at the hands of my former employers. But, I thought, the fact that I'd avenged him should, might, could enhance me in Elizaveta's eyes.

But how could I tell her that? How could I brag about my violence? First I did what I had to do and then I decided to retire from that sordid world.

What could I tell her of the criminal past of that "I"? Lawless. Uncontrolled. What could I say of my past life in which I undertook momentous acts with no consciousness of the consequences, out of habit, or on a momentary impulse?

On the other hand, how could I disclose that she and I are living on my inheritance from my American father-spymaster who made a fortune exploiting her father? Even to me, these interlocking occurrences seem truly bizarre.

My former partner Franz has me figured out, all right. Swiss Franzi knows me better than my Dad did. Again, I've lived such a life of make-believe that I myself hardly know what is real and what is fantasy. Yet I was real. Otherwise how did I become what I am today? Nationality? I have absolutely no sense of it. Certainly not for *Amerika*. Felt like a stranger the few times I was there. I'm embarrassed when Elizaveta calls me her *Amerikaner*. I'm embarrassed when Elizaveta says to someone that her husband is *Amerikaner*. Before she adds that she is Russian, proudly.

Why my sense of security back then and my insecurity now that I'm free? Free of my father and his life of deception and his responsibility for sucking me into it? I might well wonder why the pendulum has now swung in my favor and brought me Elizaveta, while my own small daughter still lies dead somewhere in the Ostfriedhof.

Yet I believe these photographs of father and mother and daughter prefigure significant changes still to come in our lives. They must be signs. If not, why did they fall into my hands? The pictures lie on the table, illuminated under the spotlights. From the table they stare upwards at Elizaveta, then extend over her shoulder toward me. They depict a destroyed family but at the same time point toward the new family of the future. Of our future. Our new family to replace the former family of her dead parents … and my dead daughter. Death. Reconstruction. Reconfiguration. Some things have always been and always will be repeated.

"Clifford, how could you have not told me about them?"

"I would've told you eventually. It's not an easy story, Elizaveta. It's part of the story of my life. And of yours too."

"You can try now. For us. There are too many blank places. You didn't just materialize from nothing that day you saw me in the travel agency. You have a background. I know that. But the blank spaces make you resemble my mother who went back to Russia such a long time ago that it seems she was never here with me. Was never really my mother. Today, I don't know if she is dead or alive. I don't want you to resemble her."

Later I'll tell Elizaveta that I tried to find out more about her mother, who was a person who believed in commitments. Ideological. Not a half criminal like me. Elizaveta couldn't imagine what the word *spy* means. Or the life the word implies. To consider that both her mother and father were secret agents rings like fantasy to her. I doubt that her mother will ever return to her old life and to Germany, ever return to look for her daughter. For normal people like Elizaveta, such stories are incomprehensible, weird fables. Yet I will go back to Russia and search again.

"Elizaveta, think about it this way: you paint and the picture you create is real. Each painting is self-contained. You can touch it and examine it and evaluate it. Why do you think I'm always touching your paintings? Like your parents, I'm always trying to touch reality."

"I thought you just wanted to leave your imprint in my work."

"Actually I touch a painting just to check that it's real, like, say, a dead pheasant in a Dutch painting."

I leaned over her shoulder and examined the photos for the hundredth time. There was something sinister about them, the sequence of her mother Masha in the first, in the second Masha and Elizaveta at the age of eight or nine, tall for her age, her mother Masha and her father Nikitin in the third. These photos, I thought, enigmatic, mysterious, are fate: they will change our lives.

"Clifford, please tell me everything you know about them, please. Tell me why."

"Your parents learned that love is dangerous," I said reductively, for how could I explain so she could appreciate them for what they were?

"Is that all? My mother abandoned me and my father was assassinated and you say love is dangerous."

"I think one reason they held together for the time they had was the loneliness of their kind of life. They stewed over the what-ifs of the past ... and the unpredictability of the future ... butterflies in their bellies ... phobias in their minds ... ghosts in their memories."

I too recall the visions of a past that could have been different. Different from the chronic hopelessness, the burgeoning evils, the outrageous miscalculations and the eternal compromises. Her parents must have thought the same. That their whole world was false. People whose real names you don't know, your own life so secret and your identity so multiple that you forget who you really are. How could Elizaveta even begin to comprehend that other world when I myself didn't understand it? I didn't try to explain that in a way we both had our origins in that same milieu, she unaware, but nonetheless the daughter of two spies. And I, the son of a spymaster, and who for a time followed in his father's footsteps. The footprints we leave behind; the footprints we follow.

For some people espionage used to be a job, a career. Now secret services are crammed with mercenaries looking for adventure; people attracted by intrigue or who see themselves as medieval knights. Others like her father are driven to seek parallel lives, thirsty for the sense of another dimension and fearful of having only one life to live. Driven by the necessity to live more fully every single hour of every single day because of their fear that each moment happens only once.

"Your father once told me that he felt an irrepressible desire to live many lives within one lifetime. Like a striving for immortality, he said. If not for another life, then another side of life in order to diminish the impact of the limited life he'd been given. Secret agents take many contradictory stands and live many contradictory lives."

"Sounds like a fairy tale."

"Yes, it does. They live a fairy tale. Yet the occurrences of their lives really do happen. Or could happen … which counts also. Who doesn't want to be free to change? Who doesn't need more living space?"

"They left me for more living space?"

"Not literally. In his different lives I think your father entered a new myth each time he felt a certain coherence … among all the incompatibles of his life." Not that he actually told me that, or that I realized it then, but when he arrived at our house in St. Moritz when I was a boy of fourteen or fifteen, I began to see him as a modern Rabelais. If he had a philosophy, it was that lived life comprises everything human. The human body, food and drink, sex, the psyche, imagination, external philosophy, illness, death. And more. Yet—or rather because of his vision—yes, I think for that reason—he became a skeptic. Disillusioned by the idea of magical solutions.

"I think your mother believed there is always space for unchanging values… like a universal spirit of equality and brotherhood."

"But what kind of a woman abandons her daughter for the life of a spy?"

"That's not fair to her, Elizaveta. Above all, your mother defended the idea of social change."

"Clifford, what importance can that have for me? She should have defended and protected me. Instead, she abandoned me."

"For a greater cause in which she really believed. In fact both of them lived in a fairy tale. In the real world they probably came to feel like fugitives. Like her own father, lost in Russia. They searched for a purer existence. But the search was futile. That's something that doesn't exist in the real world."

"But why would anyone want that kind of life in the first place?" Elizaveta insisted.

"Your father, I think, lived life as if inside one of those funhouse halls of mirrors where everything is reflected but transformed into something else and where everything is possible. In that sense too his life was a fairy tale. Once he said to me that each of us is a one-man state."

"But how do you know all this? Are you like them? Are you for real?"

"Elizaveta, that was my life for many years. I know those people—most of them traitorous and greedy. But not your parents. They were not. After your father's death, I broke away. But today's world wants to make everyone a spy. Look around you. Video cameras everywhere—big cities like huge film sets. E-mails controlled. Certain websites labeled criminal. Loitering is a security threat. In some places just walking the streets is a security breach and there's a bug in every household. The world will only be safe when every citizen is a spy."

"You describe a mad world. But I'll still never understand why they abandoned me … leaving me with a distant relative I hardly knew." Elizaveta's eyes were full of tears. "And what does all this mean for us?"

"Don't think they were immoral, Elizaveta. You can be proud of them both. The enchantment of love—and sorcery too—makes spies unpredictable. Your parents needed love. Both understood the difference between good and evil. Your father blamed the evil world in which he worked for the loss of his great love, your mother. Both of them were exploited ... and then betrayed by that world. From the start, your father—we all called him Nikitin—understood that many of the wrong people were on the side of the victors in the Cold War they fought ... and many of the right people on the side of the losers. Nikitin believed he did the right things ... though sometimes for the wrong reasons. No wonder he became a skeptic. Still, he never gave up hope. In a way that's why you and I are here together. These snapshots point the way for us. Together, we can fulfill what they had no chance to fulfill."

Her look told me that my words were not enough.

"Look, Lizzy, what about this? I'll go to Russia again. You can come with me. We'll try again."

"Most likely she's dead too. Like him."

7

I REMEMBER death. I learned it well. Death is also color and white flowers. Chrysanthemums and any white flowers are for death. You don't take white flowers to your dinner hosts. I was about twelve when I first encountered death. Then it stayed with me. All the boys in my town of St. Moritz, sons of hunters, were familiar with the death of animals but not of people. My beautiful mother of the many portraits vanished when I was still a boy. She was away on a trip, my father said. She would come back home. As long as I didn't see her, she was alive, somewhere. She could return at any time. But in my innermost self of then I knew she was dead.

The first death I witnessed hadn't seemed to regard me. My first emotion was surprise at the amount of blood in the human body. I was returning to St. Moritz on the post bus from boarding school in Lausanne, a day of June sunshine, sitting at the window seat on the left about ten rows back, when I glanced down at the winding road and saw a motorcycle just under me passing the bus. The motorcyclist's blond hair was blowing in the wind. He suddenly looked up and our eyes met through his frog-like eye goggles. The rider lifted his right hand slightly from the handlebar in greeting and grinned. In the same moment the bus suddenly swerved to the left, caught the motorcycle on some protruding hook and dragged the man the endless distance it took to halt the metal monster. The passengers rushed down to the road. I held back, uncertain if I wanted to see, until police ordered everybody out. I tried not to look at the body, ignoring death so that it didn't happen. But there was that swath of blood like red paint down the center of the road, reaching back to the point where we'd nodded at each other.

While police questioned me, the bus driver stood nearby looking at us. A young man, maybe 21, about the same age as the motorcyclist. He stared at me, supplication in his eyes, and repeated tearfully that he'd had to swerve to avoid a woman and a child walking along the roadside. I dropped my eyes, stared fixedly at the beginning of the trail of blood and muttered I hadn't seen anything. The policeman told me to get back on the bus without even taking my name. For months I didn't know who the cyclist was, which seemed to confirm my guilt.

Later I learned the boy was Hungarian, maybe a patriot, a hero who should not have died with his blood smeared across a Swiss mountain highway. Now I don't recall whether I lied out of fear or to save the young bus driver who had unwittingly caused the death of the cyclist. But as time passed the lie mattered less.

Big Cliff told me to forget it and keep my mouth shut about the accident. We didn't need to appear in any court trials, he said. Never volunteer information. You only make enemies. Keep your head down. Always keep your head down. You lift your head, you can smash it against the ceiling. I was already big and strong and vigorous and became convinced that death didn't concern me. Even that lingering sensation of death, that of my beautiful mother of the portraits vanished, as did the lie to negate it. I learned that men do two things: they lie and they die.

Beautiful Mother, upright, her thick red hair brilliant in the portrait, would have urged me to tell the truth. Tell what I saw. Justice was justice. She too was always saying what she felt was true. Still, I would've forgotten her if not for her portrait in all our subsequent houses. It might have been better to forget her. Would have lessened my, my, well, my viciousness. And my anxieties and the occasional panic attacks I suffered. The psychic implosions, the weakness creeping up my legs, the spells of unstoppable over-breathing. And if not for the Swiss-Romansch housekeeper, Romana, who whispered memories of Mother to me, the sad, insecure and violent boy I became, I would have forgotten. Tell the truth, my mother said. Then you can hold your head high. Proudly. Instead, I talked around the truth; garrulous, daring, bigger and rougher than the rough Swiss boys. I was a terror on sports fields, a vicious boxer and wrestler, the fastest man in Switzerland in the 400 meters and stood six feet four inches at nineteen. I won a soccer scholarship to Cornell that same year. Already spoke four languages before Big Cliff's people got their hands on me and taught me Russian.

Yet something was not right. Never was right. Was I not imitating my father's lifestyle? Oh God, no! Take the criminal route first. Had Big Cliff seen that part of me? The criminal side. No wonder the relentless anxiety in my solar plexus. Who is that in the mirror? Cliff, the criminal? Had Dad really wanted to save me? Is that what he meant when he advised me to just run for it? To bolt? Should've done it. But then there was the possibility of Mother's return. Had to hang around and wait. Later, Turin was not far. Nor was Paris. But little snow-bound Ithaca in New York? The other side of the world. I soon dropped out of Cornell and America and returned to the Engadine. That's when the Agency recruited me, and sent me out to spy on the world.

8

LATE winter's night. The winter terrace, I call it. Faces the main street leading to Prinzregenten Platz. Often I count back. All those years. Lies and violence and death. Yet, today, our penthouse seems to sum up my life. In Bogenhausen. In Munich. Street lamps down below reflect yellow on the unsullied icy snow. Dim lights concealing untellable secrets withheld and locked in the shadowy apartments across the way. Flickering lamps here and there, in an alley way and in the little corner park.

What could I tell others about it all? What revelations about loveless lives? Old Clifford-master spy left me his maxims, his teachings, his examples. And together with his money, he left his footprints. "Never reveal anything, Cliffy. Take care of yourself. Above all don't fall in love. Feelings are the great deceivers. Respect yourself above all." He sounded like Ayn Rand. No wonder I never knew right from wrong, good from evil. No wonder I was tempted by the criminal life. The underground world.

But after all that deceit, where am I now? One career finished. My intelligence brotherhood with Franzi closed. But I'm rich from my inheritance from a deceitful father. No wonder my hope is now cast in the present with Elizaveta. Her very proximity makes me feel hopeful. But what about old loyalties? If they were even that. Former belongings. Do such associations still linger in the shadows of my mind? Or have they all vanished like the men I gunned down in my rage on a midnight piazza in Perugia?

9

W ARM, bright, late March mornings often represent a false Bavarian spring, the time when Müncheners begin dreaming of the Italian Riviera. Of Alassio, San Remo, Bordighera. These Munich dreams are soon dashed when incessant rains of May and June cause swimming pools to postpone opening and heat to be turned back on.

When the doorbell from the street entrance rings, Elizaveta has been at her easel since six a.m. now bathed under streams of beguiling yellow sunshine from the skylight.

"*Herr Masters, bitte schön,*" a deformed voice says over the interphone.

"Who?" Elizaveta asks. "Who do you want?"

"Herr Masters?" The voice on the intercom rises into a question mark.

"I'll take it, Lizzy," I say. "An old friend." I'd recognized Ilya's voice at once, a voice deeper than one expected from the little man visible on the screen.

I say "*Dachwohnung*", and push the open button. "An old contact. A new article."

"Who is he? At this hour?"

"A Serb. The man with the Slivovitz that time. Remember? My drunk in Davos?" During the years after I returned from Russia, Ilya was my best contact in the whole Balkans. Soon after we met, I took Elizaveta to the Swiss Alps for skiing in late February when southern air begins arriving in the Southern Alps. Instead I pulled off a tremendous drunk. Ilya had brought Slivovitz from Kosovo, three golden bottles wrapped in white tissue which he had carefully rolled and tubed in maps of the burial sites of the Balkan war. He never drank a drop of it. Slavic teetotaler! I only wanted to make love with Elizaveta. I never saw a ski lift.

"Herr Masters? You're not up to old tricks are you, *Schatz*?"

"I swear this is pure journalism. My old career is behind me. Can't believe I ever did it," I protest. "You've probably never heard of the American satellite-protectorate of Kosovo. That's in Europe, not so far from here. Once the heart of Serbia. Now it's one of the biggest U.S. military bases in Europe. They bombed Belgrade to get it. Now it's theirs. A great story for me."

"Still sounds like spy stuff."

Actually she's right. Do I want back into that? Ilya, my old friend. But can I really trust him to be what he once was? Or has he too changed? Acquired new loyalties?

The knock on the door is soft and discreet. I look through the peephole. Elizaveta vanishes into her studio.

Ilya steps into the living room now illuminated like a Miami penthouse in spring. A man so small that I could easily carry him in my arms like a child—gaunt, pale, sick looking, the look in his eyes of a man who has seen much suffering.

"*Also jetzt bist Du auch Journalist geworden!* So you are a journalist now," the Serb says in German. He wraps his arms around my waist, rests his head against my chest. For a brief moment my doubts and anxieties vanish. Ilya is not the enemy.

"New role, old game, eh? Clifford, are you sure you want to get involved in this story?" he asks, speaking in his odd manner of separating each word and pronouncing each vowel. I understand immediately what he wants. He wants my involvement in Balkan matters. This is the Ilya I know well: he always drives straight to the point. "Think of your new wife, my friend. Balkan stories are always risky."

"Ilya! Ilya! Journalism is not a front. This is for real."

"*Ja, ja.* That is what all the exes say. In my country we say that once you get into this line of work, you never get out. Not in one piece."

"I did, Ilya."

"Did you really? Something of the spy nature always remains. You know that. At some time or other all spies and ex-spies go off on wild tangents. And you were always wild anyway. You shift things around, objects and ideas, and then try to pass between them unnoticed. But your nature stays fixed. Look at you! A giant. Do you think you have changed?"

I laugh silently. Doubts return and prickle. "Let's go to the kitchen, Ilya. Quieter back there. Maybe you want a drink of Slivovitz ... in memory of old times."

"*Jamais de la vie*, old friend. I still do not touch the stuff. Coffee will do."

At a table looking over an internal courtyard the silence is total. I eye Ilya sipping his coffee. The Serb has aged. We've both aged. My age shows also in my preference for morning coffee to Slivovitz. Must be because of the dead men I left on the streets of Perugia and his because of the barely buried dead people spread across Yugoslavia. And because of the shambles of his old dream of Southern Slavic unity. Ilya is a Communist. Was a dedicated leader in the Communist Youth League when we met. 'Once a real Communist, forever a Communist,' Ilya likes to say in his flowery, youthful German learned in West Berlin in the old days.

"So where are you coming from now, Ilyushka? Belgrade?"

"Straight from Pristina."

"Pristina? You mean they let Serbs stay there?"

"Only because I speak Albanian. I am one of the few Serbs remaining. But schoolteachers are always needed. I do not believe I am even suspect, so great is the confusion today after all the killing. But I do have to, uh, avoid especially your old friends. U.S. intelligence has the run of the so-called nation of Kosovo."

"Well, yeah, I know what you mean. I keep a low profile myself these days." I wonder if Ilya means they run him too. "So how did you get here anyway?" I mutter. "You surely couldn't fly from Pristina."

"Are you crazy? No, I caught a ride on a truck to Skopje. Then on to Tirana. East at night. Got to Durrës easy. And yesterday's ferry to Bari. Train to Rome and then here."

"For Chrissakes. All that just to see me?"

"I think my people in Belgrade helped somewhere. They wanted me to see you."

"Me?"

"You the budding journalist. Someone to tell the truth about what is happening in the Balkans. About the rape of Serbia. Not only today. But tomorrow too. You want to be one of our mouthpieces? Cliffy, old friend, there are many secrets hidden in the Balkans."

"There always were. And that's just what I want to learn. But let's catch up on things. So you still teach. But how did you get to Pristina? And how many years has it been since we last met? Before they bombed Belgrade I know."

"A few years before. Fifteen years at least. We were both pretty young when we met the first time that day at the Uni in Beograd. I was an intellectual then, *der ewige Student*, the eternal student. Remember?"

"And I was a hooligan disguised as a civil servant. Just back from Russia. Those were the good old days, eh?"

"Worse days for me because my people were getting ready to kill each other. Serbs killing Croats, Croats killing Serbs, everybody killing Moslem Kosovars, Kosovars killing Serbs. Back then we did not have time to think about our Russian brothers. But many people in Serbia think more about them today."

"Like everybody predicted. That it would all fall apart over there. One of my favorite countries, as you know. Well, that's now like water under the Mostar Bridge. Everybody killing anybody. What about it? What's happening there today?"

On the eve of the fall of the Iron Curtain, still in the Agency, I'd visited Belgrade as a tourist. A rather dull city it seemed at the time. No problems. I visited the language department at the university, inquiring about studying south Slavic languages. Those were grim times down there. Just when Slovenia was pulling out of the federation of southern Slavic peoples that once made up Tito's Yugoslavia. But the chief had been dead nine years and things were falling apart. That day I met a thin little man standing near a bulletin board. I've never forgotten that Ilya was carrying a big yellow notepad. His image has remained fixed in my memory that way. Tiny Ilya with his big yellow notepad ... probably at the university trying to recruit the best students.

At that point I open a drawer and ceremoniously pull out a leather-bound notebook and a fat pen, shift around in my chair and look up expectantly at the man whose age has never been clear. Nor many aspects of his life either. Never married, never even had a woman as far as I know.

"Well Clifford, you *have* changed," Ilya says, indicating my notebook. "You always had what I thought was a photographic memory. Never made a note on anything. Now do not tease me. Do not act naïve. I think you know perfectly well what is happening. Our Kosovo, the cradle of my country, is one great NATO base. Camp Bondsteel. 'Beautiful CBS', they call it. And I do not mean the TV network. That is what is happening. It is like going abroad ... if you can even get in there. The Kosovar workers on the base are the new Negroes at one dollar an hour. On the base Americans even have separate toilets. And Burger Kings and movie theaters. The base even runs its own Marathon. The Kosovo Marathon! Camp Bondsteel has a downtown, a midtown and an uptown, dance halls and bars and baseball fields, University of Maryland and Central Texas College courses, while Thai girls give massages, allegedly controlled by military authorities. And gigantic helicopters that can fly to Tehran … with a few stopovers in the string of American outposts and bases along the way. But also to Russia. The whole base is surrounded by a 2.5-meter high earthen wall, seven miles in perimeter. The largest base in the Balkans. That is what is happening just across the Adriatic from Italy. They are going to close down the Aviano Airbase in Italy, I hear, and bring it all to Camp Bondsteel. What a name for a military base. Bondsteel! Steel, steel, steel. Named after a Vietnam war hero. Sergeant James Bondsteel. All Halliburton stuff."

This is the part of the story I know well. Still, I write furiously, making a big show just to let Ilya divest himself of some of his hatred and pain and suffering … for whom is not clear.

The story behind the story is that Camp Bondsteel is the biggest U.S. military base built since Vietnam. Right smack in the former Serbian province of Kosovo, now an "independent" country, Moslem territory and a forbidding and savage part of Europe. The local people must despise the infidels on their lands, just as Bin Laden hated American troops stationed in Saudi Arabia. Conveniently, Bondsteel is close to oil pipelines and energy corridors, the U.S.-sponsored Trans-Balkan oil pipeline and the AMBO Pipeline to reach through Bulgaria and Albania and Macedonia. As a result, the Halliburton Oil subsidiary, Brown & Root Services, and a string of defense contractors are making fortunes. In 1999, in the aftermath of the bombing of Yugoslavia, U.S. forces seized one thousand acres of farmland in southeast Kosovo at Uresevac, near the Macedonian border, and constructed a military base. Camp Bondsteel became the *grande dame* in a network of U.S. bases across East Europe. A self-sufficient, high-tech base housing 10,000 troops — three quarters of the U.S. troops stationed in Kosovo, plus God knows how many mercenaries and top secret Special Operations forces, busily infiltrating Serbia too. People who know about Bondsteel call it a second Guantánamo. It hosts a CIA secret detention center, one of the black sites for torture. The U.S.-led "Battle Group East" of Poles, Ukrainians and Turks are there to guarantee "freedom of movement" for the poor people of Kosovo, the majority of whom are Moslems who would love all the amenities ... if they could just get through the steel fences and past the watch towers to see them. The town of Camp Bondsteel has 25 kilometers of roads and over 300 buildings, surrounded by ten kilometers of earth and concrete barriers. Eighty-four kilometers of concertina wire and 11 watch towers protect Bondsteel's retail outlets, around-the-clock gyms, a chapel, library and the best-equipped military hospital in Europe. Fleets of Black Hawk and Apache helicopters have already arrived.

"You know that the American Vice-President visited Bondsteel, no? Also went to Belgrade to beg for space for a U.S. base in Serbia. He told the troops in Kosovo that they had shown the world what happens when a nation fights against tyranny and decides to build a free society, a society that ... a society that never existed in this part of the world, he said. You are protecting the innocent, he said. You have been defending democracy for a decade. You are offering the security they need to build their independence and democracy and a multiethnic state."

"The usual Washington shit." I chuckle to myself over Ilya's language influences and the pauses through which he is probably asking himself what language he's thinking in or translating from. I have the same problems and appreciate his hesitations. No doubt about it, these southern Slavs are the world's best linguists. Learn new languages overnight. Even dialects. Northern and eastern Slavs like Russians or Czechs don't have this talent. Must be because of the mixture of peoples and Ottoman and Habsburg influences. I wonder why typical Americans, Anglos in general, have such meager linguistic talents.

"But Clifford, what is really happening in the Balkans and

East Europe is the underground battle between European Union countries, especially Germany, and corporate business conglomerates run by the USA. Germany wants to keep the euro as the currency for the whole region. The U.S. wants the dollar. That is why Washington undermines EU expansion to the East … and aims at replacing the dominion of Germany's Deutsche Bank. This is a clash for colonial control of East Europe and the Balkans. Part of the New World Order. Competition between capitalist blocks. Marx predicted it. Thus far the euro has won, but the future is uncertain."

"Ilya, it also means that the old nation states are dying. They'll soon be supplanted by corporations like Halliburton and their privatized military arms like Blackwater."

Ilya raises his eyebrows and peers at me hard with his dark eyes as if checking my sincerity.

Then: "Clifford, remember that eleven years ago U.S.-led NATO forces bombed Serbia for seventy-eight days and nights. An all-out war. An illegal war. A criminal war against another European country. The biggest air offensive since World War II. Over a thousand people died right here in Europe; the infrastructures of Serbia were destroyed. And tens of thousands are still dying from the depleted uranium dropped on them."

"Remember I haven't seen Belgrade since the bombing. Must be grim."

"Grim, yes, though a living city again. Lots of food and entertainment. Serbs love to eat more than they love to dance. But the ruins are brand new, in a city razed already forty times throughout history. It is hard to imagine: a war right in the middle of Europe and Europeans have forgotten it. And they keep bragging about over sixty-five years of peace in Europe. As if the bombing of Serbia did not count as a war! Many damaged buildings have purposely not been reconstructed, such as the Ministry of Defense on Kneza Miloza Street, with its cement walls buckled like cardboard. And the State Television headquarters on Takovska Street, where the current affairs office, situated between two big glass-fronted buildings, was flattened on the night of April 30, 1999. Sixteen staff members died. The city's ruins look like installations deserving the title: DESTRUCTION. Destroyed buildings dot the Belgrade landscape today. But American leaders say 'that was a long time ago'. This illegal war was a turning point toward dismantling the framework of peace and security that had governed relations in Europe … since WWII. The 1999 war in Yugoslavia and the start of the war in Chechnya that September were also the turning point in Russian-American relations. It also marked the rapprochement between Russia and China both of which are now targeted by Washington.

"Clifford, the American President and the English Prime Minister and NATO leaders claimed the bombing of Serbia was a humanitarian intervention. Truth is what Americans say it is.

"Not even a war. The generals admit they love war. They love the massacre of women and children, reducing war to collateral damages.

"Humanitarian interventions—oh Clifford, the euphemisms are destroying the sense of language, any language—an intervention to stop the genocide, they said … and the alleged ethnic cleansing of the Albanian-speaking majority in Kosovo committed by Serbian President Milosevic. His real crime was at home, against his own people. The Kosovo massacres are lies. Lies. The so-called Racak massacre never happened. Some two thousand victims were found … both Moslems and Orthodox Serbs, civilians and military, are in those graves. That is not genocide. Yet Western media still speak of genocide … and the staff of the NATO rescue mission and common people believe it. It was all fraud, the bombing and the charges against Serbia it was based on. Instead the USA and British secret services aided the KLA, the Kosovo Liberation Army, a criminal drug cartel and money-laundering gang worse than the Taliban, designed to destabilize Kosovo and create the excuse for the bombing. An organized propaganda campaign of lies. Milosevic became the 'butcher of the Balkans' and was indicted as a war criminal by the Hague War Crimes Tribunal, and died while defending himself. The thing is the general public still believes all this shit. Meanwhile the USA continues to subjugate and colonize the Balkans, peopled by sub-human Slavs. That is the way Adolf Hitler thought! First arranging it all, setting the scene, then the recognition of Kosovo's 'independence. All in the name of oil ... but the second result is the tightening of the encirclement of Russia."

Ilya falls silent, gets up, and holding his coffee cup against the pane, stares out the kitchen window. Silence falls in the kitchen. Ilya is still troubled. Though I can almost smell the aroma rising from the back gardens, I realize it is hard for him to believe we're at the center of one of Europe's most throbbing cities. That power surrounds us. Not one single person in the courtyards and backyards. Only some big blackbirds fighting over pieces of dark bread. And the reflections of a city rouged by an eastern sun arriving over the slate rooftops. All exterior sound stilled by the triple-paned windows.

What a contrast with his noisy, boisterous Belgrade. I know he needs to share some new truths that I might not want to hear. But he remains silent, the cup in his hand and his nose pressed against the windowpane. I love his infrequent guilelessness which he thinks is unreadable but which this morning is written in his eyes. Ilya is usually so talkative that his silence is disconcerting. My thoughts ramble too, remembering the times when no one in Serbia would answer you in Russian. Not the same today. Slavic pride. Russians and Serbs and Croats and Bulgars, all cousins.

His long silence means he has something important to say.

* * *

Since I have few purely intellectual inclinations, it was by pure chance that recently two unlikely encounters occurred simultaneously: I read a reference to Aristotle's discussion of possibility and probability in M.H. Abrams' book, *The Mirror and the Lamp*, which I had bought downtown chiefly for its cover and also for its appealing title, especially the word *mirror*. Besides, the book made me look good in Lizzy's eyes. And, on the same day, I read several online articles concerning the U.S. threat to "pull the trigger" on Iran.

The phony liberals who refuse to believe the probability of a U.S. attack on Iran, who think widespread torture by the USA unlikely and who reject outright the idea that the USA is a fascist nation, would do well to read up on the subject of probability-possibility. Admittedly, the question belongs to philosophy. And to history. That is something I must speak with Franz about. He can analyze anything. Anyway, I'm at the point that whatever I do at any given moment and whatever I've done in my life thus far, my images, impressions, accusations and condemnations of America are all unrelenting. I know what America is. Ilya doesn't have to tell me. I know what America stands for. I know its false morality, its pragmatic spirit that turns any lie into truth if it works, its sense of Exceptionalism, the Americanism that is destroying the world. The fear and the hate. Fear, the fixation. Hate, the fixation. First the fear of Communism. Now, terrorism. Fear and hate. In the American DNA you will find fear and hate. You wonder what else that particular DNA will reveal when it is scientifically melted down. Thank God I'm not part of that. At least, no longer. But actually what details do I know about that America? None, really. But I know the American Dream is fable. Deceit. Sham. Sleight-of-hand. I suspect American innocence is both guile and authentic. A deceptive innocence. I feel no loyalty to that. But if I'm not American, then who am I? Even if this is my home, I'm not Swiss.

Nor German. Like that Italo-Germano-Polack from Danzig I met in Perugia who said he didn't know who he was, I'm not anything.

Mathematicians and statisticians have many complex theories about what probability means. But they don't really know. Its meaning is unclear. Some people consider probability to be little more than a hunch, an expression of something that might or might not happen. For me, probability is the measure of the possibility that an event will occur. You see it in police films, the decisive probability that fingerprints or DNA match. But since apparent impossibilities sometimes happen, Abrams says that another approach is to distinguish probability from possibility and plausibility, concentrating on the terrifying consequences if the improbable does occur. I have Iran in mind. Of course just because a thing is possible does not mean it is necessarily probable. Yet the USA does have a huge nuclear stockpile and the possibility and capacity of delivering an atomic bomb wherever its mad leaders desire. Then there is the madness of human beings, the X-factor of the base nature of man which seems to predominate in these times. If it's possible to bomb the undefended city of Belgrade to get their hands on Kosovo—something like an enemy bombing Charlottesville and taking over the state of Virginia to get at Washington, D.C.—why not nuke Iran? So what might seem improbable because of its enormity—is quite possible. For improbabilities occur all the time and man does have that dark, evil stain. Man is peace-loving and warlike at the same time. Depending on his culture and ethic and environment and his nature, each characteristic is both possible and often probable. In 1919 a former semi-drifter and police spy later known as Adolf Hitler joined the small German Workers Party. Who could say at that point that Hitler's probability of becoming master and scourge of Europe in less than fifteen years was high? Yet it happened. And the scourge did what scourges do: seventeen million victims to his credit. *So, so!* We know, I mean it's much more than a hunch that under certain conditions man is capable of any atrocity. We see it daily in America's wars. In Guantánamo. In Afghanistan.

This completes the circle. The lodestone of the socio-political question then begins again. Tick, tick, tick. The struggle that has gone on since private property and class division emerged in ancient societies continues. Tick and tock, tick and tock. The dialectic at work. An old, familiar story, Abrams recalls. The proprietor-capitalist lords it over the wage earner, who in the end must change and rebel in order to survive. The capitalist however does not change and is capable of any act he can get away with to defend his privileges. He can torture or nuke as he pleases. Each acts according to his own nature, within the realms of possibility. Tick and tock, tick and tock. I share Abrams' ideas. During my career in the Agency, I experienced over and over the certitude that political leadership is capable of cold-bloodedly deciding to attack any country, committing the most abominable improbabilities. Again and again that human stain has its way.

Anyway, my attempt to make heads or tails of daily news feeds and the shortcomings of the mainstream press was an eye-opener. Now, considering possibility-probability I became aware again of what the press does not tell and what crap it chooses to print.

In my opinion what sometimes appears as American innocence in reality consists of sizable doses of both guile and guilt. A deceptive innocence. Though some claim an innocent guilt. I feel no loyalty to that, to that ... what word to describe the *people* of America? Since the nation is so distant and apart from the rest, perhaps it is truly a race. If the Allies spoke of the atrocious German race and Germans spoke of the many subhuman races—Jews, Slavs, Gypsies— to be exterminated, then perhaps despite their diverse origins Americans have become a race. Non-Americans lump them together as a race. But me? Who is that? Now, I realize, I sound like my old partner, Franzi: each according to his own nature. Franz would add that within the realm of possibility lie the most abominable improbabilities. When political leadership makes the momentous decision to nuke some distant country, its intellectuals justify the act ethically and the military executes it. That an odious act is possible becomes its ethical justification.

"Remember the summers in Milanica?" Ilya suddenly asks, turning back to me. Ilya Milanica. Milanica, also the name of the village on the Adriatic shore south of Split, north of Dubrovnik, named after Ilya's paternal Croat family. The meaning of the surname, I'd learned in Russian, has to do with love. All the Milanica lived there; their vineyards, their small inns, their fishing. When we vacationed there together in the 1990s, his Catholic Croat relations described themselves as a Mediterranean people, close to West Europe, comparable to Austria.

"We Milanica are a schizophrenic people," he says and sighs as if resigned to his destiny. A Croat father, Serbian mother. When the time came for Ilya to choose, he chose his mother's side, the Communist side. It was an easy step; from the Communist Youth League in Serbian Belgrade he entered the security service. Anything, he once told me, to distance himself from the Fascist image of the Croatia that later split from the Federation.

"Killing was an old story in Croatia. In World War Two, Croatians modeled their fascistic *Ustasha* on pre-revolutionary Russia's xenophobic Black Hundreds, the *Chornaya Sotnya*. Above all they hated Serbs. Their motto was kill, kill, kill. Kill the different ones. Croatia was the bastion, the defender of Christian Europe, on the front line against the heathens and apostates of Orthodoxy. That is how they justified their Nazism."

I know their beautiful capital city. A Latin city, Zagreb. Wide avenues, theaters and cafés, like in Vienna. The biggest surprise the non-Slav meets in Zagreb is the Croat language. It is unexpected—a Slavic language here. You might think they should be speaking German. And indeed Slavic Croatian is filled with German words.

The Milanica family tombstone in the graveyard on the hill above the village of Milanica sticks in my memory as emblematic of former Yugoslavia, both the old ideal of Slavic unity and the disaster of its disintegration. All the tensions pushing and pulling members of the same family in divergent directions marked both Ilya's spiritual self and his activist life. Curiously, the tombstone overlooking the Adriatic Sea is marked by a star on one side and a cross on the other. The site reserves space for both sides of the family: its Communists and its Catholics. The same division that earlier had cut across Croatian society too. The Croatia to which Ilya's region of the Dalmatian coast belongs. Its two cultures: Catholic and Slavic; two polarized politics: Communist and the reaction that led Croatia to collaborate with Nazi Germany and then later to absorb both Yugoslav Communism and the dream of Southern Slavic unity into its DNA. Here you feel the spiritual difference between East and West. Croatia is the boundary line. The star will have been chiseled away from the tombstone. Yet the spirit of the heritage of Yugoslav Socialism somehow survives the erased star. But strangely, Ilya's village on the Adriatic where we vacationed together remained untouched by the wars. Already then Catholic Croats thought of themselves as a Mediterranean people, close to West Europe, and were amazed that Westerners thought of them as the other peoples of the "real Socialist area".

"Clifford, you know all this. The Croats had abandoned the Soviet bloc already in the late 1940s. They were the first to split the unity of multiethnic Yugoslavia, Catholic Slovenians and Croats in the West, Orthodox Serbs in the East and Moslems in the southern regions of Bosnia, Macedonia and Montenegro. Yugoslavia was rich, successful and independent in the 1960s. Today much of the former federation is little more than an American protectorate or is clamoring to enter the European Union and NATO.

"I have secrets for you, Clifford. I would not tell anyone else what I have come to drill into your head, into your brain, into your control system, so that it conditions your entire life."

"Do I really deserve it, Ilya, your secrets, I mean? We're friends. Remember our promises, some of mine maybe drunken, some not? They were real. So don't tell me anything I can't publish."

"We want you to publish what I have to tell you. It is the core of the matter. And it will be a boost to your journalistic career … if that is what you are really doing. We hope you will shift your target to East Europe … travel there, be there … and maybe witness the coming revolution."

"Revolution? Anyway, shoot!" I say in English.

"Shoot?"

"Just an expression. I mean proceed."

"*Also gut, höre mal gut zu.* OK, now listen closely. Clearly the Western attack on Serbia and Kosovo is about oil. That is, *also* about oil. Everyone talks about the reserves in the Caspian area, oh la la. That great sea bordered by Iran, Azerbaijan, Turkmenistan, Kazakhstan and Russia. But the reality, my friend, is that if you exclude the reserves of Russia and Iran, neither of which the Western powers can control, the reserves in the Caspian Basin amount to only 37 billion barrels of oil. That is a measly three per cent of the world's reserves. The bottom of the list! Saudi Arabia alone has reserves of 262 billion barrels. This geological fact is not widely known. Or the press hides it."

Ilya pauses and cocks his head to one side, observing the effect of his words, as if wondering if I know all this. If I understand and am prepared for his summation of international events and the Balkans.

I wait.

"So why the great U.S. effort in that region?" Ilya continues rhetorically. "Why the invasion of our lands? Economically the plan is not tenable. It does not make sense. All that to-do about three per cent of the world's reserves? There is the enormous expense and complexity of the AMBO Pipeline, to get oil to the West, to lay pipes through Albania, Macedonia and Bulgaria, the many obstacles, the transit fees in each country, transport by pipes, then tankers, then pipes again and tankers again—extremely complex. America bombed Belgrade in order to force Serbia to give up Kosovo while your old friends at CIA and NATO created the Kosovo Liberation Army against Serbia. Now the KLA puppet can turn against its American puppeteer any day. And it will. We know that. Just wait till the KLA rises up like America's former man Bin Laden did in Afghanistan. The CIA first creates him to fight the Russian invaders, then he becomes enemy number one, the world's most dangerous man, falsely blamed for 9/11. The USA made Kosovo *independent*, which, by the way, was also the condition placed by Albania for hosting part of the AMBO Pipeline. You know quite well that Albania still dreams of Greater Albania, that is, the annexation of *our* Kosovo. Everybody—America, Albania, the European Union, the KLA—suddenly wants and needs our Kosovo, the cradle of Serbia. Now America has converted it into a military stronghold to protect its own interests and all the new pipelines in the whole region of the southern Balkans. Even though everybody knows it is better to pipe oil straight through Russia to Europe, pay transit fees only once. That is the shortest way to Europe and the USA."

I'm getting nervous. I know what is coming. It's my turn to go to the window to gather my wits. I stare hard at the early morning sky, following the activity of distinct groups of birds. The sky seems to be slowly revolving. I love Ilya. Ilya is always right. I know he is nearing the subject of the U.S. war against Serbia in the 1990s, when I still played a role in Agency field operations.

"So? What's your point?"

"The point is the real reasons for the USA-led attack against the Federal Republic of Yugoslavia. One thousand Western planes flew 38,000 combat missions. They dropped bombs from the skies and shot Tomahawk missiles from the seas. Out of pure nastiness, or maybe for target practice, they destroyed Danube bridges, bombed and tomahawked factories, Radio Television headquarters, refugee columns, offices of political parties, residences of government officials, even homes of foreign ambassadors, a passenger train, a religious procession, hospitals, hotels and several embassies including that of China. One still wonders if the latter was really a mistake. Yugoslavia was strewn with unexploded cluster bombs. All that destruction and death to overthrow the legal government of Serbia and to get their hands on Kosovo … and to keep the Russians out.

"Why? It seems crazy. Completely *ludo!* So why, Clifford, why? It is geopolitics, my friend. New World Order. The answer is Russia. America fears Russia. America rejects anything that can strengthen Russia. America fears the revival of the Russian empire. The USA wants to bypass Russia. But forever. Remember the old quip that the real role of NATO is to keep the Russians out, the Americans in and the Germans down. Still valid today."

I snicker and slap the table so hard it rocks.

Ilya frowns at my violent interruption and continues in an even softer voice: "Ideologically Europe might agree with America even though it makes no economic sense because Europe's interests lie in Russia. It depends on its neighbor Russia. Even Adolf Hitler knew that. Especially today for its natural gas of which Russia has the world's greatest reserves.

"Also for that reason German and American interests clash in Kosovo. In their hearts Americans say 'fuck Europe'. It counts so little in the big picture. But it is vital in the dollarization of the world.

"Serbs do not love America for the same reason. Not only because of the bombs. In my part of Belgrade you have to be careful speaking English in the wrong places. You do not see many Americans there. Not any more. Remember the pleasant neighborhood area right behind the St. Sava Orthodox church? The city skyline is still dominated by that majestic church of white marble and green copper domes modeled on the Hagia Sofia in Istanbul."

I remember. I remember the summer heat in Belgrade, when once it descends on the city, it never leaves. Until later arrive the bitter cold winds of winter. I remember well my semi-clandestine visits to Ilya's apartment. And our walks along the Sava River to where it flows into the Danube. The gateway to Europe, they call it. The Sava and Danube meet beneath the hill on which the fortress stands. It was the main fort in Ottoman Belgrade which looked down on the outskirts of the Austro-Hungarian Empire across the rivers. Then Karadjordjevic or Black George began a revolt against the Ottomans which led to Serbian independence.

"The great secret is America's maniacal fear of Russia. Why do you think that after the collapse of the Soviet Union and the end of the Cold War American military bases abroad were not closed and the soldiers brought home?"

Ilya knows that I know the answers. Sadly, Americans didn't even wonder why the troops never came back home. It was natural that they stayed "over there". In war, the winner takes all in the American mindset. Many people still have no idea of where "the troubled Balkans" are located. In any case no questions are asked about the conquest of the whole fucking Balkans. It seems natural.

"The real reason for American occupation of Kosovo, for example? It is not oil. It is not Iran. Sure you can control the eastern areas with a string of bases and extend the empire but the encirclement of Russia lies at the heart of it all. Again. And again. Crush the Russians so they never rise again. Russia and its Socialist messianism, its mission to save the world! You cannot nuke Russia because they have the bomb too … and the possibility of delivering it. So encircle them. Then squeeze them.

"Kosovo! For protection of the pipelines. OK? But all kinds of covert activities there. OK? Huge intelligence activities, CIA detention centers. Drugs from Afghanistan and recycling of drug money to support the KLA and Albania. Militarization along the strategic East-West corridors. American power moving, moving eastwards. The whole Anglo-American alliance to dominate oil and gas routes and corridors from the Caspian to the Black Sea across the Balkans. The scramble for control of the national economies of the entire former Soviet bloc. The alliance between the U.S. Defense Department and oil cartels. Imposition of the sacred dollar over the euro. That is all part of it. But never forget the containment of Russia. Crush the lungs of Russia. Smash it. Crush it. That is the fundamental point. Fucking Commies anyway! Let them drink themselves to death without regaining one centimeter of world control.

"And the second secret is: fuck the European Union too. Undermine EU expansion to the East. Chase Germany out of the Balkans. The coup de grace to Mitteleuropa. And here, Clifford, we are back to Marx again. Again the conflict between competing capitalist blocs."

"OK, OK, Ilya. I get the point. Enough for now. You just got here. Let's slow down. How about a walk? Get the feel of the territory. Reminisce some. See the town. Or are you afraid to be seen here?"

"Who knows my face here? I am harmless. Not even Munich Serbs know me. We could even go to the great mosque and no one would know me. So, yes, let us go out for a while. I can meet your new wife later."

* * *

The Angel of Peace takes no notice of us passing down the winding steps to the River Isar. It's nearly springtime in Munich when everything in nature is something about to become. Flowers and plants are still in hibernation but about ready to arouse and emerge. The magician's same legerdemain each year: winter is there ... and voilà, it's gone. At the bottom of the hill Ilya turns and gazes upwards at the Friedensengel. "It is as if she took no note of war or peace. She should have seen the blood flow in my country in the last fifteen years. She would know where she stands on war."

Ilya is right. The old lady just stands there, placidly, her wings raised toward the gray skies, alone at the top of her column, as if she were aware and conscious that there is a difference between war and peace; yet also as if she was helpless to change the continuing desire of the generals for war, to eliminate war crimes, even the destruction of the city over which she stands guard, helpless to change man's unchanging fascination with war, and apparently helpless to alleviate the massacres and slaughters and the inhumanity of war.

"*Ja ja*, Ilya, but her very name is a denunciation. She says that war is not peace ... and can never be. You know that better than I do. Each time I pass here she reminds me of that, that war scars both the defeated and the victors. And that the cleansing one talks about after a war can't remove the stain of blood and guilt. Remember that she also observed the birth of Nazism. She knew it was criminal but she knew also that the post-war denazification was a travesty of justice because of the ones who were not punished. She reminds me that the Allies went to war for the wrong reasons."

"And waited long enough to see Communist Russia destroyed first."

"Just goes to show that no one enters or comes out of war with clean hands."

We cross the Leopold Bridge and stroll up Prinzregenten Strasse. I turn and again look back. From here she's smaller, darker and less imposing. Yet she's visible from almost anywhere in this part of downtown Munich.

"Uh, Ilya, I'll need some help on all this. Too many places in the East I can't visit comfortably."

"Do you have someone in mind?"

"A good-looking young German. He's got loads of money and can finance himself … if I can get him interested. Rich and an aura of innocence about him that makes people trust him. I'll sound him out."

Ilya shrugs.

But the more I think about it as we stroll up the boulevard, the more the idea of Karl Heinz as front man grabs me. He's the kind who stumbles onto the most unexpected occurrences.

"Where are we going?" Ilya asks as we turn into the Königin Strasse. "You know I am not a tourist."

"No problem, old friend. I'm taking you to meet a curious person. You'll find you have some things in common with him. You might even know Hristo. But for now, take a look at that building over there, the U.S. Consulate General. That imposing building houses one of the Central Intelligence Agency's biggest offices in Europe. My bosses were concealed in the back section. Some of them are most likely still there. Bad people. I was detached from them in a little office over in the old town ... in the period you and I used to meet over there across the Adriatic. It seemed strange even then that Kosovo is so near. Part of Europe but a different world. Much more so now that it's an American province."

Just to flaunt their fucking secrecy oaths that I've signed and re-signed, I like to reveal secrets to people like Ilya and Franzi, my old partner, as well as to Hristo, one of my few remaining friends in old Munich. Childish, but it gives me a certain sense of power over *them*.

"It is another universe over there," Ilya mutters. "And by the way I have been in those offices twice before." He grins, delighted when he sees the surprise on my face.

"Oh yeah?"

"Either before or perhaps after your time there," he adds in his most mysterious way just to flummox me. "And Hristo? Many of them in Bulgaria. Hristo who?"

"You'll see. Oh, there's the *Reitschule*, the riding academy, just the place for us. Remember the old times? Riding in the mountains. We'll stop in the manège café later. You can see not only the manège but also the best part of the Englischer Garten. Quite a spectacle for a horse lover like you. Anyway that's his house, up there on the right. Hristo's wild wild house."

The gate is unlocked, the lateral entrance door slightly ajar. I push it open and call, "Hristo! Hristo!"

"*Shhhh, nicht so laut, verdammt nochmal,*" issues from the room near the door. "Gavrilo is having his breakfast."

A head peeks out the door, his soft words almost echoing in the hall. "Oh, Cliff, it's you. Take a look at this, would you. But come in slowly. Don't want to frighten him. He's extremely sensitive at this hour."

"Gavrilo!" Ilya mutters. "Another anarchist, eh?"

"What? What's that?" Hristo whispers. "Anarchist? He's a thoroughbred. Balkan horse."

I push Ilya into the kitchen ahead of me and watch his perplexed expression when he sees the horse's gray head and long smooth neck stretched through the window. Gavrilo is eating from a huge platter filled with special foods on a table just under the windowsill next to the sink. The sleek horse lifts his head slightly and rolls his huge blue eyes toward us, before turning back to his breakfast.

"Incredible!" Ilya whispers. "Does he live here?"

"In the front garden, where else?" Hristo says in his Bavarian accented German. He and Ilya could understand each other quite well in their own languages, so similar are Serbian and Bulgarian. But both men are international and super-polyglot. "But he takes his meals with me in the kitchen. I don't trust those assholes down at the Riding Academy stables to care for him properly. I'm allergic to cats, and dogs bark too much, and anyway like any good Bulgarian I prefer horses. Gavrilo only neighs a bit, when he's hungry. He's a real companion. Loves galloping through the Englischer Garten but otherwise he can stand for hours with his head in the window and keep me company."

"Wild Bulgarians and their horses," Ilya exclaims, chuckling. "A famous relationship."

"Our horses are special. Some so tame they're part of the family, live like household pets. Others, still wild, roam around in packs in the wilderness of old Thrace and Moesia and Macedonia. The beasts of the Balkans! Still, they sometimes wander back to civilization to tempt the tame horses to join them. Some do. Did you know that Alexander the Great's beloved horse Bucephalus was from former Macedonia and carried the emperor across the world? Alexander considered horses immortal but his died in battle, aged thirty. He named a captured city for him, Bucephala, today called Jhelum, in Pakistan. I believe Caligula's horse, Incitatus, was Macedonian too, the horse he wanted to name Consul of the empire."

"Crazy story," I comment, not so much about Alexander as uncertain whether we're sitting in the kitchen or in the stable and whether we're talking about horses or people. "A Bulgarian story," I add. "Horses and belly dancers. Bulgars, half Turks anyway."

Hristo shrugs and looks fondly at Gavrilo. Hristo is not as tall as me but is powerfully built, a bull neck and thick graying hair. He embraces me and sticks out his hand to Ilya. "Don't we know each other?" he asks, examining Ilya closely. "I think we met before."

"We did," Ilya says. "And I remember when and where. It was in the 1980's. Times were different … and so were we.

That was during the hearings and the press conference in the Sofia conference hall when your government denied charges of any role in the 1981 shooting of Pope John Paul. I sat the whole time in the back row and saw you ... a young kid like me. You kept walking back and forth, looking worried. You told me some of the background to the phony Bulgarian connection story in the Saint Peter's shooting. And we agreed."

"The whole story was the shit-trash concoction of the CIA," Hristo says. "With the help of the Italian SISMI, Gladio and God knows who else to prove us Bulgarians guilty of working for the KGB to assassinate the Polish Pope because he sided with Solidarnosc ... a threat to the Soviet Union, which was already on the verge of collapsing anyway. The so-called 'Bulgarian Connection'. The shooter, the Turk Ali Agça, told so many different versions that the CIA and BND could make a case for anything ...and its opposite. We were the fall-guys, and you knew that, Cliff."

"Of course it was so much crap," I say. "You know quite well who dreamed up such trash. Whatever that asshole American spokesman, a certain Ledeen, dreamed up or that whore of a journalist Claire Sterling reported, you could believe the contrary. Anyway, Hristo, we dropped by to see Gavrilo on our way to the Reitschule Café to watch the daily show in the manège ... even though Gavrilo is more interesting. And those old days are gone forever anyway."

"Really?" Hristo mutters, and winks at Ilya. "I think, we can stay busy, what with the American occupation of the Balkans."

"Right," murmurs Ilya, now ill at ease. "That is why I am here. To get our budding journalist here to write some exposés on the subject, especially Kosovo."

"Worthwhile endeavor, friend," Hristo says to me, dipping deeper into his Bavarian accent that he can turn on and off at will. "Why do you think I live in Munich and not back there? While you're on the subject of Camp Bondsteel in Kosovo, you both might take on the whole string of bases across the Balkans and now the Caucasus. Did you know there are thousands of American military in Bulgaria; Camp Sarafovo, the Bezmer Air Base and the Graf Ignatievo Air Base and also many Bulgarian-American Joint military facilities, all run by Americans? Why, the Novo Selo Training Range is a NATO favorite for maneuvers."

When Hristo pauses to collect his thoughts I stand up and stretch my hand toward Gavrilo's head. The gray head continues eating, ignoring me completely. I stroke the slick part of his face just above his nostrils, then yank my hand away, surprised at the horse's live warmth, almost hot.

"Big American investments there for housing and infrastructure for American troops," Hristo adds, nodding in approval at my gesture. "For sure they're there to stay. Anything to contain Russia and at the same time spread their own empire is legitimate in their thinking ... as long as it enhances their ends. And remember, I didn't love the Russians either when they ran things in my country. But we're all Slavs after all, not Turks. Some of us are Orthodox too, and we have much in common with Russia. So anything I can do to help ..."

My first meeting with Hristo, years back, was quite different. I had just finished an intensive Russian language course in Oberammergau and was waiting for my first assignment, Moscow. To get the feel they sent me to Bulgaria under a journalist cover. I was in my early twenties, he a few years older. I was sitting under an awning at a sidewalk café opposite the Beaubourg-like Palace of Culture admiring the golden dome of Alexander Nevsky Cathedral while clanging trams fought for space on the café-lined boulevard, when I saw this Greco-Roman type teasing some girls at a nearby table. All the waitresses and girls alike knew him and called his name, Hristo, Hristo. He seemed to be at home along the café strip, bumming a coffee at one table, a cigarette at another, just to get to know the girls. He laughed loudly, ran off in the rain chasing a passing girl, returned shaking his hair like a wet dog, and sat down at my table. I thought he was one of Sofia's golden youth.

Somehow these two men, wary Ilya the died-in-the-wool Communist and powerful Hristo, joyous, impulsive Bulgarian with his horse Gavrilo—named after the Serb nationalist who on June 28, 1914 assassinated the heir to the Austro-Hungarian throne, Archduke Franz Ferdinand, at the Latino Bridge in Sarajevo, thus igniting World War I—these two men fix things in place for me. Two towers of strength even though in a way they're holdovers from the past. I love them both because they don't hold my past against me. They give me a sense of permanency that I've never known before, the spirit of which I try to absorb also from my togetherness with Elizaveta and to inculcate into my elastic but porous psyche. The kind of permanency I fear might be weakened were they to learn that she's the daughter of two famous Russian spies, professional spies like the three of us sitting at a kitchen table in München-Schwabing watching Gavrilo eating his equine delicacies.

10

KARL HEINZ

WHEN Cliff's call arrived I was standing at my window looking toward the deepest part in the middle of the unruly lake and wondering why its waters were always agitated. A warning? A threat? An omen? I assumed the winds had to have something to do with it. Winds from Poland and Siberia, winds sweeping down from the Baltic across Brandenburg, zeroing in on Berlin waterways. The dark center of the Wannsee has always terrified me. The spot where the ferries to and from Kladow meet seems the most perilous.

It was early spring. Already a decade into the new century. Sixteen months had passed since *the events*. Sixteen months since terrorist bombs devastated cities across the whole continent. But I had still found neither peace nor comprehension of what had actually happened. Back at home after our exotic stay in Italy, Katharina hadn't changed one iota. Still her whorish self. Still dedicated to keeping alive my apprehensions and phobias, my jealousies and accompanying appreciations. I'm convinced she kept me on tenterhooks on purpose and even though she had begun complaining that she might be pregnant, she continued to reject my marriage proposals. Her refusal to even consider my proposal should have taught me more about myself than it did. After our adventures in Italy, the realization that I was still alone hurt me more than when she had left me years before—for my grandfather. It's said that in every couple one person is destined to love more than the other. In our case I've long been the only one to love; Katharina is instead passion's slave. I'm available to her; she uses me. I know that. I have love to give; she has none. One says that my love should be my recompense. I say, bullshit to that. I've always thought life was all about love. Truth is, I'm a case of both pent-up love and unbridled passions. Katharina wouldn't even have understood if I'd told her that love simply can't be rebuffed. And as far as her pregnancy was concerned, I never knew whether to believe her or not. In any case since she hadn't changed her wanton habits and her character and our life together was as uncertain as ever, I relied on increasingly stronger doses of my trusty lamotrigina pills, while my everyday life was one of fear and trembling. My availability and her passions! Watching her every motion in our foolish lovers' game, I hummed, adapting the popular song to myself. My song it should have been. My greatest anxieties were: first, that Katharina could leave me from one moment to the next; second, that she really might be pregnant; and third, that the lamos might lose their potency, with me doubting I could find an effective substitute.

My articles about our Perugia experience, the death I saw there, the drug rings and international spies, had stirred up momentary interest in the Berlin press. But after things cooled off following that terrible December 24, 2008 — now referred to as "the events of December 24", the day terrorist fire and fury struck the capitals of Europe; a date which lingers in the psyche and subconscious, if not the active minds, of Europeans of East and West, no less than September 11 across the Atlantic — my journalistic career was still not taking off. In fact I was stalled. Until now, I had always counted on my old sense of detachment to armor me against threatening invasions like Cliff's phone call ... and his demands for commitment. And, as Katharina charged, I simply was not hungry enough.

No, I wasn't hungry. In fact I was rich with my deceased Opa's money and property. I wasn't even hungry for fame. No ambition whatsoever. I was in too deep a rut to climb out unaided. Each morning I massaged my thinning hair with French potions, I practiced the Charles Atlas dynamic tension, and I held my narrow, pointed shoulders back as my mother had admonished me. When I noted sudden bulges in my belly region I did some sit-ups. But I still drank too much and counted on my lamos to keep my head above water. At odd times during the day I examined my tallish, lanky but thickening figure in the full-length bathroom mirror. Through my x-ray eyes I saw a still young man just barely concealing the symptoms, the contours and the threat of middle age.

In any case the call from Munich that black day was perplexing. Cliff asked point blank if I was available for cooperation in some investigative journalism that would give us both a shot in the arm. He needed me for missions in East Europe.

Despite the intrusion into my *relative* peace, I was flattered to feel needed. But I understood that these missions meant leaving Katharina alone. I fretted about how she would react and rationalized that East Europe was by now no longer far; in fact it's in Germany's backyard since old Central Europe revived ... and this time as semi-colonies of the West. I also didn't know what to think about the widespread belief that people in the East finally live in freedom after the gulag the West called their Communism. For the last two decades that conviction has been accompanied by genteel sighs of relief and recommendations that the now free peoples should enjoy their new freedoms on their own lands and not be lured westwards to upset our six decades-long peace and tranquility. Apparently few dark Moscow mysteries remain. On the other hand, knowing Clifford as I did, I knew he wouldn't have asked my collaboration were it not urgent and were it not a job I could handle.

"Why don't you just go alone?" Katharina said when I asked if she would like to travel with me. "East Europe doesn't interest me in the least. Why, people there all want to come here. Like our brothers and sisters from East Germany. Why should I waste my time in bad hotels and eat bad food? Besides I'm too busy to even consider travel ... and I do have to take care of my probable pregnancy. And, Karl Heinz, if I went anywhere, it would be to Italy."

Her indifference to life outside of herself and her fixation on Italy both relieved and disturbed me. Since our return from Perugia, she liked to speak Italian now and then. In order to retain fluency for *her* future, she said, which most certainly would include Italy. Nonetheless her enduring attraction to Italy dashed my conviction that I'd found my own shore in Berlin. Eccentric and self-centered Katharina had never understood my stewing about my existential question of where I belong.

I tried to explain. "My idea is that acquaintance with East Europe could free me from my Germany-Italy dichotomy and also my West European centrism which I thought you and my inheritance had resolved."

"You and your fixations! Bah! Right now there's life to be lived. Think about that instead!"

"In recent months I've been idle ... too complacent in our comfort. Katharina, everybody needs some, uh, challenges in life."

"Challenges! *Um Gotteswillen*, Karl Heinz. You need to relax and to, ah, enjoy me and your rich life you got from you know who."

"Got what from you know who?"

"You got me ... from your grandfather." She never missed a chance to rub it in that she had once left me for my grandfather and only came back to me after I inherited his estate. As if she were part of my inheritance!

All in all and despite my apprehensions the idea of the East appealed to me even though I know little about it. I imagined my going to the East would be like going to war must have been for other generations. A romantic appeal. Traveling from one capital to the other of Old East Europe, from Budapest to Prague and from Belgrade to Sofia. Interviewing writers and political figures in Old World cafés. Filing stories from the outposts of Europe.

A few days later Cliff forwarded me a copy of a message written by a former contact of his in Bulgaria and my initial apprehensions about involvement in a subject I knew so little about returned.

* * *

Note to Hristo Hristov from Blagovesta Doncheva in Bulgaria.

My dear Hristo, I want to share with you my answer to a well-meaning Englishman who generously offered me economic help. You will appreciate the irony of the strange suggestion of this rich West European that I should correct my diet! Yes, precisely that. Now suppose I accepted the offer that might last me several months during which I could eat better. But afterwards? I would fall back to my starvation diet of today in capitalist Bulgaria. So that is no solution. The solution, many of us here know, would be to crush Capitalism and return to our Socialist life of before damned 1989. I preferred the healthy and accessible food we in Bulgaria had under "gulag Communism" as it was called by the CIA and Mossad and all their Zionist collaborators. The Western press hasn't yet written about the direct connection between the destruction-murder of the Soviet Union and the wars of Fascist Israel and USA in the last 20 years. When will they acknowledge that the West destroyed the quality of life in the Soviet Union and the countries of East Europe? The West doesn't recognize the link between its Capitalism and the gangsterism that has now invaded East Europe. Who is going to provide me also with the free medical care we enjoyed in Socialism when we had what was called "youth acceleration"? Today it's old age acceleration. Aging has accelerated by ten years. Though 66 in calendar years,

I'm now 76, with many health problems. I need quality health care. Where is it? Now we know how capitalist health care works — or doesn't work. I have gathered examples proving that elderly patients are being deliberately killed in our capitalist hospitals. I have a list of such names. I have come to the conclusion that we have been kicked back centuries in health care. I now exist in a system like that of primitive peoples who lived in caves and simply died when they fell ill. So I cannot accept charity offers. This kind of charity solves nothing. It helps nobody. I hate it. Do the idiots who collect charities and distribute them think the poor only need food and clothes for a few days a year? The only solution is to kill Capitalism and restore our lives of before 1989 ... and to organize the same life for people in Western countries. I am an activist who opposes American meddling in the Balkans and its attempt to turn these nations into neo-capitalist client states.

"If everything was a market, people would not look after children, but only cattle." (From an Interview with Koljo Georgiev, the Bulgarian poet.)

Blagovesta

Cliff's e-mail concluded: *Karl Heinz, I need you for travel to places I can't go. You told me of your inheritance so I know you can afford it. If you agree we can meet halfway, say in Frankfurt, and talk and agree on details. This is important. Give me a call and we can decide. Tomorrow would be a good time to meet. Your Perugia friend, Cliff*

* * *

"Somewhere — maybe it was near Nürnberg," Cliff says when we meet in the station café, "I stared out the train window and wondered where the fuck I was and what I was doing." While he speaks I'm again struck by his powerful Swiss-German-Bavarian accent so different from my accentless German. Cliff, an American by nationality but, like me, by nature rootless.

"You must do that too. Anyway since I got involved in this project, I've thought of you. Since neither of us really knows who we are commitment might help us find identity. And besides, there's some good journalism involved too."

"But Cliff, I don't know my ass from my elbow when it comes to East Europe."

Still, because of Cliff, because Nikitin and Hakim had both exploded into bits on the mountain over Assisi, because they'd disappeared so violently, even in my Berlin idleness I did pay more attention than I used to to what was going on in the world. I seldom use the word *terrorist* anymore ... or use it cautiously. I learned the lesson. I speak of *resistance*. I now know the difference. Now I'm at least capable of conscientious political thought. I've acquired enough curiosity to wonder how many people have the capacity to overcome their cultural-political ignorance. I believe I'm also acquiring the capacity to reason about the reality of the socio-political situation in the West. I'm learning to *not* keep things in perspective. That's a lesson from Cliff. He says 'fuck perspective' and 'fuck impartiality too'. Like his reasons for not wanting to live in the USA — 'a mentally ill, unreal country of used car lots and plastic fast food chains,' he once wrote me in an e-mail. 'A people who suffer from an apparently incurable disease called Americanism. Exceptionalism and its delusions exempt the USA from rules of rational, civilized behavior. Besides, the country is becoming a huge cultural garbage dump.'

Even though he once worked for the *Agency crowd*, as he calls the CIA, he says it should be abolished. Obliterated, deleted, erased from the face of the Earth.

Cliff's eyes sweep over the spacious café. He grunts. "I know a bit about East Europe but too many of the wrong people over there know too much about me. Especially Americans. They would never let me into Camp Bondsteel."

"Camp what? Bondsteel? American, is it? Now what is that supposed to mean?"

"Who knows? Never understood who makes up all these names. It's an American military base. In Kosovo. The USA fought an illegal war to get it."

The Frankfurt Hauptbahnhof café-restaurant is packed. We sit in a corner hunched over a table near a big window facing the station square. Skies overhead are of a leaden gray so indistinct as to seem permanent. Not clouds or smog. Just grayness. Taxis lined up a few meters beyond the glass keep their motors running. The line moves forward quickly as people hurry from trains to important appointments. Car doors opening and shutting. All in pantomime beyond the soundproof window glass. Silhouettes of skyscrapers of this Manhattan on the River Main are reminders that this is the heart of financial Europe. The financial European Union. Nonetheless the smell of stale beer lives here, not totally unpleasant though. The turnover is so fast and the amount of spilled beer splashed over neighboring tables so great that waitresses only have time to give a lackadaisical swipe with already beer-soaked cloths in preparation for the next drinker.

"Strange," Cliff mutters following my eyes, "stale Frankfurt beer stinks in a different way from Munich beer."

"And from Berlin beer too."

"What do you think it is, the proximity of all the banks? The stink of money?"

I chuckle at his analogy. For Europe is beginning to stink of money. We look at each other and laugh. We too stink of money.

At that moment a middle-aged man in suit and tie approaches our table and murmurs rhetorically, "*Ist der Platz frei?*" and without so much as a glance at us he starts to sit down unbidden, as is the German custom. Cliff looks up at him and says softly that we prefer to be alone. The man pulls out a chair anyway. Cliff rises to his six feet and four or five inches, his thick, dark beard menacing, as powerful looking as a TV wrestler, and repeats, barely raising his voice: "I said we prefer to be alone." For the first time the man looks at him. A startled look crosses his eyes, he mutters an *Entschuldigung*, and walks away.

Cliff laughs sardonically. "These fucking Frankfurters think they own the fucking world just because of all their fucking banks."

The whole time we're together that day I'm aware of a dazed look on my face fastened like a mask. Maybe the mask hangs somewhat crookedly but the feeling is still there. I know I've changed since St. Moritz, the day of the meeting of intelligence chiefs headed by Nikitin himself, the day I sat next to Cliff's Dad and watched him die. I feel in Cliff the familiar strangeness of the same lost man I am. Of a man without overpowering beliefs or convictions. Yet he has a natural charisma, once brutal, today controlled. A quality I will never have. Killing those men in Perugia must have changed him. The brutality has vanished but the charisma, backed up by the aura of authority he emanates, remains intact.

While Cliff speaks, I feel his eyes examining my reactions. Or my lack of them. For my part I keep trying to get the attention of a waitress. And I realize we don't know each other at all.

"A crazy world," I say. "Who would've thought that getting out of that business would make it harder for you to move around the world of the East?"

"But the reasons are different now. It's my old employers who limit my movement, not our former enemies."

"*Your* former enemies. Not mine."

"That's the point, Karl Heinz, you have no enemies on either side. That's why I hope you will represent me. I will guide you … like an old spymaster. Actually it'll be fun for you … and an eye-opener too … to experience American-occupied East Europe. You're lucky."

"You think so? But how would I start? And where?"

"You go as a tourist. But also as a journalist. Bulgaria would be a good start. Very tourism oriented. The Black Sea coast. The mountains. You'll like Sofia. I started my old career there. Lots of nightlife. And you can meet American or German soldiers coming down to the capital from Novo Selo and other NATO bases. Many thousands of them there. They go to Sofia for the bars and the beautiful women. Getting away from Katharina a bit won't hurt you."

I didn't understand his last remark. Nor did he explain, just smiled ironically as if he knew something I didn't. But he had spent a lot of time with Katharina and me in those last weeks in Perugia … before *the events*.

"I'd like to hear what the soldiers have to say about their mission there. Then you might get onto one of the military bases. See the press people. Interview a commanding officer if you get a chance."

"But why? What do we want from them?" I'm getting more and more nervous. I wriggle around in the chair, look around for a waitress, and spontaneously order, too loudly, "a beer and a Dornkaat!" A grin cracking his formidable beard, Cliff does the same, I suspect just to keep me company. He doesn't realize how much I need it.

"What do we want? We want to know what the fuck *they* think they're doing down there. I wonder if the soldiers even know."

I down my Dornkaat. "But what do you think they're doing?"

"Certainly I don't believe many of them think they're there to defend America and West Europe from Iran or other vague enemies … or to fight terrorism either. Nor do I believe they're there only to protect oil pipelines. That too, of course. But it can't be all about Iran since the bases are spread also to the north as far as Estonia. What else can it be but Russia? Russia, again. Surround the fucking Russkies. That old geopolitical encirclement philosophy is still on the table. Since 1917 when revolutionary Russia dared oppose capitalism it's been right in the center of the table. Crush anything that smacks of Socialism."

"But Cliff, why? You raise lots of questions and give few answers. Is Russia threatening the West? The Red Army? Missiles? Nuclear weapons?"

"For some people Communism is always a threat, Karl Heinz. And old habits of containment of Great Russia are hard to break. When I was stationed in Moscow, even non-Communist intellectuals and dissidents talked about that old tradition. They believe U.S. hostility toward them derives from something buried in America's puritanical genetic make-up. They say Americans consider them barbarians they have to contain ... as ancient Rome did the barbarians in the wild north. That America has to encircle and circumscribe them and dictate and preach to them and look down on them ... just as one Adolf Hitler did. Maybe there is also jealousy. Envy of Russia's vast lands. For its great culture. Russia has something that America lacks. Ignorant cynics might say that it has to do with the great natural gas reserves in Siberia. In any case the source of the perceived Russian threat is a mystery ... though the memory of competition with Russia for world domination remains alive in the West, especially across the Atlantic. The reasons the USA so gleefully bombed Belgrade are clear. But Karl Heinz just stop for a moment and imagine bombing a contemporary European capital."

"So why did it happen? Did everyone go crazy?"

"Russia was the reason. Time lends transparency to events that are jumbled when they happen but which turn out to be historical landmarks. Post-communist Russia was defenseless. The USA could do as it liked in the world. Attack Iraq to get back at Russia. Get Serbia to get at Russia."

"But why Serbia?"

"Though Russia had lost many lands since 1989, it still supported its brothers in Serbia, the home of the Southern Slavs, a nation which refused to embrace capitalism. America's military establishment and their neocon pals accused Serbia of genocide. But Serbs were no more criminal than Croats and Bosnians and Albanians ... and Americans. In the

1990s Communist Yugoslavia was disintegrating. Bedlam reigned. So America bombed. Bad. Ugly.

"America was determined to crush Serbia and then detach from it Kosovo and make it another American vassal state. Today that so-called independent nation hosts one of America's biggest military bases in Europe. Camp Bondsteel. Kosovo became another link in the chain of America's encirclement of Russia. America wants to crush Russia once and for all. Surround it, squeeze it, crush it. Divide it up into little states. Get them to fighting one another while alcohol continues its work of sucking the blood from the Russian nation busily drinking itself to death."

"Sounds like Nazi Germany's plans."

"Now you get the idea. The final solution of the Russian question."

When the second round of refreshments arrives, I leap for both. Avidly. Recklessly. I'm still at war with drink. I'm not even subtle about my desire. I think of Katharina and me with our Chivas Regal and red wine in Perugia that Cliff saw more than once. He knows.

I wipe the froth of the deadly mixture from my lips with the back of my hand, and grin at Cliff. I'm the pawn. I know that. He's the puppet master. The arrangement suits me fine. "OK! It's Bulgaria. See the soldiers. Then where? And where are we going to publish all this stuff?"

"Valid questions. After Bulgaria and Serbia, you could move to the south, right into the American protectorate of Kosovo. Or maybe north to Moldova … they say Chisinau is lovely in the summer."

"Moldova? Moldova? Where is that exactly?"

"Many people wonder the same when they hear the name. It's *not* Moldavia It's former Bessarabia. Once part of Romania, then of the USSR. Four million people, six hundred thousand Moldovans abroad. An immigrant people. Orthodox. The official language is Romanian but most people still speak Russian. Since the Communist Party won last year's elections, America supports opposition parties ... also because Washington would just love to get its hands on it as it did Kosovo. Could build some fine military bases right there in the belly of Russia."

"You ever there?"

"Well, actually no. But it's an option ... a good one. Anyway, then you might also go eastwards to Georgia and the Caspian Sea Basin. We want to let the world know what these little-known East European peoples think about their new position in the world. How do they feel about American occupation? What about the U.S.-NATO military bases in their lands? How do they react to capitalism as a substitute for Socialism? We want personal testimony. Above all we want to draw a map of the U.S. encirclement of Russia. As to publishing, my Swiss papers will grab everything with joy. Your papers probably the same. Maybe more so the Italian press. You can e-mail me raw materials if you want, I'll write up the stories and sign both our names. We'll become a famous team—Beecher and Leonhard. But you can bet it will spread."

He paused. "We might even have to go into hiding."

On that I take a long swig of beer and yell to the waitress for more Dornkaat. I know I'll have to watch out for drink but today I succumb to the weight of my responsibility. Cliff raises his glass too, with a sly expression on his face. I sense he is about to say something unexpected.

"You know, we're a strange pair. Both of us suddenly rich but now engaged in a war against capitalism. Even stranger considering where our wealth comes from. Mine an inheritance from my spymaster-businessman father. Yours from a grandfather who got his money from mysterious sources ... maybe from the East. Pretty odd coincidence, eh?"

"I'd never thought of that," I say, as always uneasy about the origin of my money. My grandfather had boasted of his business acumen, his successes, his magazines and advertising companies. Only in retrospect did the size of his estate come to seem disproportionately large. Dirty money? Investments in the East? Katharina, who lived with him all those years, must know more about such matters than she admits.

"Guess I never wanted to know where my Opa really got his money. And now it's mine. Yeah, you're right. It is strange, our inheritances."

"Well, fuck it! I ignore it. It fell to me like that. Ripe fruit from the tree. Still, now I can understand how old Pharisee Saul must've felt when he had his epiphany on the road to Damascus and became St. Paul."

Cliff is most likely lying. He doesn't like even thinking about his father because the memory reminds him that he lives free on dirty money.

"What's that? St. Paul? What epiphany?"

"I mean I seem to have acquired a new vision. Something universal, I think. I tell myself that I felt a mysterious hand on my shoulder when I shot those people that night in Perugia — when your warning saved my life, and the police never even questioned me. It seems divine justice was done."

"Well, you don't seem as tough as you did before. Actually I liked you that way. And so did Katharina."

In my mind, Cliff's most admirable quality is that he lives his own life. A man who refutes the life of comfort offered by his government and has become a law unto himself. He killed according to that same law ... and for revenge. One might say that he is the right man for these immoral times. Times in which dissent is considered treason and political leaders order assassinations. I suddenly wonder if he really feels as secure as he seems.

"This way is better, I assure you," he says. "I see the whole Eastern question with other eyes now. I should've benefited more from my experience in Russia but I was too tied up in the espionage business. Now that I'm on the other side of the barricades things look different. I see the real reasons for the perverted foreign policy of the good old USA. Kill Russia! China can wait. China can share the world with us ... for a while at least. China ain't on our shit list-hit list. Not yet.

"Many changes have taken place since the Cold War and people in the West aren't even aware of it. People don't realize that NATO under U.S. command has taken over all the ex-Soviet satellites and Yugoslavia. In the first case, without firing a shot. In the second, through two illegal bombing campaigns: Bosnia in 1995 and Serbia in 1999, plus deployments of ground troops in Bosnia, Kosovo and Macedonia. Seems incredible that the ex-Warsaw Pact nations now have soldiers killing and dying under American command in Afghanistan. None of them fought foreign wars while under Soviet control."

"My god! I didn't know that either."

"Seven former Soviet republics have troops in Afghanistan ... under NATO command. While the U.S. and its allies conduct military maneuvers in the three former Soviet Republics in the South Caucasus—Armenia, Azerbaijan and Georgia; also in Ukraine and Kazakhstan. Georgia's thousands of troops in Iraq were the third largest foreign contingent there. Now they have a thousand troops in Afghanistan. Imagine! From a country of four million people. A former Soviet Republic. During the decades of the Soviet-controlled Warsaw Pact the member states never sent troops overseas. Quite a difference, eh?"

"No wonder Russia wants to rearm and uses its natural gas as a weapon."

"Now you're thinking," Cliff says.

"Last year I saw the May Day parade in Moscow on TV. They still look formidable. Anyway, Cliff, I'll do it." I gulp, reaching in my pocket and touching the package of lamotrigina nestled reassuringly in the deepest part. "I'll go to Bulgaria first. I'm morbidly attracted by the Black Sea. But first of all I need some time to study a bit."

"Right. Study. And keep in mind that in the East you can't count too much on your intuition as you did in Perugia. Old Nikitin was impressed with that quality in you. As Einstein said, 'intuition is nothing but the outcome of earlier intellectual experience.' And you have none in East Europe. Intuition about people, yes. But about geopolitics and war games, most definitely, no. Not yet anyway. Uh, by the way, since we don't have any governments behind us, here's a useful name if you ever get into trouble or need a lifeline … for yourself, or for others. You never know … you don't want to get yourself arrested for rendition down there."

"Arrested by Bulgarians?" I ask, reading the name Ilya something or other, and a Belgrade address.

"No, by my fellow paranoid Americans."

In that moment I realize that Cliff's crazy, violent world into which fate has hurled me has never let me go … no more than him. Friends of once become one's worst enemies. Old Nikitin's world has again taken hold of my life and is shaping it in the most unpredictable ways.

* * *

Like most West Europeans I have only vague ideas about East Europe. And about the Balkans I know next to nothing. I hardly know its precise location. I know about those lands down in the southeastern corner of Europe, lands of wild forests, Sylvans and Dracula and the Black Sea. Most certainly I have no understanding of Slavic mentality, the famous Slavic soul either—something I doubt the American troops stationed there ever imagine. Much less military planners across the Atlantic. For the masses of European tourists pouring into Prague to drink beer in the cellars of the city on the Vltava and walk across the Charles Bridge fighting off hucksters of indeterminate origins or those who take wine drinking cruises down the Danube from Vienna to Budapest, what was once East

Europe is hardly more than an extension of Germany. Most of the remainder of real East Europe is cast in shadow.

And the Caspian Sea Basin that the press writes so much about? For me it is a mystery shrouded in enigma. Like many West Europeans I've never been east of the Dalmatian coast just opposite Italy where I spent a couple of summer vacations with my parents when I was a kid; it had seemed like an extension of Italy. The countries on the Caspian Sea are part of the nearly inaccessible Orient, one of the remote, maybe lost, areas of the Earth that, as Marx pointed out, cannot represent themselves but must be represented. Exotic lands reaching far beyond those vague and changing concepts of the Middle East, of Arabs and Islam. Esoteric lands bordering the Slavic world; lands that throughout the millennia Westerners and especially Orientalists have wanted to represent. I feel something akin to the sensations of Paul Bowles' imaginary naïve European wandering over the Sahara and wondering about available hotels or the status of his passport. Besides, the Black Sea and the Caspian Sea awaken my old obsessive fear of bodies of water. Sometimes, during the night, I imagine being swallowed up by the sea and the horror of death by drowning. No wonder I shudder when I read or hear the torture word, water-boarding. For that reason too I'm uneasy about my possible role in the project.

I spent the week before setting out for Sofia reading about my destination country. I queried my Dad, a veteran journalist who had written extensively about East Europe. I read background articles in the archives of various leftwing publications from which I was able to draw some basic conclusions:

Of course America's military bases are there to defend oil pipelines.

Of course Americans are arrogant and stupid about the rest of the world.

Of course America is in competition with Europe for economic control of the world to the east of Germany.

But I confess that Cliff's theories about the containment of Russia as the heart of America's strategic planning leave me perplexed. However, I have more fundamental problems to deal with: geography. So I begin a study of maps and atlases, trying to get into my head basic things like just where Greece and Bulgaria border, what countries lie on the Black Sea and what lands lie east of the Black Sea. That Asia begins there. Just across the Black Sea. I'm surprised that Odessa is so near and that it is in Ukraine, not in Russia. Then I'm confused by the overlapping of the tiny countries of the Caucasus and around the Caspian Sea.

Again and again I return to those two internal seas around which humanity has lived and fought. Time ticking away, tick-tock, tick-tock. The great flood. Noah's ark. The desert of the Tartars. The top of the world. The hidden piles of skulls lining the Silk Road to Chi'in. Roads and railway tracks to Asia. Curious fixation, a romantic temptation, those railroads. The seas and deserts evoke in me the promise of adventure as challenging as scaling a peak in the North Caucasus might for young mountain climbers. Peaks to conquer. Fears to overcome. The surrounding lands still invite conquest as they have for khans and shahs and kings and emperors for all time.

On the western shores of the Black Sea, Orthodox Bulgarians and Catholic-Eastern Orthodox Romanians; Orthodox Ukrainians and Russians on its northern shores; Sunni Islamic Turks along the south shore; and to the east, the Caucasus, in Greek mythology one of the pillars supporting the world, where Prometheus was chained, now a small area peopled by Christians and Sunni Moslems of countless languages and ancient cultures. Then beyond, the great Caspian Sea, beyond the mountainous lands of variegated peoples and languages of the Caucasus, again Russia and Central Asia in the north and east, with historic Uzbekistan and mythical Samarkand and Bukhara and the great Ferghana Valley, a huge area, once the pinnacle of world civilization, now peopled by Sunni Moslems, from where famous ancient roads still lead to the Islamic holy city of Herat, today in western Afghanistan where American and Italian soldiers are stationed. And then again on the southern Caspian shores lined by the Elburz mountains, Shiite Iran, ancient Persia, and its capital city of Tehran and renowned Isfahan. Here then is Cliff's oil and natural gas-rich Caspian Sea Basin, which today, after the preceding millennia of wars and empires, of emperors and shahinshahs and kings and princes, of mystical religions and teachings, dervishes and flutes, is falling under confused conquerors from the West building walls and sacking museums and lighting bonfires to burn the testimonies of mankind's past. Lands which distant provincial America with its ridiculous Exceptionalism, its simplistic religious beliefs and its selfish and limited vision of life wants to subdue and control and include in its new world empire.

Good Christ, the complexity of the world I see in my maps and atlases! The over-simplifications and the complications, the easy roads east, the dilemmas, the enigmas, each further step demanding more and more violence and war, more and more will to conquer. And I wonder: Do I have in me the substance, the fortitude, the strength of character to penetrate even minimally that other world?

With an atlas spread before me I read online the names of the U.S. military bases spreading from West to East, along the belly of Russia. Step by step. From base to base. A new language of conquest. Creeping, creeping inexorably from West to East. Along the underbelly of deep, deep Russia, lying in wait.

How an atlas opens the world! Strange that atlases aren't banned. I've never spent enough time over them. I make lists of the names of the peoples affected by this new military imperialism—Croats, Serbs, Bosnians, Kosovars, Moldavians, Moldovans, Wallachians, Bohemians, Moravians, Bulgars, Macedonians, Greeks, Turks, and across the Black

Sea more and more ancient peoples and their lands; Georgians, Armenians, Circassians, Chechens, Abkhasians, the North Caucasians of many tribes, peoples and languages; and then Kurds, Iraqis, Uzbeks, Turkmens, Kirghiz, Persians, Afghans, Pakistani, Pashtuns. An image begins emerging. It all begins to hang together, at moments crystal clear: the ambitious goal of world domination by America with its military outposts and its armies and nuclear weapons and drones all along the line.

An atlas is a weapon.

An atlas is a diagram of world issues.

An atlas is a link to elucidate the ambitions lurking behind the issues we read of each day.

It seems the world is not big enough, the seas too narrow — or perhaps too wide — the continents too small, space too finite, maybe even the sun too near, to accommodate so many ambitions.

I'm astounded to see before me as clear as the rising sun the mythological journey of the spreading American empire unlike any other empire before — military and economic and universal. I imagine a journey over land and inland seas directly from West to East. A journey that requires no passports, no visas, jumping from one military base to another. Lily Pads, I read they are called in American military jargon. It is a journey through time and space, briefer than one might believe.

The number of Lily Pads in Turkey alone is astounding: Batman Airbase, Cigli Air Base, Incirlik Air Base, Izmir Air Station, Karatas Radio Relay Site, the Mus Air Base, all of the U.S. airforce.

I would travel by train first to Serbia, and from there on to Bulgaria and see Novo Selo. One day I hope to cross the Black Sea to the Caucasus to visit the nation-military base-protectorate-puppet state of Georgia, then south through Turkey where journalists report Israel is building up its air fleet for its attack on Iran, and to armed-to-the-teeth

Iraq. The courageous could continue on to Iran to visit the declared enemy. I could cross the Caspian Sea to the former oil city of Baku and, still dreaming, on to Turkmenistan and over the great Karakum Desert. From ancient Samarkand it's only two hundred kilometers south into Afghanistan. On and on I dream travel, over the former Silk Road, through India to China. Dreams, I fear, all dreams, for I'm no Marco Polo.

Our planet seems to stand still. In certain moments I can feel it all. A new dawn. I'm part of it. I'm part of the Caucasus and of Iraq. I too belong to the fishermen on the Caspian Sea and to ancient Persia. I too am Afghanistan. Why hadn't I understood the significance of maps before? Why, why had I spent so little time studying them earlier in my life? Geography-cartography, I realize over and over, is a much underrated subject. The ancients didn't underestimate the ultimate value of their dream-like maps. Maps bestowed special value and perspicacity to libraries of the ancient world. Maps were knowledge. Maps dealt in hermeneutics, even ontology. Cartographers were scientists and heroes. Proportion was not a fixed law. Dreams and fantasy counted more than time and space. Space only seemed unlimited, time haywire and unpredictable. Navigator peoples, the ancients, navigators all, who dreamed the adventure of life beyond the horizons. Time and space be damned. Maybe like Etruscans and ancient Greeks, the navigator peoples too were looking for markets but they were also driven by curiosity: to see what lay out there, out beyond the rim where magic still lived, where magic and strange gods were also powers; perhaps, somewhere out there, powers greater than spears and lances and cudgels and shields. Magic is cosmopolitan, a unifying power instead of the divisive force of today's religions, of the new empire, of the New World Order. Religion can renege and be renounced. Not so omnipresent magic.

Maps are part of the magic, part of dreams. How could a mere mortal dare to draw the world? Like the poet's attempt to create a world. That is the work of the gods. For a map is the visual representation of the world: its outline, the boundaries and the divisions that explain the existence of the diversity of men.

Here in Berlin-Wannsee, in springtime, the second decade of the new Millennium, the curtain of my mind has suddenly risen. The world, its empires and conquerors, all become clearer. The Romans followed Alexander the Great, then Charlemagne followed the Romans, Napoleon followed Charlemagne, European imperialism followed Napoleon, then there shone briefly Hitler's mad dream of a thousand-year empire, and now naïve and evil America appears.

I begin to imagine a universe where only the priests of power are permitted to study maps. I imagine a power structure that lives with its top secret, its limited access, revelatory atlases and maps, the secret of ultimate power, numbered and registered and stored meticulously in great security vaults, with eye identification required to view them, while *they* plot the composition of humanity in a universe in which maps are forbidden to the drugged peoples, where maps and ancient paintings depicting another world are searched out and ransacked from peoples' homes and public libraries and bookstores and burned in huge bonfires lit from one end of the empire to the other.

Struck by a memory, I return to a recently read story by Jorge Luis Borges about book burning. Borges tells the story of the First Emperor of China, Shih Huang Ti, who both built the Great Wall of China and ordered the burning of all the books before him. The two gigantic operations — the wall to oppose the barbarians and the abolition of the past — issued from one power, from one hand. Shih Huang Ti, King of Ch'in, conquered the Six Kingdoms of ancient China and eliminated the feudal system; he built the wall because walls were defenses; jealously and egotistically he burned the books because the opposition invoked them in order to extol former emperors. Burning books and building fortifications are common tasks for emperors; the singular thing about Shih was that he *ordered* that history begin with him … and the immense scale on which he operated. Borges notes that to enclose an orchard or a garden is common, but not to enclose an empire. That the most traditional of races renounced the memory of its past, mythical or true, is no small matter. Shih Huang Ti wanted to erase the past because it accused him. Shih Huang Ti forbade all mention of the word death and searched for the elixir of immortality and secluded himself in a figurative palace—maybe a Pentagon— which had as many rooms as the year has days. Perhaps like power today the Emperor hoped to recreate the beginning of time, a New World Order. He called himself The First in order to be truly the first. He dreamed of founding an immortal dynasty; he ordered that his heirs be named Second Emperor, Third Emperor, Fourth Emperor, and so on toward infinity. Perhaps Shih Huang Ti walled in the empire because he knew it was fragile and perhaps he destroyed the books because he understood they were sacred, like the maps, books that taught that which the entire universe teaches or which depict the consciousness of ordinary men. The burning of the libraries and the construction of the wall appear as operations that in a secret way cancel each other. Like the shadows cast by kings and emperors who order that nations burn their past and destroy memory and learning.

Cliff once noted that for peoples of the American empire common names like Afghanistan or Iraq or Iran or Honduras are so distant, mysterious and concealed as to seem to them mere fantasy, fairy tale lands such as Tolkien's that perhaps once had existed in history books but were no more, today never-never lands made only for dreamers and for power's inspectors and their modern mercenaries-Janissaries. My maps make me feel deprived of family in a world without frontiers, homeless, flying alone above all existence, but free to roam, free to scratch for and uncover existence, lost in the world that my maps make so small.

I read that throughout history there has always been one consolation: when the people lose their fear of the power structure and its army—and they always do lose their fear—the past resurfaces, walls fall, things turn to blood and the whole world changes.

Katharina is of a different opinion. Like the old Chinese emperor she detests my maps. Has no use for them. Sometimes, looking over my shoulder at me hunched over my maps and clicking onto the strange names and peoples, Katharina is furious.

"Your fault that I'm pregnant. Your fault alone. If you leave me here, I swear I'll abort."

"It's only for a few days. But if it takes longer you can join me … in some exotic place."

At the time I sincerely wanted to spend a long period in the East, and I hoped that she would join me and we would re-find each other. I converted my journalistic mission into exotic tourism planning too. But where out there could we be together? Somehow I doubt the North Caucasus would interest her or still her anger.

"Anyway there's nothing mysterious about Bulgaria. What about Vienna? We could take in an opera, see some castles and monasteries and drink lots of pleasant white wines. Or what about a cruise on the Danube through Budapest and Bratislava to Belgrade and Novi Sad, southwards to the Black Sea? Or we could sail from Bulgaria to Odessa in the north or south to Istanbul. Nothing adventurous."

"And me pregnant and seasick. Besides, I'm not a tourist."

I hardly hear her. I am telling myself that American soldiers based in all those countries encircling Russia, shooting basketballs and drinking up the local beer, must feel the same sense of the ordinary—no big deal. Arkansas or Kyrgyzstan. What's the difference?

11

WHILE we chat about the passing scenery, the low zigzagging Balkan mountains and the rich plains and the curving rivers, Günther, a charming German businessman sitting opposite me on the Belgrade-Sofia train, turns away from the window and says softly, "Strange but a great sadness always comes over me when I arrive in the Balkans."

His voice comes to me as a breeze, a small voice, borne on the Balkan winds. I am still feeling somewhat guilty for my enjoyable stay in Belgrade. As far as my mission is concerned they were wasted days of eating fish and baklava and visiting nightspots along the Sava riverfront in the city where I knew quite well there was no NATO presence. Maybe I should've gone to the address Cliff had given me but I had no problems. I saved it in my wallet for other times.

Günther pauses, looks toward the line of heavy trucks on the highway parallel to the railway and adds, "If you ever faced the icy silences of official Moscow during Soviet times, if you'd wandered over huge Moscow back then searching for the hardly existent old city or for an intimate café in the hope of absorbing some atmosphere, then you'd understand what I mean. But then Sofia was never Moscow … though it always imitated it. You probably know the old joke that when it rained in Moscow, they opened umbrellas in Sofia."

Günther is about Cliff's age, slender, of average height, with dark hair and the slightly reddish face of a man who enjoys life. He seems jovial and outgoing and is quite good-looking. He's dressed in a dark suit and tie over which he wears a light, blue parka he never takes off. Vaguely, I wonder why. He'd initiated conversation soon after we boarded early this morning, the two of us alone in the compartment. He had tended to his business interests in Belgrade, he said, and decided to train to Sofia instead of taking the usual flight. Like me, just for the experience. Though it's little more than two hundred miles, the trip on the Balkan Express takes all day. No one is in a hurry. No one is pressed. More than once I heard Serbs say 'we still have time to live'. They meant drinking and eating and dancing. Since he travels regularly all over this world I am out to discover, Günther is a gold mine of information. Therefore I don't regret I chose the train. Instinctively I come to trust his evaluations.

"So what do you do in places like Bulgaria?" I ask, since whatever subject we discuss Günther has something unexpected to say.

"Sign contracts," he says enigmatically, before slapping his leg and laughing. "Ideally, I really do come to sign the contracts lined up by my local representatives."

"Contracts? For what?"

"My factory in Wuppertal produces windows and doors. Any kind of fixtures. Security type fixtures for offices and stores, stuff for military barracks."

"So who buys the windows and doors from Germany? Doesn't Bulgaria produce the same?"

"My customers are special. I used to sell to Bulgarians. Now it's American and NATO military installations. Popping up all over. Supermodern barracks, huge shops and stores, security-minded administrative offices. Fruits and vegetables they buy locally but the serious stuff they buy from NATO Germany or directly from American suppliers. Of course we have to go through companies like Halliburton, which runs everything. But it's their policy to outsource as much as they can ... overcharging the U.S. government, of course. Making easy profits. War or even war planning means big money."

"I read about the NATO base at Novo Selo, near the Black Sea."

"My dear boy, that's where I'm going now. That place is literally exploding. I think they'll eventually move half the U.S. troops in Germany to Bulgaria ... or Romania. There are many other bases here of course. All kinds of space is available, though I don't believe the native people like them much. But in a poor country the bases provide jobs, so people close an eye. And what a strategic location it is. Right smack between East and West. You look straight across the Black Sea and there's Georgia, the old Soviet Republic, now an American protectorate. From there you continue directly east to the Caspian Sea and on the other side are former Soviet Central Asia and more American military bases. What a market!"

"Why is that, do you think? All those military bases, I mean. Just to protect oil?"

"*Ach ja, natürlich.* Lots of oil and natural gas there. But each time I study the maps for our marketing planning, I get a strange impression. Those bases sweep straight across from West to East, from Occident to Orient, in a straight line, right along the borders of Russia. Why, they've got so much firepower there that they don't even need Afghanistan. Don't know why they don't give up and get out of those mountain caves. Everyone else did. England and Russia too. Besides the many ancients never succeeded in beating the Afghans either. Well, actually, I do know the reason why they hang on in Afghanistan. I suppose it's because of the poppies. And you know what that means. Well, we Germans know where such ambitions lead, don't we? Anyway if I were a Russian military man I'd be worried about all those U.S. bases along my borders ... some *within* my old borders."

Again Günther stands up and tries unsuccessfully to crack the unyielding window. It's sealed. Still, he doesn't take off his parka though the temperature is far from cold. Still, the bent and fluttering trees and bushes outside mark strong winds sweeping down from the mountains. The yellow broom and mimosas in bloom simultaneously with daisies and daffodils remind me of February and March in my childhood in the little town of Anguillara hanging over the shores of Lake Bracciano near Rome. The scattered yellow petals and flying leaves show the uncertainty surrounding the arrival of spring in this mountainous part of Bulgaria.

"Besides," he continues, turning back to me, "I've found that most Bulgarians truly love Russia. Russians liberated them twice. Once from the Turks, then from the Nazis. And they have little in common with Americans. Problematic, I believe, in the long run. For NATO and America, I mean. Their differentness conditions everything."

"You should be a military man … or an intelligence expert … for Russia," I say. Günther really is politically savvy, the way he seems to know what is what. Outspoken too. I scrutinize his face, his eyes and the expressive way he gesticulates like an Italian. But I detect in him no signs of guile or mystery. In fact, a certain inextinguishable merriment resides in his eyes as he jumps from one subject to the other. He seems to be exactly what he says he is. Intuitively I like him, though I try to keep Cliff's advice in mind about not trusting my hunches about things I know nothing about. Still, I wonder why he hasn't asked me what I'm doing here.

"They know all that quite well without my help. I just sell windows and doors. I know there are lots of missiles on these bases though I haven't actually seen them. But the low ranks speak of them openly. One guy, a Captain, I think he was, told me they calculated Iran would have nuclear-tipped missiles in a few years, so that if Iran fired a bunch of them at Europe, NATO would have to shoot them all down. The problem is Russia, they say, which opposes the U.S. missile systems, especially those along its borders. Russians fear they're pointed at them, not Iran.

Russia needs the trade with Iran but is wary about it having nuclear weapons too. Frankly, I can't imagine why Iran would ever want to fire off missiles against Europe ... since America or Israel could destroy the whole country in about thirty seconds.

"You know, in my years of doing business with them I've concluded that military people of all nationalities are sick. But, they're also my customers."

"That's pretty heavy business you're engaged in. Strange there's not more secrecy. I mean, that you get right onto the bases!"

"You'd be surprised how lax they are."

"You talk as if those places were familiar. Do you come often?"

"If not here, then someplace else. Can't bear the idea of just staying home, if that's home. Wuppertal, I mean."

"Strange you say that. I've got the same problem with home. Don't know where it is really. Born and grew up in Italy. But I'm neither Italian nor German."

"I know what you mean. I grew up in Istanbul. German parents. They're still there, transplants. Yet when you go back to where you thought was home, it's all familiar, you speak like others there, but you find it's no longer home at all."

"Complicated idea. Home," I mutter. "Insidious idea that keeps returning. The idea of home must be problematic for everyone ... dangerous too."

For a while Günther doesn't answer, just keeps looking at me in an odd way. Then: "No need to keep dreaming about going home because for some of us it simply doesn't exist."

On that note he takes down his briefcase from the overhead rack and extracts a bottle of golden Scotch and two small glasses, which he fills expertly to the brim.

"Let's toast to a new adventure, the wonderful nature of which is that we never know how it will turn out."

"You must be a messenger from God," I say eagerly, tempted to chase the Scotch with a lamo to mark my arrival in this new world.

When we reach the outskirts of Sofia in the evening hours a thin mist is falling over the plain surrounded by mountains. I tell him I'm a part-time journalist and had planned some kind of tourism-oriented reportage on Bulgaria and the Balkans in general but that he has given me new ideas.

Günther wishes me luck. Then, as an afterthought he asks if I want to go with him to the Novo Selo base the next week. A couple of hundred kilometers from Sofia in the northeastern part of the country near the Black Sea ports. Get a feeling for Bulgaria. Along the way also see the Graf Ignatievo base and the Bezmer bases. "The country's an armed camp," he adds grimly. "Business for me ... and Halliburton."

I tell him I will think about it.

He hands me his business card, Günther Sachsenweger, and writes on the back, Hotel Vitosha, Sofia, and asks me to call if I decide to join him. He will be traveling by car.

When we separate under the roofs of the super modern Sofia Central Station I already know I will call him. Where better way to start than the NATO base at Novo Selo?

* * *

I begin noticing the signs soon after I leave the main station. When I read *Kosovo je Srbija* the third time, I ask the cab driver in English what it means.

The driver laughs, slaps his leather bound steering wheel and turns down the blasting Turkish-sounding folk music. He points to another sign hanging on a low building, this time in English. *Kosovo is Serbia.* "And over there, in russki," he adds, pointing to the other side of the street. He laughs harder. "No hide words here," he says.

We could be still in Serbia. A big show of solidarity here for fellow Slavs.

Ignoring the traffic he turns to me and asks if I speak German. "We surround Russia, man! They're *umringt*, surrounded," he says switching languages. "No wonder they're pissed in Moscow. Western airplanes and rockets and special troops and mercenaries. Military bases everywhere. In Kosovo and Bulgaria and Czech Republic and Gruziya too. We're all part of American empire. Now."

He worked ten years in a machine tools factory in the Rhineland. Speaks good German. His name is Hristo. Written on his taxi license. Seems every second Bulgarian male is named Hristo. These Bulgarians, I've read, don't like to leave home. Never many of them in the West but they're famous linguists all. That's one reason I love immigrants. Their languages. I have in mind the famous Bulgarian linguist I met at the University for Foreigners in Perugia. Things are moving quickly; after Günther, I've found my taxi driver for the duration. He gives me his card.

"Day or night," he says.

"Now we Bulgarians are links in the military chain encircling our best friends, the Russians. Russia has much fear," he adds. No laugh this time. "People here," he explains, "know that this encirclement scares the Holy Jesus out of Big Brother Russia, Bulgaria's historical ally and defender. And people here also know things were much better here when we had Communism."

"Really?"

"Everybody I knew in Germany believed we people of the East were all pleased to be liberated from the chains of Communism."

"But nobody is?"

"Only the big shots."

Blagovesta wrote the same thing. The people who will not be able to bear for long the deterioration in their economic and social life following the Americanization of their country. "After the end of the Cold War," Hristo says, "former Warsaw Pact nations hoped for a demilitarized

Europe. Instead the military might of America has engulfed every nation on the continent."

Cliff had briefed me: the U.S. Defense Department admits to having 700 U.S. military bases in foreign countries. The true number is probably over one thousand, Cliff and German experts estimate, in 149 of the world's 192 countries. I should have told Günther that my native Italy is a gigantic U.S. military base, an aircraft carrier in the middle of Mar Nostrum. Then, of America's official 1.5 million troops, about 400,000 are abroad. Cliff says that figure also is much too low. The real number is secret. Not only unreported regular troops jack up that number but also the Special Forces and 300,000 mercenaries, the Blackwater terror troops and secret agents and CIA and all the other semi-legal, rogue agencies Cliff harps on.

These military forces and what they really do are uncontrolled, Cliff claims. No one knows.

Foreigners—especially the targeted Russians—know far more about what the U.S. is up to in the world than do the American people themselves. Americans don't seem to have a clue. And in European eyes, they don't even care.

I read Facebook everyday about people in America concerned about the problem of buying a new pair of shoes, the new store that opened or the old one that closed, an aunt moving, a paint job for the house, how the baby is doing, a new rock group, the battle of the quarterbacks.

Ideological immobility.

Amnesiac memory.

The land of the naïve.

"You can meet the American and NATO soldiers in the cafés along Boulevard Vitosha, drinking Balkan beers and Mavrud wines," Hristo tells me, "and looking for our beautiful women. They're famous, you know. You have to be careful, friend. Our women all want to marry a foreigner like you."

* * *

My room is on a high floor in a new upper addition to the old hotel. From my windows I can see the shiny golden dome of the Alexander Nevsky Cathedral, the public gardens, and on a hill to the south the Japanese Hotel Vitosha where my new guide Günther is staying. I'll be calling him soon.

I immediately set out for the café district, passing porn shops, tattoo parlors and a McDonald's before pinpointing the Café Ulpia Serdica. The eight or nine men with crew cuts sprawled over two tables could only be military.

I sit at a table next to them. The men seem to know the waitresses. I resist the idea of vodka and instead order a beer and permit myself a lamotrigina. I listen to their talk and the blaring pop music. Elton John singing. Traffic on the boulevard heavy; Mercedes and Volkswagen, Fiat and Alfa Romeo, Citroen and Renault. I read on the menu that the Ulpia Serdica is named after the former Thracian-Roman town that became Sofia. And that "Sofia" means wisdom in Turkish.

The man nearest me catches me reading the text and when he sees the beer, grins at me, shakes his head and yells in English, "Hey, Maya, bring this man here a drink, an ice cold vodka. *Brzo!*"

"Well, thanks! Do you speak Bulgarian?"

"Nah, but he does," the Yank says, pointing at a dark-haired guy across the table. "He's Bulgarian! Immigrated to the States and here he is right back where he started, 'cept in the U.S. Army. Crazy world."

"You guys stationed here?" I ask. "By the way, I'm German. A tourist looking for entertainment."

"So are we. Well, not exactly tourists. But looking for entertainment. I'm over at Novo Selo for now. Ground troops. Some of the others are luckier, close by, at Graf Ignatievo Base. Or at our biggest base in Bezmer. We get together here. Great country. People back home don't even know where Bulgaria is. Really beautiful countryside. Reminds me of places back home. Come down to the capital any chance we get."

"Often?"

"Every month or so. Great drinks. Great women. And they seem to like us. But not everybody does."

"What do you mean?"

"Some people here hate the USA. Don't want us in their places. Most of 'em still Commies I think."

"Commies? Why that?"

"Once a Commie, always a Commie. That's what we always say."

"Don't they know you're here to protect them from Iranian missiles?"

"Oh, that old shit! Everybody knows we're here to protect the oil pipelines. Otherwise how could Americans drive those gas guzzler cars?"

"You think that's why you and German troops are here?"

"Why else? Uh, well, if you ask these beautiful girls here, ask Maya there or Dmitrov over there, they'll tell you we're here to keep an eye on Russia. Why, they even say they were a lot better off under Communism! Crazy, eh? But that's Commie talk."

"I thought the Cold War was over."

"Don't know. I never knew anything about that stuff. Don't give a shit either. This is a good job. Stay some months here and then lily pad-leap frog somewhere else. Farther on. Maybe even Afghanistan ... not that I want to go there. But a job is a job. I'd never even heard of Bulgaria either. It's a bigger country than I thought. And this is better than working in a gas station at home ... if you can even find a job back there."

"Oh well, that's stuff for the politicians."

"You can say that again. And the fucking generals!"

"So what do you guys do here in Sofia?"

"Well, just what we're doing now. Then at night we go to a mekhana and drink and sometimes dance their crazy Turkish dances and maybe pick up a girl. Want to come along? We need a civilian among us. Gives us more class.

Hey, you really speak good English. Where'd you learn it?"

"In my country nearly everybody learns English … and French too. Then I grew up in Italy and Italian makes French easier."

"My god! And to think where I live, near Mexico, nobody but wetbacks speaks Spanish. Well, I guess Americans aren't much good in languages. Something's wrong with us. We need to know more about the rest of the world."

"And Russia? What about Russia? Is it a threat?"

"Nah! We've got the big load." The GI has dropped his voice to a whisper. He looks at his buddies. He's not overjoyed by the subject. But he's a talker. "The heavy stuff, I mean. And deliverable. From one of our bases or another. They're everywhere."

"And Iran?"

"Why should those fucking Moslems bomb Europe? We'd erase them from the Earth before they even heard if their missiles hit. Look at all our airbases all over the Persian Gulf region. The attack submarines and aircraft carriers and God knows what else."

"Listen," I say, ignoring his last words, "I'm supposed to go to your base next week with a German windows and doors manufacturer. Can we meet? Can I even get on the base?"

"Oh yeah, I think so. Be his assistant or something. Ask for me. Sergeant Alvin Moore. They know me at the gate. We can have a beer together in our canteen. No vodka there. But for some reason we have lots of Calvados. Some crazy agreement with French NATO partners. They demanded it, I think … and under the counter Jack Daniels and Scotch too."

We end up back at my hotel. The mekhana is in the hotel cellar. I didn't know what I was in for. The Bulgarian-American GI, Hristo II, is with us. The cellar tavern isn't big. We're eight at the table. Half of them are soon waving five euro notes between two fingers. A gesture. A buy sign.

I finally figure out what: buying time, attention and a chance to dance the Greek-Turkish dances with another quartet of tavern hoppers. Or best of all with one of the belly dancers. Occasionally a Western tune. Down go the euro notes. Down go the tavern hoppers. Sofia seems far from the Prague of beer drinkers, and distant from sophisticated Budapest too. Much like Belgrade. No wonder they feel close.

Lots of money spent. More by Bulgarians. Hungry to spend, these Slavs. Little reverence for money, Hristo the cab driver says. Saving is something new and modern. A vague concept. You pay for what you get. And money is not everything. Well-stocked shops and public places full. Where does the money come from? Work, yes. But they enjoy life too.

* * *

Propped up in bed on the tenth floor, still half drunk and groggy from the heavy Bulgarian wine—Christ, that stuff puts you to sleep before you can even get drunk—keep in mind to avoid that stuff in the future and stick to liquor— I re-read for the zillionth time Cliff's notes written in his inimitably colorful and irreverent language, which I'm supposed to destroy before, and if, I cross the Black Sea to Georgia and the Caucasus.

Listen, don't believe the bullshit you'll hear, neither from American soldiers nor any of that gang of new Bulgarian capitalist stooges. The U.S. occupation of Bulgaria, Kosovo, Macedonia, Romania, the Czech Republic and Poland (and farther north) has nothing to do with protecting them and their so-called new "freedoms". These are now American protectorates, the best way to think of them. They're not a defense against Iran either. Why the fuck should Iran send missiles against Europe? Against anybody? You'll also hear the "insider" bullshit line of protection of pipelines to pump oil in from the Caspian Basin. Remember what I told you: they've only got 3% of the world's reserves. You think they'd spend all those billions or fucking zillions to defend a measly 3%? Look, Karl Heinz, my young journalist friend, all that U.S. military and economic might spread from Estonia on Russia's northwestern borders, southwards to the Balkans and Turkey, then in a straight line east across half the fucking world to Afghanistan, is there chiefly for one thing: to contain and destroy the Russian Commies. Who knows why America has such fear of Russia? Is it jealousy? Is it atavistic? A genetic fear? Once a Commie, always a Commie kind of thing? Someday you might even be able to document America's fear of Russia. Anyway, keep Russia in mind, man. Russia and the USA! The Cold War affected the lives of all the peoples of the region, in the Balkans and across to the Caspian Basin. They all needed Russian trade and regional cooperation. Russians, fellow Slavs, liberated Bulgarians from the Turks in the 1800s and the Red Army liberated them from Fascists in World War II. The Bulgars came from south Russia and they speak almost the same language. Yet for those peoples America is both magnet and threat. It was then. Still is today. If it's not Cruise missiles, it's the moral corruption of the American way of life. However, under the surface, the Turkish Ottoman occupation and amalgamation—that 500-year hole in their history—make Bulgarians a different race, distant from other Slavs, far from West Europe. No wonder they're the most schizophrenic people in the Balkans. Again, I repeat, America is both a magnet and a threat to them. Don't forget that, ever. And, Karl Heinz, don't neglect any ex-U.S. spies like me you might meet. And top military brass. You're the man there …

* * *

Cliff is a man of powerful passions. He lives a life of passion. A man who can squeeze the trigger. But me? What am I doing here exactly? The eternal question. Cliff speaks of investigative journalism. That's far from me. I know that. I'm just an observer.

Not an actor. Investigation means participation. It means the same kind of passion he showed in Perugia. He must have acquired that quality from his red-headed mother he told me about. A mother of flawed passions, Cliff once said. Wayward passions. Maybe his mother's estrangement is the cause of his anger, his rage that shaped him into the man who could squeeze the trigger.

But me? My only passion has been Katharina. I've never joined anything. Never participated in anything ... except in Katharina. I just watch. I watched Cliff's Dad die in the chair next to me in St. Moritz. When those men died under Cliff's guns on the streets of Perugia, I watched them fall. When my police friend died on the highway in Umbria, I watched the mourners. Observer. Bystander. Witness. Note-taker. Reporter.

Cliff has obsessions. I, curiosity. A curiosity piqued by this strange world of mekhanas and Turkish music and military might and Cliff's empire builders.

In the midst of my meditations I peel off into a Mavrud-drugged sleep. And dive into a strange dream. Men of stone, like those I once saw in the Tyrolean Alps, stone men singing in a strange linguistic mixture of German, Italian, English, Romansch and dancing with Barbara, the witch of Bolzano ... before they burn her at the stake. They have black mustaches, wear black waistbands, hold banknotes between their fingers. Are they men turned into stone or stone turned into men? The good people, the righteous people, burn her on the mountainside under an ill-portentous gibbous moon. Barbara burning and laughing hysterically "What do you want from me?" she cries to the gathered crowd. "What do you want?" Then her fading voice cries out clearly, "I'll come back ... come back ... back." In the dream I understand her perfectly, even though her words are pronounced in another strange language, it seems of the East.

I wake with a start. Come back. Come back. I'd forgotten everything in that Mavrud sleep. Katharina! Call her now.

"So where've you been, stranger?" she opens.

"Trains, interviews, newspaper stuff. And you? You ready to fly down here? It's quite peaceful here. Then I'm supposed to go see a military base near the Black Sea. We can vacation some."

"Not this time! Not this time. I took the RU486," she announces.

"The what?"

"The Mifepristone. The abortion pill. I told you I would. I don't intend becoming a single mother." Her voice sounds oddly nonchalant. But faked.

I pause. Is she bluffing? "That's silly. I told you I want to marry you."

"And I told you I don't want to get married."

Now she sounds impatient. "Besides I have to go the hospital in a few days and get scraped or something. So you're not going to become an unwed father either."

My Katharina. My joy and my hell. As Proust said, love—in this case, my love for a person who has no concept of love—can never mean happiness. I don't know whether to regret the idea of a child or to feel relief. I frankly don't believe a child would link us more. In fact, most probably a child would turn out to be divisive. A two-months old fetus is a vague concept to me, not to be compared with losing a two-year old child as Cliff did.

* * *

I e-mail Cliff about the soldiers for whom Bulgarians are still Commies who love Russia. I add that Americans say they're here to protect pipelines but that Bulgarians think they're still squeezing Russia. That Hristo the taxi driver agrees that encirclement of Russia continues. And that most Bulgarians think they lived better under Communism.

I don't write what Cliff already knows, that NATO's new ally, Bulgaria, hosts three U.S. military bases for 2,500 American troops, the first time in the 1325 years of its history that foreign troops are stationed in Bulgaria. Not even liberating Russian troops remained here. The heart of the agreement is that American soldiers can be sent from Bulgaria to third countries without specific permission from Bulgaria. Bulgaria—one great lily pad.

And now the Czech Republic has agreed to host missile shield sites. More lily pads. These are not ideological agreements. They are forms of diplomatic prostitution between opportunistic political bureaucrats representing eviscerated states and a Washington crew bent on supremacy over its former foe. At any cost.

* * *

I walk the city in squares and circles. Deconstructing it, reconstructing it. Sofia is bigger than I expected. One day I notice a group of people standing around what on closer look I see is simply a headless monument. After I ask around if anyone speaks foreign languages to get an explanation, an elderly man and his wife turn to me and explain that on top of the monument used to be the bust of Georgi Dmitrov.

I recall the name Dmitrov from my studies. He was the boss of Socialist Bulgaria when the country was part of the Soviet satellite system.

A uniformed policeman joins the crowd, frowns at the couple speaking with me and tells me that the bust was in reality that of the Russian writer-philosopher, Nikolai Berdyaev, whose writings were based on Christian Spirituality.

"Berdyaev," the policeman says in good German, "was also a Marxist and a revolutionary who abandoned the Bolsheviks. Then Lenin decided he didn't need him in the new Soviet state. He exiled him to Paris, which was best for Lenin, best for Berdyaev."

"Still," the old man rebuts, "both Dmitrov and Berdyaev believed in equal rights among people ... something we once had but don't have any longer in capitalist Bulgaria. Just look at the poor people around us." They were indeed a ragged crowd, apparently with nothing else to do but stand around the park gaping at a headless monument.

The couple and the policeman switch to Bulgarian in a heated political debate. I wander off. The rest of the day the scene remains fixed in my mind, somehow emblematic of the kind of schizophrenia I am meeting each day. I mean the clash between the former collective mentality that reigned in the Socialist world and the crass individualism of the capitalist mentality almost overnight thrust down on them.

This is an important lesson. I had perceived of that same clash in my old girl friend, Imogene, back in the Berlin of my student days, without however being able to articulate it in any understandable way to anyone, not even to myself. Though Imogene had experienced little of the collective perception of the world personally—she was too young— she knew instinctively that she preferred it. Like the old man at the headless monument. Consequently she couldn't hold out in modern Berlin. At the time I didn't understand that Imogene's interior life, projected toward the collective society, was taking control over her, her life of desires, memories and dreams of and needs for something of wider scope than herself. Like many Bulgarians standing around that headless monument today, I suspect, also Imogene concluded that her personal destiny, as meaningful as it was, in the long run was less important than the collective one. She returned to the eastern marches to search for residues of the Socialist past.

A couple of days later I call Hristo the taxi driver to drive me to the Vitosha Hotel. To see Günther about travel to Novo Selo. Hristo is his talkative self. I ask him about the headless monument. He shrugs and says of course the bust was of the national hero, Georgi Dmitrov, whatever authorities claim today. People just like to argue about it, reflecting political differences. Maybe Berdyaev's head was there earlier.

"Who knows?" he says philosophically.

Hristo is the memory bank of Bulgarian history. He knows countless legends. He recounts images of the arrival of the original Bulgars from Russia, of Cyril and Methodius who conceived the Slavic alphabet more or less as used today. Hristo knows tales of Turkish-Ottoman domination, of national liberation by Russia, the horrors of Nazi Bulgaria, how Bulgarians resisted the deportation of their Jews, and then the second liberation again by Russian armies. He knows everything about Sofia, especially those legends lying outside recorded history.

"The real story of Bulgaria is based on the unnatural changes in our history," he begins in his contorted way. "A story that may interest you as a journalist concerns the demolition of the Mausoleum built for our hero, Georgi Dmitrov."

According to Hristo, post-Soviet, capitalist Bulgaria decided to demolish the massive marble mausoleum in the center of Sofia. Like Lenin on Red Square in Moscow, Dmitrov lay embalmed right on Prince Alexander of Battenburg Square. The government made a *brutta figura* that August of 1999. Three successive explosions failed to bring down the building that was designed to withstand a nuclear attack. It didn't so much as budge after the first two attempts. The third blast only made the building tilt slightly to one side. To the left, Hristo said. In the fourth attempt they used a series of successive detonations. Finally they had to call in bulldozers. It was a ten-day show. Became a national scandal. Supporters of the new anti-Communist government spat on anyone who argued against the waste of money and history to destroy Dmitrov's memory. The story reminds me of the Chinese First Emperor burning the books and destroying history.

It's a curiosity for me also because Dmitrov is part of German history. When in 1933 the Nazis burned down the Reichstag in Berlin, the Parliament, they arrested and tried Georgi Dmitrov, in Berlin at the time, for abetting the crime.

They intended using his Communist affiliation to justify the banning of the Communist Party and the rise of the subsequent Nazi dictatorship. Hristo recounted that the Nazi prosecutor was Hermann Goering himself, who, loudly and stupidly, resorted to anti-Slav racism. But Dmitrov defended himself so brilliantly that he was acquitted. The effect of the trial galvanized anti-Fascists in Germany and around the world. "There was a saying in Germany at the time," Hristo tells me, "that there is only one real man in Germany today and that man is a Bulgarian." After his exoneration Dmitrov went to Moscow and ultimately headed the Comintern before returning to Bulgaria with Soviet troops in 1944. He became the chief of the Communist Party and the government.

He died in 1949. Some say Stalin had him killed because he wanted to unite Bulgaria and Yugoslavia and called for an autonomous federation of Bulgaria, Serbia, Romania, Hungary and Poland. Stalin feared him and his ideas of uniting the Southern Slavs.

"Dmitrov is part of European history," Hristo says. "In 1933, the French staged a parallel trial to the real one in Berlin to protest Nazi gangsterism. Also in Russia, Dmitrov had long been considered a hero. Here, in Bulgaria, he was the symbol of the tragedy of Bulgarian Socialism as well as the failure of the idea of Southern Slav unity. His influence can't be blown away by decapitating the monument or demolishing the mausoleum."

The "word", according to Hristo, the Sofia taxi driver.

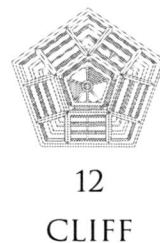

12

CLIFF

EVERY night's the same. After a few hours sleep, I wake, the uneasy feeling creeping over me. Again tonight, I'm drenched in sweat. Within moments the anxiety sweeps over me. Stealthily the stewing begins. And the doubts remain. Doubts always remain. Doubts about my true intentions today. Apprehension about my ability to do right by Elizaveta ... and Karl Heinz. As my thoughts pile up, overlap and interweave, the panic spreads. My heart pounds, my breathing accelerates. The panic races to my stomach and down my legs. I seem to be holding madness at bay with a thin cane of reason. Guilt feelings too. Guilt about my own violence. Guilt about my lost daughter. My thoughts become turbulent. From present to past and back to the present. My past is a painful memory. And the present hurts no less. Then the rage returns. Lodges in my throat. But there's also a vacuum, I think because of the missing certainties of the old violent world, a world that demanded and took more and more of me, even though I'm aware that those certainties were evil like a jungle of blood-suckers.

In my daily life, the past that rears up powerfully during the night has less and less meaning for me. I try to avoid nostalgia. Nighttime is not a battleground for normal people. I try to reassure myself that I *chose* a new destiny. A new dream, a new being, even though I'm probably still not fully cognizant of the gravity of my real situation. During the day, I become convinced that without realizing what I was about, willy-nilly I have truly created for myself a new world. And self-confidence returns. During the day I tend to forget that things happened as they really happened in my former life. Or I deny their existence. Self-deception is easier by day. Hardly a consideration.

But maybe that too is illusion.

Night is the time of truth. Of fear. During the nights of doubt, violence and guilt, scenes of the Perugia massacre inevitably come back to haunt me. I know that even though I assassinated evil rogues, the worst, the anti-Agency incarnated, they were nonetheless the Agency's own. America's own. The rogue I assassinated had been tolerated at top levels of the empire. Today, again, a little more than a year later, his type has risen to the top of the heap. The rogues have multiplied and proliferated and taken control of all our destinies. They are in command. They are the same ones watching me. Observing me. I feel their eyes. What better place to watch than in Bogenhausen under the shadow of the Angel of Peace? I can look over my shoulder and park on different streets and feel invisible all I want, but I know they are there. They are watching. And waiting. Today they are in charge. They know. They have to make me pay. They are obligated to. I take that for granted. That is just the way of things. Someday. In some way. Eye for an eye. In the end someone has to pay.

How could I have involved naïve Karl Heinz Leonhard in this affair? Neither his journalist credentials nor his Berlin and Rome newspapers could protect him if they want to take him out too.

I realize there is something terribly amiss in my reasoning. Though I once thought killing would be easy, it is not. I should wake Elizaveta and convince her that it is not easy. Though I boasted a lot, I had never killed anyone. Not until that night in Perugia. But unexpectedly something broke in me when I shot the rogue spook of whom even his own colleagues were glad to see the last. Yet he had been their colleague. But so was I. Do I count for less than that square little monster who screwed my father? No, I don't. Still, resentment toward me mounted as my name bounced back and forth between Agency stations. The resentment turned to hate when the transfers and the demotions and the purges began. Munich Station Chief Mike Garner, who never understood his Bavarian surroundings anyway, was transferred to Asia, first to Georgia, I heard, and then on to Kyrgyzstan. Serves him right, that blustering ignoramus. Garner of all people should've appreciated my contribution: that runt Fred I shot was his enemy too. But my good deed just made the older guys who survived the purge hate me more. They blamed me for what was their incompetence. "Wild John" Burton's appointment to Munich straight from Washington via Kosovo was the result. He is my nemesis. The thing about Burton, a man everyone says is at the top of his form, the thing about him is that he loves his nickname and encourages its use. He both hates me and admires me, a killer of secret agents, but also the cause of all the purges and shake-ups.

So what can I expect? What effect can the truth have on anyone? Certainly zilch effect on the real power structure. Their official reps in their dark suits and ties differ little from the military men in their uniforms with ribbons and medals on their breasts and stars on their shoulders, who, now together, have become the face of the real power of the nation. The figure of Uncle Sam, once a scary image, is shabby, his striped pants faded and baggy, his dyed beard cockeyed. Meanwhile, at home, the reality of their own situation doesn't even interest the majority of the brainwashed American people busy with their plastic dominated lives. Milk in glass bottles has become the antithesis of our plastic age. My Dad used to tell me of his boyhood when the milkman delivered milk on people's doorsteps early each morning, quarts or pints, with the cream at the top. Milkmen, glass bottles, cream at the top—emblems of another age.

Meanwhile the Agency spooks go on spinning their nonsense. Especially the new guys, the young analysts Wild John must detest, who hardly know what they're supposed to analyze. Washington warns that Iran could launch hundreds of missiles against Europe. Bizarre conclusion! Analysts have analyzed the possibility-improbability of such an attack as if it were a direct threat. Without explaining why Iran would even consider such a ridiculous thing, the U.S. military whines about the difficulties of defense against Iranian aggression. Power reasons that the attack won't be just one or two missiles, but scores, probably hundreds, and one of them will be nuclear tipped. Some arms experts admit that despite the so-called "phased adaptive array", a flexible system of moveable land and sea-based interceptor missiles, the U.S. can't even protect its own men and bases from an Iranian nuclear attack. Most of Europe would be unprotected anyway. At the same time Establishment spokesmen have admitted that though Iran has the capability of launching a salvo of missiles at Europe, it *probably* doesn't have the intent. The truth is Iran has no real beef against Europe. Only against the USA and Israel. And Iran knows that the nuclear arsenal stored in Israel would destroy the ancient nation of Persia in a matter of minutes.

So then, why the warnings and threats against Iran? Iran doesn't have a fleet of warships or strategic bombers. No foreign military bases. Its army is for self-defense. U.S.-NATO has 43 times the military budget of Iran. Anyway, why the strings of lily pad bases if they can't even defend themselves against Iran?

It must be about 4 a.m. now. Too early to wake Elizaveta to ask her opinion. It's all nonsense anyway. All bizarre. Now I understand things I was blind to when I was part of that Establishment. Iran has nothing to do with it. *Nada*. That's number one and I forgot to speak of this with Ilya. That subject requires public elucidation. Let's get Iran off the fucking terrorist threat list. That's my opinion. But no, the Establishment orders. We need Iran. We need the evil Iran threat the same way we needed the USSR in the Cold War. Keep Iran up front. Keep Iran on the front pages. Enemy number one. At least until we find a better enemy. Al-Qaida is wearing thin. So are the Talibans. Tribesmen no one has ever defeated anyway. Our Afghan straw men are already making secret agreements with them in order to clear the country of foreigners, even though Russia, experts report, is moving back into northern Afghan regions … which I doubt. So keep a tight hold on reliable Iran. Good old trustworthy Iran can always be counted on to step in just when we need a real enemy. Been around for over half a century. Keep Iran on the hooks till Russia is ready to become enemy number one again. Wait till the Russkies start pumping oil via North Stream and South Stream only to friendly European countries, first to one then the other, dividing NATO-EU Europe. Then we can clean up the Iran image and consequently up the pressure on the Russkies. Meanwhile who the fuck wants to assassinate Ahmadinejad? Apart from some nut? Or some rogue?

Again I turn toward Elizaveta in the darkness as if expecting her to respond to my doubts and answer my unanswerable questions.

I wonder if Karl Heinz grasps some of this.

I tried to lay out for him a background strategy. So that he grasps the idea that for our analysts and planners an attack or a loss that could happen tomorrow or next week is far less grave than one of next year. On the other hand a catastrophe that may happen next decade is no threat at all and not worth our attention. Therefore play the diplomatic-trade game with Russia today; our direct confrontation can be revived later. This thinking defect has been described as *time blindness*. The inability to foresee or even consider the long-term consequences of our actions and/or reactions of today.

Once you could measure imperialism by a count of colonies. Anyone with the least familiarity with history knows this. The *footprints* of America's colonies however are its military bases, U.S. influence on the national politics of its subservient nations and America's militarism at home.

But why the wars, a normal thinking person has to wonder?

No one even knows who the real enemies are. No one cares who they are. So why the U.S. wars? The truth is no one knows the real reasons why. Reasons are no longer important. Like the case of Syria. Who cared if the opposition to Assad was the same hired opposition as in Libya? Who cared if America's mercenaries executed the massacres of Syrian civilians? Truth is simply what works. Pragmatism at any human cost. The real reason for war is economics. War pays. Peace is a loser. Who in his right mind can believe that exporting democracy is the real reason for the wars? Please! Listen to me! Listen to me, Elizaveta. There are no valid reasons for the wars in Iraq and Afghanistan, in Libya and Syria. For the murder of people who've never done anything to America. Ditto for Iran. America's war stance, its deep love for war, recalls that of the ancient Greeks of centralizing Athens whose generals and armies shocked their own people when they brutally sacked the island state of Melos in order to force it into the Greek Federation. That act of war shook the people of Athens as much as each new slaughter of civilians in Iraq or Afghanistan or Libya or Syria should stun Americans today: as was customary in those times all male citizens of Melos were massacred and women and children enslaved. At the same time the peaceful Greeks were preparing an unprovoked war against Sicily just as peace-loving America is doing against Iran today.

The victims of war.

The absurdity of war.

The inhumanity of war.

The hopelessness of war.

The fucking profiteers of war.

War is a banker, flesh his gold, a Greek playwright wrote. The makers of swords and spears and helmets and shields censored all talk of peace while Athens' generals, like two-gun General Patton, sang the joys of war, crazed for sweet human blood and sorrowed at the mention of the word *peace*.

The uselessness of war. War never works, Elizaveta. War

scars the defeated and the victors alike. No post-bellum cleansing removes the stain of the blood and guilt of war. How long will it be, I ask Elizaveta silently, before we will speak of our guilt?

I should go to the toilet, take a piss, flush it down, make noise. Maybe she will wake and answer.

The great wave of patriotism generated by war! Now that's the most difficult obstacle for modern Americans. Rejection of war has become anti-American. Rejection of Washington's wars and convictions of a Washington-organized Twin Towers conspiracy, in my mind, can never be translated into anti-Americanism.

At first, the Greek wars seemed glamorous and righteous and heroic ... young men off on adventure to see the world. At first! But those wars too ended in slaughter. War pillages all men, Elizaveta. Conquerors never conquer completely and the defeated are never defeated completely. There is never a victor. The Greeks learned it. Now Vietnam and Iraq and Cuba and Nicaragua are the modern proof.

No need that Uncle Sam dictate how other peoples govern themselves while, at the same time, Americans at home are losing their own democracy ... and don't even know it. Worse: they don't even know they don't know it. Hopefully the day will arrive when people will come to their senses, stand up and scream, "Enough!"

* * *

It is 6 a.m. Elizaveta is already in her studio when I knock lightly on the guest bedroom door. Ilya and I had talked about war far into the night. No wonder my nightmare. Ilya must still be sleeping. Instead the door opens immediately. A fully dressed Ilya had been waiting.

"Ready for breakfast?"

"I was beginning to think you would sleep till noon."

"Not with Elizaveta! She's in her studio at the crack of dawn. Her aim in life is to capture the rising sun."

Ilya's presence is still a mystery. His explanation that he was sent to encourage my new journalistic career is, I believe, a lot of malarkey. But he doesn't care if I believe him or not. I'm convinced he's working a new line. Maybe he's a high-ranking agent of the *Bezbednosno-Informativna Agencija*, under some new cover. If so, he's a positive rogue in that rogue agency. He will be helpful to us all someday. The thing that worries me during the night but encourages me during the day is that from experience I know that he can be counted on to do something totally crazy.

13

KARL HEINZ

I TRAVEL with Günther east from Sofia through American-occupied Bulgaria. Along his familiar route we visit the administrative offices at Graf Ignatievo base. Then U.S. Bezmer air base. I can hardly believe my eyes. Russians vanished long ago. NATO is everywhere. According to Günther there are 25,000 Americans in Bulgaria. Plus NATO troops from former Soviet satellites and ex-Soviet republics. An armed camp. Soldiers, military vehicles, fighter planes parked on the tarmac. The contagious spread of U.S. bases Cliff had described. Extending from West Europe to the Balkans, across seas and mountains to the Caspian Sea Basin, and on and on and beyond. For me, today, that spread is centered in the heart of Bulgaria in the Balkans.

Foreign troops on Bulgarian soil is a new phenomenon. But against whom? I ask Günther. He shrugs and smiles grimly and points his finger toward the east. I believe I know what he means.

The sullen driver of Günther's Mercedes 300 makes me miss talkative Hristo in his rickety old cab. From time to time to break the monotony and liven up the atmosphere Günther opens his magical briefcase and takes out the bottle of golden liquid. That man knows how to travel. Between sips I dry swallow two lamos just to make sure of my lucidity. We stay on the autoroute as far as Plovdiv before switching to national highways to the Sliven province in eastern Bulgaria. No evidence anywhere of either wealth or extreme poverty. Just rolling hills and streams and farmlands spotted by occasional red-roofed houses.

After a night in a sterile hotel somewhere north of Bezmer, our German passports and Günther's appointment with the base commander, Colonel Jonathan Marks, earn us a salute from the two guards at the gate to Novo Selo. The base lies amidst the beautiful hills. Dark shapes hover on the horizon to the north, the contours of the Balkan Mountains.

The Novo Selo Training Range is an emblematic irony of modern European history. The former Warsaw Pact training facility, once run by Moscow, is now run by the Pentagon and used chiefly by U.S. troops. According to official Novo Selo PR, the 56-square mile area, only 44 miles west of Bulgaria's Black Sea port of Burgas, offers training sectors for tank maneuvers and nuclear, biological and chemical defense and hosts annual joint U.S.-Bulgarian military exercises. In the last two years the USA has invested over sixty million dollars in new housing and infrastructures, such as the fixtures furnished by Günther's Wuppertal factory.

As we drive down the main drag of the militarized area, Günther explains that Novo Selo is part and parcel of the reorganization of the U.S. military bases now underway: "Close bases in the USA and open them abroad," he snickers, "especially in countries that don't protest. How stupid of America to outsource its own economy, its military installations too. Closing the stateside bases will save $5.5 billion, they claim, but at the cost of 30,000 jobs in America. Is that a win or a loss? The truth is the relocation to Bulgaria and Macedonia and Kosovo, a thousand miles to the east of the expensive bases in Germany, only saves money for more arms and it positions U.S. military might closer to hot spots in the Middle East and Caucasus and to what I too have come to believe is its eventual real target—Russia."

Günther knows these things. He points out that such installations abroad bring profits chiefly to U.S. arms industries. Or to companies like Kellogg, Brown & Root, a subsidiary of the Halliburton Corporation of Houston, which build and maintain these far-flung outposts. *Ja, ja,* war and preparation for war is good business. One task of the contractors, the source of Günther's income, is to keep uniformed members of the empire housed in comfortable quarters, well fed and sufficiently amused. Some of these bases are so gigantic they require internal bus routes for the soldier-contractor inhabitants to get around, doubly secure behind miles and miles of concertina wire.

Günther, whose sales teams frequent these bases, explains that whole sectors of the American economy rely on military customers. The Pentagon reports that U.S. foreign bases contain 50,000 barracks, hangars, hospitals, and other buildings, most of which it owns outright. These are not unpleasant places to live, one claims, with the best fixtures available, Günther boasts with a certain irony. The professional military services today bear little relation to those of soldiers during World War II or during the Korean or Vietnamese wars. In America's military, chores like laundry, kitchen police and cleaning latrines are subcontracted to private military companies like DynCorp and the Vinnell Corporation. Günther claims that one-third of the 30,000 billion dollars America recently appropriated for the war in Iraq ends up in private hands.

"Everything is done to make the soldiers' daily existence resemble a Hollywood version of life at home," Günther says. "A kind of Truman Show! Remember that film? According to the *Washington Post*, in Fallujah, just west of Baghdad, waiters in white shirts, black pants, and black bow ties serve dinner to the officers of the 82nd Airborne Division in their heavily guarded compound while the first Burger King has opened inside the enormous U.S. military base at Baghdad International Airport."

Cliff had laughed bitterly when he said that of all the insensitive metaphors that have crept into the English vocabulary, none equals *footprint* to describe the military impact of the American empire as it moves eastwards. He keeps lists of those new words. "Chairmen of the Joint

Chiefs of Staff and senior members of the Senate's Military Construction Subcommittee are incapable of completing a sentence without using footprint. Who the fuck do they think they are? Genghis Khan's hordes? Establishing a more impressive footprint has become part of the military's justification for the enlargement of the empire—and a repositioning of *comfortable* U.S. bases abroad.

"However," Cliff said that day in foggy Frankfurt, "anyone who knows anything about military life knows that it can never be really comfortable … except for the under-privileged classes … or gung-ho idiots."

* * *

Mid-afternoon. The base commander, Colonel Jonathan Marks, and a purchasing agent of incomprehensible name and uncertain nationality receive us in the colonel's huge office marked by maps on the walls and an enormous Old Glory erect on a flag stand just behind the Colonel's desk. Both look at me askance when I lean forward to peer at the maps marked by tiny red, white and blue flags extending ever farther eastwards.

Marks moves to one side and stands in front of the maps and informs me that I am free to look around the base area.

Just what I wanted.

I stroll along a tar road among gray and rose-tinted, two-story barracks. All surely fitted with Wuppertal windows. Suddenly a guy stops squarely in front of me. Longish stringy hair hanging over his ears, a two- or three-day stubble on his young face, his military attire is barely recognizable as such. Tall and skinny, he is the most unmilitary type imaginable.

"Now what in God's name is a civilian like you doing wandering over this super secret base at this hour?" he says, with a wide grin. "And without a pass stuck on your jacket. Anyway, bro', I was looking for a drinking partner. You look ready," he babbles on, the grin never leaving his narrow face. "Nobody here knows what to take me for. What would you say? Idiot or corrupter of military tradition? How about it? A drinkie?"

"Sure thing! Where?"

"Where? Why in our sophisticated bar and lounge. Not far away. We can reach it comfortably by foot."

We turn a few corners and step into a pink one-story building into the almost impenetrable darkness of an igloo polar-cold cave. We stand in the doorway adjusting our vision to the darkness of a bar colder than a New York City bus in August and hear greetings addressed to my new partner whom everybody seems to know. Hallo Elmer, *Come stai? Sdrasti! Wie geht's Dir? Jak sie masz?* They're speaking in the languages of NATO's East Forces Command in the Balkans.

Elmer has a cat's nocturnal vision. Sans torch he finds a table with a view of a long bar and many flattop heads reflecting stray shards of light here and there. I find the cave beautiful after Colonel Sparks' flag-infested office.

"Elmer?" I repeat.

"Yep. Novo Selo genius-idiot and corrupter of morality," he repeats. "Tolerated because I'm a communications genius."

"I'm Karl," I say. "How old are you anyway?"

"Exactly nineteen and a half! I was wasting my time at M.I.T when I decided to enlist and lily pad around the world. Now since they need me and won't let me go on farther East, I can get by with anything. They just grin and bear it ... and pretend I'm almost a civilian. Actually I'm sloppier than usual today. Just to test them. I'd be happy to be shipped out to Kyrgyzstan. No, I really wouldn't. I like it here. Still, the empire spreads and there's always space for me out there in the new territories between Russia and China ... or the end of the world. What a life, eh? And what a quandary."

"But don't you care where ... or how?"

"Why should I? There's no stopping these anal holes. They want the world ... and still more. Did you know they speak of conquering Mars? Even if they send off their robots that just look like humans. I listen to them talk about it on their radios and secure phones. This morning I heard Caruso singing Puccini in a recording of 1902, 108 years ago. Stunning technology. So why not conquer Mars the generals and colonels wonder. The perplexing question is conquering space from whom?"

I laugh. Elmer goes to the bar and brings back four German beers.

"Seriously," he assures me, lighting up a long cigarette that emits a sweet smell. "And in secret messages some of them still talk about the Commie threat ... and the Russkies."

"What is it, do you think?"

"What is what? You mean their hang-ups about Communism and Russia? I read a report online about how a neocon false translation agency back in our nation's capital misquotes everything President Putin says. Anything to make him sound like a KGB agent in political disguise sitting around the Kremlin and singing Soviet songs like the parody of one I heard the other day, *March of the Young Soviet Builders*, and yearning for the good old Soviet Union. Holy Christ!"

"You're well read, Elmer."

"I should be. About all I have to do. Just keep the communications systems working. A cakewalk. So I read online stuff. I read it all. Surprising what you can learn there."

"So why these bases at all ... if you have so little to do?"

We drink off the first beer. Elmer continues speaking as if we were old friends. My eyes are getting used to the dark. Two tables away I spot a guy in civilian clothes. Among all the uniforms. Seems exceptionally tall even sitting. Blond, Western-looking. Wearing eyeglasses. Our eyes meet anyway. The man winks right at me. A queer? Here in the darkened bar on the big military base. A civilian employee? Blackwater?

I turn away.

"Oh, I'm an exception," Elmer says. "I really like this country. Got a girl friend over in Burgas. Stay there with her when I can get a 72-hour pass, which is pretty often. I'm learning to speak Bulgarian too. Since I'm doing so well they've promised to send me to a language school ... in Burgas."

Examining closely this eccentric soldier, I notice a small, reddened hole in his left ear lobe. I lean toward him and ask what's wrong with his ear. Elmer grins sheepishly and reveals that when he's in Burgas he wears a small but heavy earring. His good luck charm, *char* in Bulgarian, he says. Everyone needs a good luck charm. It's a *martenitsa* his Burgas friends gave him on March 1. *Mart* for March. "Red and white, it's for balance, they say, the balance between good and evil. I don't wear it here but my boss, a Captain, knows about it and warns me to be sure some visiting Senator or political official doesn't see me with an earring. Certainly not this one. I'm disturbing enough as it is. Some officers here would send me to the battlefront in Afghanistan if they could."

From time to time the kid's eyes seem to fix on something distant, something I might call eternity, most likely something much less than that in his view I'm sure. But I feel certain he has acquired here in the Balkans something unidentifiable within his own experience that forces on him a new view of life. New ideas, new comprehensions. As though he'd emerged from a cocoon. Wild eyes, wide-open eyes, seeing the real world for the first time. A secret world too. His life in Burgas is secret. His char and his martenitsa must remain secret like the source of his ear lobe infection. As though for the first time he suddenly felt the movement of the Earth, of the universe, under his feet, exactly the way I felt those weeks in Perugia with those secret people. Only in theory are you aware that the Earth revolves, but in practice you don't usually perceive the movement. It doesn't seem to move at all and you can live steadily on your feet. But Elmer feels something, I imagine, something moving things around unnaturally. Nonetheless he seems fearless. Only curious as to what it all means. He should feel fear as I did in Berlin before my story began. As I do here in the Balkans not knowing what I'm doing. I believe he is also feeling real life, maybe for the first time.

For a while we talk about this strange country. He opens the other two beers. Then I ask him point blank: "I read that the Pentagon says there are over seven hundred U.S. military bases abroad. That's a lot."

"That's preposterous. So much shit. More! Many more! We've got over one hundred in Iraq and eighty in Afghanistan. Then all the top-secret bases. CIA and Blackwater stuff. Serve no purpose. Why the fuck the nearly three hundred bases in Germany, over a hundred in Japan, same in Korea? To protect freedom? National security? Nation building? Prevent the rise of Fascism? Or another Korean war? Pure paranoia." He moistens two fingers and massages lightly his enflamed ear lobe and takes a sip of beer. "Crazy thing is we still think we're invincible ... though we don't win many wars. Look at them, from time to time marching a few troops out of Iraq and flying others in. They're sick people, our glorious leaders. Truth is we couldn't even beat the Vietnamese. Why, our leaders now claim we won in Vietnam. I hear it all the time. Can you imagine? I'm only nineteen but I know it's a myth that America won all its wars. In fact it lost most of them. Yet Americans believe pacifism is sissy, even unpatriotic. Many believe militarism is a higher form of civilization. For Chrissakes! We couldn't beat the Iraqis. Certainly not the Afghans."

"I never expected to meet anyone like you here, Elmer. Can't you get into trouble?"

I don't know what to make of him. He sounds off like Cliff but I suspect he's the kind my old boss-friend-mentor Nikitin would have warned me to be wary of—one of those who with their careless words get you into trouble. Elmer is like that. He doesn't seem to know the word restraint. For him excess doesn't exist. I could hardly imagine him at M.I.T. I just met him and he's already mouthing sedition.

"Nah, the officers just think I'm a nut. But I've learned the U.S. government tries not to divulge any information about the bases we use to eavesdrop on global communications— like right here—or about our nuclear deployments, which violate international treaties. Why, the U.S. lies to its closest NATO allies about its nuclear designs. I overhear all that shit. Tens of thousands of nuclear weapons, the bases, and dozens of ships and submarines exist in a special secret world of their own.

"At the same time their claims of a retrenchment in the empire are bullshit. It's just a changeover to new types of bases like the lily pads in remote areas where the U.S. military has never been before.

"Truth is most of our bases are chiefly in non-war zones and just our presence pisses off the locals. I read this morning we're negotiating to construct missile shield sites here. Bulgarians will really love that! Now that I speak some Bulgarian, I hear it everywhere. They hate us. Everyone except the elite: the top politicos and businessmen, all corrupt of course, who receive big kickbacks, and those few who get jobs on the bases ... for a few lousy dollars a day. People in Burgas ask me all the time what we're doing here. Truth is we just go on creating new enemies everywhere we go. While our personnel get involved in drugs or drink too much or threaten local girls or each other ... as if it were all the spoils of war. Man! Someday the payback will come."

"Wow! You're not one of those shooting off secret documents to WikiLeaks are you?"

Elmer drops his eyes, grins sheepishly, pulls at the hair over his ears and drags on his sweet smoke. Unclear whether it's a sign of admission, or regret that he's not doing it. I suspect the former.

"Raymond thinks so."

"Who? Who thinks so? Raymond? Who's that?"

"He's a guy who hangs around the base. An investigator. He's that huge fucker sitting right over there watching us. There! You'll see him everywhere. And you'll never forget him."

To relieve his discomfort I change the subject and try to avoid the tall investigator's eyes. "I met a guy in Sofia from here, Alvin …"

"Sergeant Al Moore!" Elmer says enthusiastically, glad to be out of the dead-end of secrets and, perhaps, little betrayals. "I know the guy. A typical soldier. Pretty good guy though. Good-time type. Just wants to have fun. Wants to stay here too. Not because he's really interested in the country but because he's having a good time. He'll end up lily padding somewhere else … and repeating the same lifestyle there."

"He told me to look him up."

"I know where his office is. But … hey, wait a minute; you don't have to look far. There he is now. Hey, Al," he calls to a prim type standing in the doorway. "Here's a friend of yours."

"So, the German made it here after all," Alvin says when he joins us at our table. "So what do you think of our home away from home?"

"About what I expected. Though some of the people are different than I imagined."

"Don't judge the crack American military by this character," he says, jerking a thumb in Elmer's direction.

"Out of the mouths of babes and sucklings come gems of truth," Elmer quips.

"Hey, uh, Karl isn't it? I promised you also some of our under-the-table stuff. What about a Calvados? I can't join you; I'm on duty. So I'll make it a double for you. This is coffee break after all."

Alvin goes by the rules. He's no Elmer. He's obligated to because he's a bureaucrat. I register the differences between the two men the moment he walks toward the bar in a tight military bearing. He speaks softly to the bartender who pours a drink under the counter.

"Calvados," Alvin says plopping down a water glass of the pale yellow liquid.

The differences between these two U.S. soldiers are striking. For Elmer, Bulgaria is a new world to be discovered. He's an internal dissident who reads seditious websites, dresses like a hippie, has long hair and wears a martenitsa. For Alvin, Bulgaria is not real life, but a "pretty good country", a curious theater of Turkish dancing in mekhanas, euros held between his fingers, vodka and beer and Calvados and Sofia prostitutes, a world created for his entertainment. He would find a similar world in Kyrgyzstan.

"Listen, I get off at five o'clock. What about a drive over to Burgas this evening?" Alvin proposes. "I can borrow a car."

"Exactly where I wanted to go."

"Hey, can I come too?" Elmer asks. "I need to see my girlfriend."

"Meanwhile I can try to see the press man, ask a few questions," I say.

"No problem," goes Alvin. "He's in an office close to mine. He's got nothing to do. I'll introduce you."

"Tell him about our good Captain's good luck charm," Elmer says to Alvin. "His char," he adds, I think to rib Alvin for his lack of curiosity about Bulgaria.

"Oh, that! Crazy kind of story you experience on military bases in places like this," Alvin says. "Captain Shankland, our PR man, was once sent to Georgia on a lily pad mission, I suppose to dig up some dirt about the Russian threat to democratic Georgia. While there, he bought a huge buffalo horn, apparently a prized possession in that part of the world. He showed it off at the base. Said that with it he was invincible, immune to the dangers of the world. We all envied him that buffalo horn. Until the day he went to Varna and got mixed up in some anti-American demonstration. By pure chance, he claims, he took a paving stone right between the eyes. Twenty stitches. So into the trashcan went the buffalo horn."

Unbelievable that all this is really so simple. Unclear if the people reflect the childish secrecy or if the would-be secrecy reflects the people. Buffalo horns! The lackadaisically critical and outspoken way these two men talk on this advance military base that I thought super secret, facing east, "the vanguard of a just society", "the touchstone for truth in action", "the standard for freedom". Cliff was right. He could never have stumbled into this. It's my first day here and the base and its essence, actually what it stands for, already seem familiar. I'm sitting in a dark bar, freezing my balls off, half stoned, listening to dissident talk under the owlish eyes of some civilian ghoul.

* * *

Short walk to the press office. The two lamos plus beer and Calvados have disseminated a pleasant dreamy effect in my outlook. After examining curiously my press identification, Captain Oliver Shankland, tall, with a protruding potbelly, a ruddy face and bushy eyebrows, sits down behind a clean desk, deliriously happy to give an interview. Ostentatiously I take out my notebook and pen and try to conceal the hypercritical effect of the drinks and lamos. He says he sees a lot of German journalists but was glad to be able to fit me in his schedule. I stare at him doubtfully and don't reply. Let him stew a bit.

"You will understand that there are more things I cannot talk about than information I can provide you," the Captain adds. I nod with specious understanding. But as I've learned in my off and on journalistic career, you never know. Strange things emerge from every interview … or should.

"What about the new missile sites in Bulgaria?" I counter provocatively, admittedly on Elmer's suggestion, leaning forward and staring at the white bandage on the Captain's forehead. "Hey," I ask, "what happened to your face?"

Shankland shifts around in his chair uneasily, looks at me blankly and mutters: "What missile sites?"

"The ones I read about in an online publication. The sites the U.S. is negotiating to set up in Bulgaria and Romania. But what about the bandage?"

"Well, ah, together with our good allies, Bulgarians, Romanians, Czechs, among others, we must defend ourselves." His southern accent that even I, a German, can detect, gets stronger with his every word.

"Yeah? Against whom? Who's threatening you? Looks like they already struck the first blow," I add pointing at the bandage.

"Well, ah, in this case, the threat is more against our good allies, here so close to Iran." Eye-ran, he pronounces it. "As everybody knows they've just about got their nuclear weapons ready."

"Everybody knows? How's that?" I ask, scribbling a few words on my pad. "I read that Iran denies it flatly, as do the international inspectors who spend so much time there."

"Well, sir, old Uncle Sam ain't—uh, isn't—that stupid. Of course they deny it."

"But why would Iran attack Europe? They know American firepower would annihilate them in a few seconds. It would be collective suicide."

"It's their deadly religion. Their Mohammedanism. They say plainly they will wipe Israel off the face of the Earth. They cain't contain their hate. Hate for us Americans. Hate for Israel. They want to rule the whole Middle East and exploit the world with their oil."

"Do people really believe that junk? I've read translations of speeches and documents from Iran and never saw that. They just say that time is up for Israel … and the USA."

"What are you anyway, a Commie maybe?" he asks sourly. "Coming from Italy, as you say you do. Don't think Italy would escape unscathed. Don't you people ever learn? We've got to protect our oil supplies, after all … yours too."

"So why are your missiles pointed north?" I ask, still peering hard at his bandage, hoping to get him on edge. "Ah, Captain, looks like somebody hit you with a brick."

"North? They're not pointed anywhere. But they're ready if a threat comes from Russia, if that's what you mean by north. I can testify personally that the Russkies have never changed."

I stare at him fixedly and then pretend to note down his last remark.

"They want the world. I was stationed in Georgia when Russia invaded them, an independent country, unprovoked, just to expand their empire."

"You were stationed in Georgia! My God! Doing what, if I may ask?"

"The democratically elected government there invited us to train Georgian troops to fight terrorism. I handled press relations of course."

"Terrorism? In Georgia too? Uh, did you get wounded up there?"

"It's not widely known," Shankland says, lowering his voice and leaning toward me as if about to divulge top secret information, "but Bin Laden's terrorists have been holed up in the Caucasus for years. Right there, straight east, just across the Black Sea in the Georgian mountains," he repeats for emphasis. "In a straight line, eastwards. Seems like a plan … uh, theirs of course. And Russia uses this as an excuse to pressure Georgia. Soviet—er, Russian troops so antagonized Georgia in 2008 that they provoked a Georgian reaction to defend themselves. After all, Georgia is close to NATO and we were morally obliged to help, against terrorism and against the Russians too."

"Sounds like the chief culprit in the East is still Russia. Is that true?"

"It's a mistake to misunderestimate 'em. Communism's a threat. Even here in Bulgaria, Communism is far from dead. In fact my, uh, my theory is that it has revived."

"Communism is still around?" I say, by now not even pretending to note his words.

"And thriving. And we're the guards, the sentinels, the protectors of our way of life."

"Whose way of life do you mean?" I'm having a really good time. Maybe because I'm drunk it comes easy as American apple pie to rib this potbellied Captain. I remember another thing Cliff told me: it's easy for civilians to have little respect for military rank. If you're a corporal, a Captain is a big deal but for a drunken journalist, he's a schmuck.

"Why, America's, of course. Our enemies out there are jealous. They want to take what we have from us."

"Who wants to rob your way of life, Captain?"

"All of 'em. The Islamists, certainly. And for sure the Russkies. In fact, the Soviet, er, the Russian Empire will continue to try to expand unless we stop them. With all our power. Tsars or Stalinists, it's all the same up there. Still Commies. Still Reds. People treated like cattle while the government builds up its missile sites and readies its armies to take our territories."

"Like they did in Georgia, you mean."

"Yeah, that too. That free democratic country. You see, the free people in the West don't want missiles pointed at us. And if that means we have to deploy our defensive missile systems around Russia's borders—I mean, around the borders of NATO countries—then so be it. We must thwart their threats and attacks on us. We must be strong. We have to offer friendship and assistance to those countries that want to live in peace. Our government only wants peace. But we must counter their threats by any means possible."

"Nuclear power too? Russia has a lot of it also. You want to risk nuclear war, you mean?"

"Sometimes you have to risk. We have to accept the risk of total war and accept the challenge to our destiny to create the American New World Order. We must keep the faith. Truth and good must win out over lie and evil."

Captain Shankland of the American army smoothes down the corners of his forehead bandage, then says a wild thing: "That's the point about the similarity of the good guys, us, with the bad guys, them. We both have a lot of that crazy thing called power. That's why we can't let down our guard. Too bad we didn't finish off the Russians when we had the chance in 1989. We should've done it then. But we still have time to break up that country into a bunch of little states and let 'em fight it out among themselves."

"You mean into little states like Georgia in the Caucasus? Or even smaller than Rhode Island," I say, showing off my knowledge of America's geography.

"Well, it's not the same thing. Georgia has chosen democracy and freedom … and rejected the chains of Communism. Like Poland and Lithuania, like Latvia and Estonia, like Kyrgyzstan, Georgia desires freedom."

"Uh, Captain, by the way, where are you from in the USA?"

"What? What do you mean? I'm just an American soldier. Why? Anyway I'm from Mississippi. You probably don't know where that great state is."

"Oh, I've heard of it. In fact, I've been there. Curious place, yes indeed. By the way, you still haven't explained what happened to your face. The bandage I mean."

"Just a little accident over in Varna."

Captain Shankland looks up at me from under heavy eyebrows and frowns, still condescendingly, as if wondering whether I want to pursue the subject of Mississippi or the bandage. I don't. So he stands up, signaling that the interview is over. I pocket my notebook and pen and thank him profusely for his time and for his frankness. He smiles sourly and touches his bandage again as if uncertain about my appreciation of his frankness. Actually he'd said more than I had expected to hear.

* * *

Around seven o'clock that evening we stop at a block of luxury apartment buildings not far from the Burgas waterfront to pick up Elmer's girl friend. When he returns with a small, good-looking, flaxen-haired girl, somewhat older than he, Elmer has transformed into his civilian self—a long colorless and collarless Turkish style shirt, jeans and sandals. His martenitsa dangles from his left ear. As they climb into the Ford Taunus, Lala greets us with a quick "*dobar vecher*". Enlaced together in the back seat, she and Elmer speak Bulgarian together quietly before Lala speaks to us in good English, suggesting that we pick up two of her girl friends and go to a café on the Black Sea shore. Alvin and I turn and grin at Elmer because we know he'd wanted to go to bed with her and let us go our own way.

He shrugs deferentially and mutters, "Why not?"

The evening develops in an unexpected manner. From the start everything seems dicey, and somewhat crazy, six people quickly dividing into groups of two. The girls order some mysterious pink drink, Alvin and Elmer a whiskey, I a gin and tonic. I pocket the cardboard menu. New words to learn.

Here we are, at an outdoor café facing the Black Sea. At 36, I'm the oldest, the three Bulgarian girls are in their early 20s, Elmer, nineteen and a half. It's dusk. Eastwards the sky hangs low over the sea, like in Berlin in November.

I turn my chair and peer at the flat horizon where the sky meets the water and despite my mistrust of bodies of water, dream of crossing the six hundred and fifty miles of this aquatic crossroads of antiquity from the Balkans in the west, where I am sitting, to the Caucasus to the east and to Russia and Ukraine to the north. The tide should be coming in now yet there's no perceptible movement on the water surface. Water of weak saline content fills the Black Sea, I've read; waters flowing through the Straits of Bosporus from the Mediterranean and Aegean seas, waters arriving from the Atlantic through the Straits of Gibraltar, here mixing with fresh river waters arriving from major rivers the names of which I've memorized—Danube, Dnieper, Bug, Dniester, Don, Kuban, Rioni. Maybe the Black Sea, the *Pontos Axeinos*, the Hostile Sea, as the Greeks called the Black Sea because of its storminess, really was the site of the biblical flood. The proper place, I think. Maybe neighboring Turkey's Mt. Ararat was the resting place of Noah's ark. To the south is the Hellespont, the Dardanelles, dividing Europe from Asia. Magically the Black Sea's waters flow in two directions: a surface current carrying waters from the Black Sea to the Aegean Sea of the Greeks and an undercurrent flowing in the opposite direction. Scary to consider. Must be what terrified sailors of yore. Not only terrifying but also unnatural.

The sea this evening looks like a huge lake by some quirk of nature fallen into disrepute. Smells too. Cold and humid. Untrustworthy. Hard winters here, I hear. The sea reminds me of Lake Bracciano north of Rome on the southern bluffs on which we had our weekend house. Our lake's former beauty has been reduced to environmental poverty by surrounding residential developments, traffic-packed lakeside roads, tourist hotels, boat basins and scores of restaurants. Though I grew up there and frequented the Mediterranean beaches near Rome from Tor Vaianica northwards to Ostia, Fregene and Ladispoli, I've never trusted seas or lakes. They frighten me. It's not my element.

But the Black Sea? Why Black? Even the name is scary. Not only bottomless, they say you can't see more than five meters deep into the Black Sea. What's hidden down there? Maybe another world seethes in its depths. Over two kilometers deep. Another universe. Black Sea. I smirk to myself. The former axis of the world has become a hole in the world. A hole that maybe goes much deeper than the 2,245 meters depth oceanographers speak of, like the horrendous, bottomless Lake Bracciano my father so loves. Maybe it reaches the center of the Earth. Holds the secret of the universe. Big Bang? Or just the Black Sea, black back to the origins. Nonsense, I know. But over there to the east, beyond this sea, thrives another world. On second thought the idea of crossing *the Sea*, as ancient navigators called it, terrifies me. Do modern conquerors imagine what lies over there? Do they believe they know? Or will they ever know?

I think everything over there must be different among those strange peoples. In the Caucasus. In Central Asia. But on the other hand they must be like us. Humans like me. For some reason I recall in this moment the famous Montaigne quote that "Every man carries within him the entire human condition." All I have to do is get aboard one of the ships sailing east and see for myself. But where? How? What would I do there? I, a tourist-reporter, now ashore in Bulgaria, with no hankering to defy the seas.

I stare at the horizon, feeling momentarily adrift, searching for another shore. It's the same feeling I have at Wannsee watching the perilous crossings of the ferry to Kladow. The invisibility. The omens and premonitions. Here I see only a flat water surface but I know it's deceptive. Like Lago Bracciano too. The unnatural quiet. But then there is also the horizon. A horizon means that something lies beyond. You read of their monsoons, the floods and tsunamis and earthquakes. Can it really be the same, over there? Repetitions and more repetitions of Montaigne's *condition humaine*?

I wonder what else Cliff expects from me. I read a few days ago that for the zillionth time the U.S. President has declared the Iraqi war over and withdrawn U.S. troops—except for a few. Over there, just over the curve of the horizon, not far away at all—but has tripled the number of troops in Afghanistan, a little farther east, while like daises in the Bulgarian spring new military bases pop up out there, in Balad, Al Asad, Tallil. The lily pads Elmer spoke of. The lily pad empire. America's strategic goals are as cloudy as the Black Sea waters at five-meters depth. They keep talking about hegemony over the oil-rich regions of Central Asia, lying beyond this big lake and its neighboring inland sea, the Caspian. The mythical Caspian Basin. The Persian Gulf. America is greedy for them all. Ours, ours, ours, all ours! I glance around the table. Antonia stares at me, waiting for me to speak. I instead continue to watch the Sea. Elmer and Lala whisper together. Alvin talks nonstop. Floating around on its lily pads like an evil strain of huge mobile frogs, America with its bandaged captains and technological whizzes and super weapons and lily pad bases continues its crusade against the rest of the world. Frogs leaping from one base to another. America has an evil and dark side, I'm learning—diabolic motivations for its preemptive and eternal wars, a deficiency of moral principles—at least as some Europeans see it. With each new lily pad the ethical divide between America and the peoples it wants to transform becomes broader.

To me, this evening, here on the shores of the Sea, everything seems to transform. Our world seems to be shrinking; and each of us in it is becoming smaller and more insignificant. In other places, on other shores, I imagine in China and India, their world and their populations are expanding. Things change and shift around the world. Universities in India and China will have created faculties of European and American studies. Schools of Westernists are emerging as once did our generations of Orientalists. Specialists publish academic papers and learned books about the complexities of the strange West. I wonder if also good and evil and values and morality also switch sides? Find new shores? For a moment I lose my hold on reality. I don't understand what I'm doing here on this faraway Black Sea shore with these beautiful girls while ex-pregnant Katharina waits for me in Berlin.

* * *

Antonia seems destined to be my date. I suppose because she speaks and even looks German things develop that way. Rather tall and slim, dirty blond with sky blue eyes perched above her high Slavic cheekbones, Antonia speaks high German with the north German accent of her mother. She was born in Germany before her father brought his family back to Bulgaria. When I tell her that I grew up in Italy and don't know whether I'm more German or Italian, she says it's the same for her: she doesn't know if she's German or Bulgarian. Her German mother married a Bulgarian highway engineer working in Dresden when it was in the German Democratic Republic, making her Germano-Bulgarian. That common dualism in us seals our attraction one to the other. Though not crotch high as Katharina prefers, her mini-skirt is short enough to display her perfect legs. But she neither hides nor flaunts herself provocatively like Katharina. Then, she has a curious way of cocking her head to one side when I speak, as if amazed to be on a date with a "real German", as she calls me. Gradually we isolate ourselves from the others, exchanging anecdotes about our double identities. I tell her she seems more Bulgarian than German. She says that I seem more Italian than German.

It turns out to be a strange evening, unexpected for all of us. Well, except perhaps Alvin who drinks and jokes and talks incessantly, whether anyone is listening or not. He doesn't seem especially interested in his date. Yet Antonia and I manage to remain separate. Separate from Elmer and Lala speaking softly to each other in Bulgarian; from Alvin and Svetlana, the most Slavic looking of the three girls, also nearly blond with light eyes, and who speaks pretty good English. Though at one table, we form three independent groups, three cultures, three worlds, linguistically separate but also akin in our common sense of being exiles in the world of this corner of Europe that is the Balkans.

I suspect—still my old paranoia I suppose—that my sense of exile in this moment is rooted in the influence of the Sea. And the blackness concealed under its surface. It feels like a memory of something uncertain which you can't pinpoint, something that eludes you, the recollection of something long ago, right on the edge of memory, on its very lip, that slips away. It seems linked to memories of my father in his sail boat on Lake Bracciano, to my boyhood fears and joys and dreams as from the shore I used to observe him gliding over those limitless depths, his white sail leaning perilously close to the water, while mixed emotions seethed in me and raced through my body. It seems that everything that has happened to me since those powerful emotions experienced on Lake Bracciano—my move to Berlin from Rome, my relationship with Katharina and my irascible Grandfather, the meeting with the spy master Nikitin, my inheritance, my contacts with secret power, the incredible changes in my life since—it now seems it was all written in ancient books. All inevitable. The idea of fate at work has grabbed hold of me and refuses to let me go.

I ask Antonia if it's true about the Sea's blackness five meters down. And if mysterious monsters really inhabit its lower depths? Her eyes emanate a curious light but she says she has no idea.

In that moment while she seems to look into me, it occurs to me that I haven't thought of Katharina since I paired off with Antonia. The thought comes like a sudden liberation, almost transcendental, and a resulting feeling like emancipation from invisible chains or at least from something yet unnamable in my experience. I feel unfettered— as old Nikitin might have expressed it—from an obsession that in recent months has become a phobia. I realize that I haven't taken even one lamo either. For years I've been a sick man.

When Alvin says they have to get back to the base, I announce that I will find a hotel here on the waterfront. I want to stay in Burgas. Elmer and Alvin look at me curiously.

I tell them that I want to investigate the Black Sea. They seem disbelieving, though understanding, eyeing Antonia who in that moment looks absolutely gorgeous. The spontaneous idea of staying in Burgas turns out to be magical. I didn't recognize it in that moment but staying here in Burgas was a major turning point in my life. A decision that changed everything. Antonia smiles, I think content that I will stay. Mysteriously she says: "*Aber natürlich.*" Naturally! As if she hadn't even considered the unlikelihood that I might not stay.

I don't understand what I probably should from that look, both playful and serious, expressing both the real and the unreal—of what? Of the blackness of the Black Sea? Or is it just the mystery in a woman's eyes? And then those two words: "But naturally." I have no idea why she thinks that I'm somehow fixed.

We're getting ready to leave when I see him. The same sinister man from the dark bar at Novo Selo. Unmistakable. His blond hair combed straight back, thick eyeglasses and his way of staring at me and, it seems, talking to himself. I must be imagining it. Or chance is playing tricks, again.

"Oh-oh," Alvin mutters, leaning toward Elmer. "He's here. Raymond. The nutty CIA guy. Bet he's looking for WikiLeaks," he says, winking at me. "They don't know if it's soldiers doing it … or dangerous journalists like you," he adds, grinning up at me from almost table level. "We'd better get out of here."

As we leave the man's eyes seem to follow both Elmer and me, although he doesn't show any intention of following. Only his lips move. Maybe saying I'll see you both later. But maybe it's just my paranoia.

"Elmer, wait a minute," I whisper to him when we're saying our goodbyes near the car: "Listen, man, you have to watch yourself, OK? Now I have something you might need someday. But for God's sake keep it to yourself."

With that hulk Raymond in mind and my intuition running berserk, I take out my wallet and copy Ilya's Belgrade address on the bottom half of the menu. God knows what it means but you never know, as Cliff said that day in

Frankfurt. Elmer glances at it, then at me with a funny look on his narrow face, nods, and stuffs it in his shirt pocket.

* * *

I check into a tourist hotel. My room overlooks the darkened sea. I try to relax on the wide bed. Arms behind my head, surprisingly sober, I review the day's singular events—my meeting with Elmer, seeing Alvin again, the interview with Shankland, the trip to Burgas, meeting Antonia, and now being tailed by the tall blond man with thick eyeglasses, Raymond, who is in constant communication with himself.

I write a cryptic e-mail to Cliff. About my trip with Günther, a few words about eccentric Elmer, a resumé of the interview with the press officer, the recurrent fixation with Communism and Russia that keeps popping up, vague hints about Raymond and my move to Burgas. Bent over my laptop, lily padding from one thought to the other, it occurs to me again how much journalism has in common with art and literature. Like in those wakeful hours during the night, just as an artist might recall the forgotten slash of color or the one dot that would change a painting, or a novelist the discovery of the one anecdote or the one symbolic action or the one metaphor that would clarify an invented story and link it to real life, in such a moment a journalist might hit on the one key question that would expose an interviewee such as that asshole Shankland as the stupid liar he is. All the arts have always been about truth. I know that. And truth is an eel, forever elusive. Americans seem to think that truth is believability. My journalist father has always said that facts have little to do with truth. There is such an overabundance of raw data as to be mind-boggling and in the end unusable to anyone except statisticians; statistics being a mock "science" anyway, the most ignorant and boring aspect; some kind of voodooism. The creative person must absorb and re-work facts with inventiveness. He has to interpret and recreate events.

Facts and documentations will always be fragmentary ... as is history itself. Skepticism, parody and audacity step forward with real power and make history subversive. Cliff speaks of hunches and intuition. I'm still not sure of what intuition consists. Nor do I trust my own. My instincts, as far as I can read myself, lean toward solitude and loneliness, something to be overcome. My instincts are not toward sociability or to the careful analysis necessary for uncovering secrets hidden in the facts. Still, yes, a thousand times yes—inner vision, images, imagination, invention are necessary. But then, yes, fuck the facts. In the end they become an incubus, intended for limited minds ... for those statisticians. Fuck objectivity too. All illusion. A chimera. A fata morgana. An immoral instrument of amoral power. Viva bias. Bias forever. The closest we can get to truth. I'm aware that I'm confused. It's all this new anxiety, the agitation and the eternal stewing. Zap, one idea arrives. Zap, zap, another idea. Ideas overlapping, superimposing over one another. And all the time I'm still stone cold sober. I try to find my bearings. I realize I've got to situate myself. Why, I wonder, my sudden decision to remain in Burgas? Only because of Antonia? Or intuition? I can't stop the stewing. My thoughts roam and ramble, over Europe, across the Sea, to the Caucasus, Russia, the Silk Road, Asia. Unexpected emotions pop up here and there.

I dry swallow a lamo. You never know what physical surprises await you during the night. Preventive medication for nervous crises, that's all. I've been on them for years.

Above all, I try not to think of Katharina. My awareness of the uselessness of the effort however makes my attempt not to think of her all the more impossible. It's like the attempt not to think at all. How can you not think? On that thought, a light knock on my door crashes through my internal sound barrier. Raymond again? Trepidly, I open the door and in the doorway stands beautiful Antonia.

Her not completely unexpected arrival tonight again

changes everything. In a flash, in the same instant she steps tentatively into my room I see us together in strange places, in the Caucasus someplace. Maybe in the Crimea, or someplace beyond the Sea and beyond Georgia too. I feel renewed, as if starting out again from the beginning.

Ein neuer Anfang, I think automatically and ask her how to say a new start in Bulgarian.

"*Novo nachalo*," Antonia says matter-of-factly.

Antonia looks around the room. Then at me like I'm crazy. I look at her. *Auf einmal* the room has become more inviting. Antonia sits in an armchair in the living area. On the coffee table an assortment of tourism magazines in English, German, Italian and Bulgarian. The armchairs face the plate glass French door to the balcony with a view of the Black Sea of the ancients.

I hand her a glass of lemon soda from the fridge and watch her pull her beautiful legs up under her in the feline way women have of sitting comfortably in that contorted position. The position is off-putting too, just in case I get any ideas, which I already have because of her miniskirt and her beautiful thighs.

I pour myself a beer and pace nervously, still wondering why she decided to come. Was it as spontaneous as was my decision to stay? She must have intuited something. Saw right through me. Saw my solitude. My confusion. Or maybe she saw my budding availability—that I was unconsciously freeing myself from Katharina, of whom she has never heard. Female intuition again.

I remind her that such a late night visit to a man's hotel room is suggestive. She smiles enigmatically. Christ, how I love women for their feline ambiguity. Now what did that smile mean?

She says that, yes, the view is nice. Yes, the Black Sea is definitely more suggestive of romance at night, with café and hotel lights flickering and reflecting off the quiet waters. Yes, our meeting was fortuitous.

I add that it's curious that we both feel the same ambivalence about our nationality. At the same time I have the feeling that we both are aware of the same sensation of discovery, the same presentiment that ours was more than a mere casual café meeting, the vague comprehension that something as unstoppable as it was unforeseen has happened, the awareness that not only affinity but harmony clicked between us from the first moment in the café. Because of my romantic nature on the one hand and my timidity on the other, I am probably over-interpreting. Well, at least I was until she knocked on my door and entered so naturally. Maybe she's just being hospitable, a bit condescending, as though it were her duty to patronize me, her nearly co-national, now a stranger in a strange land.

She listens to my ideas about a trip up the coast to Varna, maybe to Moldova and Chisinau, offering a proposal or two, in such a way as to suggest that, yes, she might like to join me, even though for me it's all still fantasy. These are spring holidays at her university. She's free. She shows no intention of leaving.

I tell myself not to waste time trying to analyze her behavior. I try to be as natural as she.

I feel her eyes on me as I pour her more lemon soda. I stand at the open balcony door feigning continuing fascination with the Sea. Suddenly she is standing beside me, one arm lightly around my waist. Her signal. From there in front of the French door, it turns out, it's only a few steps to the bed. She decided. *Aber natürlich*!

After love, after bed talk, Antonia sleeps. I conclude two things: this doesn't seem like a one-night-stand and I haven't thought any more about Katharina except to think that I'm not thinking of her. An astounding combination it seems in the early morning hours. I've been in the Balkans less than a week and have met Antonia, soporific like I imagine a pipe of opium—even our lovemaking was easy, pacifying, not that zany venture into frenetic madness it is with Katharina as if attempting to achieve the unachievable; something that always remains just out of reach so that satisfaction has always eluded us. From the first moment something peaceful and mollifying emanated from Antonia and now dominates our togetherness.

In my first week in East Europe I've become friendly with unexpectedly maverick American soldiers. I've visited major U.S.-NATO military bases, met a base commander and interviewed a military pressman. I've met several Bulgarians. Not bad, eh, Cliff? Kudos to me, eh, Cliff? Strange how I need the big man's approval. No, I need much more: I need his admiration, just as I once desired that of Hakim and Anatoly Nikitin.

I wake up with a song Mina used to sing on my mind. I keep humming a few bars to myself or repeating a few words of the lyrics to myself. I try to block it out but today is to be another of those days. The song is destined to become a compulsion. Another obsession. It will haunt me all day. It often happens. A song comes to me during the night and the next day I obsessively try to reconstruct the words or the melody, constantly aware of its hazy presence lodged in the front part of my cerebrum. A pop song. A ditty from childhood. Or even a national anthem. Not long ago a strange one visited me during the night and stayed for a couple of days: *Deutschland Deutschland Über Alles*. It wouldn't go away. Once it was even *God Save the Queen*! Watching too many football games. Crazy obsessions. And now this one: *Vorrei che fosse amore, amore quello vero la cosa che io sento per te* … It's fixed there. *Jawohl*. Tenacious, clinging, dogged. I hope it's real love, the thing I feel for you. For Christ's sake, where are my lamos?

Partially out of matinal guilt for my romantic escapade … and for the way I'm thinking about Antonia, but also to boast a bit about my whereabouts, I telephone Katharina. She is not even curious. Today, she says, she will be busy aborting, quickly erasing any sense of culpability or conspiracy in me. She is casual about the curettage she's to undergo this afternoon. As if it were a visit to the coiffeur. In a way her blitheness is a relief. But what can she expect from me? After all my pleas for marriage and the fact that I opposed the abortion, even though, admittedly, Antonia puts a new slant on matters.

While the concierge arranges a car and Antonia goes home to pack a bag, I walk around the city. Burgas is Bulgaria's fourth city, a major Black Sea port and has one of the biggest airports in the Balkans. The old-fashioned three- and four-story buildings make a walk through the streets a step back in time, creating a retro atmosphere resembling that of small isolated towns in Mecklenburg in the far north of Germany. I like the park along the waterfront where I can keep an eye on the Sea, as in my mind I now call the Black Sea. I daydream of a distant past, of Greek and Roman seamen, triremes and ancient navigational maps, of the Greek and Persian navigators who never trusted this unpredictable and bottomless sea.

From a bench facing the Sea I risk using my mobile to call Alvin in his office in Novo Selo. That blond man, Raymond, with his goggle-like eyeglasses still disturbs me. The hesitancy in Alvin's voice suggests that all is not well. All I learn is that Elmer didn't show up for work this morning.

"Puzzling," he adds, "He's never absent."

* * *

Occasionally looking up at the Sea, re-read one of the background documents Cliff had prepared for me, every word of which made me aware of the danger threatening Elmer.

Karl Heinz: We have to keep in mind that for the most part the mainline media is a lie machine of power. If not outright propaganda, then defense of power and power's institutions. The WikiLeaks publication of thousands of secret U.S. military files on the illegal war in Afghanistan documenting the cover-ups, the secret assassination units and the killings of civilians echo the West's imperialistic past and present. They show anyone with a sense of history how little that has changed since Vietnam. With one great difference today: the Internet. The Wikileaks whistleblower has acquired records covering years of civilian killings in Iraq and Afghanistan, revealing to those who want to know and understand how faraway societies are routinely ravaged in our name. Revealing also how much the nation of the United States has changed since the 1970s. The documents then published in newspapers like The Guardian, Der Spiegel and the New York Times are only a fraction of the interceptions. The Pentagon is of course pissed about WikiLeaks whose call for public accountability of those guilty of war crimes threatens war makers and their apologists. The Pentagon accuses WikiLeaks of promoting irresponsible moral guilt for years of systematic and systemic political murder of civilians by U.S. military forces. Official hysteria runs high, with demands that the WikiLeaks whistleblowers be "hunted down" and "rendered" or "assassinated". Following the release of the footage of U.S. killer helicopters, Wikileaks founder Julian Assange's Australian passport was confiscated. The Labour government there denies it received requests from Washington to detain him and to spy on the network. After the government in London also denied this, Assange, who went there to work on exposing the war logs, had to leave Britain for "safer climes". Having published his exposés of a fraudulent war, The Guardian should now give unreserved editorial support to the protection of its sources. Assange and his colleagues need the protection of the entire journalistic community so that he doesn't end up in prison, as have other whistleblowers in the past like Mordechai Vanunu. Remember him? He was left unprotected by the London Sunday Times, which had published documents that he supplied, alerting the world to Israel's secret nuclear weapons. As a result he was kidnapped by the Israelis and incarcerated for 18 years because the newspaper didn't protect him. In 1983, another heroic whistleblower, Sarah Tisdall, a UK Foreign Office clerical officer, sent documents to The Guardian disclosing how the Thatcher government planned to spin the arrival of American cruise missiles in Britain. The Guardian meekly complied with a court order to hand over the documents, and Tisdall went to prison. The WikiLeaks revelations about murderous U.S. activities shame mainline journalism, which is devoted to regurgitating what cynical power feeds it. That is "state stenography", not journalism. A Defense Ministry document describes the "threat" of real journalism. And so it should be. A threat. But real journalism is in danger. That threat explains the "ongoing criminal investigation" of the U.S. soldier, Bradley Manning, an alleged whistleblower. In a nation that claims its Constitution protects truth-tellers, the administration is pursuing and prosecuting more whistleblowers than any of its modern predecessors. A Pentagon document states that U.S. intelligence intends to "fatally marginalize" WikiLeaks. The preferred tactic is smear, with corporate journalists ever ready to play their part. Our role is to expose also the meretricious press for what it is.

* * *

Our destination, Varna, is about one hundred miles to the north along the Sea. I'd hesitated about renting the Volkswagen Golf though I was attracted by the idea in some morbid way, I suppose just to taunt fate. Or maybe under Elmer's crazy transformative influence I too am beginning to consider charms and destiny. The fact remains that Nikitin and Hakim were blown to bits on a mountain in Italy in the very same model. This one is blue. Peculiar, but for the life of me I don't recall the color of the VW that exploded on Mount Subasio above Assisi. Some sort of mental block because that Golf carrying my colleagues toward the hideaway I myself had uncovered in that mountainous wasteland carried them instead to their extinction. *Vorrei che fosse amore*, I sing under my breath. Oh, fuck it. Guilt again! My life companion. And today I have Elmer on my mind too. Has he been whisked away for "rendition"—that word I now understand to mean interrogation and torture—because of his possible role in WikiLeaks?

After the Burgas airport, we continue along the coastal highway past small towns and seaside resorts. We stop at a café in the village of Biala sitting on a promontory high above sandy beaches below. Antonia acts as if she were on a vacation, or perhaps a honeymoon. I try to simulate her relaxed manner. *Vorrei sentirti dire che m'ami da morire.* I want to hear you say you love me to death. Oh, God! It's still there.

"What's that song?" Antonia asks.

"An old Italian love song," I say, drinking down a Bulgarian cognac and taking her hand.

"Sing it for me."

"I still can't remember the words. But it'll come back to me."

This is all enjoyable. Enjoyable? It's fantastic—new country, new experience, new love blooming. But something is still not right. Premonitions continue to haunt me. I have no news from Cliff and have no idea if I'm accomplishing anything positive. I meet exotic women, drink sleep-inducing Mavrud wines and Bulgarian vodka and beer and snoop around U.S. military bases. All new and exciting, yes. But damned if I know if it's useful.

And now Elmer's absence. What could it mean? Have to call Alvin again in the afternoon before that G.I. playboy goes off for another night of orgy.

"*Liebst Du mich?*" I ask uncertainly, inspired by the song. Do you love me? My words ring insipid.

"*Vielleicht ein wenig.*" A little, maybe.

* * *

Varna, Bulgaria's chief Black Sea port is something else. Antonia tells me that toward the end of World War II soon after its liberation by Soviet troops from German occupation, the city was renamed *Stalin*! For some reason I find that incredible. Stalin City. Marshall Stalin. Generalissimo Stalin. But then Washington is also named after a liberating general. Another surprising discovery from my maps is our proximity to the former Soviet Union, only another one hundred miles north. The annexation of Bulgaria must have tempted the later much maligned and mistrusted Stalin despite the nationalistic aspirations of his man in Bulgaria, the one he didn't trust, the Bulgarian national hero, Dmitrov. Name a city *Stalin* and grab the whole country! With all the reshuffling of Europe's borders and spheres of influence underway at war's end, and while America grabbed everything possible, why not annex the whole country, Stalin must have thought. Make it part of the USSR. The Bulgarian Soviet Socialist Republic. BSSR. Slavic brothers, similar languages, Orthodox too. At the time Stalin had the Red Army on the spot to back him up. Possession of Bulgaria would have given Moscow control of the whole Black Sea, the Sea that once controlled the world.

But Stalin didn't even try!

From Varna, you can zip up to Odessa in several hours on a fast catamaran. Incredible the proximity. Odessa has always seemed to me to be on the other side of the world. For me it is only the city of Eizenstein's film, *The Battleship Potemkin*, that I've seen dozens of times—with the famous staircase where in the film Tsarist troops and Cossacks massacre the people demonstrating in favor of the mutinous sailors on the battleship.

Odessa and Moldova beckon from the north. Varna is a point of departure. I want to get to Moldova, and especially to the Transnistrian Republic that so recalls the recent history of Kosovo … except from a Russian point of view. If America could militarize Kosovo and nearly bring Moldova into NATO, why should Russia not do the same there in its own former territories? And after Moldova, Odessa is waiting for me personally—if only to see those monumental Potemkin Stairs, the giant staircase entrance from the Sea into the heart of the city.

Each day I'm more astounded at this varied life only one thousand miles east of Berlin, totally different cultures and peoples. Mysterious territories. Impossible borders and belongings and names. And they are all Europeans—about whom we Westerners know *nada*. Or we discount them. Look down on them. Sometimes I think Cliff organized this trip for my personal education. Or maybe it just emerged as a natural consequence in my new life.

* * *

Antonia is charmed to be in Varna. She lived here once and still thinks of it as home. More so than her birth place in Germany. Still seems odd that this port on the ominous Sea is the home of someone close to me.

"We should stay here and vacation," Antonia suggests after we've checked into a chic hotel near the port and sit on a terrace facing the Sea.

"Vacation? Antonia, I'm working, remember?"

"What work do you mean? I've still got a week more vacation and I can cut a few classes too."

"I'm trying to understand things I never did before. Trying to learn the significance of lily pads." Those two little words that sound so innocent somehow ring deadly when spoken. We order Turkish coffee.

"Lily pads?"

"Those green leaf-like pads in ponds from which white lilies grow … and frogs love to float on."

"*Da ist ja albern.* That's silly. What kind of work is that? And what does it have to with your rush to get to Moldova … and Odessa?"

"Military lily pads. That's what they call the American

military bases across the world. Like the American bases in your country. That soldiers can hop from one to the other, like green frogs with black goggles ... hopping from one lily pad to the other. NATO wants one in Moldova."

"According to Bulgarian newspapers, Russians also want a base there. If America can put a military base right in Russia's face, why should Russia not build one too? Does America want another war? Iraq and Afghanistan are not enough? What is enough? But I never heard them called lily pads. I don't know the Russian word for it. Still, I don't understand why they spend all that money on their ... their stinking military lily pads"

"Well, we'll see. Odessa is, well, another story. I want to see that staircase."

Though Antonia hasn't seen Eizenstein's film and can't understand my romantic curiosity about the staircase, she understands instinctively what is happening in the world. People here have more political awareness than in West Europe ... I'm sure much more than in America. In Bulgaria, they overestimate American power because of the chain of lily pads and the soldiers in their cities but I've concluded that innocence and naiveté are not Bulgarian characteristics, and I'm just at the start of my adventure. I've already seen that social consciousness and the sense of reality are sharper in East Europe than in the West.

Another thing about Antonia—and I believe most East Europeans, since also Imogene from East Germany had the same quality—is her ability to listen. Actually women are much better listeners than men. Men love to bare their souls to women. I tell women things I would never dare mention to another man. It must be the competition factor in the male. In this respect, Antonia is the proto-female. I know I can tell her anything and that she will listen ... and react.

But Katharina? In my life, she is the exception that confirms the existence of a rule concerning the female's willingness to listen constructively. Egocentric Katharina is completely, utterly, by her very nature, uninterested in even hearing my ramblings, my relating and my recounting of normal events of life. She has no interest in any kind of normal conversation or in my confessions or boasts or admissions of insecurity and my not knowing which way to turn. If I so much as attempt a normal everyday conversation she invariably says "What a bore" and leaves the room in a huff. "Tell me something interesting for a change," she might say. "Entertain me. Make me laugh." She is not interested in conversation, much less in any kind of speculation or abstraction. She wants to hear only concrete, positive things, stated as briefly as possible. Katharina is like the child incapable of listening to its parents. Though I feared for my father when he daunted the dangerous waters of Lake Bracciano in his flimsy sailboat, I never really listened to his journalistic tales or even read his articles. I remember his attempts to reach me. Our inconclusive discussions. As if he were searching for my inner spirit, maybe to understand what really linked us besides the sperm he had inoculated into my mother. A daughter might listen to a father; but a son, rarely. A son can only obey or not obey. But listen? Never. The relationship is too tight. Too familiar.

A woman lover must be the very best listener. You have to be totally insensitive not to react to a person who listens to whatever you dare to say. No wonder men depend on mistresses or even prostitutes. Just to get a hearing. Pay for their ear.

"Listen, Antonia Lilova — how I love your name! — listen, I spoke with Alvin … the soldier from the other night. He said that Lala's friend, Elmer, was absent today. In the military that's bad. What about calling her and asking if she knows anything? He's just a kid, a little crazy too, and mad about her."

Lala confirms that Elmer called her early this morning. He was being transferred. Immediately! He would be in touch. As if sent into exile, Lala says. He wasn't sure where. Lala is desperate. Elmer, the genius with his martenitsa and his infected ear lobe. Lily padded! Fuck security, I think, and dial Cliff's number, again relying on a hunch. I remember that Elmer had looked curiously at Ilya's name and address written on the menu. He might have had premonitions. Without preliminaries I ask Cliff to tell Ilya that a visitor might be pending ... and ring off.

"*Liebst Du mich nicht etwas mehr?*" I dare.

Antonia cocks her head to one side: "*Vielleicht doch.*"

I tantalize her with a few more words, "*Vorrei che fosse amore Ma proprio amore amore La cosa che io sento per te.*"

After another night of the new kind of love-making that leaves us both euphoric, and me with a post-coitus feeling of unaccustomed closeness to another person, a feeling of connection and union—well, not exactly unaccustomed, for as I've come to realize she continues to remind me of my old girlfriend in Berlin, Imogene, another girl from the then Communist eastern marches of Germany. I'm still puzzled as to what it is that makes them different.

* * *

The next afternoon we're in the capital of independent Moldova. The ambivalent atmosphere is immediately palpable. After all the historic changes, new and old borders, new and old masters, after being part of Romania, then Russia, Moldovans don't know where they belong.

"Life must seem like a dream to the Moldovans," I mutter.

Antonia cocks her head and looks at me expectantly.

"As if they're just waking from a dream. Maybe for some, from a nightmare. And they don't know where they are ... or what to do now. Over six hundred thousand of their four million live abroad." I ramble. I doubt Antonia can follow me. This breakaway state from the former USSR is courted by the West and also ideologically undermined by Western moles. But it is again governed by the Communist Party following democratic elections monitored by international observers. One of those East European areas almost impossible for Westerners to disentangle or pinpoint as to where it really belongs or even of what nationality its people are. West Europeans still call it Moldavia. Moldova? What's that? A country? A people? A language? If its name is unclear, its existence must seem unjustifiable. Still, Russia, Romania and NATO all want it.

"They know what they want," Antonia says. Again instinctively she understands their situation. "It's a poor country. Some of them might miss their past and still speak like Russians but most want what Westerners have."

"Yes, but many nations claim or want Moldova. I've read surveys showing that many Moldovans *want* to be annexed by someone. Even by Romania, although they know Romania is a poor country too."

"Maybe. But they have even less than Romanians. Some of them come to Bulgaria to work. And we're not rich either."

"Well, Russia would love to have it back … for strategic purposes. Keep the Americans out. West Europe wants it in the EU and in NATO in order to pressure Russia. The USA wants to put a lily pad base here … right smack in the belly of Russia."

Moldova is the former Bessarabia, another name only vaguely familiar to us West Europeans today. It was once part of Romania. Until 1991 it was part of the USSR, as the Moldavian Soviet Socialist Republic. Nearly half the Moldovan population is Russian or Russian-speaking Ukrainians, and nearly all are Russian Orthodox, where in its capital of Chisinau, in Russian called Kishinev, Russian is the street language. No wonder Moldova is on the frontline in the underground battle between Russia and the USA. It's a mini Cold War. Many deals are yet to be cut here, perhaps another test for international law after the travesty of Kosovo. A test for capitalism too. It seems to me that Moldova should say 'no' to NATO and 'no' to absorption by Western-oriented Romania. It should limit its cooperation with the

European Union too but I've seen the proof that the American eagle doesn't back down one centimeter.

As we walk through the downtown I put my arm around Antonia's shoulders. "I feel like I'm in Russia," I say, though I've no idea as to what Russia feels like. She stiffens, probably fearful of being taken for a prostitute. Moldova is famous for its beautiful women, many of whom are prostitutes. But I haven't seen any. I haven't seen any beggars either. Occasionally you see young people holding hands, though women walking with men, even younger girls, usually lay a hand in the crook of the man's arm. Something old-fashioned. Old East Europe. I feel the silence hanging over Chisinau's downtown of wide streets and empty spaces where beautiful women dressed as if for a party are really just on their way to an outdoor market. A sense of down-at-the-heels abandonment hangs over everything. A no-man's land, of lands up for grabs.

The next morning the feeling of the proximity of Russia is accentuated in the Transnistrian Republic. After exiting from Chisinau we're soon on a three-lane highway lined by modern gas stations on the 80-mile jaunt to breakaway Moldova's own breakaway republic, called Transdnestr. Just as Moldova broke away from the USSR when it folded, Transdnestr has broken away from Moldova. The self-declared republic is located on the east bank of the great lazy Dniester River that runs through the double breakaway capital city of Tiraspol and flows into the Black Sea creating that cold counter current toward the Aegean Sea.

For the international community the breakaway republic doesn't even exist. I had never even heard of it until my preparatory studies. I keep thinking of the Kosovo corollary. If the U.S. could fight a war against Serbia, bomb Belgrade for three months, overthrow its government, break up the nation, detach Kosovo, the very heart of Serbia, declare it a republic, recognize it and then build one of Europe's biggest military bases there, why could Russia not do the same here?

Antonia reasoned that way. And in this case, on its own former territory, the underbelly of Russia.

In Moldova the language issue is complex—40% per cent of the population is Russian or Ukrainian and many others speak Russian, even though the official language is Moldovan, actually Romanian, and is written in Latin script. I have Moldovan acquaintances in both Rome and Berlin who speak Russian; one in Rome did military service in the Russian army. But in the Transdnestr Republic language is a political statement. The chief language is Russian. Even the Moldovan language is written in Cyrillic as it was in Soviet times and is only one of the three official languages. Romanian is not even an official language and Latin script is banned.

Strolling along the uninviting streets of the capital city, arm in arm, almost carefree, I notice the office of the Russian-language newspaper, *Dnestrovskaya Pravda*. Antonia reads the plaque on the door: the republic's oldest newspaper. On a hunch I lead her inside where I introduce myself as a foreign journalist and ask to see the editor-in-chief. The youngish-looking, middle-aged woman, Tatiana Rudenko, who receives us, is visibly relieved when she hears Antonia speak Russian. If there is hesitation about whether to speak in Russian in Chisinau, that is not the case in the Transnistrian capital of Tiraspol—here you speak Russian first of all.

Madame Rudenko relates the history of her city, starting with its foundation in 1792 along the Dniester River east of Chisinau. The population today is 150,000 though it once had over 200,000, including tens of thousands of Jews. Decimated by the Nazis, nearly all of the Jewish survivors emigrated. Today's city is the result of a stormy zigzag voyage through two centuries of complex East European history: wars, pogroms, invasions and occupations, persecution, pressure from Russia and Nazi Germany, foreign meddling. In 1924, Moldova was transformed into the Moldavian Autonomous Soviet Socialist Republic and became part of the Soviet Ukraine with Romanian, Ukrainian and Russian as its official languages. Tiraspol was its capital until 1940 when according to secret provisions of the Russo-German Ribbentrop Pact, Russia took all of Bessarabia from Romania and integrated it into the Moldavian SSR. After the German-Axis invasion of the Soviet Union, the city was taken over by Romanian troops. Almost all of the remaining Jewish population perished. When the Red Army re-conquered the city in 1944, it again became part of the Moldavian SSR, lasting until the collapse of the Soviet Union in 1991.

As she spoke, I saw before my eyes the unfolding of a story lying outside official history. Outside European time. Actually, much of East Europe is like that for many of us. I, as a European, see also that the upstart USA could never begin to grasp, much less resolve such old hates and loves, defeats and victories, borders and boundaries and the languages and histories of peoples who themselves are uncertain as to who they are or even in what language they think. Their sense of nationality is vague and volatile. Like the cultural city of Chernivitsi, today in Ukraine not far from here, on which I spent time in my map studies. Its many names in its different languages confuse the foreigner. Chernovtsy in Russian, Czerniowce in Polish, Tshernovits in Yiddish, Cernauti in Romanian, Czernowitz in German. Once a Jewish city of the old region once known as East Galicia, with seventy synagogues, today only one remains. Jews exterminated by the Nazis, Jews deported by Russians and later, Jews emigrated to Israel. How can one grasp this bewildering region? Is it part of Europe? If not, then where is it? And who are these peoples?

After a long silence, embarrassing for me because the history Rudenko recounts makes me feel presumptuous, I go back to my original query, Antonia translating as I speak. Why does Transdnestr want to host a Russian military base today if it would stir up tensions and sharpen the Cold

War atmosphere, and in her opinion, would Transdnestr succeed in remaining independent?

Rudenko peers at me for a moment as though I'm crazy, then launches into another monologue, I'm certain reflecting the point of view of most people in this self-proclaimed, though unrecognized, Russian-speaking republic: "If America opens bases in former Soviet republics, Russia must counter each one of them. In Russian territory, but right along the line of the American military bases surrounding Russia. On the front, so to speak. After the collapse of the USSR, Russia was weak. No longer. Today, Russia guarantees our independence. Though our republic broke away from the Soviet Union, we realize that the stronger the Russian military presence here, the better for us. Russia commands here today. We look toward Russia. Much easier to go to war—cold or hot—over the Transdnestr Republic than over Kosovo.

"Now there are only 1500 Russian troops here. Here to protect the weapons warehouses of the army of the former Soviet Union. It's a symbolic force. For now. You hardly see them. They stick close to their bases. For us however it's logical that Russia deploys any weapons necessary to neutralize U.S. missile systems. Needless to say that we too are sensitive to the U.S. missile bases spread all over East Europe, in the Caucasus and in Asia. Russia's gas is a powerful weapon. But it's not enough. It's true that a Russian base here would aggravate matters between Moldova and Transdnestr, also between the USA and Russia. Still, what is Russia supposed to do? Just sit back and watch the USA take us over, and Russia too? And that, my German friend, is what Washington wants: to scare the shit out of Russia. Crush it. Dissolve it. Break it up into little countries like ours. We hope the Russian base here will help stop the American advance across the world. The greater the American presence in East Europe, in Moldova itself, the greater should be the Russian response. Strengthening Russia's military presence in Transdnestr has been unnecessary this far since Moscow continues to dialogue with Moldova, which has not wanted to use military force against our break-away republic.

"Remember that Russia can aim just as many nuclear missiles pointed at the West as the U.S. can mount from its bases in East Europe. Washington launched a strategic military thrust on Russia's borders, installing its missile sites and Air Force bases in Poland, Rumania, Turkey, the Czech Republic and Bulgaria and expanding its bases in former Soviet republics in Central Asia. Those missile bases encircle Russia ... only minutes away from Russia's heartland. Washington-NATO has launched economic and military operations against Russia's trading partners in North Africa and the Middle East. The NATO war that ousted Gaddafi in Libya has nullified multi-billion dollar Russian oil and gas investments and arms sales and substituted a NATO puppet for the former Russia-friendly regime. And now it aims at other commercial partners of Russia.

"Finally, Russia has reacted and threatens to aim its medium-range missiles at Berlin, Paris and London."

* * *

Investigative journalism works. All you have to do is knock on doors ... and then hope for answers. The words I just heard make more sense than the nonsense I read in our press in West Europe. I can't wait to e-mail the report to Cliff.

Once back on the street, Antonia smiles her feline Germano-Slavic smile and asks if she did well. On the main street of Tiraspol, capital of the Russian-speaking East European maverick Republic of Transdnestr, I stop and kiss her passionately. This time she doesn't complain about public displays of affection.

Arm in arm we stroll along the wide street leading toward the city center ... though I've begun thinking there is no real center as such. Indistinct and uncertain architecture, some buildings in marble, some in concrete slabs, of no specific style. They don't actually line the street but rather emphasize the many blank green spaces. Looks like a new city, a city yet to be completed, a Slavic Brasilia in evolution. Despite the wide avenues, not even a suggestion or pretension of grandeur. As if nothing were complete or would ever be complete. I feel the same nostalgia I used to feel walking the streets of former East Berlin. I try to picture the small town on which this new one was built. I imagine its former unsmiling peasants; dark, bearded and longhaired, pulling loaded carts down muddy roads near the river. They are men who atavistically fear devious and untrustworthy foreigners. They are men who love the joys of celebrations, men who know the difference between war and peace, between evil and good, and who worship the Orthodox resurrected God rather than the Catholic crucified one. These men however, I learned from my readings, also had a cruel streak in them, the human stain, that made them intolerant of other faiths that they blamed for their sufferings. Those anti-Semitic people must have vanished with the old town. In my imagination the new population consists of relocated individuals, not peoples, with little sense of who they are. They are stragglers, a new race, transplanted here beyond the River Dniester to cut out a new destiny for themselves. Nonetheless, the absence of the expected crowds today creates an eerie atmosphere, almost contagious.

"Hey, wait!" I cry, when I notice on the corner of the opposite street side a small crowd gathered around a newspaper kiosk. "Let's see what that's about."

The kiosk is a dilapidated structure made of metal and wood. Behind the stacks of newspapers on the front counter stands a grinning fat guy, red-faced and with thin gray hair, talking affably with his customers, taking money and giving change, while automatically stroking a big black and white cat lying placidly in front of him. Evidently newspapers have just arrived from "abroad". *Komsomolskaya Pravda* from Russia seems to be the most popular.

"Is everyone here Russian?" I ask in German, louder than intended.

Heads jerk toward me and my out-of-place language. Antonia explains that I'm a visiting foreign journalist. Answers come from all sides, all of which Antonia translates.

"I am," says a guy with a tiny dog on a leash. "I come every day to get my newspaper."

"I'm Russian too," says an elderly lady.

"I'm Ukrainian but I read the Russian papers," says another.

It turns out they are chiefly Russians. A few Ukrainians buy Ukrainian papers, and there is one old, Russian-speaking Moldovan, who says with pride that he'd served in the Red Army. He indicates on his lapel a pin that I assume testifies to his military service. Maybe a medal. A hero of the Red Army, maybe in the battle to rid former Moldavia of its Romanian Nazi occupiers.

Farther down the street, at the same time I spot a parked taxi I believe I see the tall man from Novo Selo, blond hair, thick glasses. The bogeyman of my dreams. Is it really Raymond? My paranoia? Him or not, this man too must be at least two meters tall. He smiles toward me.

On the spur of the moment I hire the taxi and ask the driver to show us the city. We turn into a square at the far side of which stands the bus and rail station. A huge Che Guevara poster stares out of the show window of what the driver says is a youth club. On the corner are big portraits of Russian leaders, Putin and Medvedev. At the entrance to the Heroes Cemetery we stop before a parked Soviet tank morphed into a monument. Later, the driver proudly points at a cognac factory. Soviet style architecture dominates this town full of Communist symbolism, a longing for the past, at least for something different from the present.

This is neither modern Russia nor the bigger Americanized countries of East Europe striving toward capitalism. The same sad torpor hangs over Tiraspol as over Chisinau; a hopeless weariness glued irremovably to its obscure existence.

We pick up our car and check into what the taxi driver told us is the best hotel in town. Rather primitive compared to West European standards, but comfortable. As we settle into the room, I realize again that in the last several days I've drunk little and today didn't even take my morning lamotrigina. I want neither now.

Still concerned about crazy Elmer, I call Alvin's office again. There is still time. He always stays precisely until five o'clock.

"What about him?" I ask.

"Like I said, I believe that boy is traveling … they can leapfrog him straight to the battlefront. Or maybe he's in jail. That silly earring and his long hair always get him into trouble."

"Or maybe the leaks we spoke of."

"Oh God, let's hope not."

"I think I saw the same guy from the café in Burgas up here where I am. He's a giant."

"Yep, must be him. You better watch your step. Not much love for journalists around here. Most know to stay away."

"So you don't really believe it's about our friend's martenitsa?"

"His what? Oh, yeah, you mean his earring. Maybe not. Must be the other thing. For Chrissakes, he's just a kid looking for kicks."

"Maybe," I mutter, and click off. We shouldn't be talking about such things by phone.

At dinner in the hotel we share a bottle of the renowned Moldavian red wine, leaving a third of it. Black bread is my wine ersatz. My compensation. I have a fixation for black bread, practically non-existent in Rome. Sour bread leavened with sourdough. *Secale* cereal, *Roggen, seigle, centeno.* And the labor that goes into it. A week of preparation. Real bread, though largely absent in the West. The East has time for it. Germany maintains the tradition, black rye bread, for me the symbol of East Europe. The heart of 'breaking bread', eating together. From the Bible too. Enough to make me miss Berlin when I'm in my Italian mode.

I stare across the table at Antonia who is looking out the plate glass window toward a suddenly busy traffic scene. Where is she in her world so different from mine? How does she react to this country? A country? Yes, but sad, unutterably worn and weary in this black hole of East Europe. Is she only registering how tame the traffic is compared to that of Bulgarian cities? Or something deeper? Does she see Chisinau and Tiraspol as I do, still the same backwater as they probably were in the former USSR? As a rule Antonia seems so urbane and cosmopolitan that I sometimes wonder if it's a role she plays to impress me, a Westerner.

Yet after my short experience here, I think that, no, East Europeans—in elegant Prague and Budapest or in the backwaters of Chisinau and Tiraspol—have a natural quality of universality about them, a quality we in the West have lost. In comparison to their largeness of spirit, we are the provincials. Maybe I had to see Moldova to understand.

"I feel so provincial here," I say.

"You, provincial?" Antonia says in her most ironic manner.

"*Ja, ja*, I mean in comparison to the ... uh, to the largeness of spirit here in the East. Our Eurocentrism in the West is too powerful for our own good."

Antonia has more than urbanity and universality; her natural elegance is without a trace of artificiality, an innate assumption of her femininity ... and a fragrance of flowers adorns her. Antonia who, I'm certain, in her thoughts, in her inner world, lives the same real life as in her everyday world. In her world doubt seems suspended, if not rejected.

I realize that I've been fortunate in meeting another unusual woman. She resembles goal-conscious, steadfast, unwavering Imogene from the eastern marches of Germany, for one year my girl friend in Berlin. Also zany, uncontrollable, forever unattainable Katharina, who, though in my mind has remained remote, is perhaps waiting for me in Berlin tonight. Antonia has the same fiber, the same strength. The three of them somehow resemble each other, these three women I've loved, or perhaps still love. I must seek out their type, strong women who both appeal to my needs and often break my heart. In any case, all three have enviable qualities. Not simply their physical beauty and graceful attributes that I forget can quickly turn out to be evanescent, but each of them is illuminated by authenticity no less than beauty. Their oneness with the world seems to strip my existential uncertainties and my scribblings of significance. At this moment, watching Antonia watching the quiet, sad town, I know that as far as women are concerned, good fortune continues to follow me.

That night however, when I should have continued on my roll of tranquility, I pay for having neglected my trusty lamotrigina and the calming effects of alcohol by plunging head over heels into a terrifying nightmare. The debilitating kind of incubus that drags me back to old realities. I am on an uncontrollable makeshift raft, adrift on the great Sea of the ancients. Terror is the dream motif. My terror of ungovernable waters. The Sea's depth. Its blackness. Near the water, from the edge of the metal and wooden raft—perhaps it's the newspaper kiosk, upside down—I peer into the blackness, quickly turn away in fear and then return to it involuntarily. Antonia takes my hand. At first we're alone on the raft on the Black Sea. Then Hakim appears. Quietly, as if he hadn't been blown to smithereens in Italy, he tries to tranquilize me and tells me not to worry. Momentarily startled by his sudden materialization, I ask him what really happened on Mount Subasio, that I thought he died there. I admit that his body was never found. He says, no, he didn't die, he made it, but Nikitin never returned. As the sun beats down on the Sea's blackness, I see images and reflections of images of underwater buildings, maybe a haunted city down there, and its indescribably horrible night creatures. Everything under and above water seems invested with horror, yet remote and unreachable so that the raft suddenly acquires a quality of security, of a safe haven, a neutral territory, and I realize that the reassuring presence of Hakim is only a mirage caused by the burning sun hanging over the devious Sea. Antonia assures me the water around us is not really deep, that I'm only seeing reflections of the cooling sun as it abandons us and that yes, she is in love with me. I don't understand her but I know the Sea is 7000 feet deep and my terror again grows. I know Antonia is lying to calm me and that an evil world lies down there. She assures me that we will soon arrive in Odessa and I will see the magical staircase of which I dream.

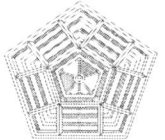

14

CLIFF

I USED to boast about my criminal inclinations. Though most people believed I was joking, I was deadly serious, especially in my hate for the Swiss petit bourgeois world in which I lived. In retrospect I have come to realize it was my natural propensity toward violence and intrigue, coupled with my father's pressure that I do 'something worthwhile' in life which eventually carried me straight into the arms of the Agency. I don't deny that the early years with that band of thugs and criminals were enjoyable, sometimes even rewarding. I mean, who wouldn't enjoy two wonderful years spent in intensive language courses in the Alps, in my case so near my home in St. Moritz? Those courses were a piece of cake for me since I have a natural language talent and grew up in Switzerland speaking different languages. As an adult I easily added Russian, Czech, some Bulgarian and a smattering of others. And then they sent me off to a new world in Russia which, even though the Agency was then passing through some of its darkest years, was exciting and my work—at least my interpretation of it—bordered on the semi-legal, semi-criminal activities so attractive to my nature. My superiors considered me a natural spy. And I was handsomely rewarded—good salary, bonuses, generous expense accounts and many perks. People envied me. Everyone except my wife. She believed she had married a diplomat. Still, in all that time, I never felt like a real spy. I was something else, maybe a headhunter in search of spies. Sometimes I think that much of so-called espionage is really a story about the spy himself rather than about the act of spying as such. My spy life consisted of talk about action, talk and much make-believe about things that might happen but usually didn't, the search for others to do the dangerous work for me. It might seem strange but I remember the people, the spies, in those places and in those times, but actually little about spying. Others took the risks for us. And some got caught. Betrayal by someone. The mafia would have despised us. Nonetheless I long fancied myself simply a criminal in disguise. And spy or not, criminal or not, my life was an endless bonanza. Not a soupçon of doubt on my part about my role. No misgivings. The years passed and I stopped thinking of alternative lives. I neglected my former artistic aspirations: I did have a few that somehow survived in secret cohabitation with the sinister side of my character. Once I had believed I would start out in journalism before then turning to literature and becoming a famous writer. I must've been bipolar. Maybe still am. Yet the longer I stayed under the wing of the American government, living, carelessly living from day to day my underground life in that kind of comfort and ease, the farther I drifted from the other me. I now think, the real me. That I could wish for anything better than the excitement of action became a dwindling dream. So, great was my surprise when the itch returned and I began to feel the unbearable weight of the chains in which I was encased. I began asking myself if the limited story I was living was to be my life story. I wondered what it was like out in real life. While I recalled my youthful aspirations for journalism, my superiors instead demanded more and more of me in their machinations. The clash was inevitable. As a result I gradually became unbearable to them. I challenged one and all. I detested their often silly games, like planting bugs in the embassies of our allies and then celebrating the meaningless results. I wriggled and resisted each step along the way, stubborn, recalcitrant, unconsciously hoping they would do for me what I lacked the courage to do for myself: eject me from the trap of that business so that I could join real life. Still, self-contradictory as usual, in conflict with my other self, when they did eject me I was so used to the power and the prestige and the rewards of the underground life that I invented a way to continue the same kind of life privately, as my own boss—my best friend Franz and I formed a private intelligence agency. Instead of exploiting the opportunity and reversing directions and becoming the artist I dreamed of, I became a mercenary.

Perhaps it was simply my destiny that I continued in same covert life of my spymaster father.

But I exacted my revenge on the system that had held me. That one night in Italy. When two of my new allies, defectors from the same secret world from which I came, died at the hands of my former bosses, I myself murdered those bosses. Those murders were the last splurges of my criminal self. Perhaps I had to reach the very acme of violence in order to find myself and re-emerge in life.

Shortly afterwards, the world as I had known it exploded that Sunday morning when Europe went up in flames. The cataclysm I had imagined. Clairvoyance? A special insight? An intuition? I still don't know. I doubt it. Anyway extrasensory perceptions are impossible to measure. My presentiment was not a permanent gift but a momentary quality. Briefly I had foreseen visions of Europe in flames. It took the excess of violence on my part and the Armageddon of the burning of Paris and Rome, of Moscow and Warsaw, to shake me from the lethargy of illegality. Then, miraculously it seemed, from one day to the next I found myself in the world of journalism where I should have been over two decades earlier. My greatest hope today is that this change toward political maturity has not occurred too late. That my latent talents have not dwindled and withered away during the wasted years. That the work that would have been pleasure back then will not turn out to be fanciful today, another chimera. That I still have enough authentic humanity left in me in order to join the rest of mankind.

I fear what a great writer once noted about people like me, that to the extent "one leans on the mighty arm of the Republic, his own strength departs from him." Like the effects of smoking on the lungs, it seems to depend on how long one hung on that powerful arm; for I have seen that many of the people I knew in that false world were incapable of any other life. They had lost the ability to live autonomously. If one was ejected from the Agency in one purge or another — it was a rare event that anyone was fired for incompetence — he was condemned to wait and mope around and hope for reinstatement or face the bitter truth and his inevitable ruin — for such a person is an alien on any other path.

I wonder if Karl Heinz understands my shame about my past? My remorse for taking so long to join real life? Does he grasp my regrets about my former violent nature that because of that one night of killings he believes still possesses me?

* * *

I decided to address in writing the direction I intend taking in order to begin to atone for my past and have attempted to record here the fruits of my experience and my convictions. After years of stewing and reflection, I, Clifford Beecher, challenge the United States of America under whose arm I spent much of my youth.

In this first confession and recommendations of a man from the secret, criminal underworld, I will begin by posing the seldom posed question: What harm would befall the United States if it decided to close its thousand plus military bases around the world which I have sent Karl Heinz to investigate? What if the USA were to dismantle the empire and bring its troops home? It is unlikely that Mongol hordes would descend on Europe and America. Certainly not on the USA, for neither a land nor a sea invasion of the U.S. is conceivable in our times.

Nor would terrorist attacks accelerate. It seems far likelier that as America's overseas footprints vanish, the probability of such attacks will also vanish.

I believe that the many countries the USA has invaded, occupied and raped while pretending to set them on the path of freedom and democracy would revive instead of decline without the U.S. presence. In any case, this is not the role of the USA, which itself is becoming a failed nation.

In other words, Karl Heinz—after a few sentences I realize my reflections are addressed to you, Karl Heinz. You are not American and are besides remote from the subject and therefore an untarnished judge of my conclusions. I believe that Washington's proclaimed warnings about what would happen to America if it dismantled the empire would prove to be the usual propagandistic lie, like Washington's predictions in the 1970s that nations in Asia, Africa and beyond would fall like dominoes to Communist domination if we did not win the war in Vietnam.

You, Karl Heinz, were not even born when the domino theory guided the entire U.S. foreign policy.

One must wonder what the world would be like if the U.S. lost control globally—apparently Washington's greatest fear and the reflection of its overblown sense of self-worth and Exceptionalism. What would the world be like if the U.S. just gave it all up? What would happen to the USA if it were no longer the sole superpower and the world's self-appointed policeman?

The fact is, Karl Heinz, it would still be a powerful nation with a host of domestic problems to be faced—immigration, a drug crisis, soaring healthcare costs, a failed education system, an aging population, aging infrastructures, unending recession, vanishing civil rights and liberties, spreading fear. None of those problems will disappear soon. None of them can even be tackled as long as the nation spends its wealth on armies, weapons, wars, intrigues and plots, global military bases and support for its roster of puppet dictators. Without the American military empire, the Middle East and

Africa would continue to export oil and even if China were to buy up what oil remains, that would force the USA to develop alternative energies. Half of Germany today exists on solar energy.

Meanwhile, whether or not the USA dismantles its empire, China will be the world's next superpower. Though it too faces myriad internal problems, China has a booming economy, a favorable balance of payments and a people determined to become an economically dominant nation-state.

Karl Heinz, while you are visiting the lily pad world, it is worthwhile to recall that the Japanese invasion of China in the 1930s spurred Mao Zedong and the Chinese Communist Party on a trajectory to power—thanks to their nationalist resistance to a foreign invader. There are many historical examples of this process in which a domestic political group gains power because it champions resistance to foreign occupation. It occurred in Vietnam and Indonesia. With the collapse of the Soviet Union in 1991, it occurred all over Eastern Europe, and today has occurred in Afghanistan and Iraq.

I can't imagine that China wants to start a war with the USA, which would mean opting for a different path than the one it has been following for decades.

Karl Heinz, the reality is that America's time is running out. As it comes face-to-face with its old infrastructure, declining international clout and sagging economy, the USA will resemble England at the end of its imperial period.

But if the USA were to dismantle its empire of military bases and redirect its economy toward productive industries; if it began making things again; if it maintained volunteer armed forces primarily to defend its own shores; if it invested in infrastructure, education, health care and savings; if it did these basic things then it would have a chance to reinvent itself as a normal nation.

Unfortunately, Karl Heinz, such a scenario is not on the horizon. I know this government will never dismantle its empire voluntarily, which does not mean that its bases will not go someday anyway. Instead, the USA staggers along, willy-nilly, according to stopgap, improvised policies, much as it drifts along from day to day in its unwinnable wars. The common talk among economists today is that high unemployment may linger for another decade. Add to that low investment and depressed spending and, I fear, the American Century will end with a whimper.

Karl Heinz, these are also the reasons why I, after my experience in the Agency, favor disbanding it. That would be a sign, a signal to the world. Not only has the CIA lost its raison d'être by allowing its intelligence gathering to become politically tainted, but its clandestine operations have created a climate of impunity in which the USA can assassinate, torture and imprison people at will worldwide. Disbanding the CIA however is only emblematic of the greater urgency, which is to disband both the system-USA and, ultimately, capitalism itself.

These are the reasons why I joined the small group of non-establishment journalists in an alternate news syndicate dedicated to telling the truth. I second those scholars who are assembling the data that will enable future historians to describe where and when the USA went astray.

15

KARL HEINZ

A LIGHT spring breeze from the Sea lifts Antonia's pink chiffon foulard, lets it flutter for an instant and then fall gracefully in ripples over her shoulder. In the same moment, a frisson of excitement swells in me from momentary visions formed by remembered scenes from Eizenstein's film. As we approach the staircase, I don't permit myself to be tempted by partial views or even mere glimpses of the historic site. I close my eyes. Playing blind I hold Antonia's arm tight and ask her to guide me. She thinks I'm crazy. I walk with my eyes tightly closed, without so much as turning my head. I want the full impact from film and history, all at once.

Then, I open my eyes. And there it is.

"I can hardly believe that I'm standing at the top of the Potemkin Stairs," I whisper to Antonia. I'm in awe. Reverence. It was so close all the time and I didn't realize it. Maybe the stops in Burgas and Varna, in Chisinau and Tiraspol, had also shortened the distances. Prepared me for the dramatic reality. Maybe that contortion of geography, the time and space distortion, the footprint mania, lies at the heart of the lily pad idea. Shorten the world. Link it. Shake it. Mix it. Make it one. But I think that those mad planners still do not realize the real distances, the separations and disjunctions, the diversity and the multiplicity of the peoples, the cultures and the customs involved. They confuse one with the other on their lily pad roll. Only to them it makes no difference. Other peoples do not count. These *other* peoples, the indistinct peoples like those of

Tiraspol and Chisinau and Chernivitsi do not count. They have never counted.

Now Antonia grasps my arm, as if searching for equilibrium, and gazes toward the Sea. I smile and hope she will become infected too. A few ripples roll in, hardly more agitated than that first evening in Burgas at the seashore café. The sea breeze is hypnotic, blowing in from the Caucasus, it seems. It's cooler here than I expected. The small boats scattered across the harbor bob only slightly. From this point, the unpredictable Sea seems pacific. But the history behind the scene before us is what makes the reality unbearably beautiful.

I translate aloud from a guidebook in English. Antonia is still curious but, no, she does not share my fascination. Though it's practically in her own backyard, she has never been here before. In Odessa. On the steps. Nor has she seen the Eizenstein film, the story of the mutiny in 1905 of the crew of the Russian battleship Potemkin against their officers who first fed them rotten meat, then shot many of them for protesting. Clearly *The Battleship Potemkin* is a propaganda film, even though the protest that provoked the bloody reaction turned out to be a real mover of history. At the Brussels World Fair in 1958 it was named the greatest film of all time. For cinema historians the Eizenstein's film is still a landmark of cinematography.

"The giant staircase appears like a formal entrance into Odessa from the Sea," I read aloud. "The stairs are the symbol of the city. They were designed to create an optical illusion. From the top the steps are steep and practically invisible. A person looking down from the top sees only the landings from the Sea. But a person looking up from the bottom sees only steps. One hundred and ninety-two steps and ten stair flights. A secondary illusion creates a false perspective since the stairs are actually wider at the bottom, 21.7 meters, than the top where the first step is 12.5 meters wide. The whole staircase is only 27 meters high, but extends for a distance of 142 meters, interrupted by landings every 20 steps. Altogether the staircase seen from below gives the illusion of even much greater length. Looking up the stairs makes them seem longer than they are and looking down the stairs makes them seem much shorter."

"The staircase is beautiful," Antonia finally says, she too now almost in a reverie.

"Come on, let's go down a couple of levels so we can look back up and see it from the perspective of the demonstrators."

This is the site of the horror scene where Tsarist troops, shoulder to shoulder, march down the stairs from the top firing point-blank on the people of Odessa on the staircase. At the bottom, mounted Cossacks wait, slashing and hacking down the fleeing people with their long swords.

Reading the history and the film sequence, I slide into a momentary trance. The guide in one hand, Antonia's hand in the other, I lift my head upwards, half close my eyes, and drift backwards in time and into Eizenstein's atmosphere. The white tunics, the wide belts and black boots of the soldiers in a tight line across the width of the top of the staircase, their identical faces blank, expressionless reflections of blind power, their rifles upright in front of them, their officer with his sword held high, row after row of soldiers in identical formation behind them ready to fill up the spaces as the staircase gradually widens. They begin their methodical descent toward us, the officer's shouted command on the level above Antonia and me, rifles now lowered, row after row of soldiers behind. I drag Antonia down to the next level, shouts of bewildered people around us, terror in the eyes of all, a mother urging her small son to hurry down toward the obscure Sea, the boy stalling, wanting to see the soldiers, their uniforms, their boots, their rifles. The officer with the sword now pointing downwards, a volley of fire, people falling around us, screams, people scrambling down the stairs, another volley of fire, an invalid without legs propels himself with his hands downwards faster than we can run. Now volley follows volley, the boy loosens his mother's hand, she is swept downwards by the terrified mass of bodies, bodies now piling up on each level, along the steps, along the lateral parapet, no way out of the inferno, no emergency exit, only downwards, down, down toward the Cossacks and fatal Sea. The mother, now near us, tries to run to her child against the current of human bodies hurtling downwards in a death descent, ever downwards. Her son lies on the steps above, she reaches him, picks him up in her arms, cries for help to the advancing soldiers of the vacuous, identical faces and blind eyes of power. Another volley and down goes the mother with her son, upside down goes the invalid, a nearly blind woman wearing thick eye glasses looks upwards toward the source of the fire until a bullet smashes through her left eye, row after widening row of soldiers, officers with swords pointed at the people-targets. Now screams from the bottom of the stairs, "Cossacks, Cossacks" goes up the cry, as the savage cavalry slashes and rips and cuts swath after swath among the trapped people, helpless in the mortal grip of uniformed, armed power. We stand on the penultimate landing and observe the carnage of the people of Odessa dying under the rifles of the faceless soldiers and savage Cossack swords. Blood everywhere. And upwards, up toward the horizon, steps, steps, ever more steps, endless steps.

"Karl Heinz, Karl Heinz, stop it, stop it now, we're at the bottom," Antonia says in my ear.

I raise my eyes; I see only stairs, climbing and vanishing somewhere above us.

I shake myself back to the present. I've read a lot about this film. The theory behind the film author's story is simple. For Eizenstein the sailors rising up against their officers and the Tsarist troops massacring the people were emblematic of the Marxist interpretation of the class conflict driving history. The thesis is the eternal clash of the bourgeoisie with the proletariat; the revolt on the Potemkin and the crushing of the demonstration on the stairs create the antithesis; the ultimate victory of the people which results in the synthesis of a classless society. Hence its classification as a propaganda film. But it was the director's creative genius that produced "the film of all time". Eizenstein harnessed the popular frenzy of that day in Odessa with his art, used here for revolutionary purposes, the realization of the dream of political writers. The inherent propaganda took nothing away from the genius of his art, which combined with history achieved what Eizenstein said, "sends the spectator into ecstasy." With that film alone he raised the bar high for true art while stimulating class-consciousness and prompting the viewer to take up arms in resistance against injustice. Unfortunately, in the West, the same technique used to sell capitalist values was easier to achieve than the transmission of values engendering revolution.

Eizenstein loved long, slow shots and a linear narrative driven by individual protagonists, shots that force the viewer to dwell on one frame at a time, to see it, digest it, live it —the frame of a baby carriage careering down the steps amid the slaughter, or a soldier trampling the hand of a child, or a mother holding her dying son in her arms—to grasp the symbolism in pure action. In contrast, pure intellectual presentation, in film or literature, bludgeons us with a blunt message devoid of action.

The revolt of the people of Odessa and the massacre symbolize the thesis of the clash of the bourgeoisie and the proletariat. The mutiny on the Potemkin: the antithesis. The revolution and the overturn of the old society, and the attempt at a new society: the new synthesis. You can't miss it. You can't misinterpret it, underestimate it, devalue it. Eizenstein's art co-exists with his message.

Standing at the bottom of the Potemkin Stairs, looking up the staircase and then out to the Sea, I mutter that Russia is not as distant and exotic as I once believed.

Antonia looks blank. "Distant? Russia? What do you

mean? It's right next to us. We drove here in the car. We're in Russia … more or less. Even if Odessa is part of Ukraine today. But everybody's still Russian here. A real Russian city. The home of famous Russian writers, Babel and Akhmatova and Pasternak. We've read them all at school in Burgas."

She is right. Even I feel that this is Russia. A historical note I encountered in my reading came as a surprise because I had assumed that German troops occupied Odessa during World War II. Actually Fascist Romanian troops did most of the dirty work. In retaliation for a resistance attack on the occupation troops in 1941, Romanians massacred 25,000 civilians, most of whom were Jews. In 1942, only 703 Odessa Jews survived. By then, more than 280,000 people had been deported, including over 100,000 Jews. After 1970, most remaining Odessa Jews emigrated to Israel or the USA and founded Little Odessa at Brighton Beach on Long Island's south shore. Then after the dissolution of the USSR, Odessa became part of Ukraine. Nonetheless, it remains a very Russian city.

"It's the propaganda, Antonia. The propaganda you and I grew up with. The fact is the Cold War is still alive. People in the West grow up believing Russia is just another despotic Eastern power. They're somewhere out there beyond the seas and the deserts waiting for the propitious moment to swoop down on us. Like the Tartars, in another famous film, who never arrive from the desert. The threats of terrorists-Communists-Tartars are the creation of power to retain control over us. Now I see Russia is much more part of the West than I realized. Part of us."

"For Dostoevsky—that's my major lit course this semester—Russia is a better West … a better Christendom too."

* * *

We check into a four-star hotel near the top of the Staircase. Antonia thrills at the luxurious setting. It reminds me of the hotel in Perugia where Katharina and I lived for those months before and shortly after "the events" that shook Europe. When I remark to the concierge on the luxury, he says in good German that the hotel is a thousand times better now than during the Soviet era. Well, hotels are not everything in life, I think. Nor is luxury. Somehow the hotel's chasseurs and waiters in black remind me of the time in a Berlin café when the Russian spy Anatoly Nikitin said that good waiters and good service were always necessary, whether in Capitalism or Communism. I wonder about this hotel. But no, it most certainly has no Russian Communist inclinations. Again I call Cliff's number from my mobile. Fuck the rules of espionage. I need to know. Useless. Still no answer. Maybe he did take Elizaveta to Russia as he had hinted.

"Herr Viktor, uh Mister Viktor! Can you …" I say to the concierge later, reading from the brass nameplate on his desk.

"*Ja, bitte schön, wie kann ich Ihnen behilflich sein?*" he answers, a wry smile at the corners of his mouth. "Just call me Viktor," he adds, still in German.

My hesitant "*Herr*" establishes my German nationality, at times still embarrassing even to my generation. Besides, as I learned in my hotel living with Katharina, concierges everywhere are especially perceptive and insightful. Magically, they are able to read into your innermost self.

"I wanted to ask what we should see here in Odessa? What are the chief points of interest for tourists?

"Are you a tourist?" he asks looking me straight in the eyes. "You and your lady friend make a striking couple. But you don't behave as tourists … nor like our nouveaux riches, especially not like the Ukrainians."

"But aren't you Ukrainian too?"

"Well, by nationality, yes," Viktor says, lowering his voice. "But I'm Russian, through and through. If we Russians here in Odessa had a choice, we would vote to reunite with Russia. Today's Ukraine is far from us."

"I'm part German, part Italian where I grew up. Today I'm a journalist."

"Well, after you see the Potemkin Steps ..."

"That was the first place we went. I've long dreamed of it. Saw the Eizenstein film many times."

"Ah ha," Viktor murmurs. Then: "Well, among the most interesting *Sehenswürdigkeiten*—you know Herr, uh, Leonhard, I love that word in German. We also have a long Russian word for 'things to see': *dostoprimechatelnosti*."

"*Mein Gott*," I say.

"That's what we Russians say when we see that German word. That's why I like to pronounce it."

"What about the Konstantinovich there on your name plate? That's pretty long."

"My patronymic. My father's name was Konstantin. Older Russian guests address me as Viktor Konstantinovich. But some of the younger nouveau riche people just say Vik. Changing times, no?"

"Your father would have been too young for the Potemkin mutiny?"

"Yes. My grandfather was also too young to be there that day but some family friends died in the massacre. Not on the steps however. That scene was fictional, imagined by Eizenstein to demonize the Tsarist regime. It all really happened on nearby streets ... where troops fired on the people demonstrating in support of the sailors' mutiny."

"Incredible. Anyway for me it still happened on the staircase. The history of that day must be alive here."

"It's alive for real Odessites. Uh, well, what else should you see? You might visit the catacombs, the great tunnels spread under the city. Once used by bandits and smugglers. During World War II, *Partizans* hid there. For months and months of cold, showing that Russians can bear things that would kill a Westerner ... like they did in Stalingrad and Leningrad. But for real sights you might see the Opera and Ballet Theater, famous for its acoustics, and some of the great city mansions like the Tolstoy Palace ... Lev Tolstoy loved the city and was an honorary citizen. And of course the Passage, something like the Galleria in Milano. Herr Leonhard, Odessa is a beloved city of Russia, always was. In Imperial Russia it was the nation's fourth city, after St. Petersburg, Moscow and Warsaw. Also it was once the home of many Russian Jews. Few of them are left here today."

I shake hands with Viktor Konstantinovich.

* * *

Later, when we come out of the Tolstoy mansion and turn down a main avenue, I see it—I'm beginning to learn the Cyrillic script—the *Russky Sotzialny Klub*. Russian? I wonder. But no matter. In we go. It is late morning. Only a few young people milling around a stage. Theater? Cabaret? What does a Russian club do in Ukrainian Odessa? Seems like a West European kind of thing. But you never know. Dissent ferments anyplace. Nobody pays us any attention. Antonia asks around. Is there someone who would speak with a Western journalist?

Robert meets us in an alcove behind the stage, pronouncing his name "Row-Bear". About Antonia's age, he's more interested in her than in me, the foreign journalist. Anyway when he comes round to being interviewed and sees that I want to record the interview, his interest is aroused and he launches into a rambling discourse, showily displaying his political aspirations for which the social club must be his jumping off point.

That evening I write up a condensed version of the interview-monologue.

Like Viktor Konstantinovich, Robert says he is Ukrainian only by nationality but Russian by descent, predilection and choice. "If we could vote on our nation," he repeated, "I would vote for Russia like most Odessites. Russia is our motherland. Not Ukraine with all its Fascists over in the western regions. We Odessites were never Ukrainians. Why should we be now?

"Western Europeans do not know that Ukraine is split between the eastern and southern parts on the one hand and its western regions on the other. The West and the East here will never be compatible. Still, Ukraine has fifty million people—the France of East Europe. Since the collapse of the USSR, Europe has pushed its eastern borders up to the frontiers of Russia. Weak post-Soviet Russia was unable to stop that advance. Not only the ex-Soviet satellite countries in East Europe from Bulgaria to Poland changed sides, but also parts of the USSR itself—Lithuania, Estonia, Latvia and Ukraine. The major problem here is Ukraine's two souls. The eastern soul holds Ukrainians close to their big brothers, the Great Russians; their western soul led rabid nationalists to collaborate with Nazi Germany against Soviet Russia. Ukraine's western soul aspires to become part of Europe; its eastern soul prefers a privileged relationship with Russia. In 2004, the American-sponsored Orange Revolution swept pro-Westerners into power in Ukraine. A year later, Russia's nominee won out in the country's first free parliamentary elections and became Prime Minister. The elections were a fatal flop for the western-looking part of Ukraine and a confirmation of the traditional division of the country.

"Three currents compete in contemporary Ukraine: the linguistic, historical, pro-Russian soul; the nostalgic, big nation, central planning, pro-Soviet soul; and a free market pro-western soul. Still, for many Russians and Ukrainians, the two peoples are nearly one and Ukrainians are referred to as Little Russians.

"Russia is alarmed about the rapid move westward of big and powerful Ukraine. In the 1990s, Ukraine contributed troops to so-called peacekeeping in Kosovo in the Balkans. It sent troops to Iraq. The Ukrainian government's desire for membership in United Europe, NATO and WTO, was the last straw for Moscow.

"Western Ukraine has close historical ties with Europe,

particularly with Poland. Ukrainian nationalist sentiment has always been strongest in the westernmost parts of the country. But it's a different story in eastern Ukraine. The Ukraine was the center of the first Slavic state, Kievan Rus, the cradle of Russia. Something like Kosovo for Serbia. During the tenth and eleventh centuries Kievan Rus was the largest state in Europe. Kievan Rus also laid the foundation for Ukrainian nationalism. A Ukrainian state was established during the seventeenth century. Then, during the latter part of the eighteenth century, the Russian Empire absorbed Ukrainian ethnographic territory."

Robert continually reminded me that a big minority of the population of Ukraine are ethnic Russians or speak Russian as their first language, particularly in the industrialized east and south of the country, where the Orthodox religion is predominant. Odessa and the Crimea were long part of Russia.

"Democracy here is as elusive as is the formation of a unified nation. Since the 2004 Orange Revolution, the ancient divisions in Ukraine between East and West have continued to stall efforts for the formation of a unified nation. The western-backed coalition government dissolved because the east and south of the nation prefer Russia and Ukraine's past. Russia is still Ukraine's largest trading partner. And Ukraine is the link on the pipeline for Russian gas exports to Europe.

"Russia retreated from West Europe for fifty years. Now with its gas as its weapon its retreat has ended. Since much of Europe's economic future depends on Russia's gas, European efforts at democratizing Russia have stopped. Only friendly relations count. Europe no longer pushes hard for Ukrainian links to the West. Not so America, which wants Ukraine in NATO and wants military bases here. Russia's gas scares Uncle Sam. America thinks it's unfair that Russia has all those resources in Siberia and wants to get its hands on them.

"Today, the tide in Ukraine has turned eastwards. The impulse toward the West of the last fifteen years has stopped. But Ukraine needs good relations with both East and West. Were Russia to raise gas prices or cut supplies, the scene would change. Keep this in mind: in a contest over Ukraine between Russia on the one hand and Europe-USA on the other, Moscow in a fair battle will always win.

"Arrogant American foreign policy is also a reason for the turnabout. For Russia, a Ukraine in the camp of the USA would be like Canada taking control of New England, or Mexico taking over Texas. Then also the European Union needs association with Ukraine. The European Parliament urges neighboring states to respect the democratic choice of the Ukrainian people and avoid any type of economic or other pressures with the goal of changing the political and economic status of Ukraine. At the same time the European Parliament has called upon future governments in Kiev to consolidate Ukrainian commitment toward general European values, to advance democracy, human rights, civic society and the rule of law, to continue market reforms and to overcome political divisions in Ukraine.

"Of course, this all rings friendly and cooperative—to western-oriented Ukrainians. To Russia and eastward-looking Ukrainians it sounds threatening, with an underlying note of economic blackmail.

"That's why Russia supports pro-Russian government leaders in Ukraine. Otherwise, the threat is revolt in the eastern and southern parts of the Ukraine like here in Odessa. But then, there is Russia's gas on the one hand which Ukraine needs, and again, America's military bases on the other, which Ukraine does not need.

"No doubt about it. Russia is again a global actor. Alongside India and China and Brazil, Russia has assumed a protagonist role. Much of the empire is gone but Russia's aspirations remain. Today Russia is showing its muscles. Moscow has tried to negotiate with Iran on the nuclear issue and has

strengthened its ties with Tehran. It is mediating with Hamas in Palestine. Still, though a weak Russia is a danger for the world balance of power, a strong Russia worries Washington. But a strong Russia to counter uncontrollable America appeals to much of the world. For many people in the world, Cold War at low risk is better than hot war in Iraq … or nuclear threats launched at Iran.

"America is never friendlier with Russia than when it is divided, poor, its economy in shambles, its empire dismantled. But Washington cannot control China or India, nor, we Odessites believe, can it contain Russia even though it aims at dividing it and crushing its influence."

* * *

After dinner in the hotel we listen again to the tape of the wordy monologue. It still makes a powerful impression. Yet, flashbacks of the Potemkin staircase predominate my mind: Eizenstein's tour de force demonstration of dialectical materialism at work … without the use of words. Today he might show America's lily pads as the thesis, the growing revolt of people everywhere to their presence and the resulting suffering as the antithesis, and a world uprising against capitalist exploitation as the synthesis.

My mental rambling calls to mind my university seminars on political theory and the famous quote from Marx: *It is not the consciousness of men that determines their social being, but their social being that determines their consciousness.* The Potemkin film is a reminder that theory becomes a material force as soon as it has gripped the masses. Strange that I'd never carried such thoughts outside the classroom until now.

Still, I have other things on my mind: Antonia, and where our relationship is going. I think that's on her mind too. She's restless, keeps roaming around the big room, from balcony to bar to bath. I tell her about my stormy relationship with Katharina, about how I'd feared that the worst thing that could happen to me would be separation from her.

Antonia seems curiously detached, not upset. Not in the least jealous. That is the past. She is a woman of the present and the future. She sits on the edge of the bed, listens to my story and then tells me she too is at the end of a relationship of two years with a man her age in Burgas. She is edging away from him because he wants to take a job as an accountant in a small business, get married and start a family.

Shortly before midnight, a strange scene takes place in our room, number 666—maybe it seemed so significant because of that famous biblical number! Is it really the number of the devil? I read that the Babylonians invented the magical essence of the number by totaling their 36 gods, 1+2+3+4+5 and so on, giving a total of 666, and I suppose one of those gods was the devil himself. *Ach, Christus und Maria*, the numbers in my life! Katharina's RU486 abortion pill. The 2245-meter depth of the Black Sea. Well, thank some god I'm not superstitious although I am beginning to accept concepts of fate and destiny. Anyway, concerning the scene in our room, which could just as well have been 555, I, the observer, want to reconstruct it and record it and hold it close to me because I believe it has a bearing on the constitution of the continuation of our life together. As usual, it is Antonia who acts out the scene; I instead have only tried to chronicle it. I recall my own peculiar sense of detachment at certain moments during those minutes ... and my participation at others. Till now our conversation has been normal conversation. Important, fundamental but normal. Normal as I imagine between normal people. Not like between unpredictable Katharina and me. And now, there is her abortion number, emblematic of Katharina's refusal of anything close to normal human life. Even Cliff is finding normality. I, instead, all this time, have been drifting on that rudderless raft of my dreams.

"I want more from life than that," Antonia begins, kicking off her shoes and removing the blue jacket I love. The light blue is a perfect frame for her Germanic blond hair. In her most down-to-earth manner she speaks of herself, the first time she has done that, always reluctant to speak of her own inner life, her desires, her dreams. "I've learned languages, am in my last year at the university and have always been at the top of my class. That has made me more daring, I suppose. Leonid thinks so. I want to live abroad, continue my studies in West Europe, probably Germany. Leonid doesn't want to understand my dreams. I've thought of doing graduate work in art history, which intrigues me. Or in comparative literature. Or both. I might aim at an academic career. Above all I want to learn how to live life right … the only life I have. Learn what is good in life. And what is evil. We debate that constantly in Bulgaria. Most people thought the end of Communism would change everything. Now people see the folly of that hope. We students also read Blagovesta's blogs. Is she right and our capitalist government wrong? I want answers. What's the right way to live? It's my life, Karl Heinz! I want to grow," she murmurs, unbuttoning her white silk blouse, liberating her perfect twenty-two year old breasts. She has never been so bold with her body. In her way, not Katharina's, she almost acts with abandon. Yet, in her, it seems natural, not an act of seduction. Not necessarily. "I want to do more with it. You're a journalist, a writer; you can be satisfied with your progress. But I'm nowhere. You might think I'm loose," she says, standing up and letting her skirt drop to the floor, an enigmatic smile on her lips and in her eyes. "Maybe you think I'm immoral, to have come away with you. Maybe in a way, I am. But just at the start. Actually I only thought of showing you Varna where I once lived. Now things have changed. I've seen how sensitive you are. I like that. Not many people in Bulgaria have the possibility or means for doing just as they like. And sensitivity dies easily … in moments of need and want. In a way, most of us in Bulgaria are more prisoners today than under Communism."

Antonia slips off her panties and stands before me in all her beautiful nakedness. Germanic appearance, Slavic soul. "At least you can decide and do what you want," she murmurs. "You make me feel free too … with you," she says playfully, fully aware of her effect and calmly pulling back the beige bed covers. Wordlessly I watch her stretch out on her back on the tight white sheets, her hands behind her head, her knees bent and her gorgeous tanned legs slightly open. Now purposely seductive and provocative, that too for the first time. Or perhaps it's her style of seduction, in action since the first evening in Burgas.

During her entire act I have either gaped at her beautiful body or tried to turn away searching for some minimum countenance and control. I'm aware of the misunderstanding of our respective roles. At one point I open the balcony door and glance at the Sea. It looks ominous. From our sixth floor, its tremendous depth, the blackness of those depths and the Sea's unnatural winds oceanographers describe and that so terrified ancients mariners give me the shivers more than does the memory of the nightmarish raft. While Antonia was still dressed, I let myself dwell on the darkness. Oh, the darkness of those depths! I was never afraid of the dark. I used to let the night hold me in its arms. The night is a comfort. Darkness is familiar. Even the sounds of silence in the darkness calm me. I used to get up early mornings just to witness the end of the night and salute it, knowing it would soon return. The end was no less beautiful than the twilight and the beginning of the night. But seas and lakes mean fear. The Wannsee and Lago Bracciano and now the Black Sea appear as a triad of terror. The still Sea lying down there in the darkness is fearsome in its tideless silence. Or, perhaps, my fixation on bodies of water might not be terror at all. Maybe it's just extreme fascination and my fear of just letting go.

Now I rip my eyes from her on the bed and open the fridge. I take out a fruit juice for her, pour myself a double vodka and take a lamo. The sudden need has risen from my guts. Caused by her beautiful body. Her nearness. Our togetherness. "*Jaden sam*," I say nervously. Very thirsty. Then "*Prosit!*"

"*Na zdrave!*" she retorts. "So you've been studying, eh?"

"It's true that I have the economic means to do anything I choose. That's a certain freedom. But not total. For can we ever do just what we want? As a rule, I'm pill and alcohol dependent. Much less so with you. But I feel useless. That's why I'm on this trip. Maybe that brought me to you," I say, unbuttoning my shirt. "But then we have to get you back to the university soon," I offer, trying to hold my ground. I'm already addicted to her constant optimism and easy manners. But this natural display of her body has changed our relationship. Again. Ah, Slavic women! Those online ads promoting Slavic wives are right.

I kick off my shoes and add, completely beside the point, "Still, I want to take you to Munich to introduce you to a friend. On the other hand, it will do me good to stay away from Berlin for a while. Antonia, listen to me. I hope you will agree. I have a feeling both our lives are going to change. But you have to promise me one thing."

"What's that, Westerner?"

"That you'll teach me Bulgarian," I mutter idiotically. "If Elmer can learn it, so can I."

For an answer she just gazes at me, a half smile on her lips and in her eyes.

"Do you want our … uh, our relationship to develop into real love?" I ask now, approaching her from a new angle. "Lasting love, I mean?"

"Oh, yes. Yes, I do."

Oh, Antonia, if you only knew! She's so young … and so beautiful. She is one of those women who take their beauty for granted. It's part of her being. She has never displayed or shown it off provocatively. Not until tonight. I wonder about her sudden departure with me. What could her parents think? And what did he, uh, what did Leonid think?

"*Dobre, dobre*!" she adds impatiently. "Enough conversation. *Kakvo pravish*? What are you doing still there? Come to bed. I'll teach you how to say other things and what they mean." Later she says, "*O, tova e dobre*. That is good." Like most women she wants to teach me lessons. I know that too.

And later, much later she says, "*Obicham te*, I believe I adore you. Already."

Her 'already' struck like a thunderbolt. Why? Can it be true? Katharina taught me otherwise. Adore me? But I know what she means.

When later she whispers in my ear, "*leka nosht*", I understand that she means it. She would not be purring and demanding during the rest of the night. She's a contented feline, ready for rest. In that moment of the beginning of a *leka nosht* I have the thought that it really will be a good night.

"*Bist Du jetzt verliebt in mich*?" I murmur in her ear.
"*Jawohl, das bin ich ... glaube ich.*"

* * *

Telephone hour in the alcove near the balcony door. Cliff and I speak in Italian ... just in case. He and Elizaveta are going to Russia. Then Lala is on the line. We speak English. She has had no word from Elmer. Not even Alvin has called. At 9:15 I reach Alvin in his office. That man's as regular as a clock. He says that in the military you have to follow the stupid little rules in order to get away with murder on the big issues. Shankland knows something about Elmer but his lips are sealed. Alvin suspects Elmer lily padded to Georgia but has no idea whether he's in or out of jail. One thing seems certain: Elmer is destined for Afghanistan. He will make a great field communications man. A quick way to die, Alvin says, for you're out there alone on some mountain all the time.

Then my guilt call to Katharina. Though it's early for her, she answers immediately, strangely wide awake at this hour. Side effects from the abortion? None. She didn't expect any. Nor did I. For her it is a non-event.

"Uh, Karl Heinz, *Schatz*"—she has never called me dear before—"by the way, I've met someone."

"Oh, yeah?"

"A doctor. An Italian. He wants me to live with him … someplace in Tuscany."

"A doctor? What kind of a doctor? Is he the one who did the scraping?"

"Oh, Karl, don't be so proper. What does it matter? He wants to get married too."

"Get married?" I keep echoing her.

"What is it about you Italians, always wanting to get married? But this time, I might. Then you'll have the whole Wannsee villa to yourself."

Surprisingly, I am momentarily overjoyed.

"If you go, leave your key."

"Don't worry your bourgeois self. This time I will leave the key. After all, it's forever this time." Despite her brutal words she sounds somewhat contrite. Unlike my old Katharina, she seems uncertain of herself. As if something had changed her. Maybe it was the pregnancy. Or the abortion. Or just age. Or could it be genuine affection for the Italian doctor? Or just the same old game afoot with a new lover? No matter at this point. This was inevitable: another breakaway, another dash for freedom. Our stay in Perugia was fine for her. It was abroad. It was mysterious. Perugia was escape. Wannsee is instead a prison for one of her natures.

After my joy, my second reaction to this turn of events regarding my life of the last fifteen years is unexpected: jealousy. Mild and attenuated and contradictory, but still jealousy. Who is this Italian she's fucking around with? Can it be true she's leaving me? Well, she did it once … and for my grandfather. I've told hardly anyone about that embarrassing interlude, an interlude that lasted over a decade. *Per l'amore di Dio*! I'm a bit numb. But I don't feel her loss this time as I did then. Not yet anyway. Not like those years of suffering over her in Rome when I nearly drank myself to death. Either it's not true, I think, after we ring off, or it's highly unlikely.

Yet when I call Berlin again in the late morning, I get her recorded message. She has already gone. After my first call when my loss was still only potential, I had only told her to leave her key. In irony. When I called the second time and she was physically gone, I felt an emptiness surge up from my guts. Her recorded message was as brutal as was her good-bye: 'If you are calling for Katharina she is no longer at this phone number, at this street address, in this city, or this country.' You couldn't get more final than that. A decade and a half of my only life left with her. Yet I ask myself again if her departure is a loss.

For now there is Antonia. Antonia, who saved my life on the raft. She can do it again. Admittedly that changes things. In my favor. Katharina was always uncertain, from the very start only potential. The future tense doesn't exist in her vocabulary. Now, I can discern the contours of a future without her. Still, despite such rationale, the feeling of the potential loss of Katharina lingers. Contradictorily, I think, the sense of real loss might ... well, though I doubt it, but if at all, it will come later.

Thinking back on the Freud seminar in my university days, I recall our reading of Freud's "Mourning and Melancholia" and of Walter Benjamin's related works. I preferred the latter for reasons I've chiefly forgotten but presumably because of his emphasis on melancholy in general. I've always been a melancholy type, I remind myself, slapping one hand in the other. I don't mean to say pathologically. I mean I'm not suicidal. Nothing like that. At the most, according to my father's psychologist friend and his Rorschach test, I could become a troublemaker because I interpreted ink signs he didn't even see. But I am not sick. Certainly I'm often uneasy. But my depression is not clinical. I'm just sad and now disoriented by the novelty of her abrupt absence from my life … as if she'd jumped off a cliff. And sadness and mourning do go hand in hand. That must be my Italian sub-nature. In any case, Freud exaggerated, I believe. Still, the fact remains that she's gone, gone, gone. I accept that. She will not come back this time. I accept that too. Like Cliff's dead daughter. Like Hakim and Nikitin. When she left me fifteen years ago I didn't accept the loss. Now I do. But I'm still sad. If not for Antonia, I would most likely sink into depression. Nonetheless I *am not sick*. My sadness is not an illness to be treated. It is just my nature, my mood, my attitude toward the world. Not a pathology. Yes, she is gone. But I've learned something new, something fundamentally important—Katharina is replaceable. She is being replaced. The proof is my relationship with Antonia. Antonia proves that I too am in constant change. I'm not the same person today that I was 15 years ago. This time I don't have to wallow in my grief and feel sorry for myself, ashes in my hair, my clothes in tatters. I'm flowing with the events, changing, changing, changing. People usually get over such events. Though, yes, something will remain. But I too am headed toward the right life that Antonia spoke of last night. Gone too, or nearly, my old phobias about Katharina. Oh, Christ! I remember them well. Phobias about her sexuality, her sexual adventurism, her preference for her beautiful nakedness, her latent or active—I never knew for certain—nymphomania, our insatiability one for the other, my jealousies and suspicions coupled with my erotic images of her together with other men, my Candaule complex. No, I will never forget Katharina. Nor my wonderful Candaule complex either. I will be sad I lost her but my melancholia is enough payment. Sufficient for my redemption. I'm already far along the road of detachment from her. Maybe I was even before I got her message. Antonia is already replacing her. Just a few more steps and Katharina will be replaced.

I pause, flip open my laptop and open my old Freud notes. There it is: "One of the craziest but most captivating implications Freud suggests is the bewildering insinuation that the melancholic's lost object is still half-alive." True, I suppose. But how devastating! Like Katharina. She is a lost object. And therefore not living. Yet the image of her I retain is not dead either since she still exists in one way or another within my melancholic consciousness. For me, she is half-alive ... like buried-alive. The pathology, if it is pathology—which I deny—of the melancholic state is that it cannot just let go. Anyway, let's face it; the rupture is not really about Katharina. This is about me and my personal freedom. Despite the intensity of our relationship, Katharina's shadow will not stay behind me much longer. Not long at all. She will depart. Depart with her Italian doctor to Tuscany and I will be free of her. Well, some memories will remain. I suppose I will miss her sometimes. I might miss and want her fire. But only a memory will remain. A shadow of a memory. Nothing wrong with memories. A few anyway. Then, maybe, as Freud says, a little bit of mourning must enter the process of my detachment from her. Yet, this time, I know she is gone never to return. That is final. For me, this time she is dead—or soon will be—and I can live, I hope, together with Antonia, in freedom from the albatross Katharina, who until just a few days ago still hung heavy around my neck. This liberating work might be slow and painful but I will rid myself of all the memories that still have some hold on me. Well, no, not actually rid myself of them. I don't know if I even want to. But at least those memories will become a pleasant part of my life, the kind you record nostalgically, wistfully, in a diary. And re-read years later ... and you remember. Memories that someday I will be able to chat with Antonia about. I should be grateful to my melancholic nature that, in this case, gives me a hand in the unification of my mind, spirit and body.

Lebewohl, Katharina. *Zdrasti*, Antonia.

* * *

Again in the alcove. Afternoon. Trying to think other thoughts. In the light breeze rising from the Sea the curtain dances playfully, gracefully, elusively around me. Small ships navigate seemingly aimlessly in the harbor. Ripples on the water today. Current from the direction of the Dardanelles, I decide. Or perhaps from the unruly Caucasus in the East. More in keeping with political reality. Is Elmer really over there somewhere? In jail? Or on some other lily pad packing his bags for Afghanistan? Where he will die? Can it be true that they are so close: both death and that different world? Useless for us to go to Munich if Cliff is not there. Maybe we should go to Russia too. But then Antonia needs to get back to school. And I want to stay close to her in Burgas. Study Bulgarian for a few months. Rent an apartment. *Um Gotteswillen*! Life is unpredictable. That day sitting in the Frankfurt Bahnhof café, drinking beer and Dornkaat, Cliff had no idea how he would change my life. Maybe today something über-consequential will happen. Or, I could just sit around and drink and make love with Antonia like those days and nights and years with Katharina. Or Antonia and I could go look for a beach along the Sea. A Russian immigrant I knew in Berlin praised a place he used to go fishing somewhere here close. In the estuary. Could look that up. But no, that's no good either. Too much to do elsewhere. I've seen the staircase ... and some of Russia in Ukraine. Time to get back to Burgas and get situated. A little fixedness won't hurt. The Elmer story is perplexing, somewhat frightening. And what about this Raymond guy? He must be involved.

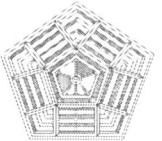

16

CLIFF

MY LIFE story has come to seem like a series of Chinese shadow plays. In my mind, reality—or perhaps its shadows—forms distorted images of a fictitious present. Or representations of a shadowy past forcing its way back into the unreal present. Maybe I have never really known the difference between dream and reality. Admittedly sometimes the difference seems minimal. My spymaster father never learned the difference either. He seemed to believe the two are separated by only a short uncertain step, an elusive thin line, a nearly undetectable shift in direction at the point the main life road divides into many alternative routes. Maybe because of the irrationality of those shadows I have never actually *tried* to recognize the difference between dream and reality. At least what I remember of old dreams and old realities is almost indistinguishable. Mindscape, I read. What is it really? Like landscape? That is what you see. But mindscape? Is it simply what you imagine? Your dream world? The world you might like to live in but never will? Sometimes I strive for mindscape and believe I want to exist in it. But I remind myself that shadow plays are deceptive and that I'm just barely past the midpoint between the old and the new.

We took the Lufthansa noon flight for Moscow-Sheremetovo. Elizaveta's first trip to Russia. Three hours later, Moscow. The fast and coldly efficient customs and passport control recalls the Frankfurt airport. It's because I booked at the revered Natsionalny Hotel, which took care of the "invitation" to Russia, visas and all the bureaucratic hogwash remaining from the old times.

I describe to Elizaveta the experience of how Soviet Russian customs control specialized in inducing guilt feelings in each foreign arrival. How the Russian uniformed official would stare unblinking at your passport for an endless time as if searching for secret coded messages in your biographical data. Endlessly fascinated, he would study the visas and entry and exit stamps from other passport controls of the world. From time to time the official looked up at you and stared into your eyes as if trying to discern the true reason you were there. His look alone made you quake in your foreign shoes and nervously finger your foreign clothes. What could you want in Moscow in the dead of winter? You didn't belong, he was thinking. What was your real purpose? Here, people were trying to survive; his wife had just had another abortion, their one-room apartment was progressively more crammed and his long-awaited raise was held up because his boss considered him a slacker.

What shady business did I, the alleged Mister Clifford Beecher Jr., have in mind in winter in Moscow?

What did I want there?

In those times each person passing that desk felt guilty. Collectively guilty. Because we came from the rich capitalist West. Was that the official's real purpose? To establish that collective guilt?

Priests tell us that guilt is only personal. Do Christians today not share guilt collectively? How many not only do not protest but openly support war and its atrocities? Our boys are over there to defend democracy. No? That is a terrible reality. Is it enough to pray for the evildoers and sinners, for the dead soldiers and the dead civilians and have faith in divine prerogative to make things right? The biblical God blamed entire peoples for their wrongs, and punished them collectively.

It seems that the more powerful the nation or the faith, the less it feels a need for morality. Today the Catholic Church of Catholic Bavaria where I live is leading a battle against moral relativism; but the reality is that without relativity, morality becomes in the end its opposite: immorality. Still, the belief in a terrible gap between morality in Western and non-Western cultures is crap.

Outside, the once gray streets are now colorful.

In the taxi, I continue thinking aloud, intellectualizing.

Elizaveta stares at me as if I were nuts.

Yet I go on. Based on the experiences of eighteenth and nineteenth century colonialism, I pronounce, the majority view among Europeans — right up until discussions of the Iraqi war and the exportation of democracy — has been that their moral values are superior to those of other cultures. Just ask our famous Orientalists in their academic institutions about it. Few think all moral values have equal or relative validity. On the other hand, a cultural abyss divides schools of thought about European moral superiority: liberal thinkers on one side and religious fundamentalists on the other. Liberal relativists believe that the truth or falsity of moral judgments is not absolute or universal but relative to the traditions, convictions or practices of a group of people. One problem for pure moral relativism is that it cannot account for the truth that practices such as the Holocaust in Germany or slavery in the United States are in any case wrong and evil. The reaction to such reality is outrage: in the Church's perception relativists pose a threat to civilized Western society. Here, however, is a pertinent counter consideration: isn't the steady degeneration facing the world today the reality that a limited number of members of a society hold great power over the rest — with the agreement of society itself? Though those with less power are stupid to agree to such an arrangement, their agreement does not delegate authority to the elite to establish what is right and what is wrong, which is what unlimited power does. The people without power do not have to accept a set of values imposed by the minority just because they agreed to give them power in the first place. If your officer orders you to murder Jews or women and children, you are not morally obligated to kill them.

All the while I observe our passage into the city in astonishment. Russian flags aswirl everywhere. White, blue and red. But I know that red flags with the hammer and sickle symbol are hidden away along this route and that they occasionally return to Red Square. You can see them in protest demonstrations on TV newscasts. Still a minority but definitely they are making a comeback. Some believe they will soon become a majority. The question is: Is that a menace or a prospect?

Elizaveta sees the city as quite normal.

The heavy traffic, the churches, the rich colors and the skyscrapers amaze me. Little Soviet architecture remains. Little Stalinist influence left. Capitalism reigns. But then there are those sporadic waving red flags.

Suddenly, my philosophic outburst still in my mind, I'm surprised by Elizaveta chattering away in Russian with the taxi driver. I sometimes forget she's Russian. Everything's upside down. I haven't been back here for decades yet it seems natural to hear and speak Russian again. Well, not natural, actually strange, but Elizaveta speaking Russian changes things.

Now I wonder: will I even have occasion to see what lies under Moscow's newfound glitter? Despite the apparent efficiency of Russian-style capitalism in comparison to the past I once knew, what will it reveal? In our case, will the new state be able to uncover, or even be interested in uncovering what we are seeking—a woman, a former KGB spy, a mother: Elizaveta's mother?

Masha Orlova might have vanished and, as we fear, been reincarnated as another person, with another name and a new family.

* * *

The Natsionalny Hotel, in my opinion always Moscow's best, is today even more magnificent, more resplendent. Efficiency, if not perfection, is the rule. "Thank God," I shout after we have settled in, "some Russian characteristics peep through the pretentious French management. The French will never impart their pomposity into the Russian soul."

Female employees on each floor still have something of the former *dezhurnaya* about them: the fat, sour and bossy woman who once controlled the keys and lives of guests on *her* floor.

Moscow's best hotel restaurant looking toward Red Square and the Kremlin is still a Russian restaurant, despite its international menu—the complex, flowery desserts are still the too sweet, calorie rich, Russian desserts.

Our spacious room is Russian. Heavy furniture and drapes and chair covers are quite French sophisticated but the room retains a Russian spirit. Pre-revolutionary, but Russian.

"I feel good here today, as I never did back then," I say, sprawling over a wide chaise longue with a double vodka in hand.

"Why is that? Did you hate it here before?"

"This was enemy territory ... and Russian officialdom treated me as an enemy. Then, the West won and everything changed. Me, as much as Russia."

"*Was willst Du damit sagen?*" What do you mean?

I try to describe that cold atmosphere. It was abnormal. Everything here was the opposite of what people abroad imagined. They were all off base. The optimists who wanted the Communist experiment to work and the Western Communists who spent vacations in Crimean spas, as well as the anti-communist critics for whom nothing in the USSR could be good. They were all wrong. None of them realized that the greatest social experiment of recent centuries had blossomed and was burning out.

While I reminisce about old times in the comfort and luxury of our rooms in the famous old Natsionalny, night falls over Red Square and the steeples of the Kremlin churches. Dimmed street lamps flicker along the boulevards. Traffic down below is heavy but noiseless, creating an unnatural ambivalence.

"It was both good and bad. Here in Moscow, I mean … in my time."

* * *

I have two potential sources of information concerning Elizaveta's mother, Masha Orlova—if that was her real name, and if she did not marry Nikitin and take his name. For that matter I was never certain that Nikitin was his legal name. He could have married her under the name Ernst Schmidt, a name that is documented somewhere. A real person. Masha could be concealed behind the same name that concealed the sleeper Nikitin for years.

From Nikitin I had the name of a Russian intelligence operative, Viktor Kataev, running a private intelligence organization. And I had an old contact in the German Embassy from the time I was stationed in Moscow. Concerning the latter, I know that embassies sometimes retain for decades unexpected information: mounds of dusty old files, or, even better, an ancient file clerk. Someone who has worked there so long that he has become as common as a piece of furniture, but whose mind teems with memories.

I had called Kataev from Munich. I think if anyone knows or can find out about Masha, this ex-KGB officer is the man. Strange that Nikitin himself had not asked Kataev for information about his great love. Perhaps he was afraid what he might uncover.

The next morning we walk to the Arbat address. The sun is warm. The streets packed with people, just as the Moscow of my times. The crowds on Moscow streets are constant, ubiquitous. Life, the real *movida*. Just as I did twenty-five years ago, I still wonder where they are all going. Soviet Russia, Russian Russia, the crowds still perform the same actions.

Elizaveta is less impressed than I. For her, this is like other big modern cities. For me, Moscow is still Moscow, though transformed, transfigured, reborn. The number of eateries of every kind is astounding. Russians eat and drink at any time of the day or night. Slavs will always be Slavs. I describe to Elizaveta how soon after my arrival at my first post in Moscow in the early 1980s, one day I walked the streets in search of a place to lunch and ended up eating only ice cream in three different cafés. Couldn't find a bite of real food. Ah, those were indeed the days!

This Moscow of red and green, yellow and ochre, soaring onion church steeples and gleaming office buildings is a new phenomenon. A new sunrise beyond the steppes and the taiga. If Tsar Peter the Great could only see this.

Kataev's institute is on the first floor of a green pastel-colored building on Ulitza Arbat in the heart of the former Moscow Montmartre. Mounting the stairs, we hear strains of music. Loud, then soft, then loud again. Someone can't find the proper volume. It's Mussorgsky. *Pictures At An Exhibition.* The Russian soul.

A man about my age comes out to greet us at the reception desk. He looks successful. Jacket and tie, shiny shoes, too much belly and a red face. Each evening he must say thanks to the concept of outsourcing as I once did. I imagine him over heavy, vodka-soaked lunches, making the same kind of deals Franzi and I used to with CIA and Saudi and Israeli intelligence agencies. He is a modern mercenary, as we were when we ran our Engadine Sociological Studies Foundation out of St. Moritz. Nikitin was right. Once in this business, it's hard to get out. In that respect I thank my lucky stars for my inheritance ... though maybe I should feel shame. The part of my father's money that didn't originate in the CIA came down to me from his business enterprises built on Agency money.

Again, there is the surprise of Elizaveta speaking Russian. No longer perfect, but Russian Russian, learned as a child from the woman we're looking for. I don't know what language to speak with Kataev. My Russian is still rusty. It will take some days to recapture the rhythm. So after the few generalities in Russian, I stick to English. Kataev seems happy with that.

"I heard what happened to old Nikitin and some of your friends. Sorry about that. It seems you came out of it in one piece."

"Not everyone did. My father died ... but of old age. But we did put an end to the Chadafö operation. I suppose Moscow didn't escape unscathed from that either."

"Did you have a hand in that?"

"A murderous hand. I killed the Chadafö boss, an American. And then I got out of the business." I realize in that moment that I relish my frank but brutal confession. My expiation. "She," I say looking at Elizaveta, "is my new life. And I've broken into journalism."

"You're fortunate," Kataev murmurs.

"But we're not here for old reasons, nor for journalism either. This is all personal. We're looking for Elizaveta's mother. I have the honor of presenting to you the daughter of Anatoly Nikitin."

Only a flicker of surprise shows in Kataev's eyes but I know he must be struck by the revelation. "He never told me a word of it when he was here the last time."

"Her name was Masha Orlova. That is, that's the name we know. If she and Nikitin married, it's not excluded that she used also the name Schmidt ... since he was legally known as Ernst Schmidt. Masha worked for your people, came back here to search for her father ... by mistake or by choice, we don't know. I think out of naiveté. In any case, she never returned. Never contacted her daughter or Nikitin. Her cover was blown in Munich. Now we want to find her."

"Of course we'll try to help. Uh, Clifford, you might not know this but our agents who returned home from abroad for one reason or another were treated well. As a rule. There must be a record of her some place."

Kataev picks up a phone. A young male assistant is there in an instant. "Zhenya, check out these names, Masha Orlova or Masha Nikitina or Masha Schmidt, German spelling. Scan all our lists. Agents at home and abroad. Ex-agents. Returning agents. Resettlement lists. All agencies. I should think from the early '80s."

"By the way, Masha's mother was Latvian," I add. "I didn't say earlier that she and her parents were living in Latvia when the war began. Then went to Germany during the war. Masha could have gone back to Riga of course ... while it was still USSR. That's abroad now, but still—"

Kataev grins. "We've still got a lot of leverage there. I would bet she did go there. The name is a problem. We forget how important are names. Then there were so many name changes in Latvia before and after the war. A country where surnames are already difficult to decipher—names of German origin, Russian origin, Jewish origin and with their peculiar Latvian endings."

"As a child I often heard the name Kalninsh," Elizaveta said. "*Dedushka* Kalninsh. My grandfather, I believe. At Christmas time, Mother told me he always became *Ded Moroz*, Father Christmas."

"Kalninsh! With that final letter 's' with the mark over it."

"Actually I think the Kalnins were of Russian origin too ... long ago. I recall vaguely a name like Dubrovka or something similar."

"You've got quite a memory, young lady," Kataev says. "Still, the real mystery is why she didn't simply go back to Germany and find you. I hope that doesn't mean that maybe she's, uh, deceased."

"That's what I wonder every day," Elizaveta answers Kataev in Russian. "Why didn't she come looking for me? *Pochemu niet?*"

"OK, Zhenya, check anything you can find in Latvia. All the names mentioned. And especially for the years after 1985 and before Latvia broke away from the USSR."

"You want me to go into the still closed files?"

Kataev gazes at the young man for an instant, then at me. Especially those, I think of the KGB files. If I could only get my hands on them alone for an hour or so.

As if in my mind, Kataev adds: "All of them."

Turning back to us, Kataev shrugs: "Doubtful we'll find anything but I would place my bets on Latvia."

"Logically, yes. But strange things happen in lives. Unexpected things. And I don't mean only death. I could be in Turin today. Instead I'm living a new life and am back here with a second wife. Masha Orlova was not too old to make a new life someplace here. In Moscow too."

"Possible."

"Look, my only other hope here is the German Embassy. Elizaveta's a German citizen. And I have an old contact there who was stationed here in the early 1980s when I was. I was a kid then but he'd been around. Knew everybody ... knew everything. He's expecting me. Helmut Bachmeier. Ever heard of him?"

"Heard of him! I've known him for years ... he's practically a friend."

"I hope to get into their archives. The Germans knew everything about every Russian in Germany then ... especially those émigrés who came back to Russia. They always hoped to find double or even triple agents among them. And that Bachmeier! He was a specialist among specialists. There might be something buried down in their cellars about Masha Orlova."

"Also in our cellars," Kataev says, and laughs an ironic laugh. "Ah, Clifford, those were the years, eh? OK. Give me a call later today. Or tomorrow morning. And, uh, Elizaveta, in the meantime we'll see what we can dig up about your mother. But I think you have to be prepared to face surprises. Twenty-five years is a long time after all."

"Uh, yeah," I say. "How I would like to get lost down in your cellars for a few days. Uh, Viktor, one last matter … for purely journalistic purposes of course."

"Of course. No problem. Tell me."

"Georgia? The little war? The U.S. military bases all around Russia? Is Russia afraid? Will Russia hold together? Will it disintegrate? What's your reading?"

Elizaveta frowns. "For journalistic purposes," I reassure her.

"Moscow doesn't like it," Kataev begins. "But we Russians have patience. That's one of our fundamental characteristics. Patience. We can wait. But we're also tenacious. Military bases don't make an empire. They will vanish with time. Tsars have more endurance. Trade, occupation, colonization, language, schools, tradition, links and more links. That's the stuff of empires. Uzbekistan, Kyrgyzstan, all of Central Asia depends on Russia for those existential things. Military bases change little wherever they are. Russia learned its lesson in Afghanistan. Now America is learning it in the same place … in the same way. Military occupation isn't enough even though Washington seems to think it is. Maybe the USA wants more than empire building. Rapid exploitation seems the direction. But Clifford, there's another dimension: America's fixation on Russia. Fear? Russia? Russia is pretty calm today. Its Tsar is calm too. And he's ready. Georgia showed that. The Russian Tsar thinks this way: OK, let them play around in Georgia, elect an idiot President, send in a few troops. But if they step over the line, wham! On the other hand, we don't have to have a clear policy on Iran. Let'em guess, Americans and Iranians too. Iran sits there and waits … like another giant trap for America. We don't have that problem. We don't like the situation in the Ukraine either—we still think of it as part of Russia. Not a separate nation. We know if things go too far, the new country of Ukraine will split.

The south, Odessa and the Crimea and the east of Ukraine will return to Russia. Similarly, the Baltic. Estonia, Latvia, Lithuania—all depend on Russia. Russia has the gas and oil now. A powerful weapon. More useful internationally than nuclear weapons of which we also have plenty.

"No, Clifford, fear lives in America. Less here. America moves in fear. We wait. We will continue to wait. No, military bases don't make an empire. The Romans learned that a long time ago.

"And as for your journalism, keep in mind that Communism has nothing to do with anything anymore. You know quite well that Russian Communism, 'socialism in one country' as Tsar Stalin called it, was pure Russian nationalism. Yes, Clifford, we can wait it out."

"But what about security? Russia must feel the pressure of all the U.S.-NATO bases around its borders."

"Clifford, you know as well as I that Europeans have forgotten the crime Germany committed against Russia in World War Two. Seventeen million Russian victims. Westerners believe in the holocaust, oh yes ... and that America defeated Nazi Germany and saved Europe from Russian Barbarians. But you and I know the truth. Eight of every ten German soldiers died on the Russian front while America waited until Russia had been nearly destroyed before entering the war. We know America wants to get its hands on Siberia's resources. America thinks it's 'unfair' that Russia has all that. The problem as I see it is that our government is still concerned with security in a traditional military and political sense. Blocs, alliances, balance of forces and interests. Too little long range strategy. That's not the approach of the USA and Europe either. At the same time, West Europeans don't feel Russia as a threat. America does. Americans are indoctrinated to feel threatened. America uses fear as a defense, as if an attack on the USA were imminent."

"But your neighbors like Ukraine and the Baltic states feel

insecure. And they don't want alliances with Russia … just trade agreements and good neighbor policies."

"Yet we hope to engage them in collective defense … like in the old times."

"Which they refuse."

"Right. Still, West Europe is not inflexible today. It needs our gas and oil, while America interprets our trade policies as disguised attempts to undermine NATO. And they are! Everybody—Russia and our neighbors, West Europe, the USA and Iran too—knows that not everything is rosy in the security sphere. NATO and OSCE will never be enough to alleviate those fears. The main problem in the world is always America. Our think tanks conclude that America aims at crushing Russia, taking Siberia and temporarily dividing the world with China. That of course is a chimera. A neocon pipe dream. America's problem is that it doesn't know the world."

"That's clear," I say, glancing at Elizaveta now fidgeting and frowning, ready to move on. She must think my search for her mother is only play-acting to cover my real interests. "One thing however is not clear," I add, now nervous myself and rushing to get in one last question. "Russian-Iranian relations. What's happening?"

"Our position is unclear. No foresight is my estimate. We support sanctions but only half-heartedly. The West wants more involvement from us. But Iran is unhappy about even the little pressure we exert on it. We're not with the West, but not with Iran either. Remember that Iran is our competitor on the European gas market. We want to block Iran as a competitor. Tough sanctions against it are advantageous to us."

"One former CIA director wants to bomb Iran's nuclear facilities. Many people agree and think it's inevitable."

"We don't agree with that. Sets a bad precedent. Iran can agree on the nuclear issues … if it wants too. A lot of national pride is involved here. Not doing anything at all about Iran's nuclear ambitions is bad. Strengthens the voice of those who want to bomb. But that's not in our interests either. Bomb Iran and you can bomb anywhere."

* * *

An unusually hot day in Moscow. Sweltering. Muggy. Midday evaporates into a sticky mass. The kind of heat that kindles fires in the surrounding forests. Brutal heat unbearable for Westerners and Russians alike. On such days *Moskvichi* go bonkers. Practically nude Slavic girls grab sun in the parks. Afternoons and evenings, bare-chested, beer-guzzling men cheer for their Torpedo or Spartak teams in Luzhniki Stadium. The pursuit of diversion exceeds avoidance of the devilish heat. Meanwhile, days have lengthened. Soon, they will seem to last forever and sleep retreats.

The German Embassy is near Lomonosov University and the Mosfilm studios, at the big bend in the River Moskva. Like many embassies around the world the German Embassy is an armed fortress. Our passports alone would not have gotten us in but my appointment with Helmut Bachmeier guarantees quick access past the guards and into a small waiting room. From every corner surveillance cameras stare down on us. We fidget. Try to act normal. Minutes later a slim, wiry man with thinning dark hair rushes in. They don't even want people in the waiting room for too long. Too many opportunities for mischief. Bachmeier's jacket is unbuttoned and his string tie askew. Although now well past middle age, his handshake is as firm as I remember it over twenty years ago.

He looks closely at Elizaveta before offering her his hand and a wry smile. "*Sie sind also die junge Dame die Ihre Mutter sucht.* So you're the young lady looking for her mother! *Kommt doch mit, alle beide.* Come along both of you. Maybe we'll come up with something … some clue."

The modern embassy, with low ceilings and bulletproof windows, at first feels cramped. Since the few remaining

Moscow townhouses that once housed embassies are security nightmares, the new building is contemporary embassy architecture. Bachmeier's office, overlooking a cobbled courtyard, instead is surprisingly spacious, its multicolored walls reminiscent of modern Dutch design. Beyond the gardens, beyond the traffic-infested avenues, the outline of the twisting Moskva River is visible.

Files and sheets of paper of different sizes and colors are spread haphazardly over his desk, I assume pertaining to Elizaveta's mother. "*Tatsächlich*!" Bachmeier exclaims, glancing at a photograph, then at Elizaveta. He offers us coffee and then gets down to business. I sip the coffee and scan the desk, the room, the windows. This space is super clean of bugs, no less than were my father's places in St. Moritz. Bachmeier looks at one file or the other. As I expected he is rich in documentation. Again I wonder why Nikitin, Elizaveta's father, didn't do this.

"Masha Orlova is listed as a regular, full-time employee of the American Committee from 1981 to 1987, registered with the German Labor Office … health insurance contributions and taxes all normal," Bachmeier reads from the first folder in the middle of his desk.

"One anomaly however," he says, switching folders. "She took a three month leave of absence in 1984, she said, to care for her sick father in Berlin. But a cross-check on Evgheny Orlov shows that he had vanished from West Berlin in December 1983. There is no documentation to tell us where she went during those three months. No visas issued, no passport stamps, nothing. She told personnel in Munich that she stayed in her sister's Berlin apartment. American security was lax. Of course much has been lost during these twenty-five years. But you must keep in mind that in that period some people went back and forth between East and West undocumented. Clandestinely. At the time, our analysts—the best in Europe of the era—concluded that Masha Orlova went to the East— East Berlin, Moscow, or her native Riga."

"That makes good sense," I say, glancing at Elizaveta. She nods, I know, disconcerted. "I remember my aunt once stayed with me at our Munich apartment ... I'd just started school and she took me there every day."

"Your mother returned to work three months later," Bachmeier continues, opening a third folder. "Two years later, in 1987—that was during the Gorbachev *glasnost* period here—she went missing. And never returned. Things were changing fast in Russia in those years. Apparently she was obsessed by her father's situation. Talked about it to everyone. Russia was changing but unfortunately the KGB hadn't yet changed. Maybe never has," he mutters, clears his throat, looks hard at the folder, then at me. "But that's another story. My conclusion is that Masha Orlova was only a low-level informant. Still, her Moscow bosses believed she was exposed in Munich and convinced her that she would be arrested if she returned to Germany and that her daughter, you Elizaveta, would suffer for it. They must have given her a new identity. We don't know whether or not she found your grandfather. I think your father, Anatoly Nikitin, a known spy, also avoided Munich to protect her and you. Then time passed. She might have met someone else in Moscow. Or in Latvia. After all, she was young enough to start a new family."

Elizaveta gasps.

"What about Riga then?" I ask. Suddenly I'm pessimistic. Things are not so clear and simplistic to me as to Bachmeier. My frustration grows. Maybe we're not supposed to learn what happened to her.

"For that we'll have to go to our cellars," he says dubiously. "Never liked that place. Helmut Amsel lives down there with his files and documentation, much of which is still uncategorized. Too disparate to file. Pieces of myriad information, stats, informant reports, diary and fake diary excerpts, travel itineraries, newspaper clippings, copies of passports, visas, assorted notes, old photographs, rumors, slanders and God knows what else. If my intelligence bosses in Berlin knew of its extent they would go crazy. They would ship it all off to Berlin and a thousand people would work thousands of hours trying to piece it all together. Never underestimate the unbridled ambitions of bureaucracy."

* * *

Dug deep down in Moscow earth, the cellar documents room is as big as a basketball court. The whole underground is reinforced concrete. Yet it is damp. Its walls sweating, almost swampy; the primordial smell of the nearby river permeating the space. Operatic music sounds teasingly from a dimly illuminated desk. You know and you do not know that this is still Russia. Unlike the modern rooms upstairs, down here the ceilings are high. Shelves over five meters high. Here and there are dispersed rolling ladders that the old file clerk, Helmut Amsel, manipulates like fighter jets. All over are strategically placed spotlights, now on dim, or extinguished. A box of switches lies under Amsel's hand: the hand of the creator of light.

"Files," Amsel says, "from way way back." File banks, file sections, file shelves, file rows. The files contain a bit of everything regarding Russo-German relations of over a century—surveillance files, phone and electronic tap files, spy reports, Stasi snitches, disinformation, Bundesnachrichtendienst reports, reports by CIA mercenaries and informants of many nationalities, and, I suspect, copies of files straight from Lubyanka surveillance dossiers and analyses of old KGB dossiers on displaced persons of 60 years ago: defectors, returnees, double agents, triple agents, and documentation on war, peace, cold war, diplomacy. Yet compartmentalization reigns in Helmut Amsel's cellar kingdom, a repository of an alternative history of modern Europe. Enough to make me feel muddle-headed.

"Orlova, Masha," Bachmeier whispers. He too seems to be in awe of the sensation of sacredness emanating from the cellar. In me, the dimness interrupted by sudden illuminations induces a suspicion of voodooism. And old Helmut Amsel is its High Priest. Mysterious little man. He has resisted time and world-shaking changes. He has hung on. Stringy hair on his scalp, wild bushes of black hairs popping from his nostrils and ears, darting black eyes. He claims he is 68 years old. That he was posted here at age 28, in the darkest Soviet times. Bachmeier had claimed he was at least 88. His service records, as far as they reach, prove it. "*Priviet*," Amsel says to Elizaveta. Without being told, he seems to know. As if he recognized her. "*Ochen priyatno. Ochen ochen priyatno.*" He squeezes her hand, looks around the sprawl and presses a switch.

"Orlova, Masha. Munich, 1980's. Moscow. Maybe Latvia. I know where she is."

The back left corner lights up like Red Square.

"She's there ... or nowhere. But I know she's there, in that corner, pretty high up."

In an instant he is back there. He slides a ladder and clambers up like a trapeze artist aiming for the heights. I imagine ropes and cords up there in the dimness. Scratching sounds echoing from the rear merge with the soft music from Amsel's desk. The scene is buried somewhere in my mind, some place where memory and my boy's imagination mingle and merge. A boy's mindscape. While he is up there on top, my memories run wild. St. Moritz, my Dad's sacred cellar he told me to stay away from. But when he was gone and Romanza and I were there alone I would sneak into his secret vault to examine his guns and peer at his files. I tried to draw the housemistress Romanza in too but she refused to enter my imagination. As a boy, my father was the reality. At the top of the heap. My absent mother was the dream; Romanza the unwilling interpreter. No wonder I'm still trying to learn the difference between dream and reality.

"Heh-heh-heh," reverberates from near the ceiling, down the sturdy steel ladder and toward us, a voice gloating and victorious, revealing the joy of his unfailing memory, his foxhound's instinct, his internal archive radar. This is Amsel's territory. His, his. His alone. Every centimeter of it. His. Masha Orlova, Nikitin, Elizaveta, Bachmeier, Clifford Beecher junior and senior. They are all the same to the file bank mouse.

Topo di archivio, I call him in my mind. He knows who I am, who, where and how we all are. The Cellar God in the German Embassy, 56 Mosfilmovskaya Ulitza, Moscow, knows us from where we appear on the page of his memory, from the physical consistency of our files: the colors, the sizes, the smells, the amount of dust we have gathered. He knows each of us in our own reality.

The trapeze artist-cellar mouse slides and glides in his descent from the heights and lands softly on his small feet. His elegant ascension, his joyous descent. He waves a thin green file. A blink, a heartbeat, and the image of my Russian literature professor at the university in Turin flashes across my mindscape. A little man too, he wrote of his enthusiasm for compiling a history of Russian letters based on the dance, that obsessive theme in Russian literature: the dancing feet in Pushkin, the obscure leaps of Lermontov's characters, the mazurkas of Griboyedov, Blok's serpentine dances, Bely's mountebanks. He believed that Russian literature itself, with its stormy heights, its continuous betting on the ultimate feelings of man: anxieties, psychoses, orgasms, terror—in comparison with which the rats of Camus' *La Peste* pale—with its propensity to change love into fire and torment, its repudiation of little Arcadias and its affection for the little man, is saved from scholars and cold analyses and clever but soulless exercises.

"She was allowed to move to Riga. 1988. A comfortable retirement. Minimal work duties. Still young. Still beautiful."

The mouse passes a black and white photo to Elizaveta. "She loved Gorbachev ... I'll copy all this stuff for you, known addresses too. Keep in mind, Elizaveta Orlova, that the person you are seeking may also perhaps be seeking you."

Spellbinding old man.

Shriveled prophet in a damned dank basement.

He looks like I imagine a *Domovoi*, the beloved old Russian household god, the shrunken old Grandpa with legendary magical powers, the *Dedushka*, ever ready to solve all the family problems. Now, with those addresses, everything has taken on a whole new dimension. Elizaveta hadn't expected it. But neither of us had known what we might find.

＊ ＊ ＊

Back at the hotel that night Elizaveta is nervous and tense. In the roof garden restaurant she fixates on the Kremlin walls.

No comments.

No reactions.

Silence.

I know what is passing through her mind: the memory of her mother from Munich is one thing. But being here on her trail, the idea of actually finding her with a new family cuts out a new scenario of her own life. How would her mother be? How would she, her first daughter, react to a sister, a brother, her mother's potential husband?

Later, we make love. Tenderly, very tenderly. Not the usual fiery way as is our nature. Then I hold her in my arms. She cuddles. I stroke her hair. She says, "That was so sweet. I needed that." She uses the word *süss*. I had never heard that description of lovemaking before. Sweet. In that context the word has a transcendental ring. I hold her as she drops off into her dreams.

17

MY FRIENDS in Soviet Leningrad used to scheme constantly for a way to get to Riga. I would night train from Moscow to experience the wonders of former St. Petersburg and they were instead plotting to drive the three hundred miles to Riga for the weekend. The marvels of Riga—the "near abroad"—the capital of the Soviet republic of Latvia, fascinated them. Almost abroad, yet at home. In the Russian mind, no distance at all from today's St. Petersburg. To Riga, to Riga. The wonders of abroad, of *za granitzey*.

Though shabby back then compared to today, Riga's shops and hotels, the old city with its cafés and nightlife offered a foretaste of Europe. Real life. European life. And everyone there spoke Russian. I liked to go to Riga in those times. I felt a link with it. I spoke good Russian, but since I spoke with neither a Moscovite nor a Ukrainian accent, many people in Moscow asked me if I was Latvian.

It's raining when we debark at the airport. We taxi to Riga's oldest hotel, the Metropole, in the old City. The rain keeps up. A strong west wind carries it in from the Baltic Sea. Wind and rain beat against the Mercedes' windows. Then against the windows of our room. A strain of music sounds through the wall from the next room. Elizaveta identifies it as Mussorgsky. Again, the Russian soul in sound, I tell her. It means Russia to me. I tell her how Russians used to love cosmopolitan Riga. Many Russians retired here. Russians in fact make up nearly half of Latvia's 2.3 million people. They don't want to go back to Russia even though pure Latvians resent them, the colonizers.

While Elizaveta arranges her things and takes a shower, I take my usual orientation walk to get my bearings. The rain has become a drizzle, lights are coming on in the city, the wet cobblestones sparkle. Today I feel less a foreigner here than before. Compared to the city I knew, Riga today is a modern, busy European city of smart restaurants, gourmet markets and fashionable shops, though the beautiful cobbled streets remain. Seems every second person is speaking on a mobile phone. I pass the white opera house where Wagner was once music director and where he wrote his first opera, *Rienzi*. Later, I step around a corner and look down a street of art nouveau buildings; many designed by the architect Sergei Eizenstein, the film director's father. I had forgotten the existence of the street. It had seemed more exotic then. Back in my day, even foreigners felt that Riga was nonetheless a Soviet city. Today you feel its Germanness, its heritage from the former aristocracy of Baltic Barons, descended straight from the Crusaders.

* * *

The next morning we visit the Moscow cellar mouse's addresses. Elizaveta is afraid of what we might find. The thought comes to me that maybe she prefers not to find her mother. What if she has another family? At the same time she's also more and more pissed that her mother never came looking for her.

"Maybe she was afraid to," I suggest, "after all those years. Afraid you would despise her for what she once was. Remember what Amsel said, the person you're looking for might be looking for you. On the other hand, Lizzy, you might have a sister or a brother. Adds joy to life."

She stares at me like I'm crazy.

We taxi to the first address. At the apartment on the third floor of a big housing block on Gogola Iela 55, near the Central Station that I vaguely remember, two old people, German-speaking, who've lived here all their lives, have never heard of Masha under any possible name. We meet the same shrugs and 'we don't know' at an attractive apartment house on the nearby Alfreda Kalnina Iela.

Farther north, we find a rather fashionable two-story, two-family house at Elizabetes Iela 65. Somehow I sense this is the place. Coincidences are beginning to tally up and run over me. The name keeps returning in my life. Elizaveta, God's promise in Hebrew, I'd read. Elizaveta, Elizabetes Iela. Years back, my first address in Munich was Elizabeth Strasse. The name of English queens, Schützen Liesl in Bavaria, Isabel in Spain, all derivations from Elizabeth. What if she had returned to Munich? Maybe she would automatically head for Elizabeth Strasse. Even number 65.

The ground floor apartment is vacant: no curtains, no signs of life. Upstairs, a Russian man listens to our story suspiciously until Elizaveta introduces herself using her first and last names.

"Orlova!" he exclaims. His eyes illuminate. "Why didn't you say so immediately? I knew your mother well." He introduces himself and asks us in.

Elizaveta's eyes narrow in a way I now understand. It's because of her own name, Elizaveta, Elizabeth, Liesl, Isabel. She, like her namesakes, sees the world as a jigsaw puzzle that doesn't make sense until she succeeds in putting all the pieces in their proper places. She is all of a piece. Though Elizaveta wants her world to make sense, she insists that it retain its soul and its spiritual side. Her mother Masha's disappearance has never made sense; the pieces of the puzzle were forever out of place. I think that's the explanation for the bright colors of her complex and mysterious paintings. Bright colors like the yellow she loves, like the light she adores. Bright color represents solution. Indicates a direction. And it also explains why she always says in German *ein Bild schreiben*, from the Russian, *pisat kartinu*, that is, 'write a picture'. Like 'write a story' or 'write a symphony'. Since painting, she insists, can never equal the power of words, she strives to achieve the utmost with her brilliant colors.

She exhales and seems to breathe in relief when it becomes obvious that Vasiliy Alekseyev is homosexual and truly adored her mother. She goes to him in her spontaneous way, and kisses him three times in the Russian manner. She has conquered Vasiliy.

While he serves tea and pastry, Vasiliy Alekseyev is eager to tell us his own story too, which he weaves in with the story of his friend, Masha Orlova. Born in Riga, he has lived in this same house most of his life. When Masha arrived here in late 1987, alone—he emphasizes—she was beautiful and very pregnant. They soon became friends.

"I came to feel like her protector. She'd spent a few weeks in two other houses nearby but somehow managed to get half of the downstairs apartment here, then the whole apartment when the other occupants left for Russia. Latvians don't love us, you know. Even though we're the majority in Riga, the countryside is chiefly Latvian. Some Russians can't hold out even though this is home also for them. But Masha didn't care. She had other resources."

Masha had her baby in early 1988, a boy, named Anatoly. "Little Anatoly brought sunshine into this sad house, a joyless house that until then had known the tragedies and the sufferings of our times. Death lived here. First my parents died here, one after the other. Then my friend and companion of many years died of cancer the year before Masha arrived. Little Anatoly brought life back into this house. He was your brother, Elizaveta."

"Was?" we both ask at the same time.

"Anatoly died at the age of twenty-six months, in a hospital on this same street. On Elizabetes Iela. A tragedy. Masha was devastated. We all were. How she got through that time I will never understand. I learned then that loss of a child leaves behind it a trail of insuperable destruction … and hurt and pain and sorrow and lasting trauma. She worshipped the baby in the special way mothers do their sons. Still today I'm convinced there was something enigmatic concealed in that baby—something hidden behind his great doubting eyes. As if he knew secrets others did not. Little Anatoly took a few tablets for influenza. He was allergic to the medicine and died thirty-six hours later. Here in Riga. In 1990. Capricious Fate. Maybe the destiny we create ourselves. Masha spoke of Providence punishing her for the mistakes of her life. The day she accepted that his death was forever and that nothing she could do would bring him back was the worst. She said that everything seemed linked. She spoke of her fragility, her growing terrors, her anxiety and panic attacks and insecurity, her guilt about you, Elizaveta. I don't know if she ever succeeded in mourning properly the loss of her son so as to close the hole it left in her. I still wonder if she has ever accepted his loss."

This is another compartment of my life I've never touched with Elizaveta: the loss of my daughter at about the same age as her lost brother. Now it bonded me with her mother Masha in a new way, and therefore also with her. Elizaveta's mother and I were survivors. Destiny? Fate? Whichever, we were now linked in a new manner. I trembled at the significance of the discovery. My Swiss friend, Franz, who had also dabbled in Jungian psychiatry, often lectured me about my unconscious, full of violence, which I blamed on my Fate. Franz said instead that I was a threat to myself no less than to others; he called the uncontrollable danger of the force of my unconscious the "internal nuclear power plant" in my psyche. For her sake and for Elizaveta's, I hope Masha took a different path to exit from her suffering.

Her eyes fixed on her hands clasped on her knees, Elizaveta doesn't respond to Vasiliy's words.

Vasiliy and I stare at each other until I then ask the question of questions: "So where do you think Elizaveta's mother is now, twenty years later?"

"About six months ago she finally decided. She left for Moscow ... to get her release was the way she expressed it. She never explained what she meant. Latvia is independent.

She has a Latvian passport. She could go where she liked. Shortly afterwards she sent me a card from Moscow but I suspect her intent was to return to Germany, to Munich, to you, Elizaveta. But she was afraid … after all that time."

"We will find her," I say, the idea of Elizabeth Strasse in Munich now fixed in my mind.

* * *

While the hotel concierge works on our reservations back to Munich, Elizaveta visits an art gallery just to pass the time. I drop into the office of the newspaper *Diena* I'd seen on my walk yesterday. I find an editor about my age in a spacious newsroom with furnishings right out of an Ikea catalogue. I speak to him in both English and Russian; he answers in English and we introduce ourselves.

"It's almost impossible to describe how much life in Latvia has changed since independence," Raudseps says after I comment on the new city. "The towers that once jammed foreign radio stations are gone. The bread, meat and potatoes of Soviet times now take their place next to mangoes, jars of sun-dried tomatoes and tubes of wasabi sauce. There have been five elections since 1991. In 2004, Latvia joined the European Union and became an associate member of NATO. But now, we again have a pro-Soviet President. Yet all the while American administrations are critical of Russia for meddling in the affairs of neighboring countries like Latvia and Ukraine."

"While backsliding on democracy at home," I can't help interjecting.

"Still, Latvians welcome attention from Washington. We see presidential visits here as confirmation of America's democratic push around the world. The Baltic States have always been a thorny issue between Russia and the West, but especially in respect of the United States, because the Baltic States were the only Soviet territories to be independent before they were occupied and included in the USSR. All through the Cold War the USA contended that the Baltic States were occupied territories. People here don't forget that. At the same time we have to deal with the reality of Russia's uneasy relationship with us, as with Georgia and Ukraine. Moscow is critical of what it labels Latvia's mistreatment of its sizable Russian minority. Ethnic Russians claim they have no rights here. They resent laws that require passing a Latvian language test to obtain citizenship."

"I understand that Russians make up nearly half the population."

Raudseps squirms nervously at that reality and nods in confirmation. "An enormous problem for us."

"The West needs Russia," I mention. "Trade and especially gas and oil."

"So do we," Raudeps agrees. "But that doesn't change the fact that we have a tense relationship with Moscow. We want Russia to acknowledge its former occupation of the Baltic States, a demand which irritates Moscow but pleases Latvians. Russia still claims it moved its troops into the three Baltic States with the approval of the governments. That creates tensions and keeps the issue of relations with Russia at the forefront. So visits by American leaders and our membership in the European Union underline that Latvia is an important and stable country ... and independent."

"Don't you think your NATO membership worries Russia?"

"Of course it does. Yet Russia too is a NATO partner and after all the Cold War is over."

"Is it really? I wonder. All these American bases along Russia's borders and, in cases like Latvia, a presence inside the former Soviet Union, can't be reassuring to Russia."

"Well, for security purposes we opted for close alliance with the EU and NATO rather than the neutrality of Finland and others ... even if it antagonizes Russia. We've been members of NATO since 2004. Our troops are in Kosovo and Afghanistan."

"Still, participation in America's wars disturbs your neighbor Russia."

"Well, that's what independence is about. A free country makes its choices."

"But American air bases here must be the last straw for Moscow."

"There are no American bases here, but admittedly Russia has had to swallow a lot. I mean, U.S. bases in other Baltic States and NATO fighter jets sometimes stationed here are big steps. Yet, at the same time, because of trade Latvian-Russian relations have improved in recent years."

"Have they really? Hard to imagine, an ex-occupied country establishing good relations with its ex-occupier in so short a time. It's easy to understand the emotional reaction of ethnic Latvians in the countryside."

"Well, we're neighbors. We're tiny and poor. Russia is big and strong and we have to have trade with them. We need a new type of relation with Russia. We have to be open with each other. Good American-Russian relations make our relations with Russia easier ... since we are America's allies now. We walk a fine line. Still, we have to conduct an independent foreign policy ... in our own best interests."

"Doesn't that make your NATO membership and its military training installations rather precarious?"

"You can bet it does. Still, we insist that Russia open its archives about its past relations with Latvia. Then create a bilateral commission of historians to clear up misunderstandings of that stormy past."

"Dreamers always imagine commissions somehow clearing up history. You Latvians must be dreamers."

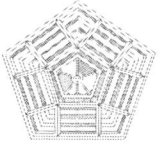

18

ELMER

ELMER was aware of Raymond's presence that night in the Burgas café. The strange giant seemed to be ubiquitous, obviously on his trail. That had been clear since the man's arrival in Novo Selo. Elmer realized that his initial reliance on the military's toleration of his eccentricities because of his particular genius was foolish. His arrogance was based on his youth. Also on his ignorance of the essence of the militaristic spirit. He hadn't known, hadn't imagined, what military power was. The army was just there like grocery stores. Had always been there. Armies everywhere. Part of existence. Part of normal society. Now he understood more. To them, he realized, he was no more than his serial number, which in his hubris he had always refused to memorize. Actually he did know the number because he remembered any number he had ever encountered in his life. But this number he consciously rejected, even though he himself had chosen to have one.

Elmer Redway was of pure English stock, from New England. In the United States he had traveled little, never south of New York City or west of New York State. Going to the beach at nearby Newport was a major event in his early teenaged years. Like English colonialists of old he had a good nose, sharp intuition and for some mysterious reason a fascination for things of the East.

He took to Bulgaria immediately, which in his mind was the first western outpost in the mysterious East. Now he felt it as an outpost of the American empire. Curiously, this country's Slavic language came naturally to him. Of all the

Americans at Novo Selo, he was the *rara avis* in that in his nine months there he acquired an astonishing knowledge of Bulgarian. He already had a circle of friends in Burgas and read about Bulgarian culture, its folklore and its legends. At the same time he was creating legends about himself at Novo Selo ... precisely because of his second life in Burgas. Wild stories circulated about him and his whereabouts as he regularly vanished on long weekends, awarded more 72-hour passes than anyone ever before. Gradually the rumors took on a lurid, mysterious tinge. Had he joined some secret Bulgarian sect? Was he even a real soldier? Had he been infiltrated there by some secret agency to spy on the men? For whom exactly was he spying? Elmer was aware that neither his fellow enlisted men nor the officers knew what to make of him, so he took advantage of his ambivalent position as an indispensable communications expert to spend much of his time in Burgas, much of that in bed with his girlfriend. Many days at Novo Selo without a breakout meant confinement to him and if there was one thing Elmer could not bear it was confinement. In the long run, it was more the legend he had created than his actual activities that was his undoing.

Quite simply, Elmer was a genius. He had been a genius all his life. Not a scientist. Not an authority on any specific subject. He'd never specialized in anything. He knew a lot about many things and to his own dismay seldom forgot anything. Sometimes he himself didn't know what he knew ... or, above all, what he should do with his knowledge. He had always been an honors student, without even trying. He won national mathematics contests. Every university wanted him. He chose M.I.T. chiefly because of its proximity to Providence, while at the same time distant enough to get him away from home. Like his academic supervisors who tore their hair over his extravagances, if his military superiors had even suspected what went on inside him, they would have lily-padded him out of Bulgaria to the East long ago. The reality was that his perfect eclecticism, his atavistic disregard of military discipline, the staggering elasticity of his thinking processes, were disconcerting even to himself. Even before the investigation began, he knew that his position had become untenable.

* * *

If Elmer was a prodigy in anything, it was in computer technology. And he loved all aspects of telecommunications. A hacker by instinct, he believed he could get into any computer, any communications system in the world. Now less than a year since he began running telecommunications at Novo Selo, the military world held few secrets from him. He only had to know what he wanted to know and he was off. At first he hadn't understood the range of his talent. Now he did.

He found it incredible what secrets technology could uncover. The fact that he could hear or copy anything said or written on any kind of radio transmission anywhere in the world still astounded him more than most other discoveries in his life. The result was that he had grasped an overall view of what the worldwide military power of his country was up to. To him the complicity between the military-financial-corporate world and the U.S. government was as clear and simple and distinct—almost audible to his sensitive ear—as if he himself had constructed the system. Elmer also understood that the military world in which he existed at Novo Selo had no inkling as to who he was—a casual visitor, or a dangerous alien in their midst. Until recently his problem had been that not only did he not know what to do with what he had already learned, but also what to do with what he was certain he would come to know in the future. It was a question of his own duality: not a physical or a mathematical duality but a dualism of his own being. On the one hand, he was integrated into a most sophisticated but cruel branch of military power; on the other hand, he, and some representatives of that power, knew, or nearly knew, or suspected, that he was alien to it. It seemed his body and his mind traveled along binary tracks, sometimes controlled and smooth and capable of acts of genius, while at other times his skill went haywire, capable of wreaking havoc and terror.

Elmer himself concluded that he was simply cynical, and skeptical about everything. Above all, what he most wanted in his present life was to sleep with Lala. Before her, he'd been practically a virgin. Sex with Lala became his only moment of unthinking and blissful oblivion. Where he could let himself drop into a thought-free nirvana.

Meanwhile, WikiLeaks could only absorb a minimum of his talents. Of his genius. That website was just a start, for he knew he had thus far only scratched the surface.

From time to time there had been mild hints that he was "suspected". Of what, he was uncertain. No direct accusations had been made but he'd received unexpected mild reprimands for minor irregularities, contradicting the general tolerance in his regard, so that he never knew exactly where he stood. At first he had thought it was only because of his differentness, of his unmilitary bearing and behavior, his long hair and fledgling beard. Then he realized that his vaunted cynicism implied to authority that he knew what was really going on in the world, and that what was happening was criminal.

That was before he began systematically collecting and sending increasingly large quantities of quality information to WikiLeaks. Naïve in everyday life, he was savvy in his field, also savvy enough to know that if he was good enough to get the stuff and diffuse it, there were others out there who could pinpoint him, right there at that computer in the communications offices in Novo Selo in Bulgaria.

A few days before the Burgas café encounter, a young Lieutenant in his section had warned him to be on his best behavior. "That Intelligence man has been asking questions about you. You've seen him. Carpenter," the officer called the mysterious giant.

"Not many two-meter tall men called Raymond come up

on my screen," Elmer bantered, as usual playful with the officer who'd taken a shine to him the maverick. "Raymond Carpenter is a name to remember."

For Elmer it was a cakewalk to ramble around inside the systems of various military intelligence organizations. Just for background he had read reports about the systematic build-up of police state powers in the USA since the 9/11 terrorism attacks—the U.S. Patriot Act and the creation of the Department of Homeland Security, the establishment of concentration camps like Guantánamo, renditions, torture prisons, and above all the assumption of greater police authority by the military intelligence agency, DIA.

It was no surprise when he found the name and even a photograph in the most obvious of places—on a secure DIA site. Carpenter was a cover. His real name was Raymond Bridges, from Tennessee, a freelance agent. One sentence referred to his special assignment—break the WikiLeaks chain and send the whole fucking bunch of them to Guantánamo for a good round of torture.

* * *

Elmer noted the investigative successes reported from locations where Raymond showed up. From Great Britain to Afghanistan, from Iraq to Australia, WikiLeaks collaborators had been harassed or jailed on outrageous charges … from rape and child abuse and pornography to tax evasion. Others had simply vanished.

Raymond moved quietly, slowly, but leaving behind him a trail Elmer could easily follow. Though Raymond was tailing him, Elmer not only tailed Raymond, but also got into his destination computers and followed his reports, movements and plans. At times he believed he was also getting into the man's mind. Once Elmer had picked up the scent, gotten onto Raymond's trail and into his mind, he realized he was predicting the investigator's next moves, sometimes, it seemed, before the ideas were even born. Psychic or prophet, Elmer didn't know. He had never told anyone of the extent of his mystical sixth sense, not even his brother back in Providence to whom he regularly confessed the weirdest of his ideas and premonitions. It was too frightening to articulate. He didn't want to know everything he knew, the cornucopia of his accumulating information. Everything was a sign of more to come. His capabilities and knowledge were progressive, in constant escalation, a spiral ever upward. That was part of his problem. The more he knew, the more he knew he would soon come to know, as if he were plagiarizing the world. The accumulation weighed heavily, often unbearably. Could his brain bear all this accumulation? At times he felt the propinquity of total yet exponentially increasing knowledge almost unbearable. He was too prolific, too fecund. It was too much for a nineteen-and-a-half-year-old boy from Providence to bear alone.

WikiLeaks, he realized, was his way of letting off steam, a safety valve for his overflowing brain.

Moreover, the thought that the gigantic goon whistleblower-breaker Raymond had no inkling about the power of the man with whom he was dealing was a consolation.

Elmer kept details of his psychic powers to himself. He never hinted to the friendly Lieutenant how easy it was to get into military communications systems. Not only formal communications systems, he was able to find the frequencies of the most remote field telephones and field radios. His skill astounded him. His intuition knew no limits. Encrypted or not, he picked up the most amazing, blood-chilling information. What he didn't actually read or hear first, he intuited and then after the fact found the proof. Anonymously, he began forwarding the best stuff to online sites, untraceable, he had believed at first. More recently he saw his materials right where he wanted them to be—on WikiLeaks.

No wonder seeing Raymond at the café in Burgas was chilling. They were closing the circle around him, he knew, though he was unsure what that meant in his case. When the Lieutenant swore him to secrecy and whispered that he was to be lily padded out, Elmer decided it was time to scram. He hadn't told anyone. Not even Lala. His thoughts were confused, chaotic. One thing however was clear: he could do without the battlefront in Afghanistan. I can live without their renditions and all the shit that goes with it. I must have been nuts to give up M.I.T for this shit.

At around six o'clock on the morning after the Burgas café date with Al and the German, he stuffed into a small duffle bag a minimum of personal belongings—random papers, some civilian clothes, shirts, pants and sneakers, his mobile phone which he knew he couldn't use, his martenitsa which he couldn't wear—and walked casually past the gate, waving to the on-duty guards who were accustomed to his going for breakfast to a nearby café. He took a local bus down to the main east-west highway and shortly after caught a ride with an 18-wheeler with German plates headed west.

The German at the wheel was one of the breed of European international truck drivers who, like big league soccer players, pick up bits of various languages, so that he and Elmer were able to communicate with a mixture of English and Bulgarian. Like all European truck drivers he knew everything concerning the relative ease or difficulty posed by customs and security controls at the borders. Herman made the Munich-Burgas run almost weekly and was glad to have company.

Herman asked where he was headed.

"To the West," Elmer said and shrugged, discarding the momentary idea of going all the way to Munich. Too many Americans there. "I thought Belgrade. I was there once and liked it."

Herman nodded, as if his nonchalant selection of Belgrade was natural. "I'm passing through there. You can ride all the way with me. About six hundred kilometers. We'll be there tonight. I sleep there every trip."

"Hey, Herman, can I change my clothes? Got to get out of this fucking uniform."

"Sure, *los*! Go ahead. *Sag mal*, you on vacation? Or ... you run?" Herman's face was one big grin.

Elmer studied him for a moment, then thought, what the hell: "I'm running!"

The clothes change ran deep. He felt like another person. His martenitsa earring made the change complete. He knew where he was going. And more than just awol. He might be nineteen and a half years old crazy, but desertion was better than rendition any day, at any age. Just give him a good computer and some radio equipment and he could continue his exposures. His flight made him feel heroic.

At first he'd thought of going to Turkey simply because it was only a stone's throw away. But the U.S. military presence there scared him. Besides he didn't know anyone there. Belgrade was farther but American presence was nil. He remembered the person he'd met there at the university communications faculty, a certain Ilya who'd sought him out in one of the computer rooms, asking for help on a communications problem. A tiny little guy, Ilya was all smiles and good will, gave him his address and told him to look him up anytime he was in Belgrade. The Ilya of the German's note must be the same one.

Within a couple of hours he would be reported as awol. It wouldn't be the first time. Returning a half-day late from a weekend in Burgas had earned him many reprimands, quickly forgiven however when he introduced some new communications gimmick that made his bosses look good. This time it was a different story because of Raymond who would understand that he was running. He wouldn't have much of a head start.

In the afternoon, as the truck hummed along the route north from Leskovac and Nish toward the Serbian capital of Beograd, Elmer dropped off to sleep. Later, the autoroute from Plovdiv to Sofia returned to him like a dream. He hardly remembered the Bulgarian capital although he knew he should have been paying attention. In his new deserter status he needed to know roads, borders and how things were done. His daring still stunned him. First WikiLeaks, now awol. He was uncertain what his legal status was. Bulgaria was not a war zone, nor was his country at war here. So did his flight make him renegade, turncoat, deserter, traitor? Was he a deserter or just awol? He was no Benedict Arnold but he knew he was on the side of justice. Nonetheless, he would probably need a lawyer someday. Someplace. But what kind of lawyer? This was a question of military law. The last item he sent to WikiLeaks must have given him away, for shortly afterwards that sinister character, Raymond, had appeared in Novo Selo. Who said his name was Raymond anyway? He had never spoken to the rumored special agent. Every time he showed up, and he seemed to be everywhere, Novo Selo soldiers of diverse nationalities snickered and pointed, and said in diverse languages, "there's that asshole Raymond".

* * *

Elmer's first filed document to WikiLeaks was his interception of an Army Staff Sergeant joking with other soldiers on a field phone about how easy it would be to "toss a grenade" at Afghan civilians and kill them.

Elmer had followed it up. Later, military investigators learned that the soldier eventually turned talk into action, forming a "kill team" to carry out random executions of Afghans. In one of the worst war-crimes cases to emerge from the Afghan war, five soldiers from an infantry brigade had recently been charged with murder for their alleged roles in the killing of three Afghan civilians near Kandahar, taking amputated fingers and scalps as tokens of their war exploits. Elmer had intercepted, recorded and publicized much of the story.

Then even that horror story came to seem less explosive than what followed. For he found a new leak which he realized was of top strategic significance. For security reasons he had submitted it to Wikileaks two weeks ago from a cyber café in a nearby town even though he realized that it too could be intercepted. Only by chance had he happened to eavesdrop on the conversation between the two high level military officers. He hadn't even pinpointed their geographical location but believed it was in either Afghanistan or much farther east, perhaps South Korea. He was again listening to a field phone conversation on a standard frequency between two soldiers near Kandahar, when a series of clicks and buzzes interrupted the exchange of the usual crude jokes and bitter complaints of combat troops of all nationalities. Two conversations then overlapped. Suddenly, the voices of two sophisticated but foul speaking males came through loud and clear. They addressed each other respectively as Colonel and General, never adding a name, though from their tone it was apparent they knew each other well. Moreover, they must have presumed they were on a secure line. As soon as he'd grasped the quantum leap in transmission quality and the level of the speakers, he flipped on a recorder so that the last minutes of that conversation were recorded verbatim.

"… *in other words, General, what about Russia in all this?*" The speaker's voice drawled in a deep southern accent.

"*In my opinion those suckers are fucked. We've got them tucked behind ever- tighter borders. Our bases in Kyrgyzstan and the new ones we'll soon have reaching from Romania and Moldova straight north and then east to Georgia have the Russkies penned inside their shrinking borders.*"

"*I'm still wary of the fucking Russkies, I confess. They're a resilient people. And now, with all that gas and oil they can squeeze and buy up Europe. You just never know what those bastards are really up to. Could make a deal with Iran and screw us royally.*"

"*Nah, Colonel, you exaggerate. They're still their usual selves. Fuck-ups. Besides they're afraid. They don't want Iran to develop nuclear weaponry any more than we do. What we have to do is keep our eyes fixed on China, Colonel. We'll soon divide up the world with it. That's the plan, straight from the horse's mouth, if you know what I mean. But only temporarily. We can outgun them too in the long run. Europe might suck up to Moscow because of the gas and oil out in Siberia but most of Europe needs us. Only us in the long run. They know what side their bread is buttered on."*

"Yes, General, but we can't keep up with China's productivity. Chinese goods are flooding Europe and their fucking yuan currency is right behind."

"Well, their fucking currency may be a problem now, but one day we're going to push it right back down their fucking yellow throats. The Japs tried it and look what it got them. An atom bomb right down the gullet. The Chinks have already got too much. After we split the fucking Russkies into tiny little kingdoms and take their Siberia from them and get them fighting each other while they drink themselves to death, we'll get Pakistan and India organized and we'll steamroller China flat as a fucking pancake—Japan and us on one side and India and Europe on the other. You just keep up your undercover work in Pakistan. Every bit of terror you can organize adds to our strength. Terrorism is a fine thing for us. Keep those Talibans fighting and keep the bombs flying against that sucker Karzai. We don't want him to think seriously that he can run Afghanistan. Jesus Christ, I don't believe it was ever a country anyway. Above all keep the poppy fields in bloom. That's our bread and butter. Meanwhile Colonel, keep your eyes fixed on the East because that's …"

The same clicks and buzzes and he was back with the field men somewhere in Afghanistan, still at their gripes and dirty jokes, and no background sounds at all.

As a rule, he gathered more down-to-earth stuff—little cruelties, like a U.S. squad destroying a gas stove in an empty hovel just for the hell of it—and, occasionally, immense atrocities such as oral accounts of the shooting in cold blood of all the males present in a family. This new leak was over his head. He didn't have the background to evaluate its international strategic significance. Russia, Siberia, China; such considerations were still beyond his scope. He would learn.

He felt a sense of having done a good deed when he sent it to WikiLeaks.

* * *

Waking from another nap, he recalled fleeting glimpses of his dream. Neither the present, nor the future he hoped for manifested in his dream world. No portents, no prophesies in which he could believe. Nothing so magnificent as augurs of new times. He was visiting the strange world of his brother in their hometown of Providence, or perhaps it was in Bulgaria. His dream self was older than he in reality. He was interested in his brother's many women. Not exactly a harem, but there were several women of various ages in his brother's hazy kingdom. His older self was sitting on a kind of extra-wide chaise longue, his legs intertwined with the legs of a woman. She said she was his brother's "woman". Sex was on his mind, and on hers. His brother arrived just in time. He didn't seem to care about their intertwined legs. But was the man his brother … or his friend? Did she belong to both of them? Or was he himself an outsider? Was he different from the rest? He looked at his brother but couldn't disentangle his legs from hers.

He had always had a rich dream life. Sometimes he recounted his dreams to friends. Or to anyone who happened to be present. It seemed like free therapy to talk about them and hear the reactions of others. Once, a couple of years ago, he began writing down his dreams into a kind of dream diary, which later made good reading. He had recorded many dreams of rooms crowded with people. Banquet tables filled with sparkling silver and women in long white evening dresses. And walks along familiar, dark and dangerous, obstacle-filled roads toward obscure destinations he felt he had to reach.

He looked at the driver Herman and decided not to try to describe the dream. Anyway the scene was already fading.

* * *

Darkness and a light rain were falling when they arrived in Belgrade. Eighteen-wheeler travel was tiring. "I'm parking in my company's depot close to the center of town," Herman said as they entered the city. "You can sleep in one of the bunks down below if you like or I'll drop you wherever you want."

He accepted the offer of a free bed. He had to stretch his meager resources. He crawled into the encapsulated bunk and fell asleep immediately.

When he slid out of the compartment early the next morning Herman was checking the tires, patting the metal monster affectionately and readying his departure. He gave Elmer his address in Munich and said he should look him up if he needed a friend. Then he pulled a map out of his back pocket. "Here's a good city map. It may come in handy. *Pass gut auf und mach's gut.*"

Elmer aimed for the parliament building. Ilya had given him an address written on the back of a theater ticket. "Palmoticheva Street 25, near the National Assembly. Ring the bell and say you're a friend."

As he tramped toward downtown, lines were forming outside the city's many bakeries. The aroma in the air and the assortment of breads on the counters were irresistible. He queued up. He ordered what was labeled a *burek*, a flaky pastry filled with meat and cheese. Looked like a meal. When he offered both U.S. dollars and Bulgarian leva, the waitress started to protest, but, eyeing his martenitsa, she shrugged and took one dollar from his hand.

She looked surprised when he thanked her in Bulgarian, "*mnogo blagodarya.*"

"*Molim*!" she said and smiled.

Elmer walked out of the shop convinced his good luck char had worked again.

It was still only about 9 o'clock when he reached Palmoticheva Street. Number 25 was a typical three-story house with six doorbells, two apartments to each floor. Ilya's name was written on a plaque, apparently for the first floor. When he rang, someone answered while his hand was still on the button.

"Who is it?"

"A friend," he said.

The door buzzed open. No sooner had he stepped into a dimly lit corridor when a door on the right opened and there stood the little man he remembered, Ilya, who acted as if he was expected.

"Come in. Quick! Nosey neighbors," Ilya said in English and closed the door behind them. "All curious about my visitors. Ah, how many cousins I have suddenly acquired. Anyway, if you stay in Belgrade you will soon be living somewhere else. Uh, what is that?" he asked, peering at his earring. "Your martenitsa?"

"I will?" Elmer asked, fingering the earring he'd forgotten he was wearing. This little Serb was one of the first to know what it was.

"My *char*," he added.

"You will if you decide to stay absent without leave … uh, you call it awol, no? And hang on to your good luck charm, you will need it in the new life you are entering."

"Yeah, that's what I am. Awol, I mean. A deserter, but not a traitor."

"Of course not. Look, Elmer—that is your name, right?— you are not alone. But as far as I am concerned, I hope you will not be the last awol to reach us.

"Come into the kitchen. You can tell me about yourself while I prepare some breakfast. You must be hungry. We Serbs eat English breakfasts. A full meal."

"So do Bulgarians ... and I had a *burek* on the way here."
Elmer sat at the table, marveling again at the linguistic abilities
of Balkan peoples. Little Ilya rushed about the kitchen, tiny
too. "Not much to say about myself. I was at M.I.T. in
Boston. A mathematician ... and I do communications too,
as I told you that time at your university. Some time ago I
started overhearing things on radios and computers ..."

"And you sent them to WikiLeaks. Then they caught up
with you and you ran."

"Well, yes, more or less."

"I have heard about you ... from friends. Tell me, why the
martenitsa?"

"I have a girlfriend in Burgas ... I'm learning Bulgarian."

"Excellent. Then you will not have problems with Serbian."

"Why did you give me your address and ... why are you
helping me?"

"This is a new idea ... for us. It is really an old one. Rat lines
to save people like you from jail ... or worse. Canada and
Sweden did the same during the Vietnam War. I met an
American who was teaching school in Finland who had
been there since Vietnam. Not a deserter. Just did not want
to die in an unjust war. Also at the end of World War II,
the Nazis set up rat lines to save top hierarchs. Not a good
comparison but still ... ! Your successful disappearance depends
on you ... and some good luck," he added, touching Elmer's
earring. "Anyway, we will be checking you. That you are who
you say you are."

Elmer stared at their plates—laden with sausages and eggs
and some green stuff—with a tinge of disgust. Still, he was
beginning to feel his accumulated hunger. Yesterday had been
a long day of truck stops with only beer and various snacks.

A fork in his left hand, knife in the other, he peered up at
Ilya: "Oh, I am what I say I am. But why are you doing this?
What's the point?"

"The point? I think you can say we are trying to understand
what your crazy America is up to. What does it want from

us? What does it want from the world? We are starting to think America is little different from Nazi Germany. It too wanted the world ... and with a no less crazy ideology, if you can call American thinking today ideology. America has gone too far. Every conqueror in history had his limits. America has now overreached ... exceeded the limits."

"But what does Serbia have to do with it? Most Americans can't even find you on the map. Why you?"

"Elmer, my new American friend, I assure you, we are not alone. We are with the rest of the world. America is more and more isolated in the world, even with all its bases from California across the continent to the Atlantic, to Europe and to Asia. History will show that America's bases are temporary."

"Maybe that's why we call them lily pads."

"And the soldiers only frogs?"

"Yeah, you might say that."

"Well, we are ready to help as many frogs who ask us. Elmer, I can tell you one short history of the effects of empires. Historically, conquerors have razed the city of Belgrade forty times. Yet here we are still. No intact building in Belgrade has stood more than two hundred and fifty years. But Serbs are still here. And now there are brand new ruins from the NATO bombings in 1999 during Europe's most recent war. As a reminder—as if we needed a reminder— our damaged buildings have purposely not been reconstructed; the Ministry of Defense with its cement walls buckled like cardboard on Kneza Miloza Street, the State television headquarters on Takovska Street, the current affairs office, which nestled between two larger glass-fronted buildings. All were flattened on the night of the thirtieth of April in 1999 with the death of sixteen staff members. Belgrade looked like it did after World War Two ... something like German cities too."

"Time seems crazy," Elmer muttered. "I spend too much time trying to understand time."

"Eternal and temporary are relative terms. As are conqueror and vassal and colony. A New World Order has been tried many times. There is only history, and its flow. But humanity continues to move at its own pace."

"Well, uh, Mr. Ilya, what am I supposed to do now? How can I live on nothing?"

"Forget the mister. Ilya is enough. Look, Elmer, we have some small funds to start with. First, we have to get you some papers. In your case, this will be easy because you are the perfect student age. We have a language teacher for you now, then later maybe the university, with a fellowship ... if you decide to stay here. And quite frankly there are not many places you can go. NATO countries will be looking for you. Serbia is not in NATO yet but is a member of NATO's Partnership for Peace."

"Hah," Elmer grunts. "NATO and peace. The peace of Iraq. The peace of Afghanistan. Lily pads for peace. Bombs for peace. Remember Dr. Strangelove, riding the bomb to finish off mankind? Oh man, the euphemisms we dream up. I wonder who invents all those slogans."

"Anyway, keep in mind that our government plans to join NATO. Maybe by 2014. America has long arms and they keep growing longer. Like Pinocchio's nose."

"So I stay here for now? Sounds OK. But I keep wondering if this makes me a traitor. I don't feel like a traitor. Though I do hate this fucking eternal war. I can't remember when America was not at war. Doesn't seem right to me. By the way, are there others like me?"

"You are exactly number three here. From different places. I will not tell you yet from where. One day you might meet the others. They are here for different reasons. You are the first to come the WikiLeaks route. You are special in that. But that is also quite serious. Your people will be looking far and wide for you. You have to be careful. Watchful always. Everywhere. We will try to protect you. Meanwhile we can find a way for you to continue with WikiLeaks, if you want to … if that is the reason you ran. Your own story could be interesting. But not yet. Not today. First step—get you underground."

"They're already on my trail, I believe. There's a guy in Novo Selo. About two meters tall. Everybody calls him Raymond. I've pinpointed him. From DIA, the Defense Intelligence Agency. Anyway, I'm here now. And I want to ask you a favor. I know you will say it's too dangerous, but I would like to get my girlfriend from Burgas here. Is it possible?"

"Ah yes, the girl behind the martenitsa. Let me think about it. Give me her name and address for now. I will get someone to call her from Germany or maybe from Burgas itself. Safer maybe. Tell her you are all right. Then, first things first."

* * *

Ilya moved him that afternoon to a studio apartment in a short, narrow street between the St. Sava Orthodox Church and the Danube port and warned him not to return to Palmoticheva again. "Too risky," he said. "There are eyes everywhere. Anyway we will be in constant contact."

He then recounted the entangled history of the old church still under construction, its white marble contrasting its green copper domes which dominated the Old City skyline: "St. Sava, the founder of the Serbian Orthodox Church, was martyred in the thirteenth century. In 1594 the Ottoman rulers unearthed his relics and burned them on the site of today's church. Three hundred years later, after the end of Ottoman rule, the building of the church was begun. Work was interrupted under the Nazi occupation and again during the 1990s civil war. Though only partially in use, this is the world's largest functioning Orthodox church. Supposed to be completed in a couple of years. Saint Sava and the Serbian Orthodox Church are central to contemporary Serbia. So, you now live in a key area of all of Serbia."

Ilya went on for a while about the St. Sava story and the ideology behind it. Elmer had to force himself to follow.

The Serbian Church, like its big brother the Russian Orthodox Church, Ilya related, is accused of caesaropapism. A church subservient to the Serbian state. Some charge that the difference between Byzantium and Serbia in this regard is that Byzantines regarded only the emperor and his court as heavenly. Serbs however confer heavenly status on the nation as a whole. Saint Sava-ism is a Serbian concept for the blend of church, state and nation established by Saint Sava, the founder of the Serbian Orthodox Church. "Much such rigmarole accounts for the charges of genocide against Serbia. NATO used the mythology to justify bombing Serbia and stealing its province of Kosovo."

Elmer's room was small with a cooking alcove in one corner. A narrow window looked onto a courtyard. Half of the wall on the opposite side was lined with computer and communications equipment.

"Wow!" he exclaimed. "Let me at it."

"That is what you are here for. And for *War Crimes Unlimited*, a new site just about ready to go. Ready for your leaks. You do your research. But please instruct me too about communications and interception and such. How does it work? How do you pick up so many signals?"

"It sounds more complicated than it is. Sometimes it's actually simple. If reception between a sender and a receiver is possible, then so is interception. You need patience and luck and sometimes a hook-up to a good satellite dish. A high frequency radio transmitter can transmit around the whole planet. The message travels to receivers thousands of miles away by bouncing off the ionosphere. In Bulgaria I relied on VHF and UHF used for tactical military communications within countries like Iraq or parts of Afghanistan and most of the Middle East. In general, all telecommunications traffic can be intercepted at the base: telephone calls, faxes, e-mails and others. Then, if you can get into NSA systems you can intercept anything.

"Actually all of this started in the United States. What they did was create this gigantic database of secret and not-so-secret materials, an archive of hundreds of thousands of cables from U.S. embassies and military installations around the world. Then they put the materials on the State Department's classified embassies' websites, but also on SIPRNET, which is the U.S. Defense Department's military Internet. That circulates to soldiers all across the world; everywhere the U.S. has got bases, like at Novo Selo. As a result, it was accessible to me, an ordinary soldier but cleared to the secret level because of my work in communications. I downloaded them onto a CD. I would listen to music and dance around my office while I was copying all that secret stuff. I put it on a USB Flash Drive, just to keep it in my pocket. Here's about all of it," Elmer said, pulling the tiny flash card from his pocket. "Right here I have 1.6 gigabytes of material, or about two hundred and fifty million words."

"Good God! Well, we are not sophisticated here but I will try to get you hooked up to some big dish. That should work out all right. And do not worry about your own transmissions. Nothing will go out directly from here. We have to find a way to transmit your stuff—and that of others—to the new site. I think it will be a roving site, one day here, one day there. With your help we will add fuel to the fire ignited by WikiLeaks. You will see!"

"I'm OK with that. But Ilya, something else important. Back in the States, I didn't realize what was really going on in the world. Few people there do."

"Not many here either."

"You know, I went awol the first time at age sixteen. Back then I came to count myself part of an uncontrollable generation ... I think because we realized we were ignorant. But I've found there's so much to rebel against. You know, Ilya, the military-corporate complex in America was just a vague theory then, barely mentioned in public. Now I know it exists. More and more people speak of an America already gone Fascist. A police state. It's the corporations! Still, I want to know more. In general I'm pretty well informed but there are enormous political gaps in my education. Besides language, I need political education."

"I have just the man for that. I will send Mirko to you. For now, your language teacher is a lady named Lyubica, written on the doorbell at the corner of this street, number two. Third floor. A walk-up. You will like her. Tomorrow is your first lesson, at five p.m. So my friend, your new life begins."

"May it be a long one," Elmer muttered, uneasily fingering his martenitsa.

* * *

His new life began, Elmer thought, in a very positive way. Lyubica was about forty years old, blond, pretty, all smiles, and literally exuded hospitality. She seemed to know his life story. He had never seen anything like her crowded two-room apartment, jammed with multi-colored lamps, shelves covering an entire wall, with two files of books, and on the other walls, paintings, signed photographs and documents, the floors covered with Turkish carpets, a table with computer and printer, a wooden desk covered in papers, open books and stacks of papers, a small divan and two armchairs. He loved it at once and felt at home.

"*Dobar dan, gospoja Lyubica,*" he said in Bulgarian.

"*Zdravo* Elmer," she answered in Serbian. "*Kako si?*"

"*Dobro, hvala,*" he answered repeating the exchange with the girl in the bakery.

Surprised, Lyubica abandoned English and from that moment spoke to him only in Serbian. Learning went fast. He found that his linguistic talents were expanding. Must come from his mathematical bent, he thought.

* * *

Ilya was a tough taskmaster. Nothing came gratis. Time was precious. That same evening, Mirko showed up at Elmer's flat.

"*Dobar vecher.*"

"*Zdravo, kako si?*"

"*Hvala, dobro.*"

Mirko, about thirty years old, tall and slim, with long, coal-black hair and a thin mustache, had completed his university studies in London and today was an associate professor of political science and sociology.

"You could be from Boston," Elmer said of Mirko's beautiful English after they'd spoken a while.

"I'm not, but I'm your political commissar anyway!" Mirko said, laughed joyously and slapped the sides of his thin legs with both hands. "Political theory is to be our subject. What do you know? Or what do you not know? Eh, by the way, is there anything to drink around here? No? OK, I brought something."

Mirko slid a bottle of Scotch from his satchel, opened it reverently, took a quick swig and passed the bottle.

"I think we're going to like each other," Elmer said, overpowered by the joyous force of his teacher, and took a polite swill of about the same length, coughed and then added: "Well, I never understood Hegel. Nor why he is so important."

"Hegel!" Mirko said, as if astonished that this kid had mentioned him. "That's a start. I did my thesis on Hegel."

"So where do we start, Professor?"

"With Socialism perhaps," Mirko said, laughed again, and passed him the bottle.

"Socialism as an alternative to capitalism is our fundamental subject," Mirko said. "I'm familiar with American hang-ups on the subject of Socialism, though I suspect you're advanced for your age. By the way," he added, "I think of capitalism with a lower case 'c' because it's burning out. Socialism instead has an upper case 'S' because it's the future."

"OK, agreed. I'll think the same."

* * *

Elmer considered Mirko's wanderings through the world of philosophy and ideology as his first real political instruction.

Mirko's message was that capitalism, the capitalist system itself and its ramifications must be replaced since the system is worsening man's condition everywhere in the world. In his view, only Socialism is a workable alternative.

"Americans," Mirko said at the outset, "are the first victims of capitalist propaganda. They're the victims of a real mind-fuck. Actually they don't know what they believe ... probably the most conditioned people on Earth. On the one hand, most people there don't know what Socialism is, while they experience capitalism and corporate power every day in their lives. And many don't like it. Socialism is by definition the nemesis of capitalism. Still, especially for Americans, Socialism would be a damn sight better than what they have. Chiefly because it's based on the idea that society's resources should serve the needs of all people, not profit a few. That's easy to understand.

"Socialism is a progressive alternative. It challenges the dominance of monopoly capital through the nationalization of banks and key sectors of the economy, combined with universal health care, free education, reduction of the work week, improvement of pensions."

"You don't question capitalism in the USA," Elmer noted. "It's anti-American to even question the system. Anyone who wishes to take part in civic life quickly grasps that being seen as anti-free market—that is, Socialist—is to become a political outcast. To criticize the system is to criticize the nation and democracy itself. It's easier to find an advocate of the colonization of Mars than to find a scholar or a mainline journalist engaged in radical criticism of capitalism. The news media have a track record of promoting the profit system. And just the word, Socialism, is taboo for most. To most Americans it sounds invasive. A threat to their individual freedoms. To their way of life. But what is it about Socialism that is so scary?"

"It's just the word. Recalls Communist Russia, Stalin. You know. For them, Socialism means giving up personal freedoms ... as if they weren't already losing them from day to day. Socialization, that is, democratization of the economic sphere scares capitalists. As does the enlargement of the political sphere. But one thing should be clear to all by now: the idea of the self-regulating market is stupid. A trickle-down effect, they claim. Absurd. A disguise for the concentration of economic power and wealth in the hands of a few. Actually, the classical notion that socialist movements would happen, not in opposition to democracy, but as its champions is much more advanced. In that respect, mere state ownership of key productive forces is not enough to create a socialist society; the people must exercise a sovereign rule over these productive forces and society as a whole. So much shit self-regulation! Society must be organized to promote collective needs. In the same way that democracy is not an accomplished reality unless the vast majority of the people rule society, so Socialism is not an accomplished reality unless associated producers control the productive forms of society and use them rationally in the collective interest. Otherwise elite democracy results. And that elite is getting smaller with every day that passes.

"Elmer! Just ask yourself why rulers in countries like France or Italy have greater difficulty cutting social programs during economic crises. Because when they look out the window they see a mass of people who would threaten their system if the vested interests attempted to turn back the clock. This makes the position of the capitalist class in such countries tenuous. But of course change is not free. The class of property will only concede fundamental rights to the rest when they fear for the survival of their own privileges."

"Still," Elmer interrupted, "just how is the Socialist paradise to be financed? That's a mystery."

"By shifting the tax burden to corporations and the wealthy and by ending foreign wars and imperialism. It's that simple. But capitalists will never do what is necessary. The world doesn't need to produce more, but better."

"The opposite of what Americans believe."
Elmer fingered his martenitsa, smoothed down his scraggly
beard and extracted from his duffle bag a still undigested
article on Hegel's ideas on Reflection. A few days before
his flight, sitting amidst the blinking LEDS in his office and
searching for something useful to spend his time on, he
had downloaded and printed the article that at first had
mystified him. He had once completed a summer seminar
in political philosophy, but when it came to Hegel, he, like
many others, simply shut down. The philosopher's language
could have been Urdu or Pashtun. Thinking of how many
Americans still turn off when they hear words like Socialism,
he recalled the crazy guy who sat next to him during the
Hegel course and who listened intently to the elderly
professor but never volunteered a word to the discussions.
When Elmer asked him if he too had problems reading Hegel,
the other smirked and said he'd never read even one line of
his work. He was at the seminar for distraction from Proust,
he claimed. If Proust had dedicated his life to those novels,
he explained, he could dedicate one summer of his life to
reading them. Not that nut Hegel.

The article warned that one must grasp the idea of
Reflection in order to understand Hegel. But his first read
of the article in Novo Selo had left him just as dazed about
Hegel as at the university, so that he had summarized and
slightly rewritten the article himself, trying to simplify the
concept:

"In inorganic nature," he read aloud to Mirko from his
own version, "reflection is the process of things reproducing,
under the influence of other things, traces or imprints of
the things exercising that influence.

"In organic nature, reflection is instead an active process,
such as in the adaptation of animals to their environment.
Properties of the organism, which are the outcome of a
long process of adaptation by the species, are manifested
actively by the individual in the immediate influence of

other bodies in the environment, which have been present during this period of development. The concept of reflection, understood as the correspondence of mental images with the material world, which is the source of those images, is the basis of the materialist approach to cognition. Water is water whether it is hot or cold and whatever the amount of solubles it contains. Yet things continually change. Like the frog that gets boiled because it does not notice the increasing temperature of the water, human beings too lay aside the quantitative changes in their Being. So we can say at this point 'A=A'."

He glanced at Mirko.

The Serb nodded. "Right on!"

"Water is good for drinking, for making concrete or irrigating crops, whatever its temperature or color. But water eventually becomes steam or ice and even poison if it contains too many salts and metal solutes. In other words, what is A one moment is no longer A the next. The capacity of one object to 'reflect' the properties of another is based on the genetic relationship between the two species. The sunflower has no knowledge of the sun but it turns toward the sun, reflecting its orientation, because of eons of evolution of the organic world under sunlight.

"Reflection of social developments in politics is something else," he concluded, looked up, and said that this must be Hegel's idea. "Still, I don't really get why all the to-do about it. It seems so obvious."

"And so it is," Mirko said. "The reflection denotes also the process whereby in any real social system, phenomena at one level reflect processes taking place at a deeper level. For example, the real content of politics is economic interest ... especially today. Changes occurring in the relations of production are reflected in changes in the political sphere. For instance, we could say that the upsurge in the women's movement in the latter part of the twentieth century reflected the movement of women into the workforce and the socialization of women's work—not the other way around. Or that the dominance of mystification in post-modern philosophy and culture reflects the extraordinary level of concentration of capital and accumulation of fictitious capital in the same period."

Mirko stopped, threw back his head and laughed his raucous laugh. "So my friend, that's enough for today. Anyway, as Adorno wrote, Hegel is the only one with whom one literally doesn't know what is being talked about. No single point is conclusive. You have to read all he wrote in order to understand the separate parts."

"Absolutely crazy," Elmer said.

"Well, this too is important," Mirko said, and took a long drink. "We Serbs say, 'Thou shalt drink!' That's always a consolation. Let's get out of here! See the city a bit."

"Ilya told me it's too dangerous. I'm nearly a prisoner."

"Ah, Ilya! He's super careful. I'll take care of you. Besides, it will be a good lesson."

They taxied to the Old Town. The tavern was chic, an "in" place. Parties going on at various tables. Beautiful women, slickly dressed men in black. Rows of champagne bottles on the tables. Belly dancers nearby. Money thrown around left and right. Money hanging from the dancers' belly buttons.

"There they are," Mirko said at their place at the long bar. "Our new capitalists. Gangsters all. Gangsters and goons. Classic capitalists, the way they've always been … in every latitude."

The live music was deafening. Shouts and toasts. A dog pranced down the middle of the table nearest them. "*Dobro! Dobro!*" they called. Suddenly, a slow piece of modern jazz stopped other noise.

"Ah, jazz, the music of life," Elmer said reverently.

"So different from the Blues I learned to love in America … the story of life's difficulties. Yet in the end, also in this music, life triumphs. As if written for Serbs."

"They don't look like Socialists," Elmer commented, as

boos sounded from the three party tables. "And they don't like this music."

"No, they're gangsters. Not real music for them. Something snapped in their souls … cut them off from the rest. Only loud sounds interest them. This is our capitalism-gangsterism," Mirko repeated. "With all its decorations, curlicues and promises to working people under the free market. Here is your free market—our inheritance from the West—right before your eyes. I want …"

At that moment a uniformed man approached them and put a big hand on Mirko's shoulder. MP was written on his sleeve. "Your papers!" he said. Peremptorily. Authoritatively.

Mirko didn't flinch. Not even a blink. He produced his papers and nodded at Elmer: "A famous foreign student," he said, turning and waving as if toward an old friend at the dignitaries at the gangsters' table.

Elmer pulled at his martenitsa, said "*dobar vecher*" in Bulgarian, and laid his false student card on the bar.

The bartender placed a bottle of champagne and two slim glasses before them. "Compliments of your friends over there!"

The MP still looked doubtful for they looked totally out of place. Still, disconcerted by the champagne, Mirko's nonchalance, Elmer's youth and his words in Bulgarian, the big man glanced cursorily at the document, took another look at Elmer and grinned at his martenitsa, shrugged, and walked away.

"Capitalism!" Mirko commented as he paid the bartender. They left the champagne untouched.

'Oh, Lala, where are you?' Elmer thought as they walked out, aware that he could never again frequent such places. It was life. But not his life. His was another choice.

* * *

September. Elmer sat on the front steps under an overhanging roof to listen to the rain. The kitten came to him out of the dark, rubbed against his leg, purred, cautiously mounted his lap and searched for an acceptable place on his knees. The little feline was agitated. She turned and twisted. Hungry for food. Hungry for affection. He held his legs together. Offered a platform. Not enough. She—he thought of all cats as feminine—wanted more. Real food. The rain fell. Music to his ears. It was chilly now. He tickled Nina behind her ears but Nina didn't like the rain as he did. He would like to take off his clothes and bathe in it. He named the feline Nina in memory of an aged cat in the ancient wooden house in the Old Town of Providence where he grew up. He called her also Autumn for her beautiful fall colors, the shades of beige-gold-brown mixing with the dark on her back and the yellow on her neck under her chin. Then he called her Baby because she was so tiny and defenseless.

He watched Nina-Autumn-Baby gobble the plate of sliced beef he served her on the steps and he thrilled that he was here: in Belgrade. In Serbia. In the Balkans. In Europe. It should seem strange that he was here. But he liked the sensation of feeling his way along the fringes. The wondrous melodic rain fell one foot in front of him. He reached out and gathered raindrops. His original Nina back in Providence had become only a memory.

Also far away was his anti-war mother who had warned him, "Look at Cindy Sheehan. Listen to her if you can't hear your mother. Anyway I didn't have you to send you off to die in Iraq or Afghanistan or Iran or God knows where else."

His mother was right. He had begun understanding late. The incredible things he intercepted confirmed every word she had said. Admittedly, when he skipped from Novo Selo, he still had no splendid thoughts of heroism. But he believed he was moving in the right direction. His anti-war ideas were springing from his own personal experience. Joining the army, he now believed, had been the catalyst for his new understanding. He could have listened to his mother and read Cindy Sheehan for years and never grasped the understanding that was now his. That seemed like a metamorphosis. Or at least the beginning of change. He had learned that he wanted no part in the awful things happening in Iraq and Afghanistan. Even their geographical proximity was threatening. Just over the horizon, eastwards along the lily pad trail. He had as if touched them with his own hands ... by means of his computers and his radios. His convictions were maturing. He felt the cracking and snapping of old ideas breaking up and rotting away and the gentle rumbling pressure of new ones breeding, spawning, sprouting, accumulating. One thing he knew for certain: he wanted no part in invading other countries and killing people. That's what the military profession had come to mean for him, even for communications operators. War is wrong. It was that simple. War cannot be justified. His mother was right. Anybody ought to know that. Where, for Chrissakes, does the war craze come from?

* * *

Elmer had quickly come to believe that the wisest thing he had yet done in his short life was to desert. His was a fortunate flight. His language lessons were going well. Lyubica's charm brought out the best in him. He was already getting a handle on the grammar. They conversed in Serb and read simple texts together—like excerpts from the novel *Haiduk Stanko* about stoical partisans who had to forsake normal ordered lives in order to fight against the former Turkish occupiers. Though he sometimes identified with young Stanko learning to live the resistance fighters' life, he also found his renunciatory existence in the present satisfying. His future could wait. His future lay in the future.

Meanwhile, his lessons in political theory with Mirko continued to open up new worlds. He felt like a child learning to read and write and to understand what was happening in the world around him. His awakening made him feel a part of life.

"The ten steps to Fascism have already been taken in

the USA," Mirko said one evening, so matter-of-factly and self-evident that Elmer only nodded in assent. "Those steps are: creation of a fictitious external threat, readying of secret prisons, formation of paramilitary forces, surveillance of citizens, infiltration of civilian organizations, arbitrary arrests, targeting key individuals, press controls, labeling criticism as espionage and dissent as treason, and subversion of the rule of law. Fascism is becoming fashionable in America as it did in Europe in the 1920s and 30s. And it spreads like a contagious disease."

"Well, one can always resist," Elmer protested.

"Of course, resistance is necessary" Mirko concurred. "But the thing is, a government can stop dissent in its tracks. Not only propaganda, promises and cooptation, but also jail and a little torture of dissidents."

From that brutal foundation, Professor Mirko proceeded into economic-social-political theory: Socialism, Communism and Nationalism. America, he said, is isolated like Serbia. It is unraveling. An unraveling mirroring that of former Yugoslavia. Even if on the surface it looks invincible, Superpower America is in its death throes. The country is collapsing. Its leaders are in meltdown. The politicians who once called for law and order have lost control. Confusion and lawlessness reign in America. Marx's vision was so right.

"And the bloody Balkan wars," Mirko explained, "were not caused by ancient ethnic hatreds at all but by the economic collapse of Yugoslavia."

"Reflection!" Elmer hazarded.

"Right! The civil war marked the end of former Yugoslavia. Criminals like those in the café that night grabbed power in Belgrade and harnessed the anger and despair of the unemployed and the desperate, just as is happening in the USA. Some greedy Serbs singled out scapegoats: ethnic Croats and Moslems and Albanians and gypsies, unleashing the frenzy leading to war. There is little difference between the Serbian militias and sects like the Tea Party and the Oath Keepers.

"We can sit here and laugh at these people but they are not such big fools as we are. Elmer, one has to keep in mind that Fascism is totalitarian. The Fascist state—a synthesis of all values—interprets and develops the whole life of a people."

"OK. So then?"

"Fascism is absolutely opposed to doctrines of liberalism, both political and economic. The Fascist state controls the economic field as it does all the others. It works throughout the entire society, in all the political, economic and spiritual forces of the nation. The Fascist state considers private enterprise the most effective instrument in the interests of the nation. And since private organization of production is a function of national concern, the organizer of the enterprise is responsible to the Fascist State."

"Oh man, if such things were only taught in the U.S. educational system."

"Fascism may not be taught formally, Elmer, but its fundamentals arise out of real life in capitalist society. It is real life experience in America too. The people are collecting the evidence every day even though are still unaware of what is happening."

"I've been thinking about the hang-up about Russia and Communism I met everyday in my short life in the U.S. military. Fight Communism. Export democracy. And contain and crush those Russian bastards, all Commies anyway. The Communist states have disappeared, haven't they? Still, the U.S. military keeps talking about Communism as if it were an immediate threat ... while the truth is that the threat you describe is spreading in my country."

"Elmer, what we see today in many places in the world is in fact the yearning for the Fascism that was born in Germany and Italy last century. That yearning is a harbinger of Fascism itself. If capitalism doesn't get the unemployed and the poor back into the economy, giving them jobs and relief from debt, then racism and violence in America, in Israel, in some ex-Communist states too, will grow. The racism, nationalism and violence within American society will become full-blown Fascism. It's nearly there. The snuffing out of hope produces angry mobs ready to kill and be killed. In times of economic collapse, the liberal elite—in the best of cases ineffectual against the rich and the criminal—gets swept aside. Then thugs and demagogues emerge to play to the passions of the mob. I've seen this drama in the Balkans. You saw some of them in that café. The same thing happens in other lands. The same stock characters, the buffoons, the charlatans and the fools, the same confused crowds and the same impotent and despised liberal class that deserves the hatred it engenders. The problem is, laws do not apply to the powerful elite. That means the death of democracy and the emergence of Fascism.

"Elmer, Fascism by its very nature protects the power relations reigning in capitalist production. Fascism organizes the nation spiritually with radical demagogic propaganda, military build-up and the creation of a mass social base. Fascism is the phalange used to break alternative workers movements in the interests of capital. Just as the Margaret Thatcher and Ronald Reagan governments of the 1980s marked the crushing of illusions of a welfare state in the USA and the weakening of the foundations of social democracy in Great Britain.

"Then, the gran finale. Once in power, Fascism carries out a palace revolution in order to be in an all-powerful position to further regiment the masses while leaving capital free to dispose of the surplus value created by the workers. The Fascist state is a monopoly organization of capital. Mussolini once claimed that all of Europe would become Fascist ... that is, corporate. His prediction nearly came true back then. He believed in the fascistification of Europe just as Lenin believed in a world Socialist revolution. In that respect Fascism was counter-revolutionary to the Russian Revolution, despite its claims that it too was social and revolutionary. The signs of Fascism are today still the same as in last century—extreme nationalism, racism, hatred for the educated class, political correctness, anti-welfare and social reform, the preaching of violence."

* * *

Elmer's several hours a day at his computers and radio equipment produced the same quality exposés he had uncovered at Novo Selo. Now his leaks went also to the new *War Crimes Unlimited*, which had quickly provoked the expected fire and fury in U.S.-NATO circles.

He imagined 'raging Raymond'. There he was in the Novo Selo bar questioning soldiers and trying to trace him. There was the DIA pressuring East European allies and Turkey to find him, the traitor. 'Find him and those fuckers like him,' his imaginary DIA warned Raymond. 'Or we'll get someone who can.'

Yet Elmer had time on his hands. Time, time, time. He petted Nina. He listened to the music of her purrs. He missed Lala. Ilya asked him to be patient. It had to be done right, for her protection as well as for his. Sometimes almost absently Elmer wandered over the web and found extraordinary but bewildering information. One night he copied a news note:

(Geneva) A step forward in revealing the behavior of the universe in the first instants of life. CERN (European Organization for Nuclear Research) in Geneva has announced that in the world's biggest accelerator, the Large Hadron Collider (LHC), temperatures of thousands of billions of degrees, comparable to those that existed in the first millionths of a second after the Big Bang, have been recreated. 'With these first experiments we have already begun to see unexpected phenomena and we are beginning a physics program to study the behavior of the universe in its first

instants of life. At the extreme temperatures now obtained, inexistent even in the heat of the stars, it becomes possible to observe primitive matter as it was before it assumed its present characteristics.'

An academic note on personal relationships perplexed and intrigued him even more than CERN's discoveries about the first instants of the universe:

In their evaluations of the possibility of success of the modern couple, scholars conclude that the first meeting promises well when at the start there is a powerful physical attraction: passion explodes immediately and creates the 'sexual chemistry' that in turn generates an emotional connection sufficient to perpetuate itself for a long time. The same conclusions apply to a sincere flirt, more typical of women: when love is reciprocated, a powerful emotional link is created from which a good sexual agreement issues, which then forms the basis for a lasting relationship.

Elmer reminded himself that he was lucky. Maybe born lucky. He wasn't in Afghanistan or in rendition and he had Lala. In theory, he added. For in reality he didn't have her at all. And his studio was a prison. The short walk down the street to Lyubica was his chief outing. Ilya even sent in food and drink. Mirko's visits now exacerbated his sense of isolation.

He had to get out. Just get out. He craved life and excitement. He rationalized that late nights were safe. He had always loved the night. The peace and the security of darkness. He shaved off his beard, clipped his hair, left behind his martenitsa and after midnight walked the city. Sometimes with Mirko. Usually alone. He liked the Old Town, Strahinjica Bana that Mirko had first shown him. Sipping beer at a bar. Admiring the array of women in various poses. He laughed sourly when a bartender told him the quarter was called Silicon Valley because of the surgically upholstered young women in its string of show-off bars. He found the cobblestone alley of Skadarlija lined with old-fashioned, vine-covered bars and restaurants. The center of the city's bohemian life was a tourist trap. But he knew instinctively to steer clear of the district for it could become a trap also for him. It was too near the main pedestrian promenade, Knez Mihailova Street, with its modern shops, bookstores and art galleries and club-like coffee bars where people met their own circle of friends: the Czar of Russia and the Opera Café with their Old World décor, frequented by artists and writers, places Mirko had warned him over and over to avoid. On the riverfront, he looked longingly at the fish restaurants. One night he couldn't resist. On an old moored ship, the Ahab, he ate a spicy fish soup for a euro and a half. He saw dancing on the houseboats moored on the banks of the Sava and Danube, throbbing amalgams of folk music and electronic beats. No wonder *Lonely Planet* named Belgrade the world's number one city for partying. "Thou shalt dance" rang the Belgrade commandment. All the places and things he had to avoid. He knew he had to stick to the St. Sava neighborhood and the banks of the Sava and Danube rivers.

* * *

October. It turned cold. Winter was around the corner. Language lessons were going well. Twice a week Mirko roamed around the political landscape—from ideology to rampant nationalism to Fascism and social democracy, and, from time to time, back to his beloved Hegel.

Elmer was a curious student, eager to learn. This was not Brown. Or M.I.T. either. Where had he been before? In his high school-university life he had never heard the things Mirko taught. What were American universities teaching? In his hubris of yesterday he had believed he knew the essentials. Today, his brief exposure to real education rally hurtled him into a new existence of which he realized knew next to nothing. He needed Ilya and Mirko and ica.

Strange, he thought, I'm getting used to these Slavic names that make up my new life. And Lala? Lala was the joyousness, the frivolity he needed. What did it all mean?

Some nights, when the soldiers in Iraq and Afghanistan had signed off, he read disparate esoteric materials online, jumping randomly from one subject to the other, following any link that appealed to his new self, the new names flitting around in his mind. Place names, personal names. Novo Selo, Beograd, Strahinjica Bana, Skadarlija, Knez Mihailova. Then, Lyubica, Mirko, Knez, Ilya Milanica. He was falling in love with those names, as Proust did with the names of Venice and Odette. Yes, he thought, names count. He let himself roam freely among names. Though Knez Mihailova was not comparable with a Venice canal, it created new images. The new names, the familiarity with and acceptance of these names, helped him adjust to his new reality. Like for Proust, the new names offered new images of what was heretofore non-existent, helped him identify with his new life. More than that: on those rare late nights on the dark streets he sought for the core of his new life. And for signs of the social world about which Mirko lectured. The secluded corners of the city and the non-mainstream people … and all their names.

A Mirko lecture Elmer especially appreciated dealt with a theme he had neglected, though it had lain there under his eyes as wide and clear and illuminated as a computer screen: indifference. "I have long tried to totalize the ultimate effect on our lives of the nature of human indifference," Mirko began one night, ignoring the rain pouring on the streets of Belgrade, as did Nina curled into a furry ball on the worn leather couch. As each wave of out-of-season sheet lightning illuminated the small apartment, Elmer imagined the city's packed cafés and its two rivers and the riverboat-restaurants and the dome of St. Saba all rendered invisible under the unrelenting aqueous pounding, and recalling the fall rains over Rhode Island, and surprised that he didn't feel one iota of homesickness. "The bored indifference of Europeans that facilitated the birth of Fascism," Mirko continued. "The indifference that permits the emergence of reactionary extremism. The sad reality is that in the aftermath of World War II it became evident that many Europeans had lost their identity. That loss, I believe, provoked their gradual departure from reality ... and the hegemony of their indifference. We have witnessed this phenomenon in the passage from the Fascist bourgeoisie of yesterday to the neo-capitalist bourgeoisie of today. The same mutation took place during the Cold War when Western propaganda depicted the image of Cossacks watering their horses in the fountains of Vatican City, thus creating a new false consciousness ... this time of the Socialist-Communist danger.

"The loss of both identity and sense of reality generated the alienation of individuals and society as depicted in Antonioni's stark cinema settings. Then came the French existentialists and French sociologists like Jean Baudrillard with his depictions of the transformation of man into an object of exchange, to be bought and sold, as if his life were an investment which must produce profit. The fundamental idea is that when material success—that is possession—is considered the highest value, relationships between men follow the same patterns as for example in the exchange of consumer goods and labor.

"In this sense, resistance must be the response. Resistance to being possessed. A person's real value, then, is proportional to the resistance one puts up against being possessed. It's a battle between resistance on the one hand, and indifference on the other. The idea is that there exists something outside us, despite the idealistic philosophy according to which nothing exists outside us. The thing is people don't perceive this crisis but they suffer from it anyway. And communication becomes the basic problem of man. Psychiatrists call this defect of our relationships with reality 'de-realization'. It's a sickness, Elmer. A contagious disease. But, there are various mediations between us and reality—like sex. The novelist Moravia noted that we can relate to reality with our bodies. Like the woman asked if she preferred to masturbate or make love. 'Make love,' she answered. 'That way you at least get acquainted with someone.'

"The bourgeoisie remains the problem. The working men and the intellectuals hovering around the fringes of the bourgeois world are potential instruments for dissecting and analyzing that bourgeois world. But as a rule the working class only yearns for the Eden of the bourgeoisie, while intellectuals within that milieu either adapt or suffer in their alienation. Since there is no escape, their anguish can only grow.

"Elmer, you have to understand the European post-war bourgeoisie in moral terms … not merely economic. As befits a well-structured class, being bourgeois is a lifestyle. And no one denies that being rich is better than being poor. Still, the bourgeoisie must also be understood in European terms. The term originated in a century of social revolution in Europe terminating in the Russian Revolution. Uncertain in their reliance on and idolization of the proletariat as the natural opponent of the bourgeoisie, post-war intellectuals gravitated toward Communism, as did much of the liberal generation in that period in Europe.

"Indifference is another story. A European-American story. As French chansonnier Serge Gainsbourg sang of his love for Brigitte Bardot: 'What does the weather matter, what matters the wind? Better your absence than your indifference.' Or Gilbert Bécaud's words: 'Indifference kills with small blows.' The indifference of one person to the other in a dwindling love affair is emblematic of the terrible impact of indifference in any field at all.

"Of the murderous twentieth century, Niemöller wrote that indifference means 'no difference'. Indifference is the destroyer of whole societies. It's an unnatural state in which the lines blur between good and evil. But I ask you, is there a conceivable philosophy of indifference? Can indifference possibly be seen as a virtue? At times indifference can be seductive. It's easier to look away from victims, close our eyes to torture and social inequalities. But indifference to suffering is inhuman. Even more dangerous than hatred. One performs great actions for the sake of humanity but indifference can never be creative in that way. It's a non-response. And in the end it benefits the aggressor.

"As inhuman as it is, indifference to suffering is bearable only as long as the suffering is invisible. Indifference to war is something else; were it not for the enthusiastic way humans participate in war we could call it inhuman. Ignorance and deaf indifference are bad enough. But today, in Europe and the United States where information abounds, we have to call conscious indifference to war and injustice, and also its brother 'indifference to indifference', criminal and evil.

"Indifference appears in all places and at all times about every subject that has no direct, personal bearing on one's own little life."

Mirko took a sheet of paper from his bag and handed it to Elmer. "I distributed this to students at my lecture on indifference. I'll leave a copy with you."

Indifference! It doesn't matter!
Indifference about the abyss between rich and poor.
Indifference about the value of labor and the working man.
Indifference about a free press.
Indifference about public corruption.
Indifference about violence against women.
Indifference about man's treatment of animals.
Indifference about arms controls.
Indifference about the government defrauding its citizens.
Indifference about national health care.
Indifference about capital punishment.
Indifference about bombing civilians from the stratosphere.
Indifference about global warming.

Indifference about war and preparation for war.
Indifference about indifference.
"Layer after layer of my new life and my new world,"
Elmer wrote in longhand across the bottom of the page.

***

Ilya was more a man of the Adriatic Sea than of the heart
of the Balkans. He took his afternoon siesta and complained
of the short days and the dark: "I wake up from my afternoon
nap and it is dark. Is it day or night? I lie in bed and wonder.
If it is night why am I fully dressed? Must I get up or try
to go back to sleep? What a quandary!"

"But what about Lala?" Elmer asked, ignoring his mentor's
laments. Ilya's sleeping problems and hatred for darkness
didn't interest him. Lala occupied that part of his mind.
What was all this worth without love?

"We are near a solution," Ilya said one evening when Elmer
was particularly discouraged and blue. "Please believe me this
time. Just a little more patience. You will be very surprised …
very soon."

Two nights later, after his usual lesson at Lyubica's and
a repetitive walk to the banks of the Danube to watch the
passage of dimly illuminated barges, he found in his apartment
a typed message from Mirko that he was to go to Ulica
Palmoticheva the next afternoon at 4 p.m. for a surprise.

***

She was sitting facing the door on a straight chair at a table
near a curtained window. She looked different from the
Burgas Lala. She was dressed in a heavy woolen coat with
a high fur collar. Elmer stood in the doorway, first blinking
in surprise, then breaking into a broad grin. Lala didn't move.
Her expression was frozen alarm. Didn't she recognize him
without his beard, long hair and martenitsa? Gradually he
became aware of the fear and terror in every feature of her
beautiful face. Her eyes darted. Shivers ran down his spine.

He took a step forward. "*Lala, kako* ..." he said, before a voice behind him in the corner behind the door growled, "Come inside and shut the door." In the same instant Elmer understood that they had caught up with him, that it was his fault for insisting and that it was probably inevitable. Lala should not be here.

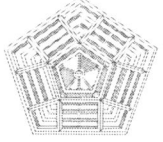

19

RAYMOND

WHEN Raymond was a teenager in Kingsport, he felt different from others, isolated from everyone because of his height. Always a foot taller than all his schoolmates, with every inch he grew, the lonelier and more awkward he felt. His destiny, he knew, was to be a loner. And a maverick. For that reason, East Tennessee State University in the small town of Johnson City suited him fine. As his college years unfolded, his feeling of awkwardness transformed into the silence of feline watchfulness. He observed life more closely than others. Eventually he cultivated that penchant for vigilance, he thought, scientifically. He noted details about everything and everyone. In his sophomore year, he began keeping notes on his observations and the people to whom they referred, which he arranged in filed notebooks hidden inside a closet.

Much to his surprise, Raymond also got on the basketball team—he didn't even try out for basketball, had never even considered it and had never especially liked the game. An assistant coach recruited him in his second year in Johnson City when he spotted Raymond's tall lanky figure walking around the campus. In those days Raymond's two-plus meters were exceptional in college basketball. Though he was never a starter, playing usually in late game minutes— which didn't bother him in the least—in one strange and inexplicable game in his senior year he excelled. The regular starter was injured and Raymond played from the first minute. For that one night everything Raymond did clicked. That night Raymond Bridges made Tennessee college basketball history, scoring 108 points; while with his every dunk the cheerleaders sang again and again, "*We are watching you,*" to the tune of the Police song so popular then. That performance changed his life. For the rest of his life, he continued singing to himself, high up in his personal aerie, the song's words, "*Every move you make, I'll be watching you.*"

It so happened that the college's administrative director, who was fascinated by espionage and intelligence, cooperated in the CIA's campus recruitment program and maintained close ties to that world so distant from his gray everyday self. He recommended the senior, Raymond Bridges, to the CIA. Though, as it turned out, the Agency itself had scarce interest in a man who stood out as physically as did Raymond, CIA personnel interviewer recognized something so special, so singular and out-of-the-ordinary in his personality that he passed his documentation on to the Department of Defense Intelligence Agency. There, Raymond Bridges' apartness and aloofness, in addition to his obsessive preciseness bordering on cold-bloodedness, fascinated first his recruiter, then his psychological examiner. The psychologist's invasive questions made a deep impression on Raymond, for no one, not even his parents or he himself, had ever dared delve into such intimate details buried deeply in his psyche. Though he was at first offended, those questions left an imprint on him, which in later years he continued to respect.

"Does your exceptional height bother you? Make you feel different? Alone?"

"Sometimes," Raymond had answered, at first embarrassed. It depended on his mood, black or rosy.

"Do you think your height bothers other people, makes them uncomfortable so they don't know how to treat you?"

Raymond was aware of the discomfort he caused but he answered, "No, not especially." No reason to reveal that the only woman-girl of his life broke up with him because, as she said, he was too tall for her.

"Do you think different thoughts up there, distant from other people, I mean?" the medical man asked. Raymond remembered how the examiner too had made a point of looking upwards at him and had chuckled softly.

"Sometimes," Raymond answered again. "But doesn't everyone?" he added. The question was, what kind of thoughts?

Raymond observed closely the slim little man, decided to risk it and took that one occasion to reveal more about his innermost intimate self than ever before, more than he ever would again. He boasted to the psychologist that he believed he was able to observe the world from another angle. That he constantly observed others often just to determine if he behaved as others did. However, he didn't tell the examiner about his notebooks and the criminal song that haunted him. That the innocent chant of the cheerleaders had become the sinister song of the stalker: *"Every move you make ... Every breath you take ... I'll be watching you."* It had become his theme song.

Both the psychologist and the recruiter recommended him most highly to Intelligence. Here was a special kind of man. So different. So clownish physically as to be above suspicion.

Subsequently the DIA trained him for lone missions. They encouraged his inclination to observe and study people and, if necessary, axe people in command ... and, in extreme cases, to kill. Actually, the DIA didn't formally hire him, he was never officially a full-fledged employee. He was something extra, undercover from the start. Outside of the bureaucratic world.

The agreement was fine with him, the loner. Raymond became an early contractor, with wide, almost unlimited authority, and rare controls. He came to think of himself as an entrepreneur.

In that gossamer vest, ghoulish, humongous Raymond began to haunt military bases around the world, observing that world from his altitude, following his hunches and investigating suspicions of military espionage or betrayal, embezzlement, sometimes even apparently petty crimes and special cases of awol in sensitive regions of the world. Raymond seemed to smell when an awol was more than simply 'absent without leave'. The DIA counterespionage sent him around the world on such missions because he seemed to sense when desertion meant also betrayal, and like a bloodhound he never gave up a scent.

The first time he saw Elmer, Raymond smelled a rat. It was his unerring instinct. Elmer's technological genius didn't impress him one whit. Not for one moment. The night he saw him in the Burgas café was the confirmation of his suspicions.

"I'll be watching you, young man," he murmured to himself. This man, he sensed, this boy with his unmilitary aspect and conduct, was headed for trouble. Bad trouble. Raymond saw only sham and simulation in Elmer's easy-going sensitivity and his popularity among officers and men. Yet, since he too found the kid attractive—Elmer reminded him of his college days, of the way he would have wanted to be, especially the time associated with his one night of glory and the 108 points—he hoped he wouldn't be the one to have to deal with his diversity someday.

Raymond had made a study of desertions and deserters. Though he sometimes felt admiration for their courage, he despised them at the same time. In his scale of values, desertion meant potential betrayal and was therefore dishonorable and depraved. Deserters were to be watched. The Pentagon reported that some forty thousand troops had deserted the ranks during the last ten years, more than half of them from the army ... even thousands of Marines.

Though most deserted in the USA itself before being sent to Iraq, some also betrayed abroad, in Iraq and Afghanistan.

Cowardice was the sentence Raymond pronounced on deserters. And as a rule, he concluded, somebody abetted them. Maybe the help was organized. A conspiracy, to corrode the military from within. From his studies of the American Civil War he was familiar with rat lines.

Yet he was disconcerted to learn that awol was a term also used by civilians to describe people like himself who just take off in life ... who at some stage go missing. Like the act of going mad. Like in the expression 'he got so mad he went totally awol.' For Raymond, this was too close for comfort, for he had been awol in that sense all his life.

Moreover, Raymond was even more intellectually confused when he learned that there are situations in which desertion is legal or even required by international law. One of the Nuremberg Principles states: "The fact that a person acted pursuant to order of his government or of a superior does not relieve him from responsibility under international law, provided a moral choice was possible for him." On the one hand, he felt a certain sense of relief, even justification, for his less than severe treatment, in fact for his unusual leniency, in the case of Elmer. In his years in the field this had never happened to him before. Nonetheless, despite considerations like morality and conscience, duty was duty. He had never had any sympathy for conscientious objectors. That a person performing military service could develop conscientious objections smacked of heresy. He had dispatched more than a few for less pressing reasons.

* * *

A secondary reason the DIA sent Raymond to the NATO base of Novo Selo in Bulgaria was its particular interest in the presence of the non-American soldiers training there. They were fertile ground for recruitment for DIA's expanding Intelligence network of agents, informers and, in some cases, even sleepers, a project that especially attracted Raymond. 'Stay-behind soldiers,' as some old hands insisted on calling them, in countries friendly to U.S. interests today. But tomorrow? What about tomorrow in an America-hating world that had to be controlled? Duty-bound in his lofty isolation and driven by pangs of conscience and commensurate responsibility, Raymond devoted much of the summer after Elmer's flight to the second part of his assignment: recruitment.

After interviews of soldiers of various nationalities recommended by the camp commander's office, and after observing them in training exercises, he settled on two — Georgy Makim, a Russian-speaking Romanian of Moldavian origin, who had a powerful physique with strong heavy hands and thumbs as thick as Raymond's wrists, a quirk which especially fascinated lanky Raymond. His second choice was a Turk from Kars, Berker Turan, also Russian-speaking because of a Russian émigré mother. Despite the latter's anomalously lean physique, he was chosen because he had grown up near the border with Georgia. Before joining the Turkish army, Berker Turan had worked in the famous vineyards of that neighboring country. He was of special interest too because of his links with extreme right-wing factions in Ankara.

Though Raymond's superiors had not established the Russian language preference — they hadn't given him a precise, specific assignment — Raymond instinctively sought them out. He knew he was scoring points. He firmly believed that his network of Russian speakers was the future. Makim and Turan convinced Raymond that the Russian threat was back and that America would have to deal with it in the near future. Besides, he knew that if ordered to do so, Makim the Moldavian and Turan the Turk would not hesitate to kill, no-questions-asked.

* * *

Though his visit to Istanbul failed to turn up anything concrete about Elmer Redway, something in the behavior of bazaar shopkeepers backed up his hunch of the existence somewhere in East Europe of a rat line to shelter American deserters. Starting then from Novo Selo and Bulgaria he eliminated one country or the other as a haven—for ideological or technical reasons—for deserters from bases in Bulgaria.

Raymond reasoned that Elmer, despite his relationship with the girl in Burgas, had most certainly left tightly controlled Bulgaria. There was too much of an American presence there. And what did girls matter anyway? They were always impermanent, temporary, fleeting apparitions in a man's life. They left you, or you left them.

The only person Raymond was ever seen with, perhaps the only person with whom he had any personal relationship at all, was Berker Turan, Turan the Turk, as his friends called him. Turan was an outspoken, garrulous type, not quite military, in a way an outsider like himself, like Elmer, who smirked at military ritual in the same way.

"Are you a patriot?" Turan asked him point blank in the darkened base bar where Raymond still spent much of his afternoons ... just to observe. "Why do you lead this life? If you're not fighting war, what do you want from life? Life is struggle. *Borba*, as Russians say. Or do you want to get into the history books as a national hero?"

"Neither of those," Raymond confessed.

"So what is it? Just personal discipline?"

Raymond glared at the Turk. Turan was too close to the truth. He'd revealed too much of himself which the Turk could eventually turn against him. Raymond suspected they were not so different from each other. The reaction was instinctive in Turan. Payback, Raymond thought, for exposing himself. He would never make that mistake again. And he would make the Turk pay in turn for having seen into him.

"It's payback," he said. "And it is a kind of war."

"Payback? Against who?" Turan pressed him. He wanted more. He was like that psychologist back in Washington who brought him into this job. But this was not a job. Nor a mission. That day Raymond actually admitted the truth to the Turk. If he could give it a name, he said, he would call it revenge. Revenge against life. His revenge was to catch and, when possible, kill the bastards so comfortable, too comfortable, in life. No one should live in their kind of comfort and ease.

"Against them all," Raymond added.

The Turk didn't reply but gazed at him, a smirk in his eyes, a twist to his lips, a firm hand on Raymond's arm ... and understood. It was if they had just signed a blood pact. Brothers in revenge.

Raymond now knew he had a killer at his side. Though he too had killed and had felt nothing, he still didn't understand what it meant. To kill. To take away the life of another. Like God. He could perhaps learn from Turan the reason for his thirst for revenge. In any case, he would take him along wherever he went.

* * *

Nearby and accessible, Turkey, he had decided, was too complex for deserters. Romania, the Czech Republic, Hungary and Poland were all too closely linked with NATO, with new U.S. military installations and U.S. Intelligence investigators, which would surely frighten deserters. He discarded also Italy. People could disappear underground in Italy but its powerful grassroots security organizations, its involvement in U.S. wars, the many-faceted CIA presence there and the Italian penchant for talk would be a deterrent to any such rat line long remaining secret. To Raymond it seemed equally difficult to go underground in Switzerland, or in big Germany too, for that matter. Of course, there was always Paris, a traditional haven for exiles, but its distance and the existence of the girl in Burgas made France seem unlikely in Elmer's case.

By virtue of elimination and his own intuition, Raymond thus arrived at Serbia, only one country westwards, with a people fundamentally inimical to the USA—also because of the theft of Kosovo—and, he knew, with a parallel Intelligence network still linked to the former Communist Yugoslavia. Serbia! That's where he would search. If Elmer Redway was there, they would find him. And the girl Lala was perhaps the bait.

He called for a meeting with Redway's superiors, the officer in charge in the Communications Systems office and the young Lieutenant, who, Raymond suspected, knew Elmer better than anyone on the base. Both officers, he knew, were more than tolerant of the kid's bohemian style. He tongue lashed them in his quietest, most threatening tones, mentioning Redway's earring and his overall unsuitable, unmilitary dress. Raymond then put on his most no nonsense mask, emphasizing his DIA role, displaying his written orders from the Department of Defense, the dangers to them both from the suppression of pertinent information, and finally invoking a question of national security. Elmer Redway had very likely defected to the enemies of the United States of America.

"So what can you tell me about him?" he asked point blank after he saw them sufficiently cowed. "Where could he have gone? Where has he been in the past? He's too young to be secretive. I believe he must have told you about his life here."

"Well, he has a girlfriend in Burgas ... and visits her often," the Captain said curtly.

"I know that. And I believe she is somehow linked to his, uh, his defection."

"Awol!" the Lieutenant said, grinning. "He has done it before. He just left one morning. We assumed he had to see that girl in Burgas."

"Desertion is what I call it," an unsmiling Raymond snapped. "Desertion, and as I said, most likely defection to the Russians. He is not stupid. And it would be stupid to go awol to Burgas, when he knew that my men and I were keeping an eye on him. I must remind you gentlemen that this young man knows as much — or more than either of you — about the U.S. military in the world. Don't be misled by his age and apparent innocence. No one is innocent in this game."

"Game?" the Lieutenant muttered.

"Let's not play with words, Lieutenant. I read some most damaging reports on WikiLeaks that I have good reason to suspect originated with your Redway."

"Sorry, sir!"

"Where do you *believe* he is? Make some educated guesses."

The Captain cleared his throat, looked at his junior officer who simply nodded gravely and said, "As a rule his traveling, as far as we know, was limited to Burgas. He's been here too short a period to have accumulated much leave time but about six months ago he requested permission — granted by me — to spend one week's leave in Istanbul. And once he visited the important Belgrade University Communications Center. With our blessing, I might add, and in the line of duty. I believe that is the extent of his travels in the year he has been here. Is that correct, Lieutenant?"

"Yessir. Correct, sir."

Raymond frowned. Waited a moment and then a beat or two longer, which made the officers squirm uncomfortably in their seats, before saying: "One last matter. I would like to search his quarters. Highly likely that a kid like him left something behind. A place. A name. We'll see."

"Fine. I'll take you there now," the Lieutenant said, displaying his relief that the grilling was over but also with signs of regret in his eyes that he had betrayed Elmer.

"OK, gentlemen, thank you for your cooperation in this extremely sensitive matter. I don't believe I need add that this conversation is top secret. We don't want Redway to suspect we're on his trail. Now, shall we go, Lieutenant?"

Elmer's room was the mess of a typical college freshman,

unexpected in a crack military installation. Raymond frowned at the grinning, tough-looking Corporal accompanying him and the Lieutenant to the room, as if he were somehow an accomplice.

"Not exactly up to military standards, I would say. Right, Corporal?"

"Yes Sir! I mean No sir," the soldier replied, trying to suppress the grin that continued pulling at his chin and deforming the bottom of his face.

Finally, Raymond too had to smile, as much at the Corporal's discomfort as at the total disorder of Elmer's small room. "Well, let's see if the kid left anything compromising behind."

He opened a few drawers, threw back the bed sheets, ran his hand along a bookshelf and examined a pile of Internet printouts. Under the bed, he found a small, old-fashioned suitcase with brass locks and buckles. Just like this crazy kid to have a bag like this, he thought, tossing it on the bed. Locked. Without a word he took a pocketknife from a back pocket and with one deft motion snapped open the flimsy lock. He picked up a book on political philosophy lying amid other books. Glanced over letters postmarked Providence, RI. Skimmed typewritten papers and handouts that he imagined were class notes. He turned his attention back to the book. Inside the cover were Elmer's name and the stamp: Property of Brown University. Automatically, he thumbed through the pages until the file card dropped out on the bed. And there it was, in Elmer's handwriting: Ilya, Belgrade University, Palmoticheva Street 25, Belgrade.

"That little idiot!" he murmured, "leaving a trail like this behind. You'd think he wanted to be discovered."

"Yessir," muttered the Corporal. "Will that be all, sir?"

"Oh yes, this is quite enough."

20

KARL HEINZ

SUMMER is pleasant in Burgas. People say that it is warmer than usual this year. Again living in the top floor suite in the same Excelsior Hotel where I stayed earlier, I sometimes forget my mission in East Europe. Once more I'm hooked on hotel living and fortunately can afford that luxury. The days and weeks pass in study and love and learning to speak Bulgarian and driving along the Black Sea coastline, north toward Varna and south toward Turkey. Every day I become more deeply intrigued by the cultural mishmash of Slav and Turk in this new world and increasingly cognizant of my debt to Cliff for liberating me from the chains of my West European culture. This is truly a brave new world. A world of philosophers like Hristo the taxi driver in Sofia, who, when I invited him to vacation in Burgas, arrived with wife and four children so that I had to rent them a vacation house on the Black Sea.

As the summer season progresses I also begin to conquer my fears of the Sea and come to think of it as a spirit, created by distant Persian and Greek and Slavic gods, as are perhaps the whole Balkans and the Slavs and their universal messianic concept of a spirit that would change and save mankind.

The Black Sea coast spans the entire eastern border of Bulgaria, from Ukraine and Russia in the north to Turkey in the south. Sunshine is endless, so different from my bleak Berlin and Brandenburg. Besides language study, I read about Slavic mythology, intrigued by those old gods which survived Christianization and, as old gods are wont to do, lurk forever deep in Slavic souls. I'm fascinated by myths of the ancient Slavs in the far north, who transform themselves into wolves for several days each year—werewolves, a popular belief in this area of the world. There is Perun, the god of lightning and thunder and the supreme god of the Proto-Slavic pantheon, Perun forever in battle with Veles, the scary god of wetness, seas and lakes, water and existence. When a three-headed snake emerged from the Black Sea, wreaking havoc and destroying all in its path in an attempt to prevent Perun from marrying Diva, Perun defeated the monster, which plunged back into its home at the bottom of the Black Sea. No wonder I've been terrified of the Sea. But theirs is not a conflict between good and evil, rather the opposition of Earth's forces: Veles and Perun, fire and spirit. Like the opposition between winter and summer. Between life and death. In Slavic mentality, I learn that the *Byelobog*, the white god, and *Chernobog*, the black god, are ever-present. The Slavic peasants accepted baptism when Christianity arrived but they persisted in performing their ancient rites and worshipping old pagan cults. This continued down through the centuries even though they eventually forgot the names of the ancient deities and myths. Christianity for them was not a replacement of old Slavic mythology but an adjunct to it. Christianity offered salvation in the next world, but for a fruitful life in this world the old religious system of fertility rites and household spirits was still necessary. Christianity has never resolved this problem, neither in Slavic lands nor in Mexico and Central America, certainly not in Africa, where the ancient rites and remains of religious cults survive. Now I understand Elmer's martenitsa. And the role of the *char*. The two belief systems simply merged peacefully—Perun morphed into St. Elijah the Thunderer or St. Michael and sometimes became even the singular Christian God Himself.

I have switched to a one-on-one intensive course at a language school near the hotel. Still, Antonia and I continue to speak German together but as I progress we try communicating in Bulgarian from time to time. Our occasional attempts fail and we soon fall back into German.

Antonia has finished the spring semester at university, earned her undergraduate degree and is enrolled in a summer seminar on Literature and Reality, led by a guest professor from Berlin, which I too follow. She uses our hotel suite as her study for enormous reading assignments and spends most nights there ... though not always absorbed in her books. "Not since my days in the German School in Rome has my life seemed so normal," I boast. At times I feel distant from Cliff and my original assignment. In the meantime Antonia has learned all the words to *Vorrei che fosse amore*, and hums and sings it when I least expect.

"It *is* real love!" I insist, at which she still smiles enigmatically and teases, "You never know for sure."

"*Liebst Du mich, ja oder nein*," I still ask, to which she answers as always: "*Aber natürlich*."

From time to time I think of Elmer and wonder to where he has been lily-padded. Antonia has tried to learn where Lala is. Lala's well-to-do parents are closed-mouth and only speak of studies abroad. Each time Antonia asks they say they will ask Lala to contact her. She never has. "*Seltsam, er ist ganz verrückt nach ihr*," I recall, though I keep my doubts to myself. Something stinks in the disappearance of first Elmer. Now Lala. Most certainly she has joined him somewhere.

One day in mid-July, I rent a car and drive out to Novo Selo to look up Alvin. Maybe I will get a chance to ask the Camp Commander about my old friend Elmer. Someone has to know something. From the gate, I call faithful, rule-bound Alvin in his office. He comes to the gate, smartly turned out in his strict military style, and vouches for me.

In the same cavernous bar, dark as night, as before Alvin brings me a Calvados and a beer. He recounts his latest adventures in Sofia, his worries about being lily-padded eastwards and swears he has no idea where Elmer is. "If he went to Georgia he would have called … I think even if he was in Afghanistan."

"Maybe he's on a secret mission," I suggest, my eyes turning involuntarily toward the door.

"You think so?" Alvin says, with a sardonic grin. "Elmer, on a secret mission? That character Raymond keeps pestering me about him too as if he thought I knew something he doesn't. He's interviewing half the troops on the base; he ought to know what's going on. Anyway the whole story is wacky. The Lieutenant who used to protect Elmer told me that there's more than meets the eye here. And the foreigners—like those over in the corner, the ones who always joked with Elmer—whisper to me not to bother looking for him. That he's gone."

"What do you think they mean, gone? Dead?"

"Awol gone. Pulled out. Disappeared. Deserted."

"Oh, Christ!"

"Yeah, but that's better than going to the Afghan mountains to be captured and tortured to death. A lot of people go awol and are never heard of again."

"I believe that ghoul Raymond is involved in all this. Don't know in what way, but involved."

"An ominous man … probably mad as a hatter."

In that moment, the door opens and there he stands. "Still following me," I mutter, as Alvin also turns toward the giant. "Not only you. He's always watching me. That man's a bloodhound … Elmer thought he was dangerous."

"Thought?"

"Maybe still does."

"Come on Alvin, tell me where he is."

"I swear I have no idea. I really thought he'd been lily padded."

"So you're saying maybe something different happened?"

"Maybe, yes."

"If he wasn't sent to the East and if he deserted, what do you think about Istanbul? He told me he was attracted by its mystery … and its history. And you know him!"

"Possible. But still, as they say, *cherchez la femme.*"

Lala's parents only say that she is 'somewhere' in England studying. Now I'm convinced that she joined him somewhere. England? I doubt it. England's too much the USA. Where else would Lala agree to go? Not that she would be attracted to Turkey, but Elmer might like the idea of Istanbul. Don't some people call Bulgars "half Turks"? All that mekhana and belly dancing and euros waving between their fingers must mean something.

While Alvin chatters about his last trip to Sofia, the kernel of an idea develops in my brain. I'll go to Istanbul and make a big show of my presence there. If Elmer and Lala are in Istanbul, maybe they will get wind of the arrival of old friends. From Lala's parents or from Alvin or God knows whom.

Back at my hotel I call Cliff from a public phone. He confirms that it's easy to go underground in Istanbul and gives me the name of a secure contact, a carpet shop in the Grand Bazaar. Told me to ask for a certain Nazar. Just asking for him will open doors. Nazar knows everything happening in Istanbul. Even if I'm wrong about Istanbul, my presence there could take pressure off the fugitive and lead the DIA man astray.

* * *

I reserve a suite at a hotel near Istanbul's Grand Bazaar and book the best seats available on the morning Metro bus for Turkey; five hours driving time, two hours border controls. The next evening we are sitting on the hotel's roof garden terrace overlooking the Bosporus and the Galata Bridge, the Topkapi Palace, the Blue Mosque, the former Santa Sophia Cathedral and pieces of the extant Byzantine walls.

The following morning is hot. America and Americans seem to have invaded huge, complex Istanbul. Because of the proximity of the Bazaar, the area is touristy, yet clean and prosperous looking. No signs of crisis here. In his book, *Istanbul*, Orhan Pamuk, the Nobel Prize winning novelist, describes his hometown as melancholy and nostalgic. But today it's the dynamism in city life that impresses the Westerner, like the excavation of a 5.5 kilometer railway tunnel under the Bosphorus. Pamuk's Istanbul seemed to be suffering from the loss of the Ottoman Empire but today's city has turned the corner and gone far beyond that. There are probably more Muslim women in head-to-toe black on London's streets than in Istanbul and maybe even more wearing head scarves. In comparison to Middle Eastern Arab cities, Istanbul is ultra-Western; hookahs and backgammon boards in coffee bars among its few exotic remaining features.

The touts hanging around outside the Bazaar are a plague, but when I ask about Nazar, one boy nods and, taking us for Italians, says "*seguitemi*" and leads us nearly on the run through a labyrinth of shops offering every conceivable kind of goods. Inside the maze agile boys dart past us in all directions, bringing tiny glasses of hot tea to the Bazaar's shops. Tea and discounts are offered to prospective clients, the traditional background for the expected haggling. Everything is on sale here, from bedspreads and handsome jewelry, from shiny cutlery to carpets from every corner of Turkey and Central Asia, to the bodies of boys and girls from anywhere in the whole East. You can spend hours, or even days, during the process of buying a single carpet.

"Nazar!" our guide says, pointing to an open doorway almost invisible between draped silks on one side and copper pans hanging on the other. I press five euros into his hand and enter ahead of Antonia. Immediately a tall, fat, dark and mustachioed figure emerges from behind a curtain, holding a gray, long-haired cat in his arms. The man is neither young nor old.

"Mr. Nazar?"

"How do you know my name?" he asks in melodious, heavily accented English.

"Clifford," I answer ... and wait.

Gaither Stewart

The man studies me for a moment before repeating: "Clifford?" as if he'd never heard the name.

"Cliff said you could help me find a certain person, maybe here in Istanbul."

"Ah, Cliff! Why did you not say so? Ah, yes, a dear old friend. We drank many glasses of tea together … and other things too." For a moment he smiles sweetly, then adds: "A friend of Cliff will always be a friend of mine."

He snaps his fingers and a boy darts from behind the curtain and rushes out the entrance. Tea is on the way. Another boy lifts breezy scarlet silken materials revealing a sitting area of three armchairs covered in dark green velour and a low copper table.

"Please, Madame," he says to Antonia, then to me, "Please, friends of Cliff, make yourselves comfortable here."

We sit down. I lean forward and begin, "I wanted to ask you if …"

"Wait! Patience!" he interrupts. "First the tea, then the, ah, then the problems which I feel certain can be resolved. I, ah, I hope you are comfortably situated in our lovely city."

While we go through what is evidently ritual—Where do we come from? Who are we? How is his friend Cliff?— he pours a pale liquid into tiny glasses, the smell of anisette immediately strong. The tea arrives and the boy carefully closes the entrance door and vanishes.

We sit in silence for some time, sipping anisette and hot tea, before Nazar asks abruptly: "Who are you searching for?"

"An American. Maybe in hiding here."

"A good American?"

"Yes, a very good American. Very young. Very different."

"Hmmm. So why is he, uh, fleeing?"

"He's a soldier who doesn't want to go to Afghanistan … or Guantánamo either. He hates the war."

"Aha! A deserter. We do see a few of them … from time to time, you understand. We try to help them. Where did this ah, good American flee from?"

"From Novo Selo, in Bulgaria."

"His name?"

"Elmer. Elmer Redway."

"Elmer?" Nazar falls silent, pushes aside his tea glass, smoothes down the ends of his mustache, pulls at his string of beads and examines the designs of the carpets hanging on a side wall. Magically his shop has grown in size. The silence weighs heavy.

"Strange," he then murmurs. "Another American has been here asking questions about, I believe, the same man. What can this mean, do you think?"

"Did you see that man, Mr. Nazar? Do you know who he is?"

"I heard about him and did see him from a distance. He is a Titan. Others here say he is not a, ah, as you say, not a good American. But for money one can buy information anywhere, anytime. Alas! Everyone selling themselves."

"Raymond!" I blurt out. "Yes, he is a bad man. A killer, I believe."

Another long silence.

Then: "Our mutual friend Cliff—or Clifford as you like to call him—might like to know that American soldiers sometimes desert from their bases throughout the Middle East. I have heard of several cases of deserters from bases in our neighboring Bulgaria. There are of course not many safe places to flee to in the world ... for an American soldier. They do not usually come here unless they are of Turkish descent."

Again, silence. This time, my disappointment must have shown on my face.

"However," Nazar said, "I know that for complex but understandable reasons some go to Serbia, to Beograd. That is, Belgrade. Who knows if your, ah, friend, the *good* American soldier went there? I have friends there. Perhaps I can learn something. If you return tomorrow morning I might have news for you. I must speak with several people, you understand. I also want to speak with my friend Cliff again."

Nazar stands up and claps his hands. The boy reappears. "Mehmet will lead you out of the Bazaar. He will meet you at the entrance tomorrow at ten a.m. Now good-bye."

"Thank you, Mr. Nazar, for your help. I hope we reach him in time ... before that, er, that Titan finds him."

* * *

The next morning Mehmet leads us back into the maze. The ritual begins again. Nazar orders tea, pours the anisette, asks again about our stay and from habit makes us a special offer on a trio of Turkish carpets. Finally, as if an afterthought, he reaches inside his extravagant purple housecoat and extracts a small piece of paper, passing it to me as if he had no idea what information it contained: "You might check with this person."

I read the name and smile: Ilya, Belgrade, Palmoticheva Street 25.

Confirmation. I wring Nazar's hands and were it not for his girth would have embraced him.

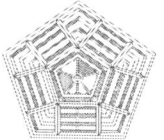

21
CLIFF

EACH morning I found excuses to go out. I had to see my publisher or meet a contact or conduct an interview. In reality I haunted Elizabeth Strasse located across the river in Schwabing. My hunch had become fixation. For hours at a time I sat in a Café-Conditorei vis-à-vis number 65, or, at odd hours, in the café at the end of the street on Elizabeth Platz where in my former life I had spent many cold evenings huddled around an antique iron stove in meetings with Russian émigrés. From the cafés I often called Karl Heinz's number in Berlin. Each time I got Katharina's message that she had left Wannsee, forever. I didn't know whether to believe it or not. I was only mildly surprised when Karl Heinz telephoned me one morning from Istanbul; he had seen Nazar.

For weeks I had hung around the tram stops and U-Bahn stations nearest Elizabeth Strasse. My intuition continued to tell me that Masha was here. There was nowhere else in Munich … unless she opted for the past and Hohenzollern Platz where she had lived in another life. Maybe I should stake out her old place too.

But no, she was here, I continued to believe, on this street. But under what name? The street was short. Uncertain of what name she might be using, I checked and re-checked names on the doorbells of every house. I showed her photograph to residents along the street … and I waited. Waited for the past to catch up with me, with Elizaveta, with all of us together. Perhaps Vasiliy in Riga would have somehow let Masha know we were waiting for her, in Munich.

A month passed. Autumn arrived. Overnight it turned cold. I had begun using the U-Bahn to reach my stakeout sites on Elizabeth Strasse. Counting obsessively on my hunch about the name Elizaveta-Elizabetes Iela, I was still certain Masha would aim for this street. Elizaveta herself adamantly refused to even go near there. But I was scrupulous in my stake-outing, thorough, no longer the happy-go-lucky buccaneer I'd once been.

One Monday shortly before noon, on a whim I switched lines on my usual travel route and headed for Hohenzollern Platz where Masha once lived with Nikitin … and later with Elizaveta. I thought I would walk around the square, check again at her old address, ask in the market on the corner, the café next door. I had the rest of the day for Elizabeth Strasse. I came up from the Underground on the square, stepped out onto a wide sidewalk into a burst of sudden sunshine and almost bumped into a woman carrying an armful of packages.

I gaped. So sudden, so unexpected, that for a moment it hardly registered. It was Masha. Masha, standing only a foot away. I would have recognized her even if she had changed her appearance. But she had not. Old Amsel, the cellar mouse, was right. It was as if the person I was looking for had found me.

I stared at her, incredulous. As Vasiliy had told us, she was still as beautiful as in the photos. She glared at me as if I were a stalker.

"Masha!" I stammered thoughtlessly. "Masha! *Vas iskal vesde i povsyudu*! I've been looking for you everywhere," I said. "I've been on Elizabeth Strasse every day for a month."

A look of alarm crossed her eyes. Not fright at first, but intense surprise at a giant stranger calling her by name and speaking to her in Russian. I could be CIA. Or from a Russian agency. "What? What? Who … who are you? I don't know you … do I?"

"No, we never met. But I know you. My name is Clifford Beecher."

At my name she again reacted with alarm. From my name she knew I came from her former world. From Nikitin's world. The world she was running from. Stunned, she let me take the packages from her arms.

"No, no, never mind my name," I said, guiding her away from the U-Bahn stairs. "Don't worry. Masha, I'm your daughter's husband. I'm your son-in-law. We've been waiting for you ... searching for you. We met your friend Vasiliy in Riga. He told us all. We know you've suffered. You don't have to worry about anything anymore."

"You were in Riga! How did you find out I was there? And Elizaveta was there too?" She released a torrent of words, of pent-up emotions as if she couldn't say it all fast enough. She had been silent so long that thoughts and articulated words were one and the same. "Yes, I've suffered. I was ill for a long time. I was sick. Confused. I'm still confused. I couldn't stay in Riga. Nor in Russia, and I was afraid to return here. Afraid I'd lost Elizaveta ... like I lost Anatoly my son, like I lost Anatoly my husband ... like I lost my life."

"Try to stay calm," I said. "You will have a new life, again a new life ... with Elizaveta ... with us. We'll go there now ... unless we want to continue this conversation all day here on the sidewalk."

"Clifford Beecher. I once knew that name from my husband. Clifford, I'm afraid she will reject me. She is right. I couldn't decide what was right. The right thing to do. I've been afraid for so long. Fear is my second nature now. I lived in fear here in Munich, like in a graveyard of my life ... my life before Anatoly, before Elizaveta. Then I lived in fear of losing her. Of losing him. Then I did ... lose all. Then I was afraid in Russia. Afraid in Riga. Since I lost our son Anatoly, life has been only imitation life. A lifetime of fear."

"No more fear, Masha. This is a new life," I dictated, casting aside her reservations, her objections, her demons, her fears. In the warmth of my success, of having struck gold, of having found the end of the rainbow, I felt myself swagger. I felt jaunty, almost devil-may-care. "Elizaveta is waiting. This will be the happiest day of her life ... and of yours."

I waved toward a taxi stand across the square until a driver saw me. Twenty minutes later we were in the Holbein Strasse. In Bogenhausen. In Munich. "This is the end of one cycle," I said as we stood at the elevator, "and the beginning of a new one."

The elevator door opened. I started to guide Masha in and stopped in my tracks. Ilya stood before us inside the elevator. Though Ilya knew little about Elizaveta's family, a secret Slavic smile cracked his face. Without a word, the three of us rode up to the top floor. Ilya impatient to talk. Masha, so terrified of the homecoming and of meeting her daughter twenty-five years later that she hardly noticed him. Her eyes were fixed on mine, seeking reassurance and strength. I imagined Elizaveta's reactions and wondered how I would react to finding my own mother a half century later.

Inside the apartment, with unseeing eyes Masha gazed around the illuminated foyer decorated with her daughter's paintings.

"Ilya, wait for me in the kitchen," I whispered. "Make some kava. Read the stack of my articles on the side table. This is a turning point in the lives of two women ... of our family."

Elizaveta came out of her studio, an alarmed expression on her face. Instead of a dangerous confrontation there in the foyer, for long seconds the two women only stared at each other.

"You're taller than me," Masha finally said, blushing and probably hoping the right words would come. Elizaveta, her usual radiance now pale and feeble, as if burnt out, didn't utter a sound.

For a few seconds longer each waited awkwardly before then embracing, at first warily, then intensely, passionately, both of them moaning softly. I had never seen the same passion of the scene being played out before my eyes. I witnessed the powerful Russian family tie win out over the inexplicable vicissitudes of Masha's shipwrecked life.

"My daughter," Masha murmured, caressing Elizaveta's hair. "Just a little girl when I left you. I hope you will forgive me."

"Mama. At last you're back home," Elizaveta said, separating slightly, her hands still gripping her mother's arms.

"Home? Yes, a long, long time ... too long ... too high a price."

"But why, Mama? Why?"

"How can I ...? Back then ... we were different, Elizaveta. Yours is another generation."

"You were different? Papa was different?" Elizaveta demanded an explanation then and there. She couldn't hold back anything. It had all been on the tip of her tongue for too long,

"I mean the times when you had to believe in something ... right or wrong. But you had to believe. I believed, we believed. But those beliefs had a high price. Too high. Then when I saw the new Russia, I knew we had lost. ... What I saw there shattered my dreams. It was the vulgarity. And everything I see here seems the same. None of it is worth you."

"But is it over now? Has it finished?"

"I doubt it, *Serdtse*," Masha said, her strength showing through, it seemed in that moment summoning up an echo of the tenacity that must have guided her former life. "I doubt it ever ends, my darling. I'm still a woman of my generation."

Gaither Stewart

22

ON THE first of September, I e-mailed Karl Heinz some collected notes on the Serbian situation:

Background on the Yugoslav-Serbian-Balkan-Russian question.

Karl Heinz: I have reconstructed for you another version of the fateful situation of former Socialist Yugoslavia. The following are views of ex-leaders of former Socialist Serbia, including a close assistant to former Serbian President, Slobodan Milosevic.

The thesis: A coup d'état executed by intelligence agencies of the USA, Great Britain and NATO overthrew Milosevic after a ten-year war against Yugoslavia, a war of attrition and mendacious, brutal propaganda against the only remaining Socialist system in the Balkans.

The objective: absorption of former Yugoslavia and the elimination of Russian influence in the Balkans.

On October 5, 2000, 16 months after the 78-day, criminal U.S.-NATO air war against Yugoslavia, the USA overthrow of the government of the Yugoslav Socialist Party headed by Milosevic. In the subsequent confusion in Serbia a battle broke out between progressive Socialist forces and reactionary forces supported by the West. The West won. Milosevic was arrested and sent to The Hague for trial by the International Court.

What stands behind this so-called "Democratic Revolution for Freedom"? This is an open question that you might look into. *After my own long years in the Agency, I know where and how such slogans are hatched. Though the anti-Serb "revolution" is not known as another of East Europe's color revolutions, it was one of the most pernicious. I personally know the origins of the "color revolutions". I once knew some of the experts who design them and choose their colors.*

Furthermore, the U.S. war against Serbia actually began in the early 1990s. Serbia resisted for 10 years, after which the CIA got carte blanche to rid the world of the "tyrant of the Balkans". And eventually to annex part of Serbia, Kosovo, to make way for the gigantic U.S. military base there, Camp Bondsteel. Great sums were invested in support of a coalition of the 18 parties of the so-called "democratic opposition", the one objective of which was to get rid of Milosevic.

The future American ambassador to Belgrade first set up an office in nearby Budapest—Hungary had already been "normalized"—where the CIA trained Serbian opposition activists. Even Wikipedia reports that U.S. government affiliated organizations such as the International Republican Institute and the US Agency for International Development, or USAID, financed a student group known as Otpor, or Resistance, which led the opposition in the presidential elections of that year in which Milosevic got 15% fewer votes than the Western-backed candidate. Neither had a majority. But instead of having a run-off vote, opposition parties charged that Milosevic had falsified the elections and went to the streets in protest against a run-off vote. The Western-backed opposition declared their candidate the winner. When Milosevic refused to resign, the Supreme Court made the peculiar decision to cancel all the votes of the province of Kosovo, which gave the victory to Kostunica and his Western supporters. Milosevic saw the writing on the wall and recognized the opposition victory.

Otpor, i.e. the Western-financed opposition to Milosevic,

refused to recognize Milosevic's surrender. The stall led to another "people's" uprising. The opposition set fire to the Parliament and occupied the government power apparatus. The coup d'état was complete. The U.S. supported opposition had won.

But why, one wonders? Why the total destruction of Milosevic? Because the image of Milosevic-as-dictator in the Western media would have been absurd if he had been removed by a democratic vote. The "counter-revolution" had to be executed with violence so that the new regime could permit foreign intervention in the state and the economy. At this point, the transformation of Communist Yugoslavia became irreversible.

Within a few months after the coup d'état, 40,000 functionaries of the old regime had been removed. Machine guns spawned new careers. Western powers created new political parties. The four major Serbian banks were dissolved by the International Monetary Fund and financial control of the banking system transferred to foreign hands.

But popular discontent grew. By the by, that discontent and underground resistance to the Western-installed government still exist today. Paradoxically, Milosevic was blamed for the suffering caused by the economic sanctions of the West and the three months of bombing by U.S. warplanes in 1999. The bombs destroyed the economy and infrastructures, aggravating the spreading social discontent. People became more sensitive to Western propaganda. This was the U.S. strategy: bombs to weaken Milosevic's power and bring about his downfall. Milosevic said at the time: "They are not attacking Serbia to capture Milosevic, but Milosevic in order to capture Serbia."

But why this aggression against Yugoslavia and Serbian-led Yugoslavia in the first place?

From the early 1990s there were NOT different wars in Yugoslavia—in Slovenia, in Croatia, Bosnia and Kosovo— it was all one war: that of U.S.-led Western powers against

Socialist Yugoslavia. Until that time, Yugoslavia had been recognized as one country since the Treaty of Versailles in the early 20th century after World War I.

Then, until the dissolution of Socialist Yugoslavia, Western powers had successfully exploited Catholics and Moslems in Yugoslavia, inciting them against the Serbian Orthodox, to counteract Russian influence in Yugoslavia. Many of these Moslem people are in fact Serbs who converted to Islam 400 years ago. They speak Serbian and call themselves Bosnians because they live in an area defined by the River Bosna. Actually, Karl Heinz, they are not good Muslims, nor good Serbs. They were good atheists till they got infected by the religious insanity with which many Yugoslav people were infected at the time. For that reason many of the attacks were on religious symbols like churches and mosques. Before the imported religious madness, these Orthodox, Catholic and Moslem people—for example in Sarajevo where I spent some time—worked, played, danced, drank and partied together. No one knew what historic religious background they came from. There were over 800,000 religiously mixed marriages in Bosnia and Herzegovina before the religious wars began. Of course that is what religion is good at—it makes people kill one another. The results of organized religions have been clear to see in the Balkans. They cause first prejudice, then wars, destruction and madness.

On the geopolitical front, in 1990, the U.S. employed the power of resurgent Germany to weaken Russia as well as East Europe, all of which was to be transformed into a Euro-Atlantic region—as one great colony. Therefore, the one Socialist survivor, Serbia, had to be removed since it remained a potential ally of Russia.

Yes, Karl Heinz, again Russia. Again it is a case of the U.S. fear of the Russian bear. Milosevic in power was the obstacle. He had to go.

The result was that the U.S. annexed Kosovo, made it

"independent" and erected there its greatest military base in Europe. Immediately after the coup d'état, Milosevic's party was crushed. Serbia became an occupied country: foreign consultants in government, army, police and secret police, and the banking system in Western hands. The economy was shattered. Privatization of big enterprises brought poverty to much of Serbia. The army was cut to four brigades, the media silenced, politicians corrupted. Montenegro was separated from Serbia and Kosovo and declared an independent nation, now recognized by many foreign countries. The former chief of the State TV was even accused of responsibility for the death of staff members who died under NATO bombs. And Milosevic and state functionaries and generals were delivered to the NATO Inquisition in The Hague for trial, where Milosevic died.

Nothing in Serbia is better today. On the contrary. New state leaders and experts, bought and tele-commanded from abroad, boast of great victories for a Serbia now on the way to adhesion to the European Union. Serbia is struggling to get on the first rung of EU membership talks but it is held back by its past and a lingering mistrust of the West and a huge segment of public opinion.

Slovenia is already a member of the EU, Croatia is next in line, and even Macedonia, Montenegro and Albania are further along the path to EU membership than Serbia, the country that used to be at the center of the most important regional power, Yugoslavia.

The multinational-dominated European Union does not reflect the real desires of Serbs and the Serbian nation; it defeats the historical idea of an independent union of the Southern Slavs — an old idea also supported by Russia. Russia again! Karl Heinz, don't forget: keep Russia in mind.

In the U.S. view another conundrum stalks the jungle of Balkan politics. The United States fears that somewhere within the Belgrade political mafia stands the former KGB agent Vladimir Putin, who also knows a thing or two about Balkan politics. The U.S. believes he is using the Kosovo debacle to revive Russian meddling in Europe. To restart the Cold War. Putin, American Neocons seem to believe, is willing to provoke a repetition of that grand chapter in Serbian history, the Sarajevo assassination of 1914, which ignited the First World War.

Karl Heinz, these are fundamental factors. They are the reality. Keep them in mind and then you will soon understand the Balkans.

Now, by the way, our friend Ilya is here. You will meet him soon. We are going to Belgrade. As he says, he wants to show you his Belgrade. The real Belgrade. You know the address. We'll meet there tomorrow afternoon. By the way, another surprise awaits you there. A pleasant one. Ilya always knows what to do.

CB

23

WE SAW the bombings as pure nastiness," Ilya said, pointing out the destruction from the bombings along the twelve kilometers into the city. One thousand U.S.-led NATO attack planes. Seventy-eight straight days of bombing and thirty-eight thousand combat missions. He indicated a bridge here or a building or an embassy there, state TV headquarters, public buildings. "Criminal bombs. For there was no official war. All that right here in modern, peaceful Europe. Soon we understood why. It was to crush Serbia ... eliminate Milosevic ... rip away the region of Kosovo ... but Clifford, above all, it was to dissolve Socialist Yugoslavia."

We rode in an embarrassed silence, looking left and right, observing the mixture of life and destruction, one overlapping the other. It had turned cold. The car windows soon frosted over. The city seemed still and quiet. I knew it was not. Belgrade was a two-headed city, one reactionary, submissive and eager for the European Union, the other still Socialist, still loyal to the past dream of the unity of the Southern Slavs and to Tito's Socialist Union of the peoples of the three faiths. Today a city of over two million people, Belgrade was submerged by a half million Serb refugees who had fled to their capital from Moslem areas separated from the union after America stole Kosovo.

"Our brilliant awol man is stir crazy," Ilya muttered. "It is hard to protect him. That boy is naïve and also too good for his own safety. Makes you want to coddle him. Indulge him. And that is dangerous. Cliff, I suspect ... no, I know, they are on his tail."

"I know. I spoke with a friend in the bazaar ... I mean the Istanbul Grand Bazaar. *They* were looking for this young man there too. The deserter, they called him. The traitor. Ilya, they don't want to take prisoners. No prisoners in this secret war, I fear."

"Elmer told me some of the story. A giant on his tail, he said. DIA, he claims."

"That giant is a killer."

"But you will know what to do."

"That's always been my job."

"I have always known that. But this time is different, Cliff. These people, the giant and his helpers, are also close to my government."

"To those in command in your government."

"Those in command. Yes."

"If only those two kids are still alive!"

"Which is uncertain. I knew his girlfriend meant trouble. She must have been the bait."

* * *

Outside the street door at Palmoticheva 25, Karl Heinz and Antonia were waiting in a doorway across the street. Inside Ilya's building, in the dim corridor, flitting shadows and undertones of whispers whirring and humming, rising and falling, like the sound of thousands of honeybees. An audible silence. The silence of the murmuring of people who understood what was happening around them on Palmoticheva Street. The roar of awareness. In Belgrade. In Serbia. In the enigmatic Balkans of Europe.

Inside, doors to two ground floor apartments stood open. The atmosphere was that of the stillness in the eye of the tornado. Total silence crept out of Ilya's apartment. The house of Ilya-Elijah, the Lord our God.

A neighbor nodded his head to Ilya, his eyes speaking his warning. Ilya looked at me. The situation was clear.

Ilya drew a pistol from his pocket.

I yanked it from his hand. "I'm better at this," I whispered, my thoughts turning to death. The death that had long been waiting for me. I feared it was waiting for me inside the Palmoticheva apartment. It seemed like my time. Still, a time for life. A time for ... but death took hold of my mind. I listened. I heard it ticking. A death clock. A new thought. Curious that it had never occurred to me before. Or hardly. Only the death of others. I shuddered. I imagined fleetingly Elizaveta together with her mother, years later, living as if I had never existed. Separation was near. Death was near. Death was waiting behind the door in front of me. My turn? My dreams cut short? My mission unaccomplished? The new generation was pushing for space. The generation waiting outside on Ulica Palmoticheva. And an even newer one inside Elijah's apartment. Relax, I told myself. Never fear. Relax and accept. Act but accept.

* * *

Suddenly I become aware of the buzzing and whirring. Am I becoming a god as Nikitin once suggested? Dizzying images flash past. A fleeting glimpse of my father dying in his chair in the Palace Hotel in St. Moritz, looking over his beloved Lej da San Murezzan, a sailboat gliding among the whitecaps, the eagle circling overhead, the rising mountains, purple below and white at the top. Paradise. Palmoticheva is premature, I think. Palmoticheva is unfair. I should have avoided Belgrade at all costs.

I enter Elijah's apartment in a crouch. The boy is standing next to a girl sitting near a window. I hear movement behind me. I understand. I know. I whirl, squeezing the trigger before I see the figures in the shadows. Screams of terror from the window, scrambling sounds from the corridor. Softly, pop pop, the silent clicks of silencers. Sounds left hanging, buried and dead, sounds saved somewhere in space or echoing in another galaxy, I think, as I feel myself falling, automatically still firing at the shadows. Cries, and bodies crashing in the shadows.

Now I feel only the prick in my chest. I hear a gasp as if in the distance. Both heat and cold sweep over me. I feel the heat. I feel the cold. I shiver and turn onto my stomach. The warmth spreads under me. Blindness comes over me like a blanket. Voices fade. I feel nothing and think nothing. Darkness lifts me and carries me away.

24

KARL HEINZ

IN A way I am glad to be back in Berlin and the certainty of the gray and cold timelessness of the Brandenburg winter. Time has seemed to stop. Things in general seem to be winding down like at the end of an era. On each of these December days enough snow falls to cover and delete the frozen snow of the day before and maintain a constant, never-ending wintry atmosphere. During the night I look forward to the chill of morning when I can open our bedroom window and let the cold wind from the lake sweep over my body. I love that sudden, stiff wind as if it were rebirth, or, at least, regeneration.

During the dark days I am aware of the past haunting this house—Katharina. My searches over the villa for vestiges of her have turned up pieces of her clothing, her trinkets from God knows where, photographs of people I never knew, her memories of our life in Perugia including a snapshot of my friend Max the assassinated Carabinieri Captain, her fashion magazines, Italian study books, their margins decorated with her strange porno drawings and the name Max written in Gothic script. Though I trashed it all except for a photo of Max, and though I have tried to eject her spirit from the house and from myself, something of her remains.

A shadow here.

A gesture there.

She was my youth—and more—and something remained; probably something always remains.

The villa had to go.

The two hours flying time to Bulgaria and Antonia's frequent phone calls to parents and friends and my weekly calls to Alvin at Novo Selo and also to Ilya hoping for information about Elmer combine to keep time alive and to reduce the one thousand five hundred kilometers distance to Burgas and the Black Sea and make the Balkans part of West Europe. We have always been close but we didn't realize it.

I had thought Antonia would need a long period of adjustment to the fast pace of Berlin as compared to easygoing Bulgaria, to the severity of the German academic world, to the West, to a new world for this girl from the East. But nothing of the sort. She is totally cosmopolitan and unprovincial. She didn't permit my assistance in her enrollment at the Humboldt-University Graduate School for literature and sociology. She let me accompany her to the Wannsee train station the first time. But Berlin? She would learn it alone.

"Did I ever tell you how you remind me of my old girl friend, Imogene?" I asked her one day after her return home from downtown.

"Another one? Are you a ladies' man, after all?"

"After all what? Me? Hardly. But she was special. Also from the East ... and had to go back home. Still, she was so very cosmopolitan. Like you."

"You think we women of East Europe are special?" she said, putting on her seductive smile, a smile lodged in her blue German eyes, her mouth slightly sardonic, somewhat crooked, the lower lip in the left corner of her luscious mouth dipping, I thought at the moment, in denial of her own eyes.

"You are, my only love. And now that we're here to stay and you're about to be a student again, I have a surprise for you."

According to my lawyer, the only remaining legal obligation concerning my grandfather's testament was to care for the aged couple of housekeepers and my grandfather's cats. I had found an amazing apartment in Berlin-Mitte near the Main Station big enough for all—us, the housekeepers and the cats.

Antonia was overjoyed when she saw it; Wannsee had never seemed like Berlin to her. Nor to me either for that matter.

* * *

A new life began.

Yet the Balkans were still part of my life. Of our lives. The events in Belgrade that cold day in October had conditioned the lives of many of us. After Cliff's cremation in Belgrade, Elizaveta took the urn to St. Moritz, where a few days later Cliff was buried near his father in the Old Cemetery on the upper part of St. Moritz Village. Ilya, Antonia and I joined her and Masha there for what was supposed to be a private ceremony. Surprisingly there was a big turnout of villagers; people who had known Cliff all his life.

Antonia had never grasped fully what happened in Ulica Palmoticheva. To explain, the afternoon of the funeral I took her to the games room of the Palace Hotel where that fateful meeting of Intelligence people had taken place, it seemed now in another life; a kind of dénouement before the deaths of Elizaveta's father, Nikitin, and his associate, Hakim ... and before the terrorist attacks on Europe. And now Cliff. She seemed even more baffled as to why this place I often spoke of held such significance for me.

"Karl Heinz, what was it was all about, the shooting and killing in that apartment in Belgrade?"

"Betrayal," I answered. "It was about betrayal. That is, traitors."

"Betrayal?"

"Very popular in the country where I grew up. Italians say either betrayal doesn't exist, or if it does, then we're all traitors. Remember that *traitor* is also linked to the word, 'deliver', like Judas handing over Jesus to the Roman authorities, thus betraying him. Since traitor comes also from the same source as tradition, the Latin *tradere*, the act of betrayal is handed down from one generation to the next."

"But Elmer is just a kid. Who could he betray?"

"He's a whistleblower, Antonia. He knows everything and delivers the secrets he discovers."

"So is he a traitor?"

"Not at all. But that giant Raymond wanted to kill him anyway ... for his delivering of America's secrets to the world. That's why Elmer is in hiding."

"Hiding? There? He wasn't even in his usual disguise."

"He cut off his beard and his hair and took off his martenitsa and looked like himself. That was his disguise. He was himself."

"They want to kill him because he's a genius?"

"No, because he wants to tell the truth. The odd thing is he didn't actually think about it much. He had the goods and the way to deliver it. He just thought it was the right thing to do."

"Poor Lala!"

"Why poor Lala? I don't believe she'll last long. Not in the solitude. Not in exile. She'll go back home soon. A man like Elmer ends up alone."

"Poor Elmer too. He needs a lot of love. More love than others."

* * *

Last month Ilya called to say he had left Kosovo for good. Since Cliff's death he had transferred some of his attention to me, as if I were Cliff's *Nachfolger*. Though I finished the remaining reportages that Cliff had sketched out and received a lot of journalistic credits myself, I don't feel like a successor to Cliff. I never will.

Ilya had left Kosovo to enter the political arena in Serbia.

He said he had had enough of U.S.-KLA domination in a country run by the Kosovar-Albanian mafia and the U.S. military and people infected with the idea of Greater Albania. He was sick of battling from his extra-parliamentary position — actually in the underground. In the upcoming elections he was standing for the Socialist Party of Serbia, the left-wing nationalist party originally formed by Slobodan Milosevic.

After we hung up I noted down his exact words: "I am sick of living stranded in anonymity," he said, "in circumstances where people have to obey the dictates of foreign and criminal power. Though it is hidden in the shadows, that black power is omnipresent. The insularity of the individual in that criminal world is unbearable."

Alvin had told me that the return to Novo Selo of Raymond's "bullet-ridden body" and the mortally wounded Turk was a hushed up affair. "Still, everyone seemed to know about it," he said. "Soldiers and officers alike were relieved to see the military plane take off with the ghoul securely in an extra long coffin. My Captain said 'thanks to whoever did the shooting … and good riddance'."

On the last day of January, Alvin called me from a safe phone in a nearby village to tell me that he was shipping out in a few days, he suspected to Georgia, and not the state of Atlanta, he added, but the country. "Strange," he said, "brigade after brigade are lily-padding to eastern Georgia or other places farther eastwards. Plus support troops, like me. I don't like the sound of it. God knows how many special troops are passing through. You'd think they were expecting another Russian attack in Georgia. But if so, why send us to the eastern corner of the country?"

I had some ideas but didn't suggest them. I returned to my maps and atlases and everything seemed clear. The eastern corner of Georgia is not pointed at Russia. Nor even southeast. It is pointed south. At Iran. Brigades and more brigades in eastern Georgia? Whatever was going on,

Elmer was right to run, for otherwise he was destined for a front line somewhere.

The next day, Ilya's online journal published a series of conversations, military dispatches and rumors, all of which bore Elmer's invisible signature, the gist of which was that target go was Iran.

25

NTONIA and I have moved downtown. The aged couple from the Wannsee villa has come with us, managing the huge apartment and freeing us for our own activities.

December days in Berlin this year seem shorter than usual. The month dwindles down toward its end, marking the end of the key year of my life. The turning point, I believe. A landmark. Still, though I find new joys in Antonia, I continue to feel regrets for the paucity of my talents and commitment.

In theory we know that the Earth revolves but in practice we do not perceive it; the ground upon which we tread does not seem to move and we live untroubled by that unperceived motion. So it is with Time in my lived life, it seems to me. Plato's conclusion that those who seek real truth are not realistic has proved to be the philosophy of our age. Pragmatism rules men and nations.

Myth becomes a substitute for reality, another misconception related to the world of illusions, based on techniques of fraud that create deceitful and speculative convictions. Since myths do not provide anything educational to the rules of society or reality, they are relegated to the area of illusion. Myths abound in the field of political history, I have learned. Whether of not people believe in the irrational contents of myth is unimportant. In particular, every religion creates its own mythology.

I have written all I know about America's lily pads and the encirclement of Russia. But when during my explorations

I met Elmer and Ilya I struck gold. We are now friends. They trust me. I am at the top of their list of press outlets for the steady stream of leaks uncovered by Elmer, who is still hanging on in Belgrade. My two Berlin daily newspapers, Italy's major newspaper and a news magazine, a British newspaper, and Cliff's Swiss newspapers are my best clients.

After Ilya's election to Parliament in Belgrade, he wormed his way onto the parliamentary foreign affairs committee, in important ways influencing all our lives. I suspect that his role in the parallel secret service Cliff had told me about is behind his sudden political rise. Since his two chief travel destinations are Brussels and Berlin, he is often at our apartment. And thanks to his new status and the political instability in Serbia, he was able to arrange for a shaky and somewhat anomalous political asylum for Elmer in Belgrade. The modified version of his name, Ilya told me, appears on his Serbian ID also in Cyrillic letters, reading Helmer Redve.

"Elmer is proud of his exile status," Ilya told me on one of his visits. "His hair is short. He still wears his earring but he keeps a low profile. Speaking Serb the way he does and considering the hundreds of thousands of immigrants and displaced persons from Kosovo, Macedonia and Montenegro flooding Belgrade, he goes unnoticed. Besides, the government closes its eyes to disturbing factors, especially anything regarding the USA and the European Union. Serbia wants no international incidents of any kind. Redve will be safe for another year or so."

26

LIFF had long believed a U.S. attack on Iran inevitable. In one of his last articles, published on the prominent back page of the weekend edition of the Zurich Herald, he described a plausible scenario for an American attack: some minor and fictitious provocation by Iran against U.S. forces stationed in the Persian Gulf area to defend the Shia government of Bahrain, in combination with alleged stepped-up terrorist attacks by Iran against Iraq. Such a false flag operation, Cliff wrote, would culminate in "defensive" American military action against Iran, "plunging the lonely USA into a quagmire reaching from North Africa to Iran, Afghanistan and Pakistan."

ATTACK ON IRAN by CLIFFORD BEECHER

(München) Iran is the U.S. fall guy. The patsy. The excuse for the United States to extend its military operations in Eurasia. Nuclear ambitious or not, Iran is the new victim on the U.S. hit list. Weapons of mass destruction were never found in Iraq. Nor will they be found in its neighbor Iran.

"Aggression on the open seas!" screams the American corporate press today about an alleged Iranian torpedo boat attack on a U.S. supercarrier parked just off the Iranian island of Kharq, an event that did not even occur. Iranian resistance to the provocative U.S. presence along its coastline in the Persian Gulf is the excuse for the USA to launch all-out war against ancient Persia. Soon the wars

in the three contiguous countries of Iraq, Iran and Afghanistan will be linked.

The alleged attack on a U.S. warship in the Persian Gulf recalls the burning of the Reichstag in Germany in 1933, the excuse for Hitler to establish his dictatorship in Germany. The alleged attack recalls the Gulf of Tonkin, where a North Vietnamese torpedo boat allegedly attacked a U.S. warship, the excuse for war against Vietnam and all of Southeast Asia.

Eurasia is the point. Eurasia, reaching from Germany and Poland eastwards, has always been the point. Former Russian-Soviet Central Asia is the center of Eurasia. Whoever controls Eurasia can control the world goes the theory. A key country is Afghanistan. So Afghanistan had to go.

After the dissolution of the Soviet Union, the U.S. established its satellites and military bases in Central Asia. But Iraq stood in the way. Saddam was not the point. Weapons of mass destruction were not the point. The existence of Iraq, the Fertile Crescent, was the point. Iraq had to be 'liberated' Syria had to be 'liberated'. Export of democracy was the slogan.

Today, Iran, ancient Persia, stands in the way. It too must go. A preemptive strike against Iran is the logical outcome of American geopolitics. Geopolitics is the art of using political power over a given territory; it is the identification of core areas and the relationship between naval and terrestrial capabilities; geopolitics in the unfolding of world history is the application of a strategy of full-spectrum dominance based on land, sea, air and space.

I paused, perplexed but convinced of the enormity of U.S. strategy. A criminal strategy for world domination. Eurasia has become central to the world. I took out my truthful atlases and there it was before me: Central Asia—Uzbekistan, Turkmenistan, Kyrgyzstan, and also Sinkiang and China. The center. The top of the world. Yes, Cliff, yes. Sacred territory. Holy lands. The transitory home relating to the origins of human civilization.

As an addendum, Cliff wrote a comment, published posthumously in a column on the editorial page of the Zurich paper. As far as I know it was his last piece of writing:

On Aggression, Freedom, Right-Thinking and Happiness.

Psychologists teach that aggression lies in the nature of the human being and is a response to frustration. One must wonder if America is paranoid and psychopathic. Schizoids tend to split human beings into "ideally good" and "ideally bad". Nazi Germany idealized Aryans and denigrated Jews. Witch-trials and concentration camps for the ideally bad are part of the history of mankind. The division of people into right- and wrong-thinkers is symptomatic of a disturbed mentality in those who do the dividing. A great hindrance to democracy today is the reluctance—or the inability—to call things by their proper name, one of the reasons why "the people" in our world never know what is really going on. Those who wonder what went wrong in the American democracy might update Abraham Lincoln's words "If slavery is not wrong then nothing is wrong" to this: "If aggression is not wrong, then nothing is wrong." The question of freedom must be considered. Freedom is also in the mind. Freedom is not to be found in imitation and right-positive-thinking. Freedom is in critical thinking. The chains of "lip service democracy" are no lighter than the chains of authoritarianism. Chains are still chains. American style pseudo- democracy is not valid for all climates. It does not deserve to be exported and should anyway never be imposed.

27

"SOMETIMES I wonder what I'm really doing," Elmer said, pacing back and forth and studying the designs on the Persian carpets of my studio. "Is my exile of any value to anyone? Providence seems far away. Not that I miss it much but just the idea of being locked up in an exile's cage is ... well, it's disturbing. Some days I feel like a canary ... and in her way Lala is sometimes a prison too. I seem to stagger back and forth between fantasy and reality. But maybe that's the way exile is ... maybe life in general."

"Still better than Afghanistan," was all I could say.

"Well, anyway, thanks to Ilya and my official exile status I got the visa to visit you. Forgive me if I'm not in a mood for New Year's celebrations."

"It's a good visit. And good for you to get away from Belgrade. Also good for Lala and Antonia. They've been friends since childhood. And good for me to be with you since for me you're emblematic of, uh, well, the freedom of choice."

"Me? Like I told you, I'm a prisoner."

Elmer had continued to shed his hippy look. He had shaved his scraggly beard and his hair was much shorter than in his military days when he had challenged authority and gotten away with it. Only a small martenitsa still hung on his left ear lobe as if a reminder of who he really was.

Some days he and I walked down Unter den Linden toward the concert halls and the opera. "Sometimes we go to the opera in that theater," I said, pointing out my favorite theater.

"How I wish I'd been born in Europe," he lamented as we walked around the university area where he seemed to feel at ease.

"You'd still be an outsider, my friend. You're a born exile."

It was true. I saw Elmer as the pure metaphysical exile, though he had the exile's documents to prove he was a political exile too.

One day we walked down the Potsdamer Strasse to Schöneberg, looking into some of the Turkish shops and observing the immigrants. Elmer seemed to feel at home among them. Nights we went out for dinner to different parts of the city—to Prenzlauer Berg, a restaurant on the Spree, to a jazz cellar in Friedrichshain in memory of my student days and of Imogene. Elmer's favorite—and where he apparently felt safest—was the dark restaurant with the-play-on-words name of *Unsicht-Bar* Restaurant. Invisible. Inside total darkness reigns. You have to touch your nose to orient your own face. Blind waiters. Spoons at twelve o'clock by your plate. While your eyes rest, your other senses revive. You feel the slightest movement of air. Hear the softest of sounds. Feel each object on the table. Conversation is magnified. Life becomes primary. Elmer commented that dining in darkness was emblematic of his exile, in which he had to continually touch himself to know it was reality.

But as a rule during his days in Berlin he and I were isolated in my study, each of us trying to come to terms with our new situation. Our relationship has matured since our meeting on the street of the Novo Selo military base. I still laugh when I recall our entrance into the dark base bar and the shouts of greeting in various languages from Elmer's admirers, I now believe because of his devil-may-care behavior. In all this time he has been on my mind. My fondness for him has grown, along with my admiration for his adaptability to an unimaginable life adventure. I could never be the protective big brother for him as was

Ilya, or the guide Cliff had been for me, yet I want to fulfill some valuable role in his exile's life—the exile I still consider myself to be too. The exile: something apart, existing in a labyrinth of many doors that seem to lead to a special place beyond the curtain of normal life but also, hopefully, to out-of-the-ordinary rewards. His condition of exile couldn't be confused with alienation, a condition of loneliness from which he might or might not emerge. His exile is separation and withdrawal. I think of Elmer as the literal exile, living temporarily away from home; perhaps I am the other kind, the permanent exile. Each person has his own exile, I continually tell myself. Our exiles mean acceptance of the existence of an impermeable wall that separates us from everything else. From much of life, even from death.

Both our situations are precarious. Berlin is my exile; Rome my freedom. Is Belgrade Elmer's exile—as he himself considers it—or is it his first tentative taste of freedom? However that may be, Elmer's, like mine, is also a metaphysical rebellion, even though he doesn't yet realize it. The difference is that his is also a courageous engagement with reality, while mine remains peripheral and metaphysical. His is rebellion against the real world that was his; mine a development of romance and fiction. Elmer retains a certain haloed dignity, a grace that makes my minor conflict of choice between Italy where I grew up and Germany where I live pale in comparison. I'm aware of the passage of my life—the death of Nikitin and Hakim, all the death I saw in Perugia. Now the death of Cliff. Elmer has just turned twenty. Life is still eternal for him. Actually he has no choice now, though I believe that in his mind he is creating different worlds from the one he knew before exile, a world in which death or even a choice of lifestyle had no place. His dialectic today concerns lived experience. He lives and thinks within his own personal history on the one hand, and on the other within the reality of the world he has discovered in his interceptions. Probably unconsciously, his direction follows all human reality. In no way could you treat the experiences of his life in the detached manner, for example, of positivist philosophers.

"Some of the ancient Roman writers I studied in school in Rome dealt with exile," I said one afternoon sitting at a front table in the elegant Operncafé. "And there were many of them. But they all missed home. You don't seem to have that problem."

"It's not that I don't miss Providence, my surroundings, my old friends ... my life there in general. It's more little things. One memory here, another there. Boyhood. Memories of something I might never experience again. Yet at other times I think I'll never want to return home."

Linen tablecloths and waiters in black and an atmosphere of discreet silence. I said we should have gone to a pub. Elmer said he liked it here. Said he'd never seen anything like it, neither in America nor the Balkans.

"I know what you mean about missing little things," I said, trying to be positive, and in that moment feeling like his big brother. "A new life doesn't blot out all that. Though you made a real break the day you went awol, I think you've got to decide whether to integrate into this new society or adapt to an exile's life. I've found that exile is not only a break with the old; it's also the start of a new life. Maybe you'll create an exile self, there in Belgrade. A new lifestyle, a new language, new people, new experiences, transformation. Exile will become immigration. It's like having two lives in one lifetime. In my first years here in Berlin I needed a kind of self-censorship of thoughts linking me to my old life. Exile means that too. Above all, for me, it means a new life. I like that part most, like a goal achieved, I think because mine was voluntary withdrawal ... not forced exile."

"Yeah, for now that's my problem too. I have Lala. I have my protector, Ilya, and my teacher, Mirko. And now I have new acquaintances at the university. But this new life hasn't yet replaced the old life. It's as if my new life were superimposed on my former life in America which now seems like a shadow lingering behind me."

"A shadow always remains, goes the old song. Anyway, you're not alone ... you're lucky."

"Lucky? Karl Heinz, I might not be alone, but I'm still lonely. I continue to think chiefly in the first person. And I wonder if my, uh, how can I say it, if my authenticity is also there ... in my loneliness."

"Exile must always be linked to flight. Usually a forced flight ... like yours. On the other hand maybe you unconsciously wanted the break with the old and chose the new. But, in theory at least, the traditional exile has the hope of returning home when the political situation in the place of his origins changes."

"I don't know. Maybe. But you know, I've come to feel exile like a disease, too. In which you live as in a permanent quarantine. Sometimes, Karl Heinz, I feel a sinking in my stomach, a wave of nausea that I'll never be able to go home again. On the other hand I wonder if I'll even want to go back. It lasts just a moment but I sometimes feel it just doesn't matter. I could just as well turn myself in as go on with it."

"I know what you mean. I think it's true that exile is also a kind of psychological experience. Really hard to deal with. Yet for sure it leads to a heightened sense of adventure. And from there, I believe, to artistic creation. Maybe you're destined to write great literature. You see things from a new perspective, different from others. In exile, you can more easily create a fictive parallel society. Look at Dante and Joyce and Pound and even Kundera. They created new worlds."

"When I start thinking of surrender and acceptance of the new life I remember the shootout," Elmer muttered. "I see all the terrible details. And that your friend Cliff died to save me. That means something, doesn't it?"

"He was an exile too, with a special intuition. We were

always speaking of hunches and instinct—and also forebodings. He once told me he knew it was due to happen ... and maybe soon. He knew what he was doing. He chose it."

"Good God!"

"But remember you and Lala changed my life when I was in a rut. You brought me Antonia. That also means something."

* * *

Elmer and Lala's bag was packed for their late morning departure for Belgrade. The four of us were enjoying a Bulgarian-style breakfast when we heard the first news from Iran on the kitchen TV. Elmer quickly grasped the significance of what was happening and without a word rushed to the landline phone.

"Hey, Lieutenant, it's me. Has it started?" A pause. "Big?" A pause. "I thought so. Take care!"

Elmer shut down the communication and said, "Well, we're not going anywhere today."

28

WE WERE following the TV news in the communications room when a flash interrupted the BBC morning news: the International News Agency reported that early that morning three Iranian torpedo boats appeared on the radar screens of the USS Abraham Lincoln anchored near Iran's Persian Gulf island of Kharg. The boats headed straight for the supercarrier.

Quoting the ship's commanding officer, a BBC journalist on board reported that "the torpedo boats emerged from the Gulf mist and sped in a provocative and threatening manner toward the carrier." According to the Admiral, the carrier at first undertook no special defensive measures. At that hour, activity on the decks of the massive vessel-fortress was minimal.

Another journalist on board testified that when the torpedo boats were about one kilometer away, they began firing at the carrier.

After repeated Iranian provocations, the Admiral's office reiterated, the carrier finally responded with cannon shots, destroying one of the attack PTs. The other two withdrew. The U.S. Navy reported that one carrier crewman had been shot dead.

"So it has finally happened!" Elmer exclaimed. "The provocation they were waiting for."

"And who knows who really shot that crewman?" I answered, now automatically thinking conspiratorially as old Nikitin had drilled into my head.

"At Novo Selo everyone felt it in the air," Elmer said. "So now it's reality."

"Those troops in East Georgia Alvin told me about were a clear sign."

"Karl Heinz, America will retaliate. And it'll be a nightmare. The war in Iraq will seem like maneuvers."

Zapping over various channels I stopped on a press briefing underway at the top of a skyscraper overlooking the Danube in Vienna. U.S. Intelligence officers had unveiled the contents of an allegedly stolen Iranian laptop computer to leaders of the International Atomic Energy Agency and a restricted group of journalists. They disclosed selections from over a thousand pages of what were labeled Iranian computer simulations. Accounts of Iranian military experiments flashed across a screen to demonstrate Iran's efforts to develop a nuclear warhead to fit atop its Shahab-3 missile. According to unconfirmed Israeli reports a Shahab-6 exists with a range of up to 5000 kilometers, about 3,500 miles.

"The Shahab can reach Israel and other countries of the Middle East," the spokesman said. The word Shahab, he explained, means shooting star, luminous, or king of the world.

The excerpts from the stolen laptop, another U.S. official stated, "disprove once and for all Iran's claims that its nuclear program is peaceful."

"Iran also obtained missiles from North Korea," the spokesman added. "Those missiles are capable of striking capitals in Western Europe and Moscow. Some of them may be nuclear-tipped. These disclosures prove conclusively that Iran has developed intercontinental ballistic missiles, posing an immediate threat to global security."

Silence fell in the conference room until a young journalist at the back stood up and without being recognized asked pointblank: "But why should Iran nuke European cities?"

The spokesman stared, apparently astonished at the naïve question, raised his arms in dismissal and muttered: "I believe the reasons are obvious to any sensible person."

"So Iran is declaring war on all of Europe!" the journalist said matter-of-factly.

* * *

"Good God!" Elmer gasped. "Well, it's time to put to good use all this radio equipment you installed. I'll contact our old Bulgarian pal, Alvin. God knows where he has lily-padded to by now. I believe I can communicate with him safely."

"How do you mean? You've taught me that anything that can be transmitted can also be intercepted."

"Yes, but there are a few tricks. Too complicated to explain. Let's see, it's close to noon in Georgia. I hope we can reach Alvin."

"And it's noontime south of Georgia too," I said, watching Elmer work. Fast, smooth, silent.

Suddenly he whispered: "Got him on the line. Put on your earphones and listen."

There was Alvin's voice. Faint but clear, wary but curious.

"Old friends here," Elmer said. "Wanted to say hello. We just heard the news."

"All grim. I'm there. Floods of us are pouring in. Exactly where I told you. Many more behind us. Don't know where they all come from ... Germany, I suppose. At this moment, everything seems quiet."

A click and the line fell silent.

In the afternoon, we listened to confirmation from NATO European Headquarters that Operation Persian Paradigm was underway. U.S. and NATO troops had crossed the Iranian border from Azerbaijan and Armenia into the northeastern corner of the country. NATO troops marched into Tabriz, Iran's fourth largest city with 1.4 million people. A center of heavy industry, Tabriz is located only 260 miles south of Tbilisi, the capital of America's ally, former Soviet Georgia. Embedded journalists alternated describing the situation as tranquil.

"Things are deathly quiet in this corner of Iran," commented the French correspondent of a Paris weekly magazine in a TV interview on France 2, adding that U.S. soldiers spoke of intentions of moving on Iran's capital of Tehran, 328 miles away but separated by the rugged Elburz Mountains. The journalist reported U.S military claims that the Azeris, the major nationality of multinational Tabriz, hailed the arrival of NATO troops with garlands of flowers for the liberators.

Unconfirmed reports mentioned sounds of small arms fire. A freelance Dutch journalist, speaking on the streets of Tabriz, said he had heard reports that two U.S. soldiers had died of gunshot wounds. Roaming foreign journalists reported many civilian victims.

NATO spokesmen in East Georgia announced laconically that no further penetrations into Iran were contemplated at this time. Simultaneously, however, the BBC confirmed reports of thousands of Allied troops crossing the border from Iraq in the southwest.

Elmer and I sat in our "communications room" waiting for the next episode. An endless interlude at that hour. While pacing the room, drinking coffee and chatting about disconnected issues we discovered we shared a love of chess. The new American war in mind, I recalled I'd read somewhere that chess helps keep mad people sane.

"Yeah," Elmer said, "but Bobby Fischer said to remember that chess is not psychology, but just good moves."

I laughed.

"And what about this? Mirko, my political teacher in Belgrade, told me the story of a Serbian chess master, Maria Manakova, who fell in love with the Yugoslav Grandmaster. In a game with the great chess master she made a series of rash moves with her king as if in surrender—probably intentional moves—and then surrendered her body to him as well. The Grandmaster liked that and married her. Psychology or good moves? Crazy, eh?"

Around midnight we began a game. Elmer seemed elsewhere in his thoughts. Off-handedly, one eye on the TV screen, Elmer checkmated me in a series of lightning moves in less than ten minutes.

Silence reigned in the apartment in Berlin-Mitte. Lala and Antonia slept. Berlin slept. I took a double dose of lamotrigina. At about three a.m. a military communiqué flashed across our screen: just before dawn U.S. troops had crossed the border into Iran from Afghanistan. By late morning, we heard, they had taken up positions around the holy city of Mashhad, a city of 2.5 million people, capital of the Khorasan province, one hundred miles from the Afghan border and five hundred and forty miles northeast of Tehran.

European correspondents inside the country reported that the Iranian military strategy was to avoid head-on encounters. Tehran's troops had headed for the mountains, they reported: the Elburz range running across north Iran between the Caspian Sea and Tehran and merging with the Hindu Kush in Afghanistan; the rugged Zagros Mountains spread from northwestern Iran to the Persian Gulf and joining with the minor range running south from Mashhad; and Mount Damavand hanging over Tehran, at 18,000 feet the highest point in the Middle East.

An Italian geologist recalled that the face of Iran is its mountains. A major nation, not the artificial land of the Fertile Crescent of Iraq.

Iran specialists in Germany agreed that the invaders were misinformed or mad to consider conquering Iran militarily.

"What kind of strategy is this?" I wondered aloud. "Cat and mouse? It was supposed to be a Blitzkrieg. And Iranians? What are they up to? Scorched earth policies? Only their mountains? Or are they readying their missiles? But against whom? Europe? And why Europe?"

"Mirko has always stressed that the U.S. invasion of Iran was inevitable." Elmer said. "I learned from my interceptions that the conquest of Iran is an old dream. It's the American military's urge to control the three linked countries of Iraq, Iran and Afghanistan."

"Persian Paradigm," I snickered. "I would bet the generals themselves don't understand the meaning ... if it has any meaning."

Three hours later came the news of the fourth wave: this time from the Persian Gulf. Following bombardment from U.S. warships and aircraft from different lily pads in the region, U.S. troops from Qatar, from the Emirates, from Saudi Arabia and Kuwait, and tens of thousands more pouring out of the bellies of the supercarriers as from multiple Trojan horses swept ashore from the Gulf. The spearhead pointed at the Iranian nuclear development center of Bushehr, on the Gulf Coast, one thousand miles south of Tehran.

Embedded journalists emphasized again and again the "Russian-constructed nuclear center of Bushehr as the target."

Bushehr is part of Russia's stake in Iran.

Bushehr is indicative of Russia's push toward the Persian Gulf.

Bushehr was a down payment on Russia's investment in the control of Iran's petroleum.

Confused tactics. Confused objectives. Confused reactions. U.S. generals demanding to march straight to Tehran and to the seat of evil in Qom. Bedlam in the diplomatic world. French, German, Dutch and Danish foreign ministries demanding a ceasefire and NATO withdrawal from Iran. Socialist France again threatening to withdraw from NATO. China backing the elimination of Iran's nuclear missile potential but condemning the invasion. Russia calling for both ceasefire and the total occupation of Iran while America is "perplexed" at Russia's plotting and aiming at restoration of its empire: Russian troops on red alert north of Georgia and displacement of its missiles to Transdnestr south of Odessa.

Silently, during the night, Iran's specialists had mined the straights of Hormuz near Bandar Abbas, sealing the Persian Gulf.

I opened my *Times Atlas of the World* to plate 27: Indo-Arabia. "My Bible," I explain to a curious Elmer. The extended American empire lay before us: the geopolitical unity of Iraq, Iran and Afghanistan, together with Armenia, Azerbaijan and Georgia in the northwest and Uzbekistan and Kyrgyzstan in the north, the Emirates and adjacent territories in the south, spaced and controlled by the lily pad chain, the center of the world, forming the geopolitical heart of the New American empire.

"Just look at this plate, Elmer. Clear as the light of day. Right here for all to see in the *Times Atlas of the World.*"

* * *

While Elmer continued studying the atlas, I went for a morning run along the River Spree just to try to think. From my new vantage point, the whole region of Georgia, Armenia, Azerbaijan, the heartland of Iraq, Iran, Afghanistan, and farther eastwards, had never seemed so near.

Yet when I looked around me at the peaceful scene along the Berlin river, the late winter mists typical of Brandenburg, dim yellow lights behind curtained windows, a face in a window, a small *Bateau Mouche* slowing for a curve or for the passage under an arched bridge, that East seemed at the same time far away. Time and space seemed unreal.

* * *

I believe that in the mind of many Europeans and in the minds of most Americans, Iran is an abstraction, a theory, a mirage from a meaningless past of Ali Baba and Aladdin's lamp, not a real, vibrant, modern society, simply wrapped in a veneer of antiquity. I have the sudden thought that for most Western Europeans, Iran, so close in distance, is on another planet, under another sun.

My atlases are right. Space is distorted, time bizarre and out of joint. Maybe it has always been that way. And, as usual, Western political power stubbornly steeped in vague academic ideas of Orientalism, still has no idea of the real reality of the East.

So now it has happened anyway. A great misunderstanding. A return to the past. War between West and East. The great war for civilization between civilizations. A huge, black, swollen, thick-skinned bellic bubble floats eastwards. America's endless war machine moves inexorably from West to East. In this moment bombs are falling on Tehran and Isfahan.

"Good-bye, blue skies!" I pull my woolen running scarf tight and sing over and over the haunting jazz piece. "Good-bye, good-bye, blue skies, good-bye. Good-bye, blue skies. Good-bye."

* * *

In silence, Elmer and I follow reactions from across the Atlantic. Cries for vengeance for Iranian chicanery echo over hysterical news channels and in the words of growing numbers of cynical neocon spokesmen speaking from the pages of the mainline press.

"Nuke the heathens," cry the fundamentalist sects and cynical neocon spokesmen.

"Nuke'em," America's enraged rednecks scream. "Persian pear-a-dig'em. Nuke those Eyeranian basterds, fucking Mohammedan Islamist fanaticists," cry agitated fundamentalists.

"Nuke 'em real good! Pear-a-dig 'em, real real good."

Cliff was right. War is addictive. Once you shoot the drug into your veins, Cliff said, you can't live without it. You can't think straight. Once you set out down the war-drug path, turning back is as difficult as going cold turkey for a heroin addict. In the haze generals live in, unpleasant realities become bunk, Cliff had repeated.

The generals and the strategists do not know that Iran is a land of ancient traditions and a powerful nationalism that has resisted foreign invaders forever. The Pax Americana is meaningless for ancient Persia.

For the generals war against Iran is a strategic opportunity for U.S. control of all of Central Asia and thus of Russia. But the new war will soon be seen as an act of strategic desperation, though, the high passes and the delusions will remain with the war addict, strung out with nothing but more war to rely on.

Meanwhile, other good people of America gather in their churches and pray. Good Christians in the great cities and across the fruited plains of America pray for things greater than themselves. For victory over the sinful Iranians. For peace. For our boys over there bearing the American message of democracy and the true faith. They pray to their Lord God that He protect "our way of life and the future of our children."

They pray that anti-American pacifists and traitors will see the light, repent their ways and face like men their just punishment.

They pray for pacification in that mysterious far away land.

But they neglect to lift a prayer for the redemption of a nation gone haywire. They still believe they are free.

"They still believe they are the chosen ones," Elmer mutters. "The exceptional ones, because their material life was once so good. They preach that killing is wrong and yet annihilate entire nations. They claim to know God but are hated by all."

"Maybe America was a lost cause from the start," I add. "Maybe its Creator was evil ... the Creator of an evil human stain. In which case, Americans must think, what does one war more or less matter?"

THE END

ABOUT THE AUTHOR

GAITHER STEWART is originally from Asheville, NC. After studies at the UC at Berkeley, other American universities and Munich University, he has lived his adult life abroad, first in Germany, then in Italy, alternated with residences in The Netherlands, France, Mexico, Argentina and Russia. After a career in journalism as a correspondent for the Rotterdam daily newspaper, *Algemeen Dagblad*, and contributor to the press, radio and TV in various European countries, he today writes fiction and journalism. He is a senior editor and European correspondent for the major American online publication, The Greanville Post. His works are published in venues throughout the world. His collections of short stories, *Icy Current Compulsive Course*, *To Be A Stranger* and *Once In Berlin* are published by Wind River Press (www. windriverpress.com). His novel, *Asheville*, is published by www.Wastelandrunes.com. He lives with his wife, Milena, in Rome, Italy.

E-mail: gaither.stewart@yahoo.it

Lightning Source UK Ltd.
Milton Keynes UK
UKOW05f0945190514

231911UK00017B/639/P